THE ALIBI

THE ALIBI

BY
GEORGE ALLAN ENGLAND

WILDSIDE PRESS

Published by
Wildside Press, LLC
P.O. Box 301
Holicong, PA 18928-0301 USA
www.wildsidepress.com

Wildside Press Edition: MMIV

To

E. O. H.

THE BEST PAL
MAN EVER HAD

CONTENTS

CONTENTS

THE ALIBI

THE ALIBI

CHAPTER I

THE BALANCE OF DISASTER

BACK and forth, back and forth a man was pacing the floor, caught in the toils of the inexorable catastrophe that now impended close. Lashed by fear, hounded by fate, up and down the room he turned, hemmed by walls of disaster. His feet, now impacting on the polished floor, now noiseless over the rugs, kept time to the mechanical repetition of the thought: "Ruin, ruin, ruin!" that ebbed and flowed in his racked brain.

Haggard and wan he paced with rumpled hair and eyes whose bloodshot glance bespoke long vigils. Save for his footfall and the busy impertinence of the clock that would soon toll midnight, the house — the house of Walter Haynes Slayton, cashier, was still. A numbing silence gripped it — a silence that could almost be heard, so deep it was. Outside, hardly a sound disturbed the frosty November night, now moonlit, now cloudy, that brooded over the suburban solitude of Oakwood Heights.

Stillness without, silence within. The night seemed waiting, big with woe. Yet through all the man's stress and torment passed a flicker of relief that his wife had not yet returned. In view of the approaching disaster, her absence on a visit was a signal blessing. His one wish now was that she might remain away till *something* could be done to stem the tides of ruin.

Back and forth — up and down — Then suddenly the
man stopped, livid, and dashed his fist against his brow and
groaned. Chill though the house had become, he felt no
cold. He burned with inward fires. A fever parched his
lips and ravaged his blood. For to-morrow — to-morrow
was his last day of grace.

"Liabilities, a hundred and eight thousand," he huskily
articulated. "Assets —"

He snapped his trembling fingers.

"Not worth *that!* And Jarboe — confound him, I wish
I had him here to-night! Jarboe's note —"

Walter Slayton cast a despairing look about his library, a
look that minded one of the hunted glare of a trapped,
prisoned animal.

"Jarboe!" he muttered. "He's reached his limit at last.
He's surely going to put me through, this time!"

With a curse he turned toward his desk, all covered with
neatly arranged papers. One of the supreme rules of life
for the cashier of the Powhatan National Bank was perfect
order in all things. Not even this crisis could disturb his
method, the habit of a lifetime.

Now even in the arrangement of the very papers that
spelled complete annihilation, irreparable disaster and in all
probability a frightful term in Sing Sing, his orderly arrangement of the data in chronological sequence was perfect.
Month by month and year by year the horrible liabilities were
sorted and tabulated, forming a trap, a web, a network of
catastrophe.

He knew them all by heart, every smallest one. How
long he had lived with them ever in his thoughts, seen them
in his dreams, found them obtruding between his vision and
every other thing — even between him and his wife's face!
Yes, right well did he know those papers on that desk. And
best of all, he knew the Jarboe letter, keystone of the infa-

mous arch. Once that arch should break no power on earth could avert a hideous collapse of the whole structure, burying him forever beneath the ruins.

In fingers that shook as with ague, under the glow of the electric lamp, Slayton picked up the trial balance he had struck, the reckoning of his terrible involvement, the sum-total of disaster.

" This is the end," said he in a dull, flat tone. " The end of eleven years of torment! The note I owe Jarboe will be the bomb that will blow the whole structure into the air. This thing mustn't happen! It can't — it *shall* not!"

Again he fell to pacing with the monotonous regularity of a prisoner in a cell. His tortured mind reverted to the first mistake, years and years ago, the first miscalculation, then swiftly ran along the well-remembered ways of progressive disaster, covered by a deeper and still deeper sinking in the mire. Every struggle to free himself had only submerged him farther and more hopelessly. At times there had been hope; then fresh misfortunes had swamped him.

And all those weary years the hideous farce of respectability, of outward calm and prosperity, of impeccable rectitude had had to be lived through. Worst of all, he had been obliged to face his wife with a smile when the heart had long since died in him.

Again the man groaned in anguish. Better anything now, even the ultimate catastrophe, than such a life!

Better anything? Even the prison cell, the striped garb of infamy? The living death of the penitentiary? No, no, not that! Never that! He felt that come what might, he would battle on and on forever, if he could, before he would submit to that!

Yet the Jarboe note was due to-morrow. It must be met in the morning. Eighty-four thousand dollars in cash must be paid. The last stand-off had been exhausted. No extension was possible. Cash was needed now — hard, cold, actual cash.

A shudder gripped him. His lean and rather clerical-looking face — a pious-seeming face that had long been of sovereign value to him in his peculations — twitched nervously. Its pallor bore a ghastly tinge in the greenish light that seeped through the electric-light shade. He blinked ominously. The glint in his eyes spoke volumes of evil.

This, he realized, was the crucial moment, the end of everything unless some bold play were made. In a kind of daze he stared at the merciless figures. He struck them with his fist. Nothing of all this must be known. The lie must still be lived!

His reputation, he knew, still stood intact. Nobody as yet even suspected him. As long as he could keep his hands on the books of the bank he might still be able to juggle the accounts.

The one absolutely essential thing was to stave off the impending calamity of the morrow. It involved taking a long chance, but nothing else now remained to do. He still knew that a good fight remained in him. Before everything should collapse and they should drag him " up the river," they should yet find how good a fight he could give them!

He shivered suddenly and drew back, glancing furtively about him as if the very walls had eyes. Close-drawn though the shades were, he feared lest somebody might be spying on him. Over to the windows he strode and pulled the curtains down a little more. Then he returned again to his desk.

His thoughts were beginning to clarify themselves a little. He realized that he would go to any length to pay that Jarboe note. The Shylock should have his pound of flesh. The last step should be taken and the last card played.

Then if he lost, the crash he would make in going down would prove him at least no petty thief.

Slayton flung down the balance again, and with a steadier hand unlocked and opened a little drawer at the right of the line of pigeon-holes that topped his desk. From this drawer he took an envelope, and from the envelope a paper with a few figures in carbon-copied typewriting.

This paper he studied a moment under the light. It was one of two copies which alone existed in all the world. Chamberlain, president of the Powhatan, had the other one. Doubtless, thought Slayton, Chamberlain felt entirely safe. The cashier nodded satirically, and for the first time that night smiled. A wan, thin-lipped smile it was, saturnine and terrible to match his thoughts, as he studied the Open Sesame that would smooth his path.

"Now we're getting down to business," he murmured. "It's a long shot, but there's a chance at least. I'll have a chance to run; I shan't be trapped and done to death like a caged rat. A chance — that's all I want!"

He smote the table with decision.

If he could only tide things over for a month or two all might yet be well. Hope revived in his face. A bolder look came into his eyes. He glanced round again, holding his breath to listen. Out on the front walk he seemed to have heard a sound. Keenly he gave ear.

Nothing.

He sneered savagely at himself. Could it be that he was getting nervous? With a strong effort he collected his forces. He folded the precious slip of paper and tucked it into his pocketbook. Then, turning to a little cupboard in the corner by the fireplace, he took down a bottle and a glass.

But he poured no liquor. His wiser judgment, infallibly sane, had quickly reasserted itself.

"Absolutely *no!*" he exclaimed.

A clear brain and a steady hand would be needed to-night if ever in his life.

"Eh? What's that?"

Swiftly he faced round. This time he felt positive he had heard a step on the walk. It seemed hesitant and timid; but a human footstep had unmistakably fallen on the concrete.

"What the — devil?"

Flash-quick, Slayton sprang to the desk, jerked open the big top drawer and swept all the damning papers into it. Just as he shut and locked it, the electric bell *brrrrrr'd* stridently in the hallway, making an astonishing racket in the tomblike stillness of the house.

Savagely he faced the door with a "Plague take you!" on his lips. "Butting in on me, the night of all nights when I've got to be let alone!"

Again the bell burst into violent alarm. With an oath more than half of fear — for Slayton's nerves, despite all he could do, were jumpy as a colt's — he stepped into the hall, listened acutely for a moment, and then approached the door.

Outside he could hear an irregular tattoo of feet on the porch, sure sign of nervousness. Whatever might be forward, the visitor lacked calm self-possession.

Slayton's fear lessened. If the other man were nervous that was all the more reason why he should not be. After all, nobody in the world had anything on him. He had always managed to cover his tracks perfectly. Boldness and assurance were now invaluable assets for him. A grim smile curved his lips as he shot back the bolt and loosed the chain.

He pressed a button. The porch-light flooded down a sudden radiance. Then he swung wide the door.

At sight of the man standing there before him a sickening

apprehension seized him. His mouth sagged open. Staring, he fell back a pace, his hand still gripping the big brass door-knob.

"You, Mansfield?" he stammered. "What — what is it? What on earth do *you* want here at this time of night?"

CHAPTER II

"AS A BIRD INTO THE NET"

THE newcomer, obviously agitated in the very highest degree, made no answer to this question, but stood in the doorway returning the other's stare.

"Thank God, you — you're home!" he cried thickly. "Oh, thank God!"

Under the downpour of light from above they formed a singular picture as they stood there, eye looking into eye, while the frosty vapors of their breath idled upward toward the light. A striking picture — the middle-aged cashier, wrinkled and disheveled, in his smoking-jacket and slippers; the young bank-clerk, immaculate and trim, in balmacaan and olive-green felt hat. Different types in every way; yet the community of some unusual emotion drew them both into the same category.

Slayton, a nerve-seasoned and ruseful man, pulled himself together immediately. He thrust out a hand of welcome.

"Come in, Mansfield!" he ejaculated, cloaking his alarm behind a very natural astonishment. "You certainly did surprise me. What's the row? Anything gone wrong?"

The young man nodded, gulped and tried to speak. Words would not come. He seized Slayton's hand in a grip that, though trembling, still had good beef behind it. Slayton winced.

"Here, here, Arthur!" he protested, trying to force a laugh that rang wholly false. "Don't take my arm off! What's up, anyhow?"

8

"I — I want to see you; want to talk to you a — a few minutes!" Mansfield succeeded in articulating. "I beg your pardon for intruding at this — this ghastly hour and all that, but — but —"

"Don't mention it, my dear fellow," Slayton returned with something of his usual suavity.

Every second now he was recovering his aplomb.

"Anything I can do to oblige you, at any hour of the day or night, I'll be glad to do," he continued. "But say, it's cold out here. Come in, Arthur; come in. We'll go into the library, and —"

"By George! That's mighty good of you!" the young fellow interrupted. The sincerity of his gratitude was pitiable.

He followed Slayton into the hall. The cashier's discerning eye appraised him as wholly unstrung; as clinging to the ragged edge of desperation.

"You're mighty good!" the youngster repeated. "Fact is, Mr. Slayton, I — I've come to see you on — important business. It's —"

"You're in trouble? In some kind of a scrape? Is that it?"

The cashier's voice tried to convey deep apprehension; but in it vibrated a strange, malicious joy.

Mansfield gulped hard and peered about him nervously as the outer door closed.

· "We're all alone here?" he whispered in trepidation.

"Absolutely, my dear fellow. Now tell me; what's the row? Speak frankly and —"

"It goes no further?"

"Not an inch!"

"I'm just a junior clerk at the bank, I know, and you're the cashier. You're —"

"Never you mind about that, Arthur! It's man to man here now!"

The crafty glitter in Slayton's eye seemed to have intensified. A subtly sly look crept into his face. Did he so soon foresee some dim eventualities, some nebulous possibilities turning to his behoof? Who should say?

His masklike expression of pietism grew dangerous and hard. On his pale lips the clerical smile widened.

" Speak out, Arthur, my boy," he bade. " Speak plainly as man to man! "

" I will! I must! "

Mansfield passed a hand across his eyes.

" Great Heavens, Mr. Slayton, there's not another soul — I could go to — for help! "

" Help? You need help? "

" Terribly! "

" Why, what's wrong? "

" Well, the fact is, I — I'm in a fix. A mighty bad fix, I guess. And I don't see any way out of it except to —"

" To get my help? "

" That's just it! Will you help me? "

" I surely will, Arthur! Freely and gladly as if you were my own son. That's the greatest pleasure I have in life, lending a hand wherever I can! "

A semblance of real sincerity made the dross of it seem almost real gold. Mansfield, in his intense agitation, accepted the base metal as pure, and looked at the cashier with eyes of unspeakable gratitude. Slayton meanwhile was thinking fast.

That singularly acute *flair* which for so many years had helped guide him through many a shallow, through many a perilous way, now told him that all his advantage lay parallel with this trouble of the junior clerk's.

Could he but probe the matter to the bottom, learn its every ramification and fully win the young chap's confidence, great things might yet befall. A strong conviction rose in the cashier that he must lend a hand, or seem to; for in this way, as in no other now, might lie safety for himself.

Boundless was his relief at realization that Mansfield's coming — at first glance so inopportune, so terrifying — might after all veer to his success. When he had first caught sight of the young fellow from the bank standing there on the front porch, a poignant dismay had assailed Slayton. Not even the appearance of a police officer, warrant in hand, would have startled him so profoundly. Through having often already anticipated such a scene he had long ago resolved to discount its emotions and had schooled himself to calmness. But to be confronted at precisely this juncture by a man from the bank itself had very badly shaken him.

Second thought told Slayton that the boy could, of course, know nothing of the vast, intricate and skilled system of theft in which he had become involved. But the mere sight of him had startled the cashier immeasurably.

And now, hearing the young fellow's plea and beholding his obvious distress, a tremendous sense of easement swept across Slayton's soul. His fears vanished like a wisp of fog before the rising sun.

"Then you *will* help me?" questioned Mansfield again with terrible eagerness. "You will, you will?"

"By all means, my dear fellow! That is, if I can."

Slayton smiled affably with a glint of white teeth. Something feline, something ominous lurked in that smile; but Mansfield, standing there pale and distraught before him, beheld only friendliness and benevolence in the cashier's face.

"Thank Heaven for a friend like you!" the boy exclaimed.

His blue eyes brimmed up with tears of reaction after long stress. Once more he gripped the elder man's hand.

Slayton clapped him on the shoulder — a broad shoulder, and capable-looking.

"Unload," said he. "Let's have it. What's wrong, Arthur? Give me the whole story."

"I will!"

Arthur released his grip on the cashier's hand, took off his hat and flung it on the table, then paced a few steps up and down, much as Slayton had been pacing. The cashier's smile betrayed amusement now. To see another on the rack, was it not rare sport?

His eye caught a reflection of himself in the broad mirror over the mantel. With quick satisfaction he noted that now he showed but few signs of perturbation.

"Even the little success I've had in amateur theatricals," thought he, "is helping me now."

He felt a sense of gratitude for that experience. It might yet stand him in good stead.

Arthur stopped on the rug beside the table, confronted Slayton and squared himself for the confession that the cashier now foresensed.

Mansfield's face showed strong lines, even though immature and not yet wholly formed — lines of nascent character that bade fair to be one day powerful and dominant. His head poised itself well; the chin was firm and good, the nose broad at the parting of the brows, the eyes steady. A thatch of rather rebellious hair — yellow hair that contrasted well with the blue eyes, hair that inclined to curl despite every effort to make it lie flat — crowned intelligent brows.

This man, on the whole, stood well above the dead-level of humanity. And as Slayton appraised him more critically than ever before — for till now the cashier had noticed him as only one of three or four young clerks at the bank — and as he sensed the innate honesty and ingenuous frankness of the boy, a thrill of exultation warmed his cold heart.

"Clay to my hand," thought he, "if I can only mold him as I must. Clay that will harden to adamant in time. Fate knew I needed him. Fate sent him. Fate is good!"

Suddenly Arthur spoke.

"I — I am a thief!" he blurted, in a terrible voice.

"A —?"

And Slayton, with well-feigned surprise, gripped the table-edge.

"A — *what?*"

"A thief! There! Now you know the worst. You know all there is to know — except why I did it. When I say that, I say everything — the whole business. I've stolen — stolen money from the bank. It isn't much, but that's no excuse. To me it's a lot — a terrible lot!

"It's more than I can pay for a year or two. But I'm going to pay it, every cent. Principal and interest! All I need is time — time, that's all. And so I come to you. You can help me through this. You can pull me out o' the mud and give me chance to make good. To make good and be a man again — honest — square. For God's sake, help me — help me!"

His words, which had been rushing in a stream, grew choked and incoherent. They broke; they ceased. Mansfield suddenly covered his face with both hands, dropped his head and stood there racked with anguish. His pallor, the tremors that shook him, the wordless groan that issued from his lips all told the story of his crucifixion.

Unmoved, Slayton studied the young fellow with a cynical coolness, much as if he had been a peculiar biological specimen impaled on a pin. Then the cashier nodded again, and once more the pale-lipped smile disclosed his teeth.

"As a bird into the net of the fowler," thought he, "so art thou delivered unto my hand!"

CHAPTER III

"COME, come, my boy," said he, his voice seeming to speak volumes of friendly comfort. "Brace up! Things can't be half so bad as you try to make out. You're unnerved, half-hysterical, far from yourself. You're exaggerating the trouble, whatever it is. There'll be a way out — there must be. If there isn't, I'll make one for you!"

Overcome, Arthur clung to the other's arm.

"I — I knew you would!" he managed to articulate. "If you ever succeed in getting me out of this, I'll owe you a debt of —"

"Nonsense, my boy! My natural liking for you, as well as my Christian duty toward my fellow man, dictates that I should lend a hand wherever possible. That's my only religion, Arthur, to do whatever good I can in life — that and the Golden Rule. So you see I'm only following my natural bent in helping you. Don't thank me, please!"

"But I do, I do!"

"You mustn't. Tell me the whole thing; that'll be more profitable. Let's have the story in as few words as possible. It's getting late. Why, bless my soul, it's nearly midnight! What's the trouble, Arthur? Out with it!"

He smiled at the boy with as good a simulation of cordiality as he could muster, though inwardly he was cursing this young bungler who at an hour so very inopportune had dropped into the midst of all his plans. This interruption would surely delay and might perhaps wreck his arrangements. Something must be done, and at once.

His mind alternated between rejoicing at the possible uses to which he could turn this incident and the certain loss of valuable time it involved. A returning sense of the imperativeness of immediate action forced upon him the realization that unless he could speedily rid himself of Mansfield, the few remaining hours of night would be forever lost. With the morning, should it find his plan unaccomplished, ruin would dawn.

A thrill of nervous anxiety, of sudden fear, shot through him. Now that the diversion of his ideas by Mansfield's abrupt entrance into the scene had somewhat abated, a burning eagerness began once more to possess him. He must be at work! Every moment now was golden. But he held his grip upon his nerves. Biting his lip, steadying his voice, forcing a calm that belied his racing pulses, he once more exclaimed:

"Let's have it all, my boy! All, and immediately. The sooner you get this thing off your heart and conscience the sooner we can begin repairing the damage. Now sit down in that big chair and—"

"No, no; not there! I couldn't sit down, Mr. Slayton; indeed I couldn't. I—I guess I'm too nervous to keep still. You see, it all started by—by—"

"Well?"

Mansfield floundered, flushed, paled, and remained speechless. The cashier shoved a box of cigarettes across the table.

"Maybe a little nicotine might help?" he ventured.

"No, no. I've cut that all out, along with—everything. No more. I'm done!"

"So?"

And Slayton reached for the box. He lighted one of the cigarettes, inhaled deeply and gusted thin vapor toward the ceiling.

"That's good," he commented. "Glad to hear it. Do

I infer that — er — a tendency to dissipation has got you
into this — hmm! — this difficulty?"

" No, not that. Oh, I haven't been an angel, or anything of that sort! But since I — well, got to going with
Enid — with Miss Chamberlain, you know —"

" Ah, yes; of course! You *have* been paying some attention to Miss Chamberlain. I forgot about that. Naturally that factor makes your position all the more difficult. It hasn't any direct bearing on the case, I hope? I
mean, in order to keep up appearances and all that, you
haven't —"

" No, no; nothing of that sort! "

And Arthur seemed to repel the idea by swiftly thrusting out his hand.

" Much as I — love — Enid, Miss Chamberlain I'd give
her up a thousand times over, before I'd be a — thief to win
her! "

" Very well said; very well-indeed! It *would* be an odd
situation — wouldn't it? — for a bank-clerk to woo the
daughter of the bank-president with money stolen from the
bank itself. That certainly would complicate matters.

" And by the way, Arthur," Slayton added with an attempt at merely casual interest, " before we go any further,
just what are your prospects with the young lady? Pardon
my asking. I do so only because it may — well, may possibly have rather an important bearing on the case."

" My prospects? " queried Mansfield.

He passed trembling fingers through his hair.

" Well, I don't just know, for certain. Pretty good, I
guess. I've been entertained at their house five or six
times. And then I've been their guest at the Edgemere
Country Club, and once I went yachting with them, last summer, as far as Mount Desert. They've been just bully to
me! I — I guess they kind of look on me as — as —"

" As a future member of the family? Is that it? "

"I guess so. Enid does anyhow; I know *that* much. That's what makes all this so terrible. If it ever gets out just think of what'll happen! It won't be only a case of about killing my father and mother, but Enid will have to suffer. I don't care what happens to *me!* It's —"

"Of course; of course! But enough of this, Arthur. Let's get down to specific facts. You've misappropriated funds; is that it?"

"Stolen, you mean! Stolen! Yes!"

The boy's head came up sharply. He faced the older man, eye to eye. Slayton's glance was first to fall.

"Stolen!" Mansfield repeated. "I'm a thief!"

His look belied him. Not shame now, but a kind of strange, wild pride burned in his face. At sound of the words, Slayton changed color. Then, stammering and abashed despite his every effort, he demanded:

"What amount? How much did you — steal? And how did you take it? And when?"

"How much? Twelve hundred and fifty dollars. I stole it last week on Thursday afternoon and Friday morning. I can show you just how I got away with it, to-morrow. I'll give you the falsified accounts. It was only a matter of a few ciphers and a decimal point or two. You know, it's not very hard to do that sort of thing, sometimes. Such things can be put through for a while, and got away with."

"Of course, of course," assented the cashier nervously. "Well, well, Arthur! The facts are out at last. Twelve hundred and fifty, eh? Hmm! Not a vital matter after all. Not irreparable by a long shot."

"You'll give me a lift?"

"Gladly! On one condition."

"What's that?"

"On condition that you tell me what you took the money for."

The boy turned a shade paler than before. He thrust
out a denying hand.

"No, no! Not that, Mr. Slayton. Not that! I can't
tell you that!"

"Why not, pray?" And Slayton's eyes narrowed, as he
blew another lungful of smoke across the room.

"Why can't you? It can't be any more disgraceful than
the fact of the theft itself! Come, come, Arthur! Make
a clean breast of it! Playing the races, eh? Nothing to
the ponies, my boy; nothing to them! Or was it the little
ivory ball on the spinning wheel, or the pasteboards, or the
bubbles in the tall glass, or the —"

"None of those, none of those! Not one! No, nor the
other thing you were just going to ask. Nothing of all
that, so help me!"

Arthur's fist struck the table a smashing blow.

"Nothing at all like that! It's a clean reason anyhow.
Absolutely clean. Yet I can't tell you. I simply can't!"

"But you must, Arthur. You must. Otherwise —"

"I can't! And you'll help me just the same; won't you?
My God! You've *got* to help me! If you don't, if you refuse to lend me enough to cover the deficit before the examiners call to-morrow —"

"The examiners?" ejaculated Slayton, startled out of
his mask-like pretense of calm. "To-morrow, I — I forgot about that! Let me think, Arthur. Let me think!"

He felt a sudden, deadly pang of terror. How could he
have overlooked that vital fact? To-morrow was November 15. And the Federal examiners would be there!

The thought of this new contingency lashed him like a
nagaika. Money! He must have money to straighten out
his accounts! If any theft were to be discovered it must
not be laid to *him!* That note must not go to protest; no
question must be raised as to his solvency.

Money! He must get his hands on it at once! He must

have cash — hard white and yellow cash from the canvas bags, or yellow-backs from the sealed packets. More than a hundred thousand he must have by morning from the farthest recesses of the vaults!

That meant only one thing: he must get to work at once. A fine sweat began prickling on his brow. Unseeing, he stared at Mansfield. Past him and through him the cashier stared, seeming to see striped clothing, rows of cells, high-barred windows; to hear the clank and jangle of huge keys; to scent the foul, carbolic-acid stench of the Pen.

To-morrow! To-morrow morning he must have more than a hundred thousand dollars!

The urgency of the situation dawned on him with fresh, full, terrible insistence. No longer could he cherish at the back of his brain any hope that perhaps the job could still be postponed another day or two. Even were Jarboe's note not due, this other contingency would force him to act at once.

And so, now suddenly struck by the instant necessity of the crisis, he stood there staring, making no answer to the agonized young man before him.

Mansfield's cry of despair hardly reached his consciousness — the cry of:

" So, then — you won't let me have it? "

" What? " asked the cashier, confused.

" I can't tell you why I stole it — I can't, *can't!* " the boy cried in anguish. " It wasn't for myself anyhow. It was for — for — No, no! I can't tell! "

Dazed for a moment and unable to collect himself, Slayton shook his head in vague negation.

A glint of lamplight on steel caught his eye.

" Here! Drop that! Drop it, you young fool! " he shouted, leaping.

" Stand back! " cried Mansfield in a choking voice. " Look out now! If you won't give it to me I've got noth-

ing to live for! I'll lose Enid and disgrace her and everybody; I'll go to Sing Sing, and —"

Swiftly the cashier struck, with surprising strength. The
pistol spun through the air, clattered across the table and
thumped to the floor.

"You young idiot!"

And Slayton caught it up.

"None o' that, now; you understand? None o' that here!
No cheap melodrama in my house!"

He flung the weapon into the desk-drawer and slammed
it shut. Mansfield stood there staring at him, white to the
lips.

"I tell you," he quavered, "if I don't get that twelve
hundred I'll surely do it, one way or another. There's
plenty of deep water between here and New York, and —"

"Drop your nonsense!"

Slayton's voice had gone rasping and harsh.

"Suppose you did do it, you lunatic? What possible
good would that do? It's stupid, to begin with, and the
worst possible kind of welshing. No thoroughbred quits
that way. And talk about wrecking Enid's life! What
could possibly shatter her worse than that?

"Would it accomplish anything? Would it put back the
twelve hundred? Would it clear your name, or —"

"Do I get it or don't I?" demanded Arthur, livid.

"You don't deserve to; but —"

"I'm going to get it? You'll give it to me?"

"Damn you, yes!"

"Thank God!"

"Better thank *me*, you fool! Come to my desk at nine
in the morning, and take the envelope I hand you. You're
saved temporarily. In a day or two I'll arrange —"

"Oh, how can I ever —?"

"Come now; come, come! Cut that! This is no philan-
thropy. I'm simply doing my duty, my Christian duty; that's

all. I'll lend you the money. You can pay me in monthly installments. As I was going to say, we'll arrange suitable terms."

" I'll be your — your slave as long as —"

" Don't talk rot! I'm tired now. Here it is almost midnight. A nice *quart d'heure* you've given me, I must say. Get out! I've seen enough of you. Go on — go home! And mind now, no nonsense! And be at my desk at nine, sharp. You've got just time to catch a train for the city.

" Not a word! Not a word! Get out — and devil take you!"

CHAPTER IV

THE DAWNING OF AN EVIL PLAN

MOTIONLESS, Slayton stood listening a moment to make quite sure Mansfield was on his way. The outer door thudded shut, reëchoing through the silent house. Steps crossed the porch and made off along the walk with diminishing sound. These faded into silence. Mansfield was gone.

"Good!" ejaculated the cashier, nodding with content-ment. "*He's* out of the way, at all events. Nearly spoiled everything, damn him! But as it is, things are turning my way again."

The prospect was bright with encouragement. This accident of fate might after all prove a blessing in disguise. Slayton was not slow to understand that the boy might after all prove wonderfully useful to him.

"If my brains haven't turned to ivory and my heart to water," thought the cashier, "I can use him on a pinch, and use him hard! Twelve hundred, eh? And all ready to blow his foolish head off for that trifle? And wouldn't tell why he stole it?"

Slayton rubbed his sleek hands together with satisfac-tion. He began to catch glimpses of some deep motive in the boy's actions — something far deeper than wine, women, song; than cards, roulette, the ponies. What that some-thing was he could not even guess as yet; but he felt cer-tain it existed.

And once he could discover that something, he believed,

he hoped — yes, already he definitely calculated that he could — mold young Mansfield to his purposes as a potter molds his clay.

The clock, striking midnight, started him from his reflections. The time had come for action if anything were to be done to avert impending disaster. He rubbed his sleek hands together, then faced suddenly about and glanced at the clock.

"Say, this won't do!" he exclaimed. "*I've* got to be getting busy. Time enough, but none to spare. Fifteen minutes before train-time. It'll do."

He produced a bunch of keys from his trousers' pocket, unlocked a lower drawer in his desk and took out a neatly-wrapped parcel. The very care with which this had been done up typified the man. Methodical, cold, precise and neat in all his ways, suave and outwardly impeccable, he stood for all that may be summed in the one word: "Respectability."

Slayton opened the parcel, took out a gray wig, a false beard and mustache and a pair of gold-rimmed glasses. These properties, saved from the amateur theatricals of the previous winter, now bade fair to assume a rôle of great import.

In five minutes the metamorphosis was complete. With intense satisfaction Slayton surveyed himself in the glass. He had become wholly unrecognizable. Nothing now remained of the personality that had been. In place of the well-groomed, suave and immaculate bank-cashier of forty-one, an elderly man of broken-down and seedy appearance stood there on the rug before the fireplace.

"Grand!" ejaculated Slayton. "Why, I might pass for my own father!"

He felt a sudden sense of security. Nobody could ever be able to assert that he had been out of his own house that night. He knew that if ever he were suspected of the crime he had now definitely planned to commit, Mansfield's testimony would give him an alibi.

Mansfield could be made to swear that he had left Slayton at home, close to midnight. He could be made to swear that Slayton had not taken the 12:17 train to St. George's and the ferry; and this, Slayton knew, was the last train till morning.

Exultant, the cashier continued his preparations. He was just beginning to realize what a stupendous piece of bull-luck it had been all around that had driven Mansfield to see him. If the thing had all been planned in advance it could not have worked out more beautifully.

Slayton threw the string of the parcel into the fire, then carefully put back into the desk-drawer the paper that had enwrapped his disguise. One might have thought so slight a matter as a sheet of brown paper could possess no possible importance; but Slayton believed otherwise. Now that his mind had been fully made up to the deed he meant to do, he intended no step to fail, no link of the chain to show the slightest flaw.

His intelligence, logical and incisive to almost a super-human degree, weighed every chance and analyzed every contingency. One possibility in ten thousand existed, per-haps, that the disguise might be called into question. By wrapping up the things again in the original paper that still bore the name of the dealer from whom he had bought them he could strengthen his case. He could establish a claim that the disguise had never been out of the parcel since the time of the theatricals. Ninety-nine persons out of a hundred in opening a package will throw away the paper. Slayton was the hundredth. He saw possibilities even in a sheet of manila.

Having locked up the paper for further use, he put on his boots and discarded his smoking-jacket. Then he went out into the hall, and from the closet under the stairs took a

disreputable old coat and overcoat, also a battered felt hat
— clothing he sometimes used for working round the gar-
den, in rainy weather. He slid an electric flash-light into
one of the pockets, and made sure he had a pair of gloves.

" No finger-print evidence for me!" he muttered.
" That little detail is worth looking out for. Well, now "
— surveying himself in the mirror of the hat-rack —" I
think I'll do! "

As an elderly, rather shabby but still respectable citizen
he stood there smiling at himself. Then he returned to the
library, took the memorandum of the safe-combination that
was written on the little slip of paper, and pocketed his keys
and a bottle of machine-oil which he found in the drawer of
his wife's sewing-machine.

Lastly he put on a pair of old, well-worn rubbers, and
buttoned the shabby overcoat tightly up about his throat.
One last look in the mirror convinced him that all was perfect. He was about to extinguish the electric lights when
an idea struck him. " Eh? " said he. " Had I better?
Mightn't it lead to — to more than I intend? "

Hesitant, he debated the question in his mind. Suddenly he shook his head.

" It will lead to nothing! " he decided. " I know perfectly well what I'm about. My self-control is absolute.
No harm can come of having it. And as a bit of protection in a pinch, it may be invaluable to bluff with. Yes, I'll
take it."

Once more he returned to the desk, opened the drawer
into which he had thrown Mansfield's pistol, and took out
the blunt-nosed, brutal weapon. Critically he weighed it
in his hand, a moment.

 " Big enough caliber, I must say," he commented.
" Forty-something, at the very least. If that infernal idiot
had made good on his threat, he'd have blown the top of his
head clean off, in a shocking manner. He'd possibly have

involved me in a charge of murder that might have played the devil with me. He'd certainly have delayed me so that I couldn't have put this business through, to-night. In any event, it would have been fatal to me."

Cool as Slayton was, he shuddered at the thought of what might have happened there in the library; and a sense of fear assailed him as the new idea flashed to his mind that under those circumstances he might easily have been convicted of murder.

In any event, Mansfield's suicide would have forever destroyed all hopes of his clearing himself from the financial web that now enmeshed him. It would have fatally delayed him and have banished every hope. Slayton realized how closely he had verged ruin, and cursed the boy under his breath.

An ugly set of the jaw betrayed Slayton's inner character. "He'll pay for this later, damn him!" the cashier muttered. "He'll pay. But now — enough of this. Time's up. I must be going."

Swiftly he extinguished all lights, left the house, made certain the door was locked, and then struck into a brisk walk toward the station, a quarter-mile distant. Already off to southward he could hear the piping whistle of the locomotive. Everything had been figured to a nicety. He would arrive exactly on time. There would be no delay, no lurking in the roadside bushes to wait for the train; no enervating suspense on the station platform, should he venture there. Slayton smiled again.

"It's all fitting together like a Chinese puzzle, bit by bit," said he. "A few hours more and this burden, the intolerable horror of this menace, will be lifted from my shoulders forever."

Exultant, he strode along, breathing deeply the frosty air of late November. A magnificent night that was, to be abroad — a night that should have turned his thoughts to better things; to wonder at the beauty and majesty of nature; to thoughts of uprightness and honor; a night the like of which only a few each year brood over earth and sky. ′

No snow as yet had powdered the world with fairy jewels. The light from a gibbous moon, now and then obscured by vagrant clouds through which it seemed swiftly to stoop, limned with surprising clarity each house and wall and tree. The tang of approaching winter vivified the air. Never had Slayton sensed a greater fulness of life, of power. He pulsed with a plenitude of energy, with purpose, with keen and conscienceless strength.

To him the night seemed one fitting to witness his act of liberation. He felt that freedom now lay close ahead. It seemed inevitable. His will, his purpose would make it so.

Scornfully he thought that only weaklings bow before threats of disaster. Real men, strong men with capable hands and brains, he reflected, know how to meet each peril and weather every storm.

Inflated with a sense of his own power, the cashier strode on and on. Of a sudden the train slid into view, a long checker of bright spots running swiftly through a patch of oak forest. Far across the night were flung raucous echoes from the screaming locomotive as it signaled the next stop. Slayton quickened his pace a trifle.

As the train ground to a stop, with brake-shoes spouting cascades of fireworks, he mounted the steps of the platform. A figure in a balmacaan and an olive-green felt hat was moving directly toward Slayton, to enter the smoker.

Firm as a rock the cashier stood there. Mansfield, he clearly saw, was suffering from an extreme attack of nerves. The boy's sidelong glance was furtive. Ordinarily his blue eyes held steady, clear and unafraid. Now they shuttled uncertainly. The clamp of his teeth on the pipe he had forgotten to light supplemented the shiver that racked his body. Plainly Arthur was about " all in."

For a second or two Mansfield's look rested full on the cashier's face there under the gleaming lamps of the station. But no sign of recognition appeared. Slayton knew that his disguise was absolutely perfect. He had not been detected, and he would not be.

"Bo-*ard!* *All* a-board!" chanted a brakeman, swinging his lantern.

Slayton smiled very grimly to himself.

"Perfect alibi," thought he as he entered the train. "He and I are the only passengers to get on here. He'll swear if need be that I was at home when he started for the city, and that nobody got on to the train here except a nondescript old man. Perfect!"

Mansfield went into the dim-lit smoker. Slayton followed, and sat down two seats behind him to watch his actions. The boy's nervousness did not decrease. It seemed rather to grow more and more acute. Half a dozen times he lighted his pipe before they reached the municipal ferry, and half a dozen times it went out. He shifted in his seat, picked up a discarded paper, tried in vain to read, threw it down, took off his hat and replaced it.

The cashier, almost alone with Mansfield in the car — for only one other passenger sat there, drowsing at the extreme rear — buried his chin deep in the upturned collar of his old coat, pulled down his formless hat and feigned sleep. But under the hat-brim his slit-closed eyes kept gleaming watch. And hidden in the big false beard his lips were smiling ominously.

Mansfield ventured a glance behind him, saw only a gold-spectacled man asleep, and felt relieved. Presently, as the train swayed racketing through Stapleton, the cashier saw him take a photograph from his pocket, gaze at it with rapt intentness and passionate fervor, then suddenly press it to his lips.

"The young fool!" thought Slayton.

All that he could see in Mansfield's love was that it bound shackles on the young chap's wrists. An impediment such folly was — a giving of vast hostage into Fortune's keeping.

On and on clashed the almost empty train, over switches, through sleeping suburban towns, past red-eyed lights that glowered in swift trajectories, away, away! Finally a long skreel of the whistle blared its announcement that the terminal was near, at the ferry.

Mansfield slid the photograph of Enid Chamberlain back into his pocket and buttoned his coat tight. Again he glanced around. Slayton saw that the boy's eyes were gleaming — wet with tears.

A sneer rose to the cashier's lips.

"Idiot!" he muttered.

And of a sudden, deeper and more ominous thoughts began to cluster — birds of evil omen — in his brain.

"Perhaps it might be done," he whispered, fixing his hard eyes on the boy. "Perhaps it might be done, after all. Who knows?"

CHAPTER V

THE ROBBERY

NOISELESSLY the flat key, which Slayton had carefully oiled so that it should not squeak, turned in the lock. Silently the grillwork door of steel, likewise treated to a few drops of oil, swung inward. And in silence Slayton entered the bank enclosure, listened a tense moment, holding his breath, then soundlessly closed the door behind him.

Temptation whispered:

"Leave it open! In case of trouble you'll need to have it open for a quick get-away!"

But with superior intelligence he resisted. It was essential, he knew, that he should leave everything in normal condition as he passed. An open grill, if discovered, would precipitate disaster.

He listened eagerly, there in the gloom of the bank office, lighted only by the glaring incandescent that hung before the door of the huge safe, fifty-eight feet to his left. Slayton knew it was just fifty-eight feet. There was no major measurement of the building he had not familiarized himself with. Not that any very definite idea of robbing the vaults had ever been borne in on him till that night; but rather on general principles. His methodical mind, coldly impersonal, had a passion for information of every sort. No telling when it might come useful!

So there he stood and listened. Not a sound. Already he had penetrated close to his goal without a sign or signal of discovery. A few minutes more without interruption and success — golden success — would fall into his grasping hand.

Just a few minutes more — a few terrible, nerve-racking minutes — each an eternity of possibilities! How precious every second was! Yet Slayton did not hurry. Calmly, deliberately, with perfect self-control and careful thought, he was executing each move precisely as he had planned it.

In this supreme moment, as in all the moments of his life, system and calculation ruled him. Through all his nervous tension he realized the prime necessity of coolness. One false step now would mean — What would it *not* mean? Everything in life now summed itself in just this: Ten minutes more of undetected work.

" Ten minutes! " thought the cashier, harkening with terrible intentness. " Just give me ten minutes without that old fool of a Mackenzie butting in, and I'm safe! "

So far everything had gone with perfect success. Slayton had watched Mansfield descend into the subway entrance at South Ferry; then, sure that the young fellow was safely on his homeward way, had briskly walked up Broadway to Cedar Street, down which he had turned.

A few minutes later, quite positive that no patrolman had observed him and that old man Mackenzie was down in the safe-deposit vaults, he had let himself in at the side door of the bank.

This door he had noiselessly closed after him. Quickly he had removed his disguise and had thrust the glasses, wig, beard and mustache into his overcoat-pocket. In his own likeness now he stood there within the enclosure. Nobody in the world had seen him, *as Walter Slayton,* in the city. His plan was working to perfection.

Once the job should be done, he knew, two or three minutes would suffice to put the disguise back again. He would return to Staten Island as he had come, an old man. And meantime, if Mackenzie should just happen to discover him, what could be simpler than to make him believe — believe —

An uncomfortable doubt assailed the cashier. Right well he knew how hard-headed, shrewd and suspicious the old Scot was, with all the canny wisdom of his nationality. Here, had Slayton been willing to face the fact, lay the weak link in his chain — the possibility of Mackenzie's inopportune arrival on the scene.

Still the cashier lulled his anxiety to sleep with the belief that on a pinch he could convince the old man all was well. And really, after all, what was there to fear? Not one chance in a thousand existed that Mackenzie would discover him.

The old man, he well knew, was down-stairs in the safe-deposit vaults, where he had a comfortable chair with a well-padded cushion to ease his aching bones. From long years of studying Mackenzie's habits, Slayton possessed absolutely unimpeachable data on them. Mackenzie acted with the fixed precision of an automaton.

With the oncoming of age he had fallen, like many old men, into precise, mechanical ways. Now Slayton could have taken an oath as to the watchman's location. The fact that the hour was 1.37 vouched for his presence in the vault. From 1.15 to 1.30 A. M. it was his invariable custom to make a round of the offices, the big barred enclosure guarding the safe-doors, the rear rooms — those of the directors, officers and one or two others — and then finally to descend the steel stairs to the subterranean chambers.

Here, his duty done and all the recording-clocks duly punched, he was wont to sit for an hour or more, reading certain mathematical treatises whereof he always carried one or two, well-worn, in his pocket. Mathematics formed the only love of this solitary old man, now as since his youth. Once he had dreamed of being a professor, with

letters after his name, but fate had been unkind and had
amused herself by making him a night-watchman in a bank
— an exemplary night-watchman, be it said; a paragon of
a night-watchman.

But still he clung to formulæ, sines and cosines, equa-
tions and quaternions. He read Binomial Theorem as other
men read novels; found ecstasy in Conic Sections, thrills
of joy in Logarithms, pure nepenthe from all his woes in
the complicated mazes of the Higher Calculus. A harmless old man, withal, though sternly devoted to his duty,
with incorruptible Presbyterian zeal. Sturdy, too; rude of
fist — on a pinch — and keen of eye, with an accurate trig-
ger-finger. No man, this rugged Caledonian eccentric, to
play trickery upon.

Slayton, however, still felt perfectly secure. He knew he
possessed the old fellow's great good-will. The gift of
many a second-hand book had long since won his heart.
And, furthermore, Slayton felt positive that at this precise
moment Mackenzie was absorbed below-stairs in some dizzy
flight of triangulation or in mental gymnastics with x and
y and z.

"He won't be up for half an hour at the inside," muttered the cashier, advancing with extreme and noiseless
caution through the passageway between grills, toward the
door of bars guarding the safe. And half an hour will
far more than suffice. Fifteen minutes, even ten, would
bring success. "All I need is ten minutes — just that, no
more!"

Slayton paused again to listen, then again crept forward,
crouching, furtive, ominous. Making a slight détour to
the right along a side passageway past the bookkeeper's cage,
he pulled down the shades in front of two windows through
which the safe-door could be seen from the street in the
glare of the sixty-four candle-power incandescent dangling
before it.

A certain risk, by no means small, was involved in this act, but it had to be done. Only the patrolman on the beat would ever notice that the shades were down, if he should chance to pass; and Slayton knew he was not due yet for more than thirty minutes. With the shades up, however, any chance pedestrian might see him at work and raise the alarm. By all means those shades must be lowered.

This, too, was part of his elaborate plan. Though Slayton's definite decision to carry out this coup had been formed only a couple of hours previously, the major outlines of it had long been taking shape in his brain. All he had had to do was fill in those outlines. And this his keen intelligence had readily accomplished, even in the limited time at his disposal.

He smiled again shrewdly. Another step had been safely accomplished. All that the job needed was system, a level head, and steady nerves. Once more he advanced to the attack of the safe, his rubber-shod feet perfectly soundless on the tiling. Through the bars of the enclosure that guarded the vault of concrete and steel, with its massive laminated door that carried an intricate machinery of wheels, levers, spindles and pinions, he could now clearly see the goal of his salvation.

He chose a key from the bunch he carried. A moment, and he had unlocked and swung wide the door of massy bars. This he passed through and closed again, but left unlatched, so that at an instant's notice the way of retreat would be open.

And now, tense with excitement in spite of all that he could do to hold his aplomb, with narrowed eyes and gloved hands that trembled a little, with uncertain breath and hammering pulses, he stood close before the safe itself, directly under the cone of light from the incandescent.

Not all his coolness and skill of planning, not all his steeling of the nerves, nor yet the dispassionate coldness of his blood, could keep the cashier from sensing a violent emotion at this, the moment of his first " break."

His previous crimes had all been subtle thefts, the juggling of figures in massive ledgers, the falsification of totals and balances. There had existed no soul-racking crises, no climaxes of emotion. Now, however, all was different. Here he stood before the safe, a burglar, brother to the yegg, differing from him only in the adventitious fact that he possessed the combination, in place of " soup," to open the huge doors.

Slayton began to shiver annoyingly. Under his breath he cursed himself. At this stage of the game was he going to stand there and get stage-struck? An attack of nerves just now would surely be the climax of misfortune. With a strong effort he tried to pull together. He was finding out that for an inexperienced man — no matter how conscienceless — to plan a robbery is one thing; to execute it another.

Despite the fact that he had already lived this scene in imagination, now the reality of it gripped and shook him. Impatiently he tried to thrust aside his introspection. Forcing himself to action, he reached up and snapped off the incandescent. The drenching glare of its illumination, flooding down upon him, would make him a shining mark, a target of targets, should the old man by any chance happen upstairs from the vaults.

Then in complete darkness he drew from his pocket the little electric flash-lamp. His pocketbook yielded up the slip of paper bearing the precious carbon-copied figures — the cipher to the combination recently changed; a cipher whereof only two records existed, one in the hands of President Chamberlain, the other now held in Slayton's gloved fingers under the light-pencil of the electric ray, as he stood there keenly attentive.

A week later Slayton could have accomplished nothing.

The bank was on the point of installing a time-lock, before which nothing save nitroglycerine or thermite will avail. But now only a combination faced the cashier. And, armed with the little piece of paper, it possessed no more difficulty than A B C. He read:

R 5 to 40; L 4 to 50; R 3 to 25; L 2 to 91; R to stop,

Deftly he turned the knob, sensing with satisfaction the play of the tumblers. Through his mind passed a grim amusement at thought of the way in which he would circumvent all evidence against him. His gloved digits were leaving no telltale marks. And in the morning the slip of paper with the combination would be found locked in his desk. He could prove it had never left the bank. He could prove he had never quitted his home that night. No possible chance existed of attaching the crime to him.

Nodding with greater confidence, his nerves now steadying, he worked. And now again he glanced at the paper.

With a slight, an almost imperceptible click, the tumblers fell into position. Slayton's eyes gleamed as he turned the brush of light from the dial to the wheel of polished metal at his right hand.

He rotated the wheel, drawing back all bolts. Then he seized the handle and pulled. At the familiar action — the very same thing he had already done some thousands of times — the door swung easily and gently outward. And yet how very different now the feeling of it was!

Slayton snicked off the current that operated the little flash, and for a moment stood in complete darkness, seeing nothing save some vague gray patches far across the bank-windows giving on the street. He seemed to glimpse bars across these windows. Bars! A vague *frisson* of prescient foreboding insinuated itself into his consciousness, but with impatience he shook it off. Still a glimpse of barred windows *was* disquieting.

" Damn my nerves!" he growled. " Going back on me, are they?"

Another moment he remained there, listening with terrible intentness, breathing through his mouth for greater silence. Was there anything to hint at trouble?

Nothing.

A heavy and oppressive stillness brooded over the darkened bank at this eerie morning hour — an hour of the ebb-tide and dregs of human life. Through the hushed black of the rooms the *click* of the electric timepiece jumping forward a minute sounded with startling loudness. Slayton's muscles tensed. Even that slight disturbance, that little impingement of energy on the muted inertia of the place, seemed of ill omen.

Outside, a dull, vague murmur bespoke the city's lethargy. A distant tram-gong seemed an impertinence in face of the vast sleep, the entire paralysis of life that marks the Wall Street section after midnight. From the East River one or two drowsy, booming whistles drifted up. The hoot of a motor siren over on Broadway mocked the sleep-numbed city.

Convinced that he still remained quite undiscovered and that no danger menaced, Slayton now once more switched on the beam of his search-light. Quickly he threw back the bolts of the inner door of the safe. Then, hesitating not a second longer, he stepped boldly into the strong-room of steel, the goal of all his thought and toil and peril.

Money, hard cash, specie in huge masses exerts a peculiar, almost a maddening, effect on the average man. When confronted with the chance to dig both arms to the elbows in real currency he is apt to lose his better judgment, to run amuck, to do hasty, ill-considered, incriminating things. If he steals he will often steal in stupid and unscientific ways that not only limit the amount he can get away with, but also lay open the way to his subsequent detection.

Not so Slayton. He stood far off from the beaten paths of averages.

For long years and years he had daily and hourly handled money as the commonest of all commodities. He knew money as he knew nothing else. He understood money, thought money, lived money.

To count, handle, appraise, estimate, check, weigh, pay out, and take in money had for many years constituted his life. Now, confronted by all those bales, stacks, rolls and bundles of the familiar stuff, he found his emotions subsiding.

Well, was he not at home there in that vault in face of all this currency? The cash soothed and calmed him. At sight and touch of it his *sang-froid* returned; his pulses ran normally; the fever left his blood. Again he smiled, but this time confidently, masterfully, the smile of a connoisseur who sets his hand to something that he dominates and knows and loves.

Methodically now, without a single false move and without the loss of a second's time, he began his work. To a " T " he knew exactly the place of each denomination, each medium, each kind of specie, bills and other assets in the vault. Leaving aside the compartments devoted to commercial paper and securities, and likewise shunning the canvas sacks of metal, he thrust his hand into a certain pigeon-hole where reposed two hundred and fifty one-thousand-dollar bills in neatly sealed packages of fifty bills each.

Well did he know that the number of each of those bills was recorded in a certain ledger. Even as he abstracted three of the packages and slid them into his inner pocket, he was preparing for the next step in his procedure. He could have taken more, but that might have increased the subsequent peril; and his idea was not to make a haul, but merely to clear himself from his complications, with a generous margin to turn around on. No; he would take only one hundred and fifty thousand dollars. That would do very well indeed. And the next step would effectively block all tracing of the bills.

To this end he took down the ledger containing the entries of the banknote numbers, turned to the pages thumb-indexed " 1000," and ripped them clean out.

These pages he folded and stuffed into his inside coat-pocket, thereafter replacing the ledger in its proper position on the shelf.

He reflected a moment, then nodded with assurance. An important step toward a perfect alibi had now been taken. The theft would assuredly be fastened on somebody in the employ of the bank. No outsider would ever have thought to tear out those pages. Slayton neither knew nor cared about where the blame would fall; but at the back of his mind that nascent idea kept glimmering out again — the idea that if it should become known that one of the junior clerks was in financial trouble, suspicion could not help pointing its finger that way.

"Well, anyhow, it's no affair of mine," said he, preparing to retreat, now that his work was done. "Let them figure it out for themselves."

For a moment he scrutinized the interior of the vault by the rays of his search-light. He paid particular attention to the floor. Nothing had been dropped, he assured himself — nothing that could in any possible way incriminate him. He had left no finger-prints. Should any tracks of his rubbers be detected that would amount to nothing. The rubbers were of a style and pattern sold by the million; moreover, they were worn quite smooth.

Cautiously he returned to the door of the vault, flashing his little antenna of light ahead of him. A few minutes more of non-interference would liberate him, would put him back on the sidewalk again, disguised and safe. Only a few minutes more! Already he seemed to breathe the outer air again — the frosty, life-inspiring air of liberty!

When — hark! What was that?

Recoiling, Slayton gave ear. Back into the shelter of the vault he shrank, peering out tensely into the black.

A step?

Could that be a step out there somewhere in the corridor leading from the safety-deposit vaults below-stairs to the bank office?

All Slayton's blood seemed to coagulate round his heart and clot there and stifle him.

A step!

A step indeed — the old man's step! Mackenzie's!

CHAPTER VI

L OUDER now it sounded, louder and nearer still. It paused a moment as with nascent suspicion; then came on and on again, shuffling a trifle, yet alert.

Livid, Slayton switched off the light of his electric beam and crouched there breathless in the dark. Terrible curses rose to his lips, blasting imprecations, furious maledictions against the old meddler who now for the first time in weeks, perhaps, had just taken it into his head to break his schedule, to mount the circular stairs, to make an extra turn about the bank.

On came the step, and on.

In a few seconds, Slayton knew, Mackenzie would reach the office door, would see that the incandescent before the safe had been extinguished, would start investigating.

The end — the end of everything in life for Slayton — now all at once on the ultimate verge of success — had hurled itself to smite him down. Failure mocked at him, ruin, destruction.

And a sudden tigerish hate leaped into the cashier's heart as he crouched there in the blackness of the big safe, watching. He felt no personal hate against the simple-minded, honest, faithful old Scot, but hate of him as a tool, a means, an instrument of wreckage in his path.

For the first time in his life Slayton felt a thrill of the lust for blood. He comprehended, as with a lightning flash of apperception, how man can raise his hand to strike his brother down. But *he* would not kill, whatever might befall. Of that he felt entirely positive. Subconsciously he

41

knew he would not kill. Let come what might, he would not stain his hands with murder.

Yet a strange, persistent shudder quivered through his body. He felt a fever that singularly seemed a chill. Only by clamping his jaw could he stop the castaneting of his teeth. And in the dark his lips parted in a snarl of hate and malice.

Now all at once a little wavering will-o'-the-wisp of light became visible in the bank office, a spot of white illumination that wandered vagrantly over desks and grills, along the walls, across the windows.

" Mackenzie's flash-light! " thought Slayton.

His heart sank. In a second now the old man himself would appear. Everything would be lost. Ruin would smite him down.

Slayton heard a grumbling voice. Obviously old Mackenzie's suspicions had been aroused by something. The watchman was talking to himself as he advanced. Then, just as a vaguely dark form moved in the gloom through the far doorway, Slayton understood.

The watchman's light had found and was resting on one of the lowered window-shades. Like an inquiring eye, it held its gaze a moment there. And again Slayton heard the burring accents of the old Scotchman in self-communion.

Mackenzie moved forward. The light jumped sharply. Slayton knew the old man had noticed that the incandescent before the safe had been extinguished. A sound of breath, quickly inspired, told Mackenzie's surprise. Then the dark form pushed forward with determination.

Swiftly the cashier thought. Was there any means of escape? Could he still retreat around the vault, gain the corridor, reach a door, a window?

Even as his fevered mind leaped for the hope of safety, he knew it was futile. Every window was barred with steel. The only door he could hope to reach was in plain sight of Mackenzie's sharp eye. And in that stillness any slightest move might now betray his presence. Nothing re- mained to do save crouch down and wait and hope — hope against every possibility that in some way or other he might yet escape detection.

But now already Mackenzie was advancing.

The watchman had at last become convinced something was amiss. The incandescent might have burned out; but the window-shades could not have lowered themselves. Mackenzie knew trouble was afoot. And with the bull- dog courage of his race, with an admirable and self-immo- lating sense of duty, the Scotchman hesitated not, but ad- vanced to ferret out this mystery.

Even through his welter of hate and venom Slayton felt a stab of admiration for the simple directness of the old man's courage. He rang in no alarm, summoned no help, waited not to reconnoiter or to estimate the peril; but as if going his usual rounds pressed forward down the grilled passageway toward the safe.

" Somethin' wrang, the noo! " Slayton heard him solilo- quizing. " Somethin' surely wrang. I dinna ken whut, but I soon shall, or me name's no Sanderson Mackenzie! "

As he came on and on, grumbling to himself, he sprinkled the floor with light from his flash, like a priest throwing holy water. Suddenly the flash stopped short, resting on some object that lay upon the floor.

" Whut — whut the de'il is *this?* " Slayton heard the Scot exclaim.

Tensed in panic-stricken observation as he cringed there peering round the edge of the safe-door, he saw the vague form bend as though to pick up something. Then the little silvery beam of light played over an object held in Mackenzie's hand. Hand and object stood out with star- tling vividness by contrast with the dense curtains of the sur- rounding gloom.

" Eh?   Whut?" the old man ejaculated.

Slayton, peering, felt a sudden weakness turning his bones to water.

The thing that old man Mackenzie was staring at in mute amaze was — *Slayton's wig!*

With some strange cynicism of mockery, fate had ordered that this cursed object should drop from the cashier's pocket and that it should now have fallen into the hands of the enemy.   Probably at the moment when Slayton had drawn the search-light from his pocket he had also pulled out the wig and let it fall.

Now there it was, an absolutely damning bit of evidence against him.

Without it some slight chance of escape by clever ruse and dodging might still have existed.   With it no hope whatever could possibly be conceived.   Slayton's whole salvation depended on the alibi that Mansfield could be forced to give him.   But with that wig in evidence the entire defensive case would drop apart like a rotten fabric.

Slayton felt suddenly very sick.   He could imagine the impending scene, the investigation, the disgrace, the anguish of his wife, the horrible penalties already surely hanging over him.   He seemed as if meshed in the hideous complications of a nightmare; and yet he knew that this thing was only too terribly, too inescapably real.

Even at this minute if he could get out of the bank and away unseen, that infernal wig of his would damn him. Not only would it start a train of thought in Mansfield's active brain — a train of thought which would be fatal to him — but it would inevitably produce investigations that could only have one ending.   The thing could not fail to be identified as his property.   A score of persons might recognize the peculiar wig as that which he had so successfully used in those accursed amateur theatricals.   So long as that damnable object were not recovered the future could mean absolutely nothing for Slayton except prison stripes, barred windows, utter ruin, endless and infamous years of Hell.

Another and a different passion all at once was born in the cashier's chilled heart — the primal instinct, deepest-rooted of any in the universe — self-preservation.

Now all at once, a staggering choice had been flung up at Slayton — the choice of certain punishment or of some possibility in risking far, far more that he might win complete freedom.

And like cloud-wrack before the breath of tempest all the cashier's antipathy against murder vanished. He knew in a flash that Mackenzie must die.

Must die if he, Walter Slayton, were to live!

Once more his hand sought his pocket. It closed there on the corrugated butt of Mansfield's automatic. Eagerly his fingers clutched this harbinger of quick salvation.

He realized that the shot would be easy. The distance was not over twenty-five feet at the outside. He could fire through the big steel bars with perfect ease. He could not miss.

Steadily now with heart of ice and nerves of iron, steadily, silently, rigid with purpose, he withdrew the weapon. He poised it, ready, waiting, eager; and as his flexed forefinger tightened on the trigger he smiled again. This time the smile was of joy.

Never had Slayton felt so great a thrill of happiness. The touch of that gun to his hand was a benediction. Down came the grim snout of the pistol — down, down, along the edge of the safe-door. Steady it held, and true, perfectly aimed against that massive rest. The barrel, as it found its mark, froze to accurate position there.

Slayton's heart, which had been thrashing rather wildly, now once more was beating with normal pulsation. An extraordinary calm, poised and highly efficient, had succeeded the cashier's earlier emotion. With businesslike precision he drew a careful bead on the dark blot of the old man's form, vaguely outlined by the reflection of the search-light's little beam.

His gloved finger tightened, tightened still more.

All at once Mackenzie made up his mind to act. He turned, ready to go.

The crash of the report, though loud, seemed less so than Slayton had expected. Quick echoes snapped back at him. Then all grew still again.

Silent, eager, perfectly self-possessed, he waited, giving ear for any sound of danger. He heard none. Old man Mackenzie's form had vanished. No groan arose, no cry, no murmur. All was silent as the grave.

Ice-cold, calm, watchful, the cashier stood there, the pistol still in hand. Was Mackenzie merely shamming? Had the shot really taken effect? Or was some ruse in preparation? Slayton could not tell. But with wily astuteness he waited.

If no policeman had happened to be in the vicinity he knew a very good chance existed that the single shot might have passed unnoticed. There was more than a good chance. The detonation could not have carried far, hemmed in, as it had been, by those thick walls of masonry.

A minute he remained there — two minutes — three; and each was an eternity.

Nothing.

No sound. Not a breath. Absolute silence still reigned, interrupted only by the nervous *click!* of the electric chronometer.

Then Slayton advanced, *en vedette*. Through the door of the great steel cage he passed, and entered the grilled runway where Mackenzie had stood.

Suddenly he stopped.

" Got him ! " he ejaculated.

The electric light, falling from Mackenzie's hand, had

rolled to one side and stopped there. Now its single eye
of radiance was fixed on a terrible something, motionless
and grim. A something that, half-glimpsed, set the hair
bristling along Slayton's nape, stopped his breath and racked
him again with sudden chills.

A something of his making; a something that silently cried
out against him with a terrible, still voice, never again to
be put away or forgotten, never again to be shut out from
him, any more.

A something which he trembled to approach; which he
dared not see; yet which, with resistless force, grappled him
toward itself.

A something —

Death !

Right in the light-circle of the lamp the dead face lay,
waxen, wrinkled, appealing in its supreme helplessness, with
glazing eyes uprolled, with open mouth distorted hideously,
with gray hair drabbled in a viscous, black, varnish-like
liquid — a liquid that even as Slayton watched it, shuddering, quivered with the falling of another drop upon its
spreading surface on the tiles.

"Got him, first shot," muttered the cashier. "No cry,
no struggle, nothing. Just dropped him, that's all. Devil-
ish neat shot, I think."

He spoke dully, as with no very clear realization of the
event. His actions seemed mechanical. His staring eyes,
rimmed with white, blinked strangely as he stood there peering into the dark.

Dazed, he drew nearer, and shoved the pistol back into
his pocket. He felt a certain pride through it all that his
shot had been so extremely effective. Yet horror overbore
all other sensations. He moved mechanically.

"Mackenzie! Oh, Mackenzie!" he loudly whispered.

The light went out. Now all things lay folded in curtains
of velvet gloom. This was far worse than anything the

rays could show. He produced his own light and cast its rays here and there, seeking the wig.

There it lay, still clutched in the old man's fingers. Slayton snatched it up and crammed it into his pocket.

He was safe now, at any rate — safe from the charge of robbery. Yes, but — the other, the vastly more terrifying charge?

All at once his teeth began to chatter violently. Full realization had just been borne into him that he had killed a human being — that he was a murderer.

He had wanted only to steal, not to take human life. He had not wanted to kill. He, Walter Slayton, was not that kind of man. And yet he *had* killed. And there before him lay the body of Mackenzie!

"God!" he whispered. "I've killed him. Killed a man!"

Very sick, he recoiled.

"Oh, I didn't mean to do it. When I came here, I — I only meant to steal. I didn't mean to take human life — to kill!

"I'm a murderer! If they catch me, if they catch me *now* —!"

He shrank away. Before him seemed to rise a vision of the death-house, the narrow door, the pitiless cement chamber under its glaring reflectors; and, in the midst of all, a terrible thing, black, ominous, waiting — the Chair.

Cowering, striking the horrid apparition away from before his eyes, he retreated. Back he recoiled, anywhere out of that hideous corridor of death; back from that place of terrors, where already the heavy, salty odor of fresh blood poisoned the very air. Haggard, he peered about him. What now?

With a kind of desperation he realized that something must be done at once to lay the guilt of this, as of the other crime, upon other shoulders than his own. At once, or it

would be eternally too late.   He must get back to Oakwood
Heights, change his clothes, conceal the money and be ready
— fresh, shaven, alert — to return to New York on his usual
train.

Not one iota of variation must be observed in his conduct.   He must prepare himself for an ordeal of acting
such as would tax the abilities of a consummate artist.   And
time was growing now so terribly short!

With a violent effort the miserable man pulled his nerves
together.   He went over to the water-cooler, drank two
brimming glasses of ice-water and felt a trifle relieved.
Then he stood there, pondering.

Obviously he would gain nothing by locking up the safe
again.   Now that the old man was murdered there could be
no delay in the discovery of the theft.   Nor would there be
any advantage in putting back the money.   That would only
bring about his bankruptcy and help fix suspicion on him.
No; as he had begun, so he must go through to the end —
to the very end, whatever that might be.

He shuddered, and for a moment leaned against the steel
bars of the vault-cage to steady himself.   Then suddenly he
recoiled.

Bars!   Steel bars!   Couldn't he get away from the damnable things?

Once more he took thought.   His only way, he decided,
would be to prove a perfect alibi.   He had left no tracks, not
even a finger-print or foot-print.   Let them suspect all they
pleased, they could prove nothing.   He must remove every
possibility of proof.   He must fasten the crime on somebody
else.   Some other man must take this medicine; not he!

"Somebody else!" said the cashier.   "Somebody else
must suffer for this.   But who?"

Pondering, he once more began to resume his disguise, for
already the peril of staying too long in that fatal place was
growing acute.   Not only was the light increasing, outside,

but the awakening sounds of the city's life warned him he
must be gone. Adjusting the false beard and mustache, he
began his preparations for flight.

"I can make it, all right enough," said he. "There's still
time. Time enough, yet, before nine o'clock!"

As he reached into his pocket for the wig, which he had
stuffed in there, his hand fell in contact with metal. It recoiled as from the touch of a viper.

The automatic!

"Ugh!" Slayton grunted wordlessly. The feel of that
cold, murderous thing, which only five minutes before had
flicked out a human life, sent shudders of repulsion rippling
through his unnerved flesh.

But almost at once a different thought possessed him.
Again his hand sought the weapon.

"Well!" said he. "It's his, isn't it? It's Mansfield's?"

Startled by the wide-flung possibilities all at once opened
out before him, he stared as if petrified.

"It *is* his!" he exulted. "His! And so — and so —
why not?"

A croaking laugh of triumph rose to his pallid lips.

"Yes, by God!" he gulped. "It can be done! It can —
it shall!"

CHAPTER VII

THE "·PLANT"

SLAYTON'S mind now definitely made up to foist the guilt of this black murder upon a perfectly innocent man, he proceeded with his usual well-calculated coolness to carry the infernal plan into execution. With intelligence of a high order and with the deliberation he now felt was essential to success, he faced the problem, adjusted himself to the new conditions that had so unexpectedly arisen, and prepared to meet them.

In the cashier's personality lay nothing of the hysterical. His nerves could not be stampeded into any rash or ill-considered action. Everything he did was done with reason, care and purpose. Now that he had become a murderer, thief and criminal, he had suddenly developed into the most dangerous of all kinds — the cold, intellectual, scientific type.

Facing the body of the aged watchman, not yet stiffened in death but still warm and limp, he took thought how best to fasten the accusation of the murder on young Mansfield. He must, he understood, build up a rather elaborate structure of circumstance. By no word of his, by no accusing finger must the charge be brought. The unanswerable testimony of the facts and nothing else must make the charge of "Guilty!"

Slayton did not go to work at once. He understood that a moment's calm reflection might now win the whole battle. So, he reflected. He even brought a chair, sat down, rested his elbow on his knee and his chin on his hand, and deeply pondered the case. Not until the outlines of the process should have been worked out in his incisive mind would he so much as move a finger to execute his plan.

One single false step now might not only ruin his scheme, but also retort the charge of murder on his own head. At all hazards he must proceed with caution and intelligence. So he sat there scheming as Dante pictures Satan ruminating darkly in the deeps of the lowest Pit.

Finally, light in hand, he got up and approached old Mackenzie's body. The scent of blood was highly distasteful to him — for Slayton was a man of peculiar refinements and easily offended — but he did not draw back. He turned the old man over to see where the bullet had struck. At sight of the wound behind the right ear he critically pursed his thin lips. Then he let the limp head fall back again. With the greatest care he avoided staining his gloves with blood.

His electric light still burning, he proceeded, in a businesslike manner, to carry out his plan. First he went noiselessly to Mansfield's desk, looked it over and tried the drawers. All were unlocked.

Slayton carefully examined the drawers. In one drawer he found a pair of gloves, and took them out. In another he came upon a box of paper-clips, with a few pins and trifles mixed in. Among these he saw a button. At sight of it his eyes brightened with satisfaction.

He recognized this button. It matched the boy's usual business suit. Evidently it was one of the little sleeve-buttons. A few threads still adhered in the holes. Slayton took this button in his gloved fingers and studied it closely, turning it under the rays of the lamp, which cast ghostly reflections up over his thin, pale face, mask-like and sinister.

The threads, he thought, had been cut off by a knife or by scissors. He figured that the button had worked loose, and that Mansfield, careful and prudent, had cut it off and put it into that box against such time as he could have it sewn on by a tailor — perhaps even by Enid Chamberlain;

who could tell? Slayton's satisfaction was large. The importance of this button, if rightly used, might be tremendous.

With the gloves and the button he knew he had enough in his hands to convict the boy. He must avoid too great profusion of proofs. He might add one or two more bits indeed, but he must be careful not to overplay the game. Just a few pieces of unimpeachable evidence, he felt, would prove far more effective than a dozen, which, by their very abundance, might give rise to suspicions of a frame-up.

Slayton listened a moment for any possible sounds of peril. He heard none. Beyond the usual dull night-murmur of the city, all was still. And yet he knew the patrolman would be along now in a few minutes. He had no time to waste. It was imperative that he get to work immediately.

He pulled the threads out of the button and tucked even this tiny bit of material into his waistcoat pocket. Broken threads formed part of his scheme, but cut threads did not. His mind grasped even this detail; and so he kept the threads.

With the gloves and the button he returned to the body — having closed the drawers of Mansfield's desk — and dropped the button near the corpse. The tiny bit of bone rolled round a couple of times, finally coming to rest near the grillwork. So far, so good.

Next he took one of the gloves — the right — and dabbled three of the fingers in the old man's clotting blood. He then loosened Mackenzie's coat and waistcoat and ripped open the old watchman's shirt. He took off his own right glove, put on Mansfield's, and thrust the blood-stained fingers in against the dead breast over the heart. Then he withdrew his hand again, making sure the glove was leaving its mark there.

This done, he replaced the boy's glove with his own, took Mansfield's gloves and pistol and prepared to descend to the basement of the bank-building. He had two doors to unlock before he could reach it, but he knew where Mackenzie always kept the keys hanging and so had no difficulty. Thus he soon found himself confronting the steam-heating plant, with which he now had business.

The fire in the furnace, banked by the janitor before that worthy man had departed for his home on Canal Street, now glowered dully. Slayton opened the furnace door and tossed in the pages torn from the ledger. A considerable quantity of ashes fell out. With these he buried one of the boy's gloves — the one with the blood on it — leaving only a bit of it exposed. He then threw the other glove in upon the red coals and watched it shrivel and blacken to a crisp.

After this he tore up the paper with the cipher of the combination and burned it, all save three small fragments. These, he made sure, had some of the carbon-copied typewriting on them. He dropped them casually on the basement floor.

Then he threw the pistol with which he had shot Mackenzie — the pistol that belonged to Mansfield — over behind some ash-barrels. He pondered the whole train of evidence, smiled, nodded and returned upstairs.

" It will do, I guess," he judged. " There's no flaw in it anywhere that I can see. It will do."

He now made ready to depart for his home at Oakwood Heights. All at once a thought struck him. One weak link in the chain might be fatal. And he had just realized that there existed one such link among those he had so carefully forged.

Where had Mansfield got the cipher with which to open the safe?

In this frame-up the possession of that cipher was going to possess great weight — or rather proof that the paper had been in Mansfield's hands. Slayton's claim, of course, would be that he had kept it locked in his upper right-hand desk-

drawer, which it had never left. If Mansfield had got hold
of it the boy must have forced the lock. Very well, then;
obviously that drawer must have its lock forced.

But Slayton had no tools with which to force it, and time
was growing terribly short. Only a few minutes for action
still remained. If he should miss the 2:55 boat to Staten
Island he could not regain his home, and he would have to
appear at the bank in new clothes just purchased. That
circumstance alone would throw suspicion on him. It was
imperative that he reach home! Not a minute was to be
lost.

That meant that he could not return to the boiler-room to
look for tools. He must use whatever he could find.

Slayton swept his light over Mansfield's desk again. A
steel letter-opener was lying there; a little tool with " A.
M." rudely scratched on it. He caught it up, returned to
his desk, unlocked the upper drawer, and inserted the point
of the steel tool in the lock. There he broke it off short.
He then dropped the broken opener into the pocket of a coat
that hung on a hook near the assistant bookkeeper's desk —
a coat belonging to that bookkeeper, a man named Holmes.

The last step had now been taken, the last bit of evidence
rendered conclusive. With a rather extraordinary finesse
Slayton had even made it appear that Mansfield had tried to
lay the blame on Holmes.

He chuckled to himself, rubbing his smooth hands together. Rather neat he thought the arrangements. Rather
phenomenally neat, indeed!

An idea suddenly occurred to him. Unless the usual " O.
K." were rung in on the watchman's alarm-system, the police
might become suspicious and send over an officer from the
nearest precinct station-house to investigate. Slayton accordingly rang in this alarm, punching the clock as Mackenzie would have done. He nodded and smiled with satisfaction at his extraordinary keenness.

He now resumed his disguise, made sure he had left no incriminating traces, and finally let himself noiselessly out of the bank after having once more turned on the incandescent in front of the safe and put up the shades again. Under the shelter of the doorway he listened keenly, peering about for any possible danger. He saw none, and so issued forth boldly on to the sidewalk.

Thus with one hundred and fifty thousand dollars in his inside pocket and shielded by a profound conviction that his own personal safety was secure, he proceeded confidently homeward. He made no effort to avoid anybody. The few pedestrians afoot hardly vouchsafed a glance at him. He passed a couple of policemen, one on Cedar Street and one near Bowling Green, but neither one molested him.

And the glimmer of the harbor, with here and there a dim-eyed moving blur of red or green, gave him a strange sense of liberty, of vastness, of escape. Freedom now from debt and hounding and threats; freedom from the long years of subterfuge and deception; freedom from Jarboe's prying investigations — all had been won by one bold coup and by one single shot. He could have run and shouted for very joy! Now he could pay off Jarboe's note of eighty-four thousand dollars and all his other twenty-odd thousand of obligations — all — all — and more!

No sense of guilt or fear rose up in him now, as he reached the ferry and made his way aboard. Leaning over the rail, watching the black water that asked its age-old questions, never-answered, he felt no drawings of remorse. The dead eyes of the old man gazed not at him, searching out his soul. No; calm, cool, resourceful, he succeeded in shutting away all such disquieting memories and introspections. Other things more vital still had to be thought out; and above all surged and soared the glory of that new and splendid exultation, Freedom!

Slayton settled himself in the men's cabin, lighted a cigar

and plunged into thought. He deeply pondered the inevitable events now impending. For a time he weighed the possibility of incriminating Mansfield still more by forcing the boy in some way to leave New York at once. When the young chap should appear at the bank in the morning, all unconscious of the charge now certain to be raised against him, some slight possibility might exist that he could succeed in freeing himself. He might conceivably prove an alibi. The finger of accusation might turn toward Slayton himself. If the cashier could only concoct some scheme which would force Mansfield to run away, it would set the keystone of proof in the arch of assumption.

But no; Slayton decided this would be quite impossible. Moreover, Mansfield was of fighting stock. He would not run, in the first place; and in the second he was no quitter. He would fight. Even if he could be made to leave New York, once he should be accused he would hurry back to face the charge and see the thing through. And that, in itself, might react in his favor. No; decidedly no; there could be no advantage in trying to stampede him.

The boy must be let alone to walk into the trap that had so cleverly been baited for him. Only by absolutely overwhelming him with masses of damning evidence could he be beaten down. Well, Slayton would overwhelm him, that was all.

The cashier realized, with a thrill of anticipation, how perfectly all the lines had been laid. He felt content to await the outcome of the morning, confident that not one chance in a thousand existed that Mansfield ever could get clear.

Thus he returned home to the dark and deserted house in Oakwood Heights, unseen, unnoticed and secure. The hour now was just a little after 3.30 A. M. First he took off and hung up the old clothes in which the murder had been done, making certain no spot or touch of blood had sullied them. He then wrapped up his disguise in its original paper and

locked it into its accustomed drawer in his desk. He burned
a number of incriminating papers relative to his indebtedness
— now on the morrow to be wiped out.

Finally he sat down at his desk and wrote a letter to his
wife, taking good care to date it " Wednesday, Midnight,"
and to say that young Mansfield had been down to see him.
Slayton mentioned nothing of the boy's errand, but said he
had just gone back to town on the last train. As a bit of
subsidiary evidence this letter — calm, normal, familiar, betraying no slightest hint or sign of nervous perturbation —
might have considerable value.

Slayton went out and posted this in the box on the corner.
Then he returned and went to bed as if nothing whatever
had happened. He took good care, however, to set his alarm-
clock so that he should run no risk of oversleeping in the
morning. Should anything prevent his putting in an appearance at the bank at his accustomed hour, serious results might ensue.

Resolutely suppressing all thoughts of the murder now
blackening his soul, he slept. His self-control surpassed belief. With that fresh crime but a few hours old, he slum-
bered quietly, soundly, restfully.

But Mansfield did not sleep. Burning as with fever, haggard and pale, haunted with terror, he passed a night of
fear, remorse and agony in his boarding-house room.

Would Slayton really help him? Mansfield asked himself
a hundred times. Would he keep the shameful secret? Or
would he crush him, after all?

Would ruin be Mansfield's portion — ruin and the loss of
name, of future, of good repute, of Enid, of all that made
life worth living? The bitterness of Hell he plumbed that
night, and drank the dregs of pain.

Thus he, innocent of the greater wrong that soon was to
be laid on him, agonized in the long hours of that fatal night.

Thus Slayton, his hands reeking with blood-guiltiness, slept calmly on.

And as the one kept vigil and the other slept, old man Mackenzie lay silent, rigid, terrible, on the bank floor, his dead eyes glazed, his limbs now stiffened in the *rigor mortis,* his blood now clotted in a black pool beneath his shattered head.

CHAPTER VIII

THE cashier was awakened, a bit dazed and dull, by the clangor of the alarm. The first shock of remembrance startled him rather severely; but, strong of nerve and will, he presently mastered his emotion and in a businesslike manner began preparing for the inevitable ordeal. Like an actor making up for a difficult rôle, he set about preparing himself for the part he must act in the drama to be staged at the bank. His make-up in this case meant one of the most exacting of all dramatic tasks — the assumption of an absolutely natural appearance and demeanor under hard stress.

A cold bath, followed by a vigorous rubdown, a shave, and clean linen throughout, made him fit and keen. At his accustomed hour, absolutely normal, so far as the outer man was concerned, he set out briskly for town. Sixty-five of the one-thousand-dollar bills he left in his bedroom, securely hidden behind a picture, against any possibility of the house being searched. He knew that, tucked in between the thin board backing of the picture and the print itself, they would be absolutely safe. In his pocket he carried eighty-five thousand dollars, with which to meet the note he owed Jarboe. Whatever happened, *that* matter must be settled at once.

On his way to the Oakwood Heights station he met Ashley, of the International Life. He walked along with the insurance man, talking on indifferent matters. With satisfaction he noted that Ashley observed nothing at all unusual about his speech or manner. He could tell positively that he was attracting no attention. Inwardly he congratulated himself on his success so far.

The trip to the city passed without event. He breakfasted at the restaurant he usually patronized when his wife was away, and simulated interest in the paper he forced himself to read — the paper that as yet contained no news of the murder.

As he was leaving the place, cigar in mouth, the first real blow went home on him. Only with difficulty could he hold his composure. The nasal cry of that newsboy on the corner: " Bank murder! Bank mur-der!" shot a bolt of apprehension through his soul. He felt suddenly as if everybody were looking at him, pointing at him, mocking him, and mouthing one terrible word:

" Murderer!"

The thing was, of course, an illusion, an absurdity; nobody in the world knew anything of the truth. He, Walter Slayton, was perfectly and absolutely safe. And yet — and yet —

A fine perspiration began to prickle out all over him. His eyes grew dim for a moment; he turned a sickly, leaden color. He realized now, for the first time, just what he was facing. The murder was known, of course; he knew it would be known long before he could reach the bank. The papers had it already, in their special editions. Already reporters, police, detectives would be swarming. Already there would be a morbid, pushing crowd around the place where he — Heaven help him! — must thrust his way in, acting that part of his, always acting that part, for very life's dear sake.

And at realization of all this, now definitely borne in on him, a kind of cosmic weakness seemed to take possession of him, a loosening of all his bones and joints and muscles, a disintegration of the soul, a terrible, sick fear — stage-fright, in a word; only on how vast, tragic and fatal a scale!

As a drowning man fights to grip some support, so the

cashier fought now to recover his nerve and strength. Life
and death it meant; no question about that. Once the very
slightest act of his should awake suspicion, two and two
would be put together and he would be watched. Detectives,
police, experts would fasten on him as weasels fasten on a
rat; and all the complex, potent machinery of science, of
chemistry, of blood-analysis — things terribly dreaded by
the layman, who overestimates their possibilities — would
be used to drag him down to death.

In a second's glimpse Slayton saw how crude, after all, his
" plant " had been. Or so it now seemed to him. If the
great, steady eye of investigation should turn on him, he
knew he would be lost.

Could he, guilty, compete in the appearances of innocence
with the boy? He knew he could not. He understood that
once any charge were made against him, he must break and
wither under it.

A terrible fear and hate of Mansfield was born in him.
He feared and hated those clear blue eyes, that healthy,
normal face, those manly brave tones and inflections of the
voice. Everything about the boy, he felt, would cry out:
" Innocent! " whatever might befall. And should the boy
and he be weighed in the balances, one against the other, only
too well he knew the outcome.

But then this thing must never come to pass. No suspicion must arise! The accusation against Mansfield must
come with such sudden and crushing force as to sweep all
before it like a bayonet-charge, leaving no force behind it to
attack him, Slayton.

Yet could all this be done? The cashier, shaking now,
seemed lost and sunk in boundless abysses of despair. That
one blow, that shock of the cry: " Bank murder! All about
the Powhatan Bank murder! " had in a flash shot him to
pieces with its terrible connotations of what he now must
face.

Slayton stood there as if transfixed, unable to go ahead, powerless to move. One or two men glanced at him curiously. His lips twitched in a sickly smile. He understood perfectly well that if he remained there much longer he would become conspicuous and awaken comment. Yet he could not move. And still the newsboy's raw yell of "Bank murder!" pierced his ears. Slayton could have smitten the urchin down and trampled him. This boy here was flinging Slayton's crime to the whole wide world — and must he, the murderer, hear the horrid accusation?

A film passed before his eyes. He put his hand out blindly, grasped a railing and steadied himself. Then by a supreme effort of the will he walked on up Broadway. And ever that cry: "Murder! Murder!" rang in his soul — and other cries reëchoed it; the whole city seemed howling "*Murder!*" at him. "*Murder!*"

Cursing, he turned aside and entered an office building to get out of the glare of daylight. The light, he thought, was what distressed him most of all. Everybody could see him so plainly in the light. An obsession got hold of him that there was a spot of blood on his right hand, inside his glove. He knew that there was no blood there, but still he could not convince himself of that fact.

And he dared not bare his hand to look at it. For even in that half-lighted hallway he felt that somebody would notice and interpret the act. Torture wrung him between fear of looking at his hand and burning eagerness to look. He swore again, and stood there trembling and panic-stricken.

The hallman, he now felt positive, was observing him with curiosity and undue interest. He turned to go again. Just as he reached the revolving doors a newsboy thrust a paper in his face.

"Paper, boss? All about th' bank moider!"

Slayton caught a glimpse of huge black type with other type below in vivid red — the paper, then, was printed in blood? The curse he launched against himself for his folly in entertaining such a vagary made the newsboy stare.

"Gee! Some nut, hey?" muttered the boy, as Slayton emerged once more on the street — the merciless, pitiless, all-seeing street, Broadway, under the light of a pale November morning.

The cashier realized that he had not yet mastered his fears. But he must act; he must move; he must keep going. Only in motion now could he find safety and a chance to pull together.

What had become of all the assurance of only a few hours previously? Whereas the night before in the darkness he had felt absolute confidence in his astute plans and clever ruses, now all at once — under daylight and amid all these hurrying thousands of his fellow-men — he found himself stripped bare of courage.

For a second it seemed to him as if all the dikes of self-control were breaking before that flood of unreasoning terror; as if he must run amuck, flinging his arms wildly, screaming:

"Look, all you people; I — I am the murderer!"

But by an effort that wrenched his soul he lashed his routed forces into discipline again. His panic, having reached its climax, now began to subside. After all, nobody had noticed him to any serious degree. Nobody knew him; nobody had understood.

He turned aside from the morning throng, all so busy and so eager; he put his foot upon an iron rail in front of a steamship company's office; and retied his shoelace. This little act, this small respite from facing the eyes of human beings, gave his stampeded resolutions time once more to form in battle line.

And as he stood up again, again looked men in the face and drew a deep breath, he knew that he had conquered.

Once more he had whipped his wavering soul back to the firing-line. He still was master in his own house.

Still weak, though with returning strength and self-confidence, he resumed his course up Broadway. Jarboe's office lay close at hand, in Trinity Place. Thither he now directed his steps. The note must be met at once; moreover, to carry eighty-five thousand dollars in the stolen one-thousand dollar bills back to the bank itself would be the acme of rashness. At all hazards he must rid himself of those bills immediately.

Jarboe had just got in when Slayton arrived. The rat-eyed little usurer, disfigured by a large wen on the forehead, showed him into an inner office, a veritable spider-web of iniquity and extortion, whence but few flies ever escaped with whole wings. Rubbing his hands together and leering with disgusting insinuation, the old Shylock awaited his money.

Slayton made no words with him, but counted out the cash, took the note, and without even a " Good morning! " started to leave.

" Awful tragedy up at your bank, sir. Awful, indeed! " the old man mumbled. " But it's an ill wind blows nobody good."

Slayton's face paled to a dull gray.

" What do you mean, you infamous scoundrel? " he demanded.

" Mean, sir? Oh, nothing; nothing at all, sir. Why do you ask? "

" Do you mean to insinuate —"

" I insinuate nothing, sir. It's nothing to me where or how a client of mine raises the money to pay his just debts. If I get my honest dues that's all I'm concerned with. Only — Mackenzie was such a fine old chap; now wasn't he, sir? And —"

Beside himself, Slayton whirled on the creature, his face a mask of hate.

"Look out, you hell-hound!" he flung at the usurer in a low voice of passion. "Look out that you don't get as much, some of these days, from one or another of the men and women you enjoy ruining, you blood-sucker!"

"There, there, sir," returned the usurer, grinning with toothless gums. "Don't get excited, sir. What happens outside of this office is no concern of old Jarboe's. We all of us have secrets. Skeletons rattle in every closet, sir. They rattle in mine. All well and good. Let them. Maybe they rattle in yours. I don't care. None of my business. If you have anything on me keep it to yourself. I'll do the same by you, sir. And maybe we'll do business again some of these times. Good day, sir; and thank you."

Speechless with rage — rage so intense it swallowed even any alarm that old Jarboe's pregnant words might have awakened — Slayton left the office, slamming the door behind him. Only when he once more found himself in the street did he recover his full wits. But with the return of entire rationality he found all his residue of fear was gone. The interview with Jarboe had — for a time at least — banished it. And, too, the feeling that after all these weary months and years of dickering and bargaining and begging and usury he once more was a free man, out of Jarboe's gnarled clutches, filled him with a vast, assuaging sense of relief.

In vain now news-stands and shouting urchins assailed him with their visual and auditory shocks. Tall headlines and strident cries had lost their power to dismay him. Slayton felt as if he had been inoculated against emotion. His first severe panic, caused by his first hearing of the shout: "Bank murder!" had now, in subsiding, left his emotions a sterile medium.

The fires of fear had purged away most of the consumable panic-material in his soul. He had received his necessary training. Now he felt a new boldness. A certain eagerness began to possess him; an impatience to meet this peril, to face it down, to have it over and done with, once for all.

" The quicker now the better ! " he growled, striding along with renewed strength.

His intense anger at Jarboe had infused fresh virility into his look. His face betrayed no more emotion than might naturally have been expected there, now that the whole down-town section was reëchoing to the news:

" Powhatan Bank Murder ! "

Suddenly he bethought him that he had not yet bought a paper. This in itself might look unnatural and give rise to suspicions. Surely he must have a paper. He purchased two — one yellow, the other moderate in tone — and thrust them into his overcoat pocket.

It was impossible for him to force himself to read a single word of the story. Irresistibly it repelled him. But headlines flung themselves at him as he paused at the news-stand, and would not be denied:

NIGHT-WATCHMAN MURDERED IN COLD BLOOD!

ROBBERY THE MOTIVE — $150,000 STOLEN !

Slayton knew he ought to read something of the murder. He understood perfectly well that the papers might contain information vital to his welfare — warnings, perhaps, or hints of conduct he might employ to strengthen suspicions of Mansfield. Yet, strive as he could, he found himself unable to fix his thought on the printed columns as he walked on and on. Now that he was approaching the vortex of the crime, a resistless force seemed to be drawing him onward, downward, as into a whirlpool. All he desired now was to reach the bank and with his own eyes see again his horrible handiwork; with his own ears hear the infamy discussed; with his own mouth speak the words that should send an innocent boy to the electric chair. Hastening his step, he pressed on.

Everywhere, he felt positive, people were talking of the tragedy. His exaggeration of its importance had become almost an obsession with him. In knots on curbs and corners men were gathered. What else could they be discussing save that? He saw open newspapers in office windows, with clerks and brokers reading them. They were reading details of the murder, of course; nothing else mattered now but this crime of his.

As he walked down Cedar Street he thought the drift of traffic was setting toward the bank. A policeman on William Street was obviously headed that way. As all roads lead to Rome, so now all Slayton's thoughts and sense-impressions drew toward that fatal spot where old man Mackenzie, shot down by his hand, lay rigid in the eternal mystery, death.

Slayton reached the last corner, took a firmer grip on his resolution, and swung into the street itself where the bank stood. Now that the supreme moment was almost upon him, an icy coldness of determination had possessed his body, mind, and soul. A sphygmograph would hardly have registered his pulse as higher than normal.

His face was pale and just a bit drawn about the mouth; but who could question that? Mackenzie had been his friend for many years. Had he not shown some natural emotion would it not have been strange indeed?

As he approached the bank he saw the street was almost blocked by the crowd that, morbidly curious, had clotted round the door. A number of policemen were doing their best to keep the traffic moving, but without any very marked success. A motor patrol stood backed up to the sidewalk. Slayton caught sight of the uniform of a police surgeon.

In the buildings opposite, eager faces crowded at the open windows, faces wherein no sympathy showed, faces merely gaping with pleasurable excitement. In one of the windows a moving-picture operator was steadily turning a crank. This scene would ere long appear on a multitude of screens as part of the news of the day.

A shudder of repulsion passed through the cashier at sight of the sensation-seeking New York mob now clustering round the place of death, like flies on carrion. With this repulsion he felt at the same time a kind of strange and perverse pride that he, Walter Slayton, should be the cause of all this commotion. For a moment he understood the psychology of the low-grade murderer who cannot rest till he has returned to look once more on the face of his dead enemy.

As he came on and on through the outskirts of the crowd, slowing through the thick of it, a reporter snapped a focal plane in his face. Slayton felt no emotion. Nothing in that photograph, though printed in a half-million edition, could harm him. He realized that, after all, his appearance could not matter much. A good deal of perturbation could pass unnoticed or be taken as quite natural. The sequence of circumstantial proof above all — this must be the determining factor in convicting.

Slayton's relief became greater. He held his head well up now as he elbowed his way to the front.

"Let me pass, here!" he commanded. "Let me pass!"

A policeman halted him.

"Nothin' doin', mister! Nobody else ain't allowed in the bank!"

Slayton flashed his card. With apologies the officer cleared a way for him.

"Has the coroner come yet?" asked Slayton.

The officer nodded.

"He's just gettin' through viewin' the body," he answered. "He only come a few minutes ago. We had trouble locatin' him," he added, while morbid bystanders craned and crowded to catch a word.

"Any verdict?"

"Not yet there ain't. But it's a job, all right. Somebody croaked him sure, and —"

"Anderson found him? The janitor found him? Is that right?"

"That's right. When he opened the place the old man was layin' there cold!"

Slayton pushed on through the big revolving doors into the lobby of the bank. Now finally he had reached the dreaded yet the longed-for place where lay his victim. Now his ordeal of self-control was crowding close upon him. Now at last the moment of supreme peril was at hand.

CHAPTER IX

W ARILY, yet with the boldness that now alone could save him, the murderer advanced, his every sense alert for peril.

A strange, unnatural tension reigned in the bank. None of its usual morning activities had as yet begun. Paralysis lay upon its entire life. Not a single one of its people could be seen in any of their accustomed cages. Here and there an officer in uniform or a plain-clothes man stood silently watchful. At one of the glass shelves on the left a man was busily writing — scrawling hasty lines on cheap paper. Slayton recognized a reporter and shuddered.

Near a pillar at the end of the. hallway a little knot of men, all unknown to Slayton, stood talking in low tones. One or two of them looked up at him. He felt again that horrible sensation that his guilt must be apparent to everybody. Once more he knew there must be blood upon his fingers. But with a strong effort he collected himself and advanced toward the little doorway that gave admittance to the grilled area of the bank.

Through this grillwork Slayton could see another group of men, some of them employees of the bank, some strangers. One he recognized from newspaper pictures he had seen as Coroner Roadstrand. With the coroner was a medical-looking man.

Slayton caught a fugitive glimpse of himself in a mirror. He perceived that he was very pale, but that his face betrayed his crime he could not see. His thoughts were rac-

ing like a sluice. He hardly knew whether to bless or curse
the delay in the coroner's arrival. That delay explained,
of course, why the body had not been already removed. In
some ways this might make the situation harder for him.
In others, he instinctively felt, it might help him.

He shrank from viewing the corpse again, and yet he
knew he must conceal this emotion. At that precise moment of all moments the most acute peril would assail him.

Where, he wondered, could Mansfield be? It was already past the usual time for his appearance. Why had
he not arrived? Slayton felt a burning eagerness to have
him arrive, to be at work on the plot against him, to see the
meshes tightening about the boy.

And yet the cashier knew that Mansfield's tardiness would
help the plot along. If by any chance the young chap
should fail to come at all, that would be of tremendous importance. Every moment of delay now possessed enor-
mous possibilities.

His mind whirling with the strain of the situation, yet
dominated by the overmastering determination to play the
game to a finish, he approached the gateway in the grill.
His re-awakening emotions exceeded anything he had calculated on. He had believed himself now cold enough,
calm and calculating enough, to preserve his poise even
under these circumstances.

But he had not reckoned on the reality. A glimpse of a
still body, lying there under a blanket that had been drawn
over it, sent his heart plumbing downward in sick horror.

Sheridan, the paying-teller, glanced up as he approached,
turned, and came toward him. One or two others in the
group by the body looked at him.

"Hello, here's Slayton! Slayton's come!" he heard
voices.

A hand fell on his arm. He started with a nervous shock.
God! Arrests were made in just that way! The touch of

that hand left him shaking with terror. For a second he thought catastrophe had smitten. Staring, he faced the man beside him.

Another reporter!

" Confound you, what are you doing in here? " demanded Slayton with passionate anger, reflex of his groundless fears. " What do *you* want, anyhow? "

" Have you any opinion as to the identity of the murderer? " queried the reporter.

" If I had, d'you think I'd tell *you?* "

" I represent the *Evening* —"

" I don't give a damn what you represent! In a case of this kind, where the personnel of the bank itself may possibly be involved— Get out! Not a word; you understand? I refuse to be quoted for a single word! "

Slayton flouted the reporter and strode on. His confidence had suddenly risen several degrees again. Those few words of his, he knew, had been a master-stroke. Already the reporter was scribbling. Inside an hour, Slayton felt confident, staring head-lines would fling to the world:

EMPLOYEE SUSPECTED OF BANK MURDER!

Could things be working out more admirably?

Slayton smiled to himself. He opened the gateway and entered, removing his hat, wiping the sweat from his forehead. Sheridan met him. Two or three others drifted his way. A hush fell on the low-voiced conversation in the group about old Mackenzie's body.

" Why didn't you 'phone me, Sheridan? " demanded the cashier. " The first news I had was through the papers when I left the boat."

" 'Phone you? We did! You must have started for town, though. Nobody answered."

" Missed me, all right. And my wife's away. Chamberlain down yet? "

" Not yet. But we've got him on the wire. He's started.
My Heavens, Slayton, this is the limit! Worst thing that's
ever happened here. A hundred and fifty thousand gone
clean, and the old man —"

" I know; I know. They haven't moved him yet, I see."

" No. The coroner has just got through. Murder, of
course. Person or persons unknown. And — by Jove,
I'm glad to see you, though. We're all more or less
up in the air here.— Frankly, I don't know what to do,
and —"

" You haven't talked, I hope? Haven't said anything to
reporters or the police? "

" Well —"

Sheridan looked embarrassed.

" Not much. That is —"

Slayton laid a finger on his lips.

" Nothing! " bade he. " And don't let any of the others
talk. We've got to wait for Chamberlain. Time enough
then. And, by the way, cable Williamson at once. We'll
need him."

" All right. Mighty unlucky, I think, that our vice-
president should just happen to be in the Isle of Pines when
this happens. He's got some head for a case like this."

" Right! But it won't take long to get him back. Everybody else here? "

" Yes."

Slayton glanced round with a new sense of power. He
was decidedly beginning to get his grip on the situation. The
manner in which they were deferring to him as the highest
bank official present was encouraging. Suspicion could
not possibly rest on him, he felt positive. He was finding
himself again.

" You say they're all here? " he demanded.

" Why, yes. That is —"

" Where's Mansfield? "

"Oh, Mansfield? Well, he's not down yet. I forgot."

"Hmmm! Not down? Isn't he late?"

"Why, yes. A few minutes."

Slayton seemed to ponder. His lower lip protruded; his eyelids closed to slits.

"Hmmmm!" he grunted again, but said no word.

Sheridan regarded him narrowly, a new suspicion now obviously dawning in his mind. All at once, in so low a tone that nobody else could overhear it, the cashier shot a question at him:

"How are Mansfield's accounts?"

"Why — all right, so far as I know."

"So far as you know, eh? No shortage anywhere?"

"Not that I know of."

"Have you inspected his books lately?"

"Well, no. That's not part of my duties —"

"Make it part of them, then. Look them over immediately. Give everything of his a careful going over."

"Why, sir? You don't suspect —"

"Never mind. Do as I say. Either inspect his books or have them inspected at once. Privately, you understand. And report to me. Then —"

"There he is, now!" interrupted the teller, nodding toward the side door. Slayton turned sharply, his motion so acted as to give any beholder the idea that he and Sheridan had been discussing the young clerk.

Mansfield had, indeed, just entered. At sight of him the cashier's heart leaped up with joy. Where he had previously felt ninety per cent. safe, he now felt a hundred.

The boy, honestly upset by the news of the tragedy — which he had read with intense horror while on his way down-town in the subway — had hung up his hat and overcoat in their accustomed place, and now stood surveying the scene with mute wonder and repulsion.

His face, pallid and wan from the sleepless night he had

just passed and the racking emotions of the crisis he had weathered, expressed astonishment and fear. His hair was rumpled. In his perturbation he had neglected to shave. His boots, muddy and unpolished, still showed signs of the trip down over the country roads at Oakwood Heights. His clothes were creased and wrinkled. He had not gone to bed at all the night before, but in his distress had paced the floor of his room until in exhaustion he had flung himself down for a little sleep.

From this he had awakened too late for any change of clothes. At nine he knew he must be at Slayton's desk to get that envelope — his salvation. Breakfastless, unnerved, and haggard he had rushed down-town. Then, on top of everything, this ghastly news had capped the climax of utter confusion.

He knew the murder might prove fatal to him. His sorrow for old Mackenzie was overlaid by this stern fact. The deed might wreck all his plans for restitution. He must see Slayton at once and make sure of that money! Otherwise — ruin confronted him, the loss of his position, his good name, the girl, everything in life!

Yes; and the infamies of prison faced him, too. No more horrible calamity could have befallen him just at that juncture, than this disturbance of the bank's routine. What wonder then that the boy stood there haggard and distressed?

But now his eye caught Slayton's. Yes! The cashier was certainly looking at him. The boy saw Slayton's head move and his eyes beckoning. The message was unmistakable:

"Come here!"

Hope revived. The cashier then, in spite of everything, was going to keep his promise! Mansfield felt the wellsprings of joy and gratitude gush up. He forgot all about the murder for a moment in the ineffable relief of that beckoning nod. His head went up again. Confidently now and with a firm step he approached Slayton and the teller.

But now, to his surprise, Slayton was regarding him coldly. Others were looking at him, too, with wonder and dawning mistrust. The coroner, leaving the body, was moving toward him.

Confused by all this, Mansfield hesitated. He realized that the moment was most inopportune. Even at the risk of exposure, he must not intrude at such a time. But Slayton had surely summoned him. Absolutely at a loss, the boy stood there, overcome by stage-fright, a prey to harrowing indecision.

"Well, Mansfield, what do you want?" demanded Slayton curtly.

"I — Nothing, sir."

"Very well. Go to your desk."

"Yes, sir."

He stared at Slayton a moment, realizing that the man had betrayed him and that everything was lost. For a second a kind of shimmering black haze seemed to dance before his sight. His hand went out, caught hold of a chair, and gripped it desperately.

Then he pulled himself together, turned, and somewhat unsteadily walked to his accustomed place in the bank. He sat down heavily in his chair. A curious, light sensation seemed to have taken away all his strength. He had had no breakfast, and had slept but little. His physical unfitness now gave free play to the ravages of the mental anguish assailing him. He swayed as he sat there. His head swam. The pallor of his face was terrible to look upon.

Every eye in the bank was on him. Already ugly suspicion has begun to raise its head.

But Slayton appeared to take no heed of this. He turned to the paying-teller.

"Sheridan," said he, "please have the men go to their

desks. Have the curtains lowered at all the grills. We can't do any business for an hour or two — maybe more. We've got to see just how hard hit we are financially, and get our bearings before we pay out another dollar. Understand?"

"Yes, sir."

"All right. Get busy!"

He faced the coroner, and held out his hand.

"Coroner Roadstrand, I believe?" asked he.

"Yes. Mr. Slayton?"

They shook hands cordially. Then Roadstrand turned to the keen-eyed medical man with — a shrewd-looking doctor of more than middle age, with shell spectacles.

"Dr. Nelson, Mr. Slayton."

Another hand-shake.

"Dr. Nelson often helps me with my cases," explained Roadstrand. "I think we'll need him this time. Have you any theory. Any suspicions — any data?"

Slayton shook his head.

"Not till we've examined the evidence," he parried. His eyes — involuntarily, as it seemed — turned for a fraction of a second toward the pallid, shaken figure of the boy now fighting for self-control at the desk in the corner. Roadstrand and Nelson exchanged a significant glance.

"Quite right," assented the coroner. "Evidence is all that we must go on."

He turned toward the body, grim and rigid beneath its blanket.

"Evidence," he repeated. "Let's examine it."

CHAPTER X

U NDER Sheridan's orders the bookkeepers and clerks slowly dispersed to their posts. Miss Leavitt, the stenographer, and Miss McDonald, an assistant bookkeeper, who had just come in, were bidden to withdraw to the little room used by the women patrons of the bank and to stay there till further notice. One or two of the men made so bold as to smoke. Though this was against the rules, the nervous tension of the moment drove them to it, and Slayton did not stop them.

Thus they waited, isolated from each other — waited with dread the inevitable ordeal now facing them. Each man knew himself absolutely innocent, yet the stress of the forthcoming inquisition weighed heavily upon them all. Evidence — circumstantial evidence above all — sometimes plays such fantastic tricks that not one of them felt secure from the possibility that the ultimate horror, the murder charge itself, might hang over him.

Mansfield alone among them all did not feel this fear. He sat there in the darkened bank under the gleam of the incandescents — for Sheridan had ordered all shades drawn to keep the morbid crowd outside from peering in — and gave no thought to this new possibility of dread. As a matter of fact, it never even occurred to him. The stress of the actually impending ruin now precipitated by Slayton's treachery left no room for any other suffering. Anguished and shaken, he sat there, staring at the ink-stained blotter on his desk, his mind racked with visions of the inevitable destruction now close upon him. But of the murder charge as having any connection with himself he took no slightest thought.

Not so, however, the others. *They* had already fixed the guilt, passed judgment and condemned him. As they took their places at their desks and counters, and as here or there a little roller-curtain was pulled down before a grill, scarcely one of them but turned curious eyes upon Mansfield — eyes hard with hostility, eyes of repulsion and accusation, eyes that expressed no sympathy, no pity. Not all the boy's previous popularity, not all his fine, frank ways and hearty young manhood could stem the tide of that suspicion. Already the shadow had fallen athwart his head. Though he himself realized it not, already the meshes of the net were closing round him.

But of all this Slayton seemed to remain entirely unaware. He overheard no muttered syllable. He saw no look oblique with accusation. Dispassionate as fate itself, calm and judicial as a supreme-court justice, he had attention now only for the evidence that Roadstrand and the doctor could lay before him. However the tides of opinion in that little world of his, the bank, might run, obviously he could not be influenced thereby.

"The evidence! That's what we want, and nothing else," he echoed Roadstrand's words. "The quicker we see what we've got now and what it all means, the better."

He stopped by the body.

"Poor old chap!" he commiserated. "He died game, anyhow. No widow to grieve, I'm glad to say. An old bach. Brother in Troy, I believe. Otherwise without family."

He bent and drew back the blanket. His hand trembled a little, and for the fraction of a second a nervous twitch contracted his face; but his eyes held steady as he examined the body, lying there stiffened in the blood he himself had spilled,

The old man had fallen on his right side. The distortion of his posture was not great. He seemed to have died instantly — to have fallen prone, shot through the vital respiratory center behind the ear. The waxen rigidity of his face looked less appalling now than when half seen by the gleam of the electric flash the night before. When Slayton realized that the ordeal of this inspection was one he could endure without flinching, a great burden seemed lifted instantly from his soul.

Sheridan quietly returned as the cashier was gazing at the body. He joined the little group. The four men silently studied the corpse a moment. Then Slayton spoke.

"What was the idea in leaving him here so long?" asked he. "I suppose Anderson found him at seven?"

"Yes," answered Sheridan. "He notified the police at once. By seven-fifteen everything was under surveillance."

"Well, why wasn't the body taken away sooner?"

"It couldn't be moved, anyhow, till I'd seen it," explained Roadstrand.

"Oh, of course! And you were on a case?"

Roadstrand nodded.

"It's Hell the way I'm rushed," said he. "We're all up to our eyes in work all the time. Think of a city the size of New York with only five coroners! I got here as soon as I could, anyhow. And after I'd viewed the body the doctor and I agreed we'd better leave it till President Chamberlain could see it, too. That might have some bearing on the case."

Slayton shook his head.

"No; none whatever," he answered. "I'm sure Mr. Chamberlain would be very glad indeed to avoid any such experience. He's getting along in years, you know, and — well — I think he can very well be spared this ordeal if it can possibly be arranged otherwise."

"You'd prefer to have the body removed as soon as you've

seen all the available evidence? You'll be responsible for
the bank in having us take such action?"

"Yes."

"Very well. As a matter of fact, Mr. Slayton, the body
doesn't present much evidence of importance — only the
wound itself and a few slight marks."

"Let me see."

And Slayton knelt by the body, keenly critical.

Dr. Nelson turned the old man's head a trifle, the shoulders moving with it, for the full rigor had now set in.

"The bullet struck here, you see," he explained, pointing. "I judge it must have been fired from about twenty-
five feet. Probably from the safe-door there."

He nodded toward the door, still open and guarded by a
policeman in uniform.

"You see for yourself, it didn't come out again. It's
in there somewhere. We'll find it, all right enough, at
the autopsy."

"Autopsy?"

"Of course. That bullet may be of great importance."

"When will you recover it?"

"As soon as possible. This morning. At the morgue.
I've already telephoned up for them to make preparations.
We'll have that bit of lead before noon, at latest."

"Good!" ejaculated Slayton. "You surely do get the
facts in an efficient way."

His lean, pale face remained quite impassive. He
blinked reflectively.

"Anything else?"

"Three marks on the breast," answered Roadstrand.

"Marks? Wounds, you mean?"

"No. Just blood-marks — finger-marks — see?"

He opened the old man's shirt a little more. It already
gaped where Slayton had torn it apart with his own hands.

On the left breast the cashier now plainly saw the three marks he had put there with Mansfield's glove.

"So then," said he, "there must have been a struggle."

"No, not that," said Nelson. "The murderer evidently put his hand in there to see if the heart was still beating — to see if life was fully extinct."

"That's right; that's right," assented Slayton, getting up again. "You professional men have it all over us business drudges when it comes to an analysis of events and so on. I'd have surely said there was a struggle. But I see how it was now. In some way or other the murderer got his hand into the blood here on the floor, and then put it over the old man's heart. But then — haven't you got a valuable clue? Finger-prints there, and — and on the knob of the safe?"

Nelson shook his head.

"No; none at all. None — worse luck!"

"How so?"

"The criminal wore gloves."

"Oh! Gloves, eh? It was all thought out beforehand, was it? Premeditated, and all that?"

And Slayton, once more casting a glance — a glance that was pure art — toward the annihilated Mansfield, drew out his cigarette-case.

"Premeditated?" repeated Nelson. "Not necessarily; that is, so far as the murder itself was concerned. The robbery, of course, was well planned. The criminal has left no footprints of any value. He took care to conceal those as well as his finger-marks — wore rubbers or something of the sort. Yes, he must have planned things very skilfully.

"But so far as the murder goes, that may have been done on the spur of the moment, in a pinch. The old watchman probably discovered him unexpectedly and — and got killed, that's all. The premeditated murder charge won't hold. It may even have been a case of self-defense. We don't know — yet."

"I see," assented the cashier, lighting his cigarette. "You men fairly make my head whirl with your reasoning. I know I'm breaking the rules and setting a bad example to smoke here; but, confound it, in a case like this —"

He turned to Sheridan.

"We've seen enough, I guess," he judged. "Don't you think so?"

"More than enough," assented the other. "I think we ought to have this taken away. Mr. Chamberlain would never get over it if he had to see it lying here."

"Right! Better take it now. I understand all you've shown me, and can testify to it if need be. So can Sheridan."

"Of course I can," affirmed the teller.

"All right. Let's clean things up here."

"Very well," said Roadstrand. "And after that we'll look at two or three other interesting bits."

He summoned the policeman who stood near the door, and gave a few curt orders. Presently, while the various employees, isolated and interned at their desks and in their cages, watched with silent awe — with now and then a hateful glance at Mansfield — a couple of policemen with a stretcher came in, clumping heavily over the tiled floor.

Two minutes later, under the white woolen blanket, old man Mackenzie had forever left the bank, his duty done, his story at an end, and all his debts fully paid. The eager crowd about the doors experienced a momentary thrill at sight of that stark figure. Then the stretcher with its light burden was shoved into the motor patrol. The policemen climbed in after it and drew the doors close behind them. The engine accelerated, the siren screamed, the patrol plowed away through the throng and headed northward toward the morgue.

Old man Mackenzie, now but a piece of evidence, was on his way toward the autopsy-table.

Within the bank, Slayton inhaled a lungful of smoke and blew it out with nervous energy.

" Sheridan," said he, " have Anderson clean this up — if he can — and put fresh sawdust over it.   We'll have new tiles laid in a day or two; but for now tell him to do the best he can."

He turned to Roadstrand and the doctor.

" Now then! " said he.   " Let's go over the rest of the evidence.   The quicker we get at the bottom facts in this terrible affair and have the murderer behind bars, the better."

CHAPTER XI

ROADSTRAND motioned toward the directors' room. "It mightn't be a bad idea to have a little more privacy than we can get here," suggested he. "We've already got our hands on one or two matters of interest. Suppose we go in there to examine them — eh?"

"All right," assented Slayton. "Come on, Sheridan. You're in on this, too."

The four men approached the private room. Their way led past the safe door.

"Just a minute," said the cashier.

He examined the combination, swung the door open, stepped inside the vault, and almost closed the door. For a brief moment he was there, alone. Swiftly he cast a glance around, particularly at the floor.

Had he left any sign, dropped anything, given any clue or hint of the crime? No; he could find nothing. Relieved, freed from a small but insistent fear that, like an obsession, had for some time been gnawing at his soul, he opened the door again and peered out.

"Shot Mackenzie from here, you think?" queried he.

Nelson removed his spectacles, scratched his bald spot, and nodded.

"It looks that way," he judged.

"And after that robbed the safe? You think the robbery followed the murder?"

"Probably so. At any rate, the robbery was no hurried affair. The criminal evidently knew all about the location

86

of the different kinds of funds, and, moreover, he understood the bank's system of books and accounts."

"How so?"

"Why, don't you know? He took only one-thousand-dollar bills, and he also mutilated the ledger containing records of the numbers of those bills."

"No! You don't say so!"

"I do say so. That's why — that's one reason why — we've figured that only an employee of the bank could have done it; that, and the fact that the safe was opened with the combination. No finger-prints here at all," and Nelson touched the shining combination-knob. "No violence of any kind. The thing was all planned out in advance, and was surely pulled off by a man who had access to the cipher of the combination. That means a bank employee, doesn't it?"

Slayton raised his eyebrows.

"I'm afraid it does," he answered. "I'm very — much — afraid it does. And if I'm not mistaken —"

"Well?" demanded Roadstrand.

"Oh, nothing! We mustn't form any opinion at all without the evidence. Let's see, now."

He re-entered the safe. Sheridan followed him.

"What does the loss total, Sheridan, so far as you know?"

"A hundred and fifty thousand."

"All in those one-thousand-dollar bills?"

Slayton pointed at the ravaged compartment.

"Yes. And — see here?"

Sheridan indicated an empty place in the file of the bank's books, standing on their carpeted shelf.

"He didn't take the whole record-ledger, did he?" demanded Slayton.

"No. It's in the directors' room. But all the pages with the one-thousand-dollar-bill records are gone. You'll see."

"Hmmm! A clever idea, at that!" Slayton muttered. "We aren't dealing with any fool, believe me, gentlemen! We're up against a slick proposition — a long-headed fellow, and no mistake.

"Well, enough of this. Now let's see that ledger and whatever else there is that bears on the case."

They all proceeded to the directors' room. Slayton closed the door. Outside in the bank itself, isolated anxiety continued to hold the clerks and officers in bonds of terrible suspense. Some were smoking, some making a pretense of work, some aggressively assuming indifference.

Mansfield was doing nothing of the kind. Plainly in a blue funk, he was sitting at his desk, elbow on the blotter, face hidden in hand, a picture of the most absolute despair and misery. And back and forth passed looks from clerk to bookkeeper and from messenger to clerk; and here a raised eyebrow, there a dour grimace, yonder a shrug of the shoulder told their thought.

Indifferent to it all, Mansfield sat there, buried in his anguish.

"I am ruined," he was thinking. "Position, honor, reputation — everything is gone. I am lost. Enid is gone forever. Everything's all over now."

Through the glass of the door, Slayton caught a glimpse of Mansfield, and saw a look that passed between Parker, the messenger, and the assistant bookkeeper, Holmes. He thrilled with joy. Even though he should say no further word, should never raise his hand to point at Mansfield, should never give this thing another moment's thought, he felt positive the boy would go to Sing Sing, maybe to the chair.

And, realizing the perfection of the frame-up, he felt a glow of pride. If this were not a masterpiece of deception, had one ever been conceived and executed since time began?

Slayton faced the others. Still cold and unmoved, his lean face showed rather more than its usual pallor. Sheridan, of ruddy visage and portly build, frowned with anxiety and nibbled at a pencil with perturbation.

"Shall we sit down?" asked Roadstrand.

Slayton nodded. All four of them — Roadstrand, Nelson, Slayton and Sheridan — drew up chairs about the broad oak table of the bank directors. The cashier lighted another cigarette. In spite of every effort of the will and every self-assurance of safety, he found himself a bit nervous again.

All this suavity, all this seeming acquiescence with his ideas, might they not be only part of a trap to lead him on and snare him in the end?

He trusted nobody. Were he to come through this thing alive and free, it must be through his own wit and nerve and energy. The slightest misstep might cost him liberty, might cost him life. Not for one second must he relax his watchfulness or leave the way open for psychic shock or physical surprise.

Thus, weighing the others' knowledge and motives, he sat there with them at the table. But on no face appeared the slightest tinge of ruse or suspicion. The doctor, the coroner, the paying-teller all seemed honest, frank and unsuspecting. Slayton felt positive that, so far at least, he had made good his bluff and kept the assumption of his innocence intact.

"Let's see the ledger," said he. "That may give us some clue."

Sheridan handed it to him, bringing it from the mantel where it had been lying.

"Well, well!" said Slayton, opening it and studying the mutilations with keen interest. "He made a clean sweep, didn't he? And, so far as I see, there's nothing here to tell us what hand ripped the leaves out. Is there?"

The doctor shook his head.

"Absolutely nothing," he answered. "But as a piece of subsidiary evidence, to show the high mental caliber and keen wit of the criminal, the ledger possesses considerable value."

Sheridan took the ledger away. Roadstrand, meantime, had pulled a little bundle from his pocket. He now undid the rubber bands that held it and opened it out on the table.

"Here," said he, "is something of vital moment. It has already led me to form certain theories. Let me have your opinion and see if it coincides with mine — with the doctor's and mine."

Speaking, he took out a soiled, ash-covered glove, and handed it to Slayton.

"What do you make of that?" he asked.

"Where did you find it?" queried the cashier, suppressing his elation. "A great deal depends on that."

"Right! A very great deal indeed. Well, we found this in front of the furnace, buried in ashes."

"Have you got the other?"

"Not yet. I think we'll find nothing but the metal snap. Undoubtedly that will turn up in the ashes under the furnace, when sifted."

"You mean then," asked Slayton meditatively, "that the murderer meant to throw both gloves into the furnace, but in his hurry and excitement dropped one, and the ashes fell over it when he opened the furnace door?"

"Something like that. Now do you recognize the glove?"

Slayton turned it and examined it carefully, then shook his head.

"No," said he. "There are no distinguishing marks. I can't tell anything about it. Hello! What's this?"

He pointed at the fingers. Three of them were stained with dull red, to which ashes adhered in minute flakes.

"That," answered the doctor, "is blood."

" So then — This is the very glove that was on the murderer's hand when he felt of old Mackenzie's heart?"

" Good reasoning!" commended Roadstrand. " Now, if we can only prove the ownership of.the glove!"

" Anything else?"

" Yes; several things. See here!"

He took a small button from the package and gave it to the cashier.

" That," said he, " was found about four feet from the body, near the grillwork."

" Torn off in the struggle?" asked Slayton.

" Don't know. We don't think there *was* any struggle. The old man was probably shot from the safe, you remember. Death must have been instantaneous. Don't you think so, doctor?"

" I'm sure of it," affirmed Nelson.

" So then, this button —?" interrogated the cashier.

" Probably just happened to fall off. It must have been loose. Perhaps when the murderer thrust his hand into the old man's breast he scraped the button off. We don't know; can't tell; but here it is, anyhow. Can you identify it?"

The cashier studied it attentively, turning it over and over in his bony fingers.

" Hmmm!" he grunted, a world of meaning in the monosyllable.

Roadstrand and the doctor exchanged a keen glance.

" Well, whose is it?" demanded the coroner.

" I can't say positively."

" Have you an opinion?"

" Yes."

" Well?"

" I'd rather see some more of the evidence before making any statement."

" *All* right! Here's something of still further interest."

Roadstrand unfolded a paper that had been inside the parcel, and spread it out on the table.

"What do you make of that?" he asked.

Slayton, now for the first time facing the unexpected, beheld six or eight gray hairs, stiff and rather wiry. He blinked with involuntary alarm.

"What do you make of those?" demanded the coroner again.

"Make of them? Why, nothing. What are they?" countered the cashier, sparring for time, if only a few seconds, to collect his thoughts.

He failed to comprehend what was coming now; but with extreme wariness he was steeling himself against any surprise or attack.

"What are they?"

"Gray hairs, of course."

"Yes, I know; but what have they got to do with this case? Where did you find them?"

"In the gripping fingers of the old man! Now, how shall we explain that?"

Slayton felt suddenly very sick. In a flash he knew the truth, the answer to the riddle. Those hairs belonged to that wig he had worn — the wig that old Mackenzie had picked up — the wig that had been the direct cause of the crime itself. When he had pulled the wig away from the dead man's hand a few hairs had come out. Now those hairs constituted a menace terrible in its possibilities; a deadly peril as unexpected as it might prove fatal.

The cashier realized only too well on how slight pivots the whole machinery of justice may turn, and how minute a bit of evidence may lead a murderer to the chair. Had he possessed a million dollars he would have given them all, and more, with eager joy, to have those few hairs in his keeping, to destroy them, to remove them forever from the searching ken of scientists and lawyers.

He knew that he was paling; he knew his face had altered, despite his every effort at indifference; and to conceal his emotion he took the paper with the hairs in it, bent his brows, and studied them with intense application.

Then finally he shook his head.

"I don't make anything of these at all," said he. "Unless, of course, the old man might — might have —"

He paused, seeking the idea that would not fully come. Then with inspiration he concluded:

"— might have clutched at his head in agony and pulled these out."

"Very good," put in the doctor. "But they aren't human hairs at all."

"They're *not?*" ejaculated Slayton, terribly shaken.

"No! Even a cursory examination with a pocket lens convinces me of that. They belong to, well —"

"To what?" the cashier demanded.

Sheridan leaned forward eagerly.

"Some animal, I think," the doctor said.

"Animal? But how the devil could they get into his grasp, then?"

"That's exactly what puzzles me," answered the doctor. "The circumstance is most baffling. What this means I frankly don't know. But, if rightly interpreted, this single bit of evidence might go far toward solving the mystery."

Though Slayton felt a horrible sinking sensation at the pit of his stomach, he managed to remain calm.

"This clue certainly ought to be followed," he suggested.

"It will be," affirmed the doctor, "to the end."

The room seemed swimming before Slayton's eyes, but he still sat there resolutely, staring at the diabolical little wisps of hair on the bit of paper. At the very outset, he realized, he had received a blow that might yet nullify all his plans and land him in the chair. To his mind recurred the old saying that even the cleverest criminal always leaves some loophole open, or drops some clue, that may convict him.

"That wig! That infernal wig!" thought he.

A thousand times better would it have been had he gone to the bank undisguised than to have left this terrifying evidence in the old man's dead fingers.

Holding his nerve by a supreme effort, he shoved the paper back toward Roadstrand.

"I can't offer any suggestion about this," said he, forcing his eyes to meet the coroner's. "Let's leave it aside for a while. Have you anything else of value?"

Roadstrand drew out his pocketbook, extracted from it an envelope, and laid it on the table.

"Here," said he, "is something of the highest importance."

Speaking, he folded the hairs up again in their paper and replaced them in the little parcel.

"We haven't succeeded yet in locating the pages torn from the ledger; but, judging by the use the criminal made of the furnace in the basement, we're pretty positive he must have burned them there. This envelope here "— and Roadstrand took it up again —"contains three bits of paper that he dropped when he tore up and burned something he knew had to be destroyed. We found these three tiny scraps on the basement floor about an hour ago. Please see if you can identify them."

Slayton prepared himself for a fresh shock in case this new evidence should also be something dangerous to him. He watched eagerly as Roadstrand shook the contents of the envelope upon the polished wood.

Then with relief he recognized the minute bits of paper he had purposefully "planted" on the basement floor — the little fragments of the cipher with which he had opened the safe. His heart leaped for joy. Here now was one more step toward the goal, one more factor in the working-out of his plan.

He picked up one of the bits — another; then the third. He studied them and turned them over; then, thrusting out his lower lip, he frowned and said:

"Why — it's the cipher! The combination!"

"It is, eh?" queried Nelson. "You recognize it, then?"

"I certainly do! See this ' 5 ' here and this ' sto '? I ought to know this carbon-copy — I made it myself! Only two of these ciphers existed. Chamberlain's got the original. And —"

"What does that ' sto ' mean, anyhow?" put in Road-strand.

"It's part of the word ' stop.' The cipher read: ' R, so-and-so; L, so-and-so to stop.' The murderer just happened to let this piece fall, when he tore it up and threw it into the fire. Understand?"

"Yes. That's what I thought it was — the combination. Nelson didn't quite agree, but I knew I was right. What I don't understand, though, is how the crook got hold of that paper in the first place. Where did you keep it?"

"Keep it? Why, locked in my desk, of course," answered Slayton, sensing a disagreeable measure of inquisition in the coroner's question.

"Which drawer?"

"Upper right hand."

"And you're sure it was locked in there last night when you went home?"

"Positive!"

"All right. That accounts for it, then."

"Accounts for what?"

"For that drawer being broken open. One of the things we established after the first essentials had been attended to was that your desk had been tampered with."

"The lock picked, you mean?"

Roadstrand nodded.

"This is what I took out of it," said he.

From his waistcoat pocket he produced a pointed bit of steel.

"That was broken short off in the lock," he explained, turning it in his wiry fingers. "What do you make of it?"

"It looks like a paper-cutter or something of that sort," judged the cashier. "Now, if you could only find the rest of it, you'd have some mighty valuable evidence. Evidence, I should say, that ought to convict."

"We *have* found it already," smiled Roadstrand.

As he spoke he drew the broken letter-opener from his upper vest-pocket. "Now, whose is it?"

"Where did you find it?"

"In a gray coat hanging near the assistant bookkeeper's desk."

"A gray coat?" Slayton exclaimed. "Why, that's Holmes's! I never would have believed —"

"Don't get excited," cautioned Roadstrand, while the doctor smiled tolerantly and Sheridan nervously rubbed his shaven chin. "The mere fact that it was in a certain man's pocket doesn't prove it belongs to that man. In fact, it might rather prove the contrary. The opener might have been dropped into that coat-pocket as a blind. Look at it, please, and see if you can identify it."

He handed it to Slayton. As the cashier took it he felt his heart thump violently. Now that the first opportunity had arisen to make any direct accusation, he found his nerves were jumpy as a cat's. Desire whispered:

"Accuse directly and with boldness."

Caution bade:

"Not yet! Go slow!"

And caution won. Shaking his head, he answered:

"I can't tell whose it is. There are several in use here.

They're all pretty much alike. Do you recognize it, Sheridan?"

He gave the broken opener to the teller. Sheridan scrutinized it beneath bent brows, then looked up sharply.

"What's this ' A. M.' scratched in the handle here?"

"' A. M.'?" demanded Slayton. "Is there an 'A. M.'?"

"See?"

Sheridan pointed. Yes, there the letters were rudely scratched, as with a penknife, in an idle moment.

"' A. M.,' sure enough," said the cashier. "Why, there's Moore; but his first name is Edward, and there's — there's nobody else except — well —"

"Mansfield?" demanded the doctor.

Slayton nodded.

"What's his first name?"

"Arthur."

The silence that followed was vast in its potentialities. Roadstrand broke it.

"I think," said he, "we'd better have a little talk with that young man."

CHAPTER XII

SLAYTON regarded the coroner for a pregnant moment, without a word. Then, leaning forward across the table, he forced himself to look Roadstrand fair in the eyes.

"You mean —?" he whispered tensely.

"Call Mansfield!"

The cashier's heart surged with exultation. A dizzying sweep of joy surged over him. Already he had forgotten the accursed possibilities dormant in those white hairs found in Mackenzie's stiffened hand. He motioned to Sheridan.

"Get Mansfield," he repeated the order.

The teller rose, stood there a moment beside the table, and, resting his knuckles on the wood, looked first at Roadstrand, then at Nelson.

"Gentlemen," said he slowly, "as far as that boy's concerned, I'll take my oath —"

"No matter about your oath," snapped the coroner angrily. "Your oath isn't worth a damn in this case. Here's evidence that points directly at him. His appearance this morning is damaging. Things would look black for the angel Gabriel himself with that kind of proof against him. We want to talk with this Mansfield fellow. Bring him in here right away."

"All right; but you're making a fearful mistake, just the same," retorted Sheridan with some heat. "That kid's as square and white as —"

"Can that!" exclaimed Roadstrand. "Go get him!"

Slayton snapped peremptory fingers.

"Are you going to get him, or shall I?" he demanded.

The teller, yielding to authority, turned and walked reluctantly toward the door. But he did not open it. Instead, he faced round, stood there motionless, and directed a keen, suspicious glance at Slayton — a glance by no means lost on the cashier.

"I'll be damned if I will!" he suddenly exclaimed. "That boy's got no more to do with it than I have. I'm not going to be the bearer of any such message to him. I won't be a party to any such an accusation, even to the extent of summoning him in here."

Slayton laughed sneeringly.

"You're a fool, Sheridan!" he snarled out. "Suit yourself, though. It doesn't matter. But I tell you right now your attitude is liable to be misconstrued —"

"What d' you mean?" demanded the teller, clenching his fist. "Are you insinuating —"

"Sit down and shut up!" commanded Slayton. "Or else get out!"

Their eyes met angrily. Sheridan, eagerly desirous of being present in Arthur's behalf at the interrogation, subsided. He came back and sank down into his chair by the table again.

"That's all right," he growled. "But I know Arthur, and I know he's straight. And if you mean to infer that I —"

Slayton reached out and pressed a push-button at the side of the table. A buzzer sounded outside. Parker, the messenger, started up as if the current had passed through his body and came to the door of the directors' room. He opened it and stood there, pale and scared — but no more frightened than every living soul out there in the offices and cages, waiting in terror for the catastrophe that might strike like lightning where it willed.

"Tell Mansfield we want him," bade Slayton.

"Yes, sir!"

And Parker departed, vastly relieved that the finger of accusation had not been leveled at *him*. He stopped by Mansfield's desk.

"They want you in there," said he with rare tact. "I guess you're in bad."

"What?" asked Mansfield dully. "Who wants me?"

"*They* do — in there!"

Parker jerked his thumb over his shoulder.

"What for?"

"Search *me!*"

"They didn't say what for?"

"Go an' see," the messenger answered coldly. "I guess you know, all right, all right!"

A confused murmur rose in the bank. With dour suspicion everybody was eying Mansfield. He stood up, blinked for a moment, and looked first one way, then the other. Somewhat dazed, he turned to Parker.

"In there, you mean?" he queried. "In the directors' room?"

"Uh-huh! An' you better be on your way, too. They don't act as if they was very patient."

Mansfield, moving as if in a dream, slowly started toward the room down the grilled passageway. A score of hostile eyes followed his every step with cold analysis and condemnation.

"Thumbs down!" the verdict was already, before a single bit of evidence had been adduced.

The boy, his mind wholly occupied with the disaster that had come upon him through Slayton's treachery — for no slightest suspicion of any greater peril had even so much as occurred to him — hung his head and sagged along, pallid, disheveled, haggard. Eagerly the others watched him as he passed that grim, sawdust-covered spot on the tiles.

No sign there? He gave no sign, showed no repulsion, quivered not with horror of the place?

"The scoundrel!" muttered Parker, frowning blackly. "Hard as a rock! There's a nice, mild character for you; what? Guilty as Hell, and never bats an eye!"

Mansfield, oblivious to all this hostility — or, subconsciously noting it, attributing it only to his theft, which now must surely be known — reached the door of the directors' room. He paused there a moment to gather himself together, a little. Then, very pale, but with his jaw hardclosed, his eyes half questioning, half defiant, he swung the door and entered.

"You sent for me?" he questioned huskily. "Well, I'm here."

"Yes; so we observe, Mansfield," answered Roadstrand with a grim smile. "Come in and shut the door. We want to ask you a few questions."

"All right; I'm ready."

He closed the door and advanced toward the table.

"What is it you want to know? I'm ready. I won't hide anything. It wouldn't do any good, anyhow. Mr. Slayton here knows all about it. I thought he was going to help me —"

"Mansfield! Look out!" exclaimed the cashier. "I warn you now you'll gain nothing by lying."

"But you *did* promise! Last night! You won't deny that, will you?" demanded Arthur, amazed. "If you'd kept your word I could have —"

"No more of that now!" interrupted the coroner. "This isn't a wrangling match or a joint debate."

He turned to Slayton.

"In a word, what's this he says about you? What are the facts?"

Sheridan, an odd look coming into his eyes, leaned forward eagerly.

The doctor squinted interrogatively through his spectacles. Slayton smiled with a glint of those white teeth of his.

" Mansfield called on me last night at about eleven-thirty," said he, " at my house in Oakwood Heights.   He told me he was twelve hundred and fifty dollars short in his accounts, and asked me to lend him enough to cover the deficit.   I refused and —"

" That's a lie ! "

" Silence ! " shouted the coroner.   " You, Mansfield, keep still there ! "

" But he said —" persisted Mansfield.

" Sh-h-h-h, Arthur ! " cautioned Sheridan, clapping him on the shoulder.   " One at a time.   Don't get excited.   The facts will all come out in due course.   Let him speak."

" All right," answered the boy.   " But I know what I know ! "

" I refused, of course," continued Slayton.   " He entreated, but in vain.   He even threatened me with an automatic pistol; but I held firm, and —"

" My God, what lies !   What infamous —"

" If you don't keep still, young man, I'll — I'll have you gagged ! " roared the coroner in a passion.   " Not another word till I tell you to speak !   Understand ? "

" Shall I continue or not ? " demanded the cashier.   " You understand, naturally, I can't give a connected narrative with these crude interruptions."

" Go on," directed Roadstrand.   " Interruptions, eh?   I'd like to hear him interrupt again.   Go on ! "

" I refused, and held to my refusal.   He left me at about eleven-fifty, I think, and caught the midnight train to St. George's.   I read a while, wrote and posted a letter to my wife, and then went to bed.   That's all the direct testimony I can give.   The rest is up to you."

" Thank you," said Roadstrand.   " Very clear and very concise.   That explains a number of things."

He turned to Mansfield.

" Now then," he interrogated, " you admit the shortage? "

" Yes, sir. I'm not going to try to hide that, or anything."

" Is that amount correct — twelve hundred and fifty dollars? "

" Yes, sir."

" Why did you take it? "

" I — I can't tell."

" You refuse? "

" Positively! "

" Put that down, Nelson," directed the coroner. " Make an especial note of that. He refuses to tell why he stole."

" Merciful Heavens, Arthur! " exclaimed Sheridan in deep distress. " What's this you say? You — you're really short? You took that much? "

" It's a fact, Mr. Sheridan. I admit it. Only I thought Mr. Slayton here was going to help me out. He promised to, but for some reason or other changed his mind. So now I'm in bad — right up against it."

He paused. Slayton's sneering laugh was more effective than an angry outburst. That laugh said:

" Oh, yes, indeed! I, Walter Slayton, the respectable — I would be likely to compound a felony, would I not? As likely as to — commit a murder! "

Tense silence held the room in thrall. One could hear the boy's quickened breath. The ticking of the little alabaster clock on the mantel sounded strangely loud. For the space of five seconds no man spoke. Then all at once the coroner leaned forward, jabbing a finger at Mansfield.

" Remember now," said he sharply, " anything you say here may be used against you. I'm a judge, *ex-officio*. This is an official preliminary hearing."

" In that case," interposed Sheridan, " this boy must have counsel."

"Sit down and keep still," directed Nelson. "We're running this interrogation, not you."

"I'm within my rights as his friend to insist that he say nothing until he had been advised by a competent lawyer. I volunteer to produce such a one inside of five minutes."

"If you can't keep out of this, Sheridan," exclaimed the cashier angrily, "you'd better leave the room."

"Order, here!" cried Roadstrand, rapping the table vigorously with his knuckles. "Now then, Mansfield, you needed money badly?"

"No, sir. Not any more than the twelve hundred and fifty dollars. And I'd have put that back, all right, and made good if *he* hadn't double-crossed me —"

"No more of that!" exclaimed the coroner sternly. "We'll leave out all accusations. Don't bring anybody else into this. We're dealing with you, and you alone. You admit being at Oakwood Heights and having a pistol?"

"I—"

"Arthur!" exclaimed Sheridan, taking him by the arm. "See here! You don't know what you're saying. You're all balled up. They'll tangle you up here inside of five minutes so tight that the devil himself couldn't untangle you. You keep still now! I'm going to 'phone for a lawyer, and —"

"Silence!" shouted Roadstrand, turning quite purple in the face. "I simply will not and cannot have these interruptions! I've got authority here as much as I'd have in a court-room. This interfering with a witness can't be tolerated, and sha'n't be. Go on now, Mr. Sheridan. Leave the room, and don't let's have any trouble about it!"

Sheridan gasped with rage and clenched his fists, but Slayton now had risen and was facing him.

"Are you going to obey the legally constituted authorities of the County of Manhattan, or shall we have to use force?"

demanded Slayton. "There are two or three officers outside there. It's up to you!"

Sheridan turned on him with a snarl of passion, of loathing, of intense suspicion.

"Don't worry!" he exclaimed. "I'll go, all right. And,
what's more, my resignation from this bank takes place immediately. No more job for me in a place that tolerates a
skunk like you! So much for *that*.

"But there's another thing. You won't be through with
me when I go out of that door. I'm going to watch this case
right through to the end. I see how it's drifting and I'll
watch it, never fear. You're smooth, Slayton; you're oily,
slick and suave. But you can't put anything over on me.
So now you know. That's all for *you!*

"Arthur!" and he seized the boy by the hand. "You
take my advice. Don't tell anything. Don't admit a single
thing! Don't speak a word till you've seen a lawyer. That's
within your constitutional right. Remember now — and
God help you! Remember!"

He released Arthur's hand and strode to the door.

"See here, you!" cried Roadstrand. "I think you'll bear
a little watching. Not a step outside this building do you
stir till this thing's settled. So don't try it. Now get out
of here and stay out!"

"Don't you worry about my leaving," sneered the teller.
"Next thing I know you'll be trying to put this over on *me!*
All right; go to it. I'll stick till Hell freezes, but I'll see
justice done that boy!"

The door banged vigorously behind him. Pale with consuming anger, he returned to his desk, leaving Mansfield
in the hands of the inquisition.

"Lord! If he only remembers what I've told him!" muttered the teller. "If he only remembers and keeps still!"

Roadstrand, meanwhile, was exchanging a significant
glance with the doctor.

"Extraordinary actions, I must say," he remarked, swabbing his face with his handkerchief — for anger always made him sweat. "That fellow will bear watching, believe me. It wouldn't surprise me if he —"

"You think so?"

"It's possible — as an accessory, you understand. We'll have tabs kept on him, at any rate. Now then!"

Once more he turned to Mansfield.

"Enough of all this matter of the robbery. Enough for the present. Let us pass to other things. You admit having had a pistol, do you?"

Arthur hesitated. His eyes sought the glass door through which Sheridan could now be seen, seated at his desk. Should he answer any questions, or should he refuse, as Sheridan had told him?

"Come on, Mansfield! Speak up!" directed Slayton. "What did you do with that automatic after you left me?"

The boy gaped at him, amazed.

"What — what did I *do* with it?" he stammered, trapped into the damaging admission. "Why, nothing, of course. Seeing that you took it away from me and put it in your desk drawer and kept it, how — how could I have done anything with it?"

The cashier smiled triumphantly.

"Don't lie, Arthur," he cautioned. "It can do no possible good. After you threatened me with that gun, in case I wouldn't help you —"

"After I — *what?*"

"You deny having threatened me?" demanded Slayton truculently.

"It's a lie! I never!"

"You see, gentlemen," said the cashier, turning to the others, "we can't get anywhere with this fellow. He's more devious than an eel. He —"

"A rotten lie! I never so much as thought of threaten-

ing you!" exclaimed Arthur, stung into action by the lash
of the false accusation. "You know it's a lie, too! I only
said I'd kill myself if you didn't help me out, and you
promised —"

"Order!" cried the coroner. "This is no debating society. It's obvious you had a gun, anyhow. Now, where
is it? What have you done with it?"

"*He's* got it!"

And Arthur jabbed an angry finger at the smiling cashier.

"He took it away from me. Told me not to be a damned
fool, and all that. Put it in his desk drawer, and —"

"Nothing of the kind, gentlemen," affirmed Slayton.
"When he left me he took it along. It's his word against
mine. Choose for yourself. He came to me, confessed
his theft, menaced me, and then when I had pacified him,
took himself off with the gun in his overcoat pocket — the
right-hand pocket. I remember seeing him slip it in there."

A moment's silence, while Arthur, gasping with rage,
could find no word to lay his tongue to. Then subtly a
change of expression came across his features. His eyes
narrowed slightly, his mouth hardened, and a dangerous glitter came into his pupils.

"What — for God's sake, what are you people trying to
put over on me, anyhow?" he managed to exclaim huskily.

For the first time now some glimmer of suspicion had begun to dawn in his ingenuous mind of the abysses, the yawning pits and snares laid ready for his feet.

"What are you driving at, anyhow?" he demanded again.
"You — you aren't trying to — make out that — I —"

"Driving at?" smiled Roadstrand, dangerously suave all
of a sudden. "Why, nothing except the truth. That's all
we're striving for — to elucidate the truth from all this mass
of confusing details. The truth, nothing less and nothing
more. You surely can't take exception to that, can you?"

Speaking, he had fixed his eyes keenly on the boy's coat.

He seemed to be studying the buttons there. A peculiar look came into his eyes.

" Just as I thought," he muttered. " Precisely as I thought ! "

Arthur, too confused to answer anything, too violently shaken by the new and horrible suspicions that now, like sudden tempests, were whirling and ravening about his head, stood there peering at him as a trapped animal will sometimes peer at its captor. His face twitched, especially the mouth; and on his forehead a few little glistening drops of sweat began to appear. He put out his left hand and took hold of the back of the chair where Sheridan, his only friend, had been sitting.

Thus for a moment silence came again upon that group of beings, between whom and around whom the lines of destiny were drawing with a savage, ever-increasing tension. And in that moment, through the revolving doors of the bank, two figures entered — entered, and came into the lobby; stopped there, looked about, and once again came forward.

CHAPTER XIII

THE TRAP IS SPRUNG

ONE was the Hon. Edward Bruce Chamberlain, president of the bank, a man of about sixty-five, gray and rather markedly wrinkled, yet of military bearing, keen of eye, alert of mind, confident of manner.

The other, Enid Chamberlain, gave one an impression of sunshine and spring, of warmth and life and happiness, even on this dull, gray November morning. One could hardly see her clearly as yet, for the screened windows of the bank shut out the daylight, and the electric lights seemed only pale and ineffective; but one could see she had a little trim, white toque on her black hair — a toque with a single, slashing, crimson feather — and that her long white coat draped a figure of great elegance and beauty. Her eyes were black — or were they a dark blue with liquid depths? Now, as they glanced about the lobby, they mirrored sorrow, pity, wonder; they seemed questing somebody they could not find. Plainly they asked:

"Where is he now?"

They could not find the one they sought, for he was facing three inquisitors there in the stillness of the directors' room — facing them with a new, strangling terror clutching at his soul.

"You don't — mean to say you think — I —" he stammered half unintelligibly, his eyes, frightened and pitiful, going from one face to another, his whole body beginning to tremble in a racking shiver.

"We don't mean to think anything but what the evidence points out to us," answered Roadstrand grimly. "Please look at this and tell us whose it is."

With a sudden gesture he flung the bloodstained glove down on the table, right in front of Arthur.

"Well, whose is it?"

Mansfield fixed unseeing eyes on it for a moment. They could not focus. Everything seemed to blur, to swim. Then, as out of a mist, vision returned. He perceived the glove. Mechanically he took it up and turned it over. At sight of the blood a kind of yellowish tinge spread across his drawn face.

"Blood?" he gulped. "Blood — on my —"

"It's yours, then? You admit it?"

Helplessly the boy peered at Roadstrand, as if not quite seeing him, not quite understanding.

"Mine?"

"Yes, yours!"

"*I* don't know how any — blood —"

"I'm not asking you about that blood — old Mackenzie's blood —"

"Mackenzie's? On *my* glove?"

"You admit it, then? It's yours?"

Arthur let his head fall, and stood silent and shaking there before them, some measure of realization of the truth making itself felt in his numb soul. He could not yet grasp the total of this infamy against him; but, conscious of even a part, he gripped the chair to keep himself steady; and so, mute and pallid, stood there before his merciless accusers.

"He admits it, doctor," announced Roadstrand in a professional voice, which showed a little exultation despite his efforts to render it quite neutral. "Note that down. Exhibit A. Identity admitted before witness."

Outside in the lobby, old Chamberlain was talking with a plain-clothes man. The officer was requesting him not to hold any conversation with any of the employees until such time as the investigation then under way should be completed. He pointed out the spot where Mackenzie had fallen; and Chamberlain, advancing with commiseration and horror, peered through the grill at the patch of sawdust on the floor.

Enid shuddered a bit and turned away. Her mind was on another topic. A line of anxiety had drawn itself between her straight, dark brows. Her eyes, eagerly questing, failed to discover what they sought.

"Where — where's Arthur?" she asked frankly. "You don't suppose they're going to examine *him,* too, do you?"

"Everybody must be examined," answered the old man, smiling vaguely. "Even I must answer questions, I suppose. In an affair of this kind, a tragedy of this kind, no pains are too great and no sacrifices too bitter in serving the ends of justice. Justice is stern, Enid; but pure and mighty. No innocent man need fear. Only the guilty need tremble. So have no uneasiness; have no uneasiness, my dear."

"I know, father; but Arthur —"

The old man smiled again and looked down tenderly and wisely at the girl, so eager and warm and brave.

"Arthur has nothing to fear," said he. "By the way, where *is* the boy?"

He turned to the plain-clothes man.

"You don't know who is being examined now, do you?" he queried.

"Search *me!*" answered the officer. "They've got a young feller in there with 'em. He's been in there about ten minutes. It'll be all right if you go in, of course. They want you."

Chamberlain laid a hand on the girl's arm.

"Sit down here, Enid," he bade her, "and wait for me. I'll find out about Arthur. Don't be troubled, my dear. Everything will be all right — all right in every way!"

Enid, nervously twisting her long white gloves together, sat down in a deep leather chair in the little alcove reserved for women, glanced about her, bit her lip, tapped her boot on the carpet, and in a dozen ways showed extreme distress. The glances of admiration that — despite their worry — two or three employees could not help leveling at her, fell unnoticed from her shield of indifference. Only one thought possessed her now:

"Where is Arthur?"

Where was Arthur, indeed? On the brink of the pit! On the sheer edge of the abyss that has no bottom and no end. There he was standing, clutching in desperation at any hold and finding none!

Out of the vague and formless vapors seeming to rise from that depth he heard a voice speaking to him again. And the voice said:

"Is that your letter-opener?"

He stared at a bright metal object, blinked, and made no answer.

"Examine that letter-opener, Mansfield," said the voice. "It is broken, you see. The broken end was found in the lock of Mr. Slayton's top drawer. That was where he kept the combination of the safe. On the handle of this utensil you will observe the initials 'A. M.' Kindly tell me — does that letter-opener belong to you?"

Mansfield nodded. Useless now to combat that even, horrible, betraying voice. Helplessly he looked at Roadstrand, whose face had now also emerged from the mists.

"Yes," he admitted in a flat tone. "It's mine. But how it got broken —"

"No matter about that. Later such matters can be discussed. It's yours; that's enough for now. Doctor, enter the data. Letter-opener acknowledged also before witness. Exhibit B.

"And now," the coroner continued, "now finally here is a

button. This button was found near the body of Mackenzie. Do you recognize the button, Mansfield?"

He laid it on the table close before the shivering boy. Arthur stared at it, unseeingly.

"Off his sleeve," whispered Slayton, pointing.

The doctor, rising, pulled the sleeve around into full view under the electric cluster in the ceiling.

"One button is gone, you see," the cashier remarked. "And — well, you can see for yourself; this one matches the other two, there."

Unable to make any answer, on the ragged edge of collapse, Mansfield stood there, hanging on to the back of the chair.

"It's yours, isn't it?" demanded Slayton with malice. "Maybe you can explain how it came to be found beside the body of the murdered man, and —"

"Gentlemen! Gentlemen! What is this? For Heaven's sake, what does this mean?"

Slayton, half starting from his chair, faced the door, an oath on his pale lips. In the doorway stood President Chamberlain, peering at the strange scene with eyes that, unable to believe their testimony, seemed to understand nothing.

"What does this mean, gentlemen?" repeated the old man.

He raised a trembling forefinger, pointing it at Mansfield. "What is this? What —?"

"My dear Mr. Chamberlain!" exclaimed the cashier, and flung a protesting hand outward at him. "I beg you —"

"You aren't accusing Arthur, are you?" demanded the old gentleman, taking a step forward. "Not that! Not that!"

Roadstrand stood up so suddenly that his chair clattered over backward.

"Mr. Chamberlain," he cried, "*we* are accusing nobody! If there is any accusation, the hard, cold facts of the case are making it!"

"They're all lies, lies, lies! Foul, horrible lies!" cried
Mansfield, turning toward Chamberlain. "They've got
some — some kind of frame-up on me here!"

His voice rose wild and trembling; his hand vibrated at
the table.

"Look a' that there, will you? They say I broke into
Slayton's desk with that letter-opener and took the cipher
of the combination! They say I shot Mackenzie —"

"Shot Mackenzie!" cried Chamberlain. "*You?* Father
above! You — shot —"

"They say so! They —"

"The *facts* say so!" interposed the doctor, also rising,
with indignation.

"Damn the facts!" cried the boy in a wild outburst of
passion. "I know what I know! I never was in this bank
last night! I went home to my room —"

"After threatening to kill me in my house if I didn't give
him money to make good his thefts!" shouted the cashier,
in a white heat.

"Arthur! You — you've been stealing?"

"Yes, by God! I have! But murdering? No, no, no!
But they're trying to put it over on me, just the same.
They've got one of my gloves and put blood on it, and they've
put a button off my coat beside the body, and — and now
they're claiming —"

"*Arthur!*"

At the girl's cry of anguish everybody faced the door.
They caught a glimpse of a pale, wild face, of outstretched
hands, of eyes that stared in terror. Then the old man
whirled toward his daughter, arms outspread, to shut away
the sight of that terrible room from her.

"No, no, Enid!" he cried. "You mustn't come in here!
You mustn't —"

"Arthur! Arthur! What are they doing to you? Oh,
what are they doing?"

"Enid! *You* believe me, anyhow, don't you? As God lives, I never killed Mackenzie!"

"Killed him? Killed him? They say you —?"

"No, no! No, *no!*"

And the old man, seizing his daughter by the wrists, held her back, as she would have run to Arthur with open arms of trust and comfort.

"None of that now, Enid! No scene here!"

He forced the girl back, away, out of the room. The door closed behind them both. From without came sounds of anguished sobbing.

Three or four men started toward Chamberlain and Enid. Pale with rage and resentment, Sheridan ran to the old man.

"Of all the rotten frame-ups ever spawned in Hell," he cried, "this is the —"

Chamberlain raised a trembling hand in protest.

"Water, quick!" he entreated. "I think Enid's going to faint!"

Inside the room, sudden battle had flashed into fire. Now Arthur was smashing into all three men.

"Go on! Arrest me!" he shouted. "You, Slayton, you sanctimonious hypocrite, perjure your damned soul! But I'll give you something to remember first!"

His fist cracked like a pistol-shot on Slayton's lantern jaw. The murderer, cursing, plunged headlong across the table, strewing the exhibits right and left.

"Come on, you!" defied Arthur, the lust of battle in his blue eyes, which now had cleared again. "You've got me framed up, all right — but I'll land a few good wallops before you get me!"

Roadstrand lunged at him just as the doctor closed in from behind. Arthur parried the blow and drove home hard with his left. Before he could swing on the doctor, that wiry person had flung an arm about his neck, unbalancing him and dragging him down.

Unmindful of discipline, bookkeepers, clerks and reporters came crowding. In the door appeared a policeman, stick in hand.

Holding his dazed head, which rang and echoed with Arthur's blow, Roadstrand shouted:

"Officer! Your duty!"

The stick, descending, crashed a shower of sparks through Arthur's brain. All strength abandoned his tense body. His head drooped forward; his arms relaxed; his legs, doubling beneath him, let him slip down, down to the carpet of the disordered room.

Then consciousness lapsed. Insensibility drew the mercy of its pall across his agony.

The trap so cleverly, so malevolently set by Walter Haynes Slayton, cashier, had sprung at last.

And in its jaws — mangled, helpless, doomed — lay Arthur Mansfield.

CHAPTER XIV

FAITH SUBLIME, AND A LETTER

ONLY three persons in a whole world of accusers arose to defend Arthur Mansfield. One was the boy's mother; one, ex-teller Sheridan of the bank; the third, Enid Chamberlain.

Shall we stay, a while, to see how she was bearing all her grievous burdens and to learn the depth and breadth of her unshakable faith? To know how she was struggling, boldly championing him despite the torrent of prejudice and falsehood now sweeping him away to death?

Enid's bedchamber fronted the whole western sweep of sky above the Hudson and the Palisades. A wide bay-window, glazed with magnificent curved panes, jutted toward Riverside Drive; and nearly all day long, when any sun at all blessed the world, sunshine gladdened the soft-carpeted, vaguely perfumed, charmingly furnished room of the old banker's daughter.

To-day, however, no sun was shining through the broad and polished panes. None warmed the girl's sad heart. Day was verging toward its close; and as it died, the glow on the ceiling grew ruddier, from the hickory coals in the fireplace at one side of the room.

In a low wicker chair Enid was sitting in the sweep of the window, drooping like a broken flower. One arm, bare to the elbow in the short sleeve of her loose, silk-embroidered Chinese house-gown, had fallen nervelessly over the side of the chair; and from her relaxed hand a photograph had dropped to the floor. Half a dozen letters lay in her lap. From one, a faded jonquil peeped out. What had its pressed and faded petals to tell her, now? Everything? Or — nothing?

Pale and with reddened eyes, Enid gazed unseeingly through the window. Her busy little Sèvres clock chimed four silver notes, but she did not raise her head. For an hour she had been sitting there, indifferent to the moving panorama of the driveway traffic, unseeing the wide gray reaches of the river, beholding not the buttressed shoulders of the Palisades.

There in that window where only three nights before she had waved her hand at Arthur Mansfield in affectionate *au revoir* — that very window where she best loved to sit and read his letters, or write to him, or dream (as girls will dream) of " sometime," now she was trying to think and fight her way through the terror that had suddenly enmeshed her. As a wounded animal will creep to some familiar lair to lick its wounds and strive for life — or die, if die it must — so Enid had found no other place in the big mansion that seemed *home,* now, save this one chair in this one window.

Pondering — not very coherently — she had through blurring tears watched the dull, glowering haze of light that marked the sun's place as it sagged lower, ever lower down the cloudy, snow-threatening November sky — down over the leaden river toward the dun silhouette of the wooded heights beyond.

At one blow, Enid Chamberlain's happiness and all her joy of life had been struck down and shattered in the dust. An immense and formless cloud, cold, dour and forbidding, had in a second of time eclipsed the sunshine of her soul. Now, though the girl could hardly analyze it, she seemed herself to have become part of the wintry landscape. Her June had altered swiftly to November. In the midst of dreams of sun and field and flower, of green, wav-

ing grasses, of blue sky and song of birds, she had awakened to the shivering reality of "biting wind, and snow,
and rain," of fear, of horror. The laughter on her lips
had been transmuted to a cry of pain. The light in her
dark eyes had by some cruel magic been congealed to tears.

Enid pressed a strong, slim hand against her bosom, and
shuddering bowed her head. You could see, now, how very
pale she had grown. All the roses in her cheeks had died
and vanished. In her white face her eyes now looked unnaturally dark, and her ripe lips showed vivid, passionate
and full.

The masses of her splendid hair had all fallen down,
loose and uncared-for, over her shoulders and the back
of the wicker chair. In the warm little valley just at the
base of her throat, you could see the pulsing of her heart —
too fast, too fevered, too eloquent of pain.

Thus the girl sat there, grieving, now that the first gush
of her anger, the first shock of her emotion had somewhat
subsided. And so the dull blur of the sun slid still a little
lower down the leaden arches of the sky; and into that
sweet room the twilight pressed, dimming every outline,
softening every contour. Out from the corners of this
sheltered place that breathed the most intimate spirit of the
feminine, shadows crept thicker and thicker still. Lights
began to spangle the Drive, the misty stretches of the Hudson, and far across it, the Jersey shore.

Still Enid sat there with those letters and that dead jonquil in her lap, seeing nothing — nothing but a steel cage
in the black, forbidding, horrible infamy of the Tombs.

She shuddered at realization of even a little of what that
meant — the Tombs! Arthur was in the Tombs! Again
that cry welled up in her; it came to utterance as a whisper,
now:

"O Arthur! Arthur! What are they doing to you?"

Thank God for one thing, at least, one little respite amid

all this torment! There in the Tombs he could be safe from prying interviews, from raw sensationalism, from the maddening goads of publicity. True, the press could continue to crucify him, but he was shielded from the ubiquity of the reporter and the camera-ghoul. Enid was thankful for this, and for the shelter of her room. Here in this wicker chair, in the bay-window, she too could be free a little while from the torment and the horror of that persecution.

Their grief and agony, she reflected with a peculiar bitterness, had served no purpose as a shield to keep them from the morbid, prying eyes of the sensation-seekers. No, it had all been quite the reverse. That very anguish, his cry of "Innocent!" and her loyal trust that had re-echoed it, had all poured oil on the flames of the indecent fires of sensation.

The girl writhed inwardly with hate and loathing of the yellow press; with shame, with hatred of such outrages. A kind of desperate anger possessed her at thought that Arthur and she had been and still must be mangled to make a New York holiday. She pressed her hands to her eyes as though to shut out the horrible papers with their violent headlines, their columns of lies, misstatements, innuendoes, diagrams, illustrations, analyses. She seemed still to hear the snapping of cameras at her father's door, as she had tried to leave the house, that morning. How shameful and horrible a thing it was that New York's jaded palate must be stimulated by such vicious and debasing methods!

Yellow journalism had, indeed, fairly taken the bit in its teeth and bolted. Romance, robbery and murder had woven a triple skein of excitement. "Heart-interest" had mingled with bloodshed and loot. Newspaperdom, gloating, had dipped its pen in red ink, and scrawled frantically. Raw, crude, blatant, some sheets had run wholly amuck. An orgy of journalistic viciousness had swept the city.

Obscure, the night before, Arthur Mansfield in an hour had become the most talked-of man in the city, and Enid had been forced to share with him every step of his Calvary. As a bank-clerk, quietly performing his duties, Arthur had possessed no news-value whatever. As a self-admitted thief who would confess neither his motives nor a vastly larger theft; as an accused murderer who had assaulted three men and been quelled only by police clubs; and — above all — as a social intimate of the powerful and prominent Chamberlain family, his value in the way of a " feature " had become incalculable. There was even some betting on the outcome of the impending battle. Thus the Mackenzie murder case assumed almost the dignity of a sporting event in New York City. The metropolis breathed deep, and prepared itself for the spectacle.

The People of the State of New York, versus Arthur Mansfield! Rare title to how rare a play!

Fate could not have thrown a more juicy morsel for the space-writers and scandal-mongers to roll under their tongues, than the quasi engagement of Enid and Arthur. In various phases the crimes and the romance were capable of infinite enlargement, endless speculation. Enid, prostrated there in her darkening bedchamber, with the poor relics of happier days lying in her lap, felt hot tears seep through her fingers at thought of all that had been, all that now was, all that yet must be.

In her greater suffering over Arthur's accusation of murder — an accusation she never for one second would admit as just — she forgot his real crime, the theft of the twelve hundred and fifty dollars. That matter had become deadened, nullified, overlaid by the other and vaster woe. Why had he stolen? She did not know. She doubted even that he had. Though he admitted it, this must be only in order nobly to cover some defenseless head. But after all, that mattered not. Nothing mattered save that they were parted, and that upon her boy now rested the brand of Cain.

Enid raised the letters to her lips, kissed them and talked to them, whispering there in the dusk, cherishing them to her breast, giving her soul to him who now sat alone under the shadow of death in the steel cell.

She realized that in all probability the end of everything for them had come. Perhaps the knell had sounded for all their hopes and dreams and wonderings of " sweet togetherness." Innocent though Arthur were, she felt instinctively he might not be able to free himself from the toils. A certain savagery on the part of press and public had already, in the first two days of the case, poisoned the world against him. What jury could be fair, what judge impartial now? She knew that Arthur's fight — brutally exaggerated by the press into a murderous assault on the coroner, the doctor and his own " benefactor " and " best friend "— had greatly injured him. She knew the public was beginning to consider him a dangerous wild beast of a man, whom society in its own behalf would do well to eliminate.

Her boy, gentle, brave and kind, a murderer? Impossible! Womanly instinct told her it was but a scurvy jest of fate that he, so big, clean, strong, loyal, had been swept, like a leaf before a gale, to infamy.

And yet, there he now stood before the hateful eyes of the world, pilloried on that bad eminence, already overwhelmingly condemned by public opinion, already facing the little door, the narrow door, that leads nowhere save to death.

Enid shuddered, groaning.

" No, no, no! " she whispered. " Not that! Not that! "

She heard voices in the hall below.

" Can that be father? "

Gathering the letters and the faded flowers up in her silk kimono, she rose from the low wicker chair and looked out of the window. A few flakes of snow had begun to fall, shimmering about the lights of the big limousine now just growling away from the curb.

"Thank Heaven he's here, at last!" she exclaimed. "He's got news — he must have news of Arthur!"

In her haste, she spilled letters, dead blossoms and all out on her beautiful and immaculate bed, and ran to the door, through it, down the hallway to the big oak stairs.

"Father! Is that you?" she called, eagerly.

"Coming! Coming, Enid!" Chamberlain's voice replied, from below. She heard him say something to the butler. Then his boots sounded on the parquetry, and now she saw him, under the glow of the alabaster bowl that hung inverted in the hallway.

"Any news, daddy?" she demanded, her fingers gripping together till her rings ridged the white flesh. Her eyes now seemed quite black, with glints of light from the beautiful and costly lamp of translucent, sculptured stone.

"Hello, Enid!" And he started up the stairs, toward her. "How's the headache? Better?"

"Good news? Is it good news, father?"

His heart went out to her in pity and love. The blow of this crime, the horrible campaign of sensationalism it had engendered, the shattering of Enid's happiness, had staggered him. And yet he felt that truth was truth, and that to face it honestly with her was best.

"Don't ask me that, dear," begged he.

"Why not? Oh, why not?"

He paused a moment on the landing, and looked up at his daughter, his only child, with eyes of infinite sadness, compassion, wisdom.

"Don't ask me!" he repeated, in a low voice.

"Oh, but it is good, isn't it?" she cried, running down the stairs to him. "It is, it is, it *is!* I know it is! It must be — it's got to be — it *shall* be — !"

She flung her arms about his neck and hugged him tight.
"Daddy mine! Tell me it's good, good news!"

"Enid," answered the old man, unloosening her clinging
hands with gentle firmness, "we can't talk this over, here
and now, in this manner. I've just come from talking with
Hillis & Ballantyne. I've got a great deal to tell you, a very
great deal, indeed, and you must listen carefully. We must
see where we stand and what's to be done. We're facing
a sad problem, my girl — a sad, heavy problem. Suppose
we go to your room, for a little heart-to-heart? Ever since
God wanted your mother so much that He couldn't let me
keep her any longer, that room has been more home to you
than any other in this great, big, empty mockery of a place.
Let's go up to your room and talk it all over, and see where
we stand and what's right and what's wrong, and what must
be done and what we're going to do. Come, Enid!"

The old man drew her head to his heart, a moment, and
kissed her unbound hair.

"Come!" he whispered.

His arm encircled her. In silence, together, father and
daughter went on up the broad staircase under the alabaster glow.

CHAPTER XV

SADLY they climbed the stairs. The old banker's step lagged wearily. His shoulders drooped into an unaccustomed curve. In the two days since the murder, ten years seemed to have weighted him with the lead of a burden that never can grow lighter — old age. His eyes showed dull and lifeless; and under them the loose skin was pouched as never before. For the first time in his active, vigorous life, Edward Bruce Chamberlain looked his years.

But the merciful twilight of the upper hall and of Enid's room soon hid all this, even as it concealed the girl's pale cheeks and wistful eyes of pain. At the door, Chamberlain's hand sought the electric button, but hesitated and fell again. Repellant, now, was the idea of light. Save for the vague red warmth upon the ceiling, cast by the hardwood coals in the fireplace, and the pale reflection of a street-lamp through the broad windows, the room lay in shadow. That shadow soothed and comforted the man. After the day of pitiless searchings and questionings, after the inquisitions and the staring eyes of publicity, the sweet warm dusk of this upper room fell like balm upon his wounds.

Enid, released from his encircling arm, turned to him and laid both hands upon his shoulders and peered into his eyes, where the firelight pointed itself in little gleaming dots. Her face showed as a dim white blur in the dusk. For a moment of firelit silence, father and daughter faced each other there.

"Daddy — good news, or none!" she whispered, pleadingly. "Oh, it must be good! It shall be!"

"Sit down over there, Enid," he bade her, loosening her hands. With a sudden impulse of father-love he drew her to his arms again, and kissed her forehead, patting her shoulder as though she had been a child.

"Horrible affair!" he suddenly exclaimed. "Wreckage of everything! And the infernal publicity and sensationalism — brutal, hideous!"

"Nothing matters, father," she answered, "so long as Arthur is innocent."

"Sit down, and listen," he said, abruptly, releasing her. "But first, promise me something!"

"What is it?"

"Promise me you're going to be my own brave, strong, sensible girl, through all the inevitable grief and strain of this terrible affair — through everything, even to the very end. Promise me that!"

"I promise!"

"Promise me you're going to act in every way as your mother would have acted — wisely, rationally, nobly, come what may. Do you promise that, too?"

"Yes! But tell me, why are you asking? Do you mean that he — that Arthur —?"

She hesitated, a chill dread in her heart. Her eyes peered eagerly at the old man's face. She gripped his right hand in both of hers.

"Father! You don't mean —?"

"Now, now, Enid, remember your promise! You mustn't get excited and you mustn't jump at conclusions. You must control yourself, my girl. You must listen to all I have to say, judge reasonably, accept evidence like a rational being, form just conclusions and stick to them — in a word, be the only kind of girl that Edward Chamberlain could possibly have for his daughter!"

Enid sighed, brokenly.

"I'll — I'll do everything you say, father," she answered. "If you only — tell me —"

"I'll tell you everything. But you must sit down, first, and be quite calm and reasonable. At a time like this, my dear, we must put sentiment aside and be guided by intelligence. We must view matters dispassionately, not allow personal feelings to influence our judgments, and —"

"I know, father, but Arthur —"

"Arthur is a man like other men, my dear. He must stand or fall by the same laws with all others. He must be judged by the same standards and measured by the same —"

"Father! What are you coming at?" she cried, suddenly. "What are you leading up to? This kind of prelude doesn't lead to a verdict of 'Innocent!' It leads to 'Guilty!' Well, if you think he's guilty, tell me so at once! Speak it right out — 'Guilty!' But don't try to gloss it, and conceal it and work up to it as though I were a child! Tell me, tell me, do you think — he —?"

Chamberlain nodded, firmly.

"Yes, Enid, I do!" he answered. "If you insist on asking me, in plain words, whether I think Arthur is guilty, I must answer in the affirmative. And I am voicing the opinion of Hillis & Ballantyne, in saying so. For three hours, to-day, they — probably the best criminal lawyers in the country, certainly the best in New York — went over all the available evidence, with me. And at the end of that time —"

Enid released her hold on the banker's hand, turned and walked to her low chair, sank into it and let her face fall into the warm hollow of her elbow, along the broad arm of the chair. Very much a woman, she began to cry.

"I don't care, I don't care!" she sobbed. "I don't believe it, and it isn't so! Arthur didn't do it, because — because he couldn't — he wouldn't — never, never, never!"

"Enid, you promised —"

"What do I care about your criminal lawyers or your —?"

"My girl, my girl! Listen to me! You gave me your word you'd be reasonable and weigh the evidence!"

He walked to her, stroked her hair soothingly, and patted her beautiful, shapely head.

"My dear!" he protested. "This is no way to keep your promise or to get at the truth. This is doing precisely what you said you wouldn't do! Now, now, calm yourself, I beg you. Let us approach this thing rationally, see where we stand, and examine the factors —"

"I don't care for your factors or your evidence, either!" she exclaimed passionately. "You may know all about those and everything else in the world, but I — I know Arthur!"

She raised her head, now, and looked at her father with tear-wet eyes that gleamed in the firelight.

"Arthur — my Arthur — couldn't have done those things!" she cried, splendidly, defiantly, bravely. "Impossible! A thousand times, impossible! If the whole world should rise up and point at him and charge him with that crime, I wouldn't care! If all the evidence under the sun were heaped against him, it would mean nothing to me! I know, I know, I *know* he's innocent!"

Chamberlain made a despairing gesture with both arms, and let them fall at his sides, hopelessly.

"My dear," he protested, "if you adopt that attitude, of course there's no use in my talking to you. If you abandon your promises, and raise the flag of absolute defiance to all the standards of proof as universally recognized, naturally there can be no benefit in my expounding this matter to you. It's your prerogative to adopt any arbitrary opinion you may choose, and hold to it, and close your ears to reason. But I must tell you, Enid, you're not serving Arthur by any such tactics. You're only injuring him and your-self. I do sincerely beg of you, Enid, to hear the case dis-passionately, and try, in so far as your heart will let you, to judge it on its own merits."

"You mean you want me to agree with you and those lawyers, whose whole stock in trade is lies, deception and fraud? To say he's guilty, when I know he's *not?* To —"

"Only to listen to the facts, Enid, my girl. Only that, nothing more."

"Facts all distorted so as to prove him guilty!"

"No, my dear. Only plain, irrefutable realities that can't be overlooked, evaded or misinterpreted. Much as this blow has wounded me, much as I have liked Arthur, and hoped for his future and built upon his happiness and yours in every way, nevertheless, I have used my reasoning facul-ties. I have faced truths, and listened to deductions, and even formed my own. I have accepted grief, Enid, and pain — more than you know, since it involves you, too — and made up my mind to let justice work itself out, unim-peded. And —"

The girl faced him, suddenly.

"You mean, even if he were guilty, you'd let them kill him?"

"I'd let justice take its course, Enid. Wouldn't you?"

"But he isn't! He isn't, and I know it!" she reiterated, with sovereign feminine evasion. "And I don't care what they say, I never will believe it! Never!"

"You don't even want to know the evidence?"

"It means nothing to me!"

"Even when they've found the very pistol that killed poor old Mackenzie? Even when they've recovered the bullet, and found it fits the gun? Even when that gun is —"

"Not his! Not his, father! Not his!"

She flung out her hand in passionate denial.

"Not his!"

She was not weeping, now. The fighting instinct that had made her father a power in the land, the instinct that had lived through all the race of Chamberlains, had blazed out, at last, in Enid. The man she loved was being meshed in webs of trickery and lies, she knew. Horrible conspiracies were being woven round him. She felt the impulse to rise up and shout his innocence to all the winds; to run to him, defend him with her body and her blood, free him, win him back to good repute and happiness and joy once more.

"Not his, father! Not his!"

Chamberlain smiled very sadly, and nodded that massive head of his, with its mane of white hair.

"Yes, my dear, but it *is* his!" he answered, in a deep and quiet voice. "It was found last night behind some ash-barrels in the basement of the bank, where he evidently threw it in his haste and panic. He has acknowledged it as his. That fact, joined with the others, has completed the circle of proof. There exists no doubt, now, as to the indictment. It cannot be for less than — less than —"

"Murder?" She spoke the word in a quivering whisper of horror. "Murder?"

"Yes, Enid."

"Arthur — indicted for — murder? *My Arthur a murderer?*"

"Yes."

"But — he didn't do it! He never did it, father! Somebody else did it, and — laid it off on him! Somebody —"

"Nobody else could have done it, my girl. In no possible way could anybody have done all the various things and left all the different trails which converge — every last one of them — to one focal point, where Arthur stands! We have motive, we have ability, we have means, we have results, we have proofs. In my earlier days, Enid, I studied rather deeply in law, and though I never was admitted to the bar, I am not unversed in its history and practise. I know, if I know anything, that not a jury could be impaneled in this whole country that, on the evidence alone which has so far come out, wouldn't convict!

" I don't tell you this to wound you, grieve you or crush you, Enid. God forbid, my darling! You know I'd lay down my life for you in a second, if I could save your happiness. But, my girl, you're now facing a situation where neither your father nor any other man, nor any power on earth, can lighten the blow or avert the shock. You've pinned your faith and given your love to a man, outwardly noble, strong and good, but inwardly rotten. A man who has not only confessed to having robbed the bank of more than a thousand dollars —"

" Yes, yes, I know that! But I know he didn't take it for himself. There was some reason, some big, fine motive —"

" My child, emotion blinds you! You are not reasonable, to-night. Suppose we postpone this till to-morrow? Sleep on it, if you can, and with the morning light, perhaps you may be calmer and more amenable to truth. This tragedy has disturbed your just perspective, blunted your judgments and troubled your sense of right and wrong. I suggest that we wait until morning for the continuation of this talk? "

" No, father. No, not that. You're mistaken. I'm quite calm — or if not, I will be. You see — I couldn't possibly wait, now, to hear it all. You've told me part. I don't believe it, anyhow, but I know what they're saying. Well, tell me everything. Everything, father. Don't keep anything back, now! "

" And when you have it all, Enid, and understand the perfectly conclusive nature of the evidence, you must admit the truth. Mr. Slayton's desk, from which the safe-combination was stolen, was opened by Arthur's own paper-cutter. One of Arthur's gloves was found in the bank cellar, with blood-marks on the fingers — marks that corresponded to others on old Mackenzie's breast. The other glove was burned in the furnace; only the metal snaps were discovered. Bits of the paper were found, too, on which the combination had been written. Arthur must have dropped them, when he burned —"

"Father! You're assuming everything and proving nothing!"

"On the contrary, Enid, I'm stating facts proved as certainly as signs of Holy Writ. I'm giving you what Hillis & Ballantyne have given me —"

"They're prejudiced, just as you are!"

"I, prejudiced? When I'm spending a lot of money to see if some loophole doesn't exist to free that boy? Good God, Enid! Prejudiced?"

"I don't care, father, I know it's all, all a horrible, brutal, ghastly mistake! He didn't do it — he couldn't have!"

"Perhaps you'll deny that when he was questioned he turned on Mr. Slayton like a wild beast, and would have certainly assassinated him right there in the directors' room of the bank, if the coroner and the doctor hadn't interposed? Perhaps you'll deny that he had to be knocked insensible by a police club, and be rather badly cut up, before he could be arrested at all? Perhaps you'll claim actions like those are the actions of an innocent man?"

Enid shuddered at thought of that brutality. Despite herself, she thrilled with pride at thought of that battle royal. Arthur, unjustly accused, had fought! He had resisted, at any rate. He had not yielded, meekly; he had not begged and supplicated. No, right manfully he had struck out — and only force had conquered him.

"He's innocent, and he's a *man!*" the girl exclaimed. "Whatever they say, whatever they do, I trust him. And I love him, too, and nobody in the world shall ever take that away from me! No, not Slayton, nor lawyers, nor coroners, nor doctors; not jurymen or judges; not jailers or executioners; nobody shall! Nobody in this whole wide world — not even you!"

The banker shrugged his shoulders, in despair.

" Enid," said he quite slowly, " I fear we shan't get anywhere, just now, even if we discuss this matter all night long. You view Arthur as a hero and a martyr, though Heaven alone knows how you can idealize crime to that extent. The world views him as a criminal of rather unusually dangerous tendencies, because endowed with more than usual intelligence. No doubt the law will deal severely with him. You and I and all of us have got to suffer much galling publicity. The bank will suffer. We'll all suffer. Poor old Mackenzie, alone, won't have to. His brother has arrived and will take care of his remains; the bank will pay for everything. In some ways, the good old chap is to be envied. I'm sure Arthur might well envy him, at least. He might well envy him, indeed!"

"Arthur will yet go free, and we'll be married some-time!"

" Eh?"

" I wasn't quite sure I loved him, before. *Now* — I know it!"

" You mean to say you're going to cling to that — that —?"

" Father!"

" You're going to — keep up —?"

" I'm going to stand by, that's all. Of course you know I've written him, already, and sent some things. Well, every day I'm going to do that. And everything that money can do in the way of lawyers, shall be done."

" By you, Enid?"

" I've got my own money, haven't I?"

" But, my girl, think of the publicity! You'd far better

take a trip to Palm Beach, or the Riviera, or — or anywhere, till —"

Enid laughed, for the first time since the murder.

" I'm your daughter! " said she. " Remember, I'm the daughter of Edward Bruce Chamberlain! And you talk to *me* about being afraid of publicity? You talk to *me* about running away, in a pinch, when the man I love needs me? "

In sudden shame, the banker dropped his head.

" Enid, forgive me! " he whispered, reaching out and taking her slim, strong hand in his wrinkled, corded one. " My daughter — yes, you're my daughter, all right. I see that now, plainly enough. You *are* the daughter of Old Chamberlain — thank God the metal still rings true! "

She rose and threw her arms about his neck and kissed him, fervently.

" My daddy! "

" Enid? "

" He *is* innocent, isn't he? He is, he is, he *is?* "

" God knows. Faith like yours could move mountains! "

" Mountains? Worlds! Universes! It shall move everything! Arthur shall be vindicated; he shall go free! "

Tears started hotly in the old man's dimming eyes.

" Let me go now, Enid," he begged, gently pushing her away. " To-morrow, when we both have slept on this sad problem, we may have more and clearer light. But for now — good-bye."

" Good night, father. Don't condemn me for my faith! "

" Condemn you? God forbid! Mistaken though it be, I love you for it! Love you for it, Enid, even though I can't share it. Even though my analysis can't answer ' Innocent! ' "

"Don't analyze, father. Only have faith! Only trust my boy. If you knew him as I know him, you'd trust him just the same as I do!"

Chamberlain made no answer. Silence fell between them. He took the girl's eager face in both his hands, looked for a long minute into her dark eyes, vaguely seen in the firelight, and sighed. Tears dimmed his vision.

"Your mother had eyes like yours, Enid," he said very slowly, very gently, "and faith like yours, too. Once I gave her cause to test that faith — and it held true. Maybe your faith may yet be justified; God knows. It doesn't seem possible, Enid. Too many lines of evidence converge on Arthur, to make it seem possible; but still, it may be. I hope so — oh, you can't know the fervor of that hope, for your sake and for his! So perfect and sublime a trust deserves to live. God grant it may not suffer disillusion!"

He kissed her forehead and her hair, and then her eyes — those eyes where he still seemed to see the spirit of the woman dead and gone away forever from his love.

"Good night, Enid, and God keep you!" he whispered brokenly.

Then he left her there, silently, in the warm sweetness of her firelit room.

She turned to her broad window, where now the thickening snow fingered silently against the panes, ghost-white and swirling like shrouds of spirits driven by the wind. She laid her arms along the window-sash and stood there peering out into the moving whiteness of the night.

"Thicker than snowflakes the lies are drifting, swirling, falling on my boy," she murmured. "Lies, lies, lies! But the sun of truth will shine, sometime, and melt them all away. Love will banish them — justice shall be done —

"Love and faith, if they're only big enough and strong and pure and true enough, can work miracles, can move mountains. Can't they set my Arthur free and give him back to me again?"

At the same hour, had you peered into a certain steel cage in the dismal recesses of the bastile rightly named "the Tombs" you would have seen Arthur Mansfield, sitting in an attitude of unspeakable despair on his hard bunk. Silent, motionless, alone he sat there, shoulders bowed, head drooping, eyes fixed upon the dirty cement floor. Above his head a raw incandescent, slightly swaying, threw harsh lights and shadows over his wavy hair, his broad forehead — cruelly cut and bruised on the right temple — his unshaven cheeks, now sunken with grief, anger, and the fever of his violent emotions.

His blue eyes had grown dull and lifeless. From his face the fresh, healthy color had departed. Nerveless, his hands hung over the knees of his torn and wrinkled trousers. Less than eight-and-forty hours' experience of the majesty and dignity of the Law had altered the boy almost beyond recognition.

Flowers somewhat tempered the air of the cell with their sweet breath. A little photograph of Enid all in white — a breezy, woodsy, camping-out picture, reminiscent of one of their happy times together — stood on the bare board shelf in the corner near the crumpled letter that had brought it to him — the letter she had written with tears as bitter as his tears in reading it; the oft-read letter; one of those that by their faith and trust and womanly tenderness and love had thus far sustained him through the Valley of the Shadow.

Beside him on the bunk another letter lay. Sighing, Arthur picked it up and once more looked at it with hollow eyes. He knew its every line and word by heart, yet still he searched it through for some word or meaning to bear him hope from the desolated home whence now all hope was banished.

" Piling in pretty fast just now, isn't it? " he whispered. " Pretty fast and pretty hard! "

The letter said to him:

MILLARTON, New York, Friday.

MY BOY:

Your mother will stand by you, come what may. I know this whole thing is a terrible conspiracy of lies. You are innocent! Yes, Arthur, I know it.

I am only an old woman, now, and crippled as I am I can't go to you. Dr. Harris says it might kill me to go. I'm needed too much to take any risks. But even though I can't see you, Arthur, I can send you all the love and help and devotion of a mother's heart.

God has put heavy burdens on to us to bear. Our money is nearly gone, as you know, but the old house is worth a few hundred dollars, and I'm dickering with Swasey now. I can raise enough for legal fees that way. The case can't be long. Just let you get your story to the jurymen and you'll be freed. I know it, Arthur; I know it! You're innocent, and that means you'll soon be free!

The news of your arrest on this trumped-up charge struck your father down as if he had been shot. That was yesterday noon. Cyrus Barker told us the news. He was as kind as could be, but it just missed killing him outright. He was sitting in the big rocker by the stove in the kitchen when Cyrus came in. As quick as he understood, he jumped up and cried in a terrible voice:

"Murder! They've arrested Arthur for —"

That was as far as he got. He fell and cut his head on the stove. It was another stroke. This makes the second, and he has been lying paralyzed ever since, and unconscious most of the time. Dr. Harris says he hasn't very much chance. So he may be taken away from us, my boy, before you ever see him again.

He and you are all I have now, and you're in jail and he's at death's door. Oh, Arthur, Arthur! If tears were dollars to free you and bring him back again, Heaven knows the payment would be full by now.

Don't worry, dear, about what will become of us. If they really indict and try you it will be better for your father to go now and get home where there is rest and peace. As for me, Arthur, I

don't care. I can work for you, and will! There is still strength
in this heart and in these hands.

That's all I want in life, now — to work and free you and clear
your name. Can I ever feel tired, then? If I did I wouldn't be
your mother.

Poor Enid, that dear girl of yours! I will write her, telling her
to have faith and trust in you, even as I have. I know what
such a tragedy must mean to her. Night and day I will pray and
work for you.

I have retained Lawyer Swasey, of Swasey & Hardacre, to defend
you. He will start for New York to-morrow. Be not downcast.
Truth is mighty and will prevail. After these storms will come
calm. God knows best. All my kisses and all my love to you,
my boy!

MOTHER.

P.S.—Lawyer Swasey has just been here. He seems unwilling
to take the case after all, though he won't say why. It surely can't
be that he thinks he would fail to clear you. I will see Dutton
at once and engage him.

Maybe Swasey is afraid he would never get his money. He tells
me your father's business is in bad shape, and in spite of the twelve
hundred and fifty dollars you made on that Rio Hondo investment
and sent us — like the good, dear boy you are — everything is
very much involved.

But don't worry, Arthur. There will yet be a way. God can
make one for you, as He did for the Israelites through the Red
Sea. Remember, He can do everything!

Read the Twenty-Third Psalm, especially Verse 4. God keep
and bless you, my poor lost boy.

MOTHER.

For a few minutes Arthur held the poor, painfully written letter in his hand. His eyes dimmed as he gazed upon
the halting lines, blotted with tears. Then he crushed it to
his mouth and kissed it passionately.

"If she can only be kept from knowing the truth about
father's business, and why he needed that twelve hundred
and fifty dollars!" thought he. "If she can only be kept
from knowing where I got it!"

A pang transfixed his heart. *That* much at least she

would have to know. That much was all admitted. But
his father, stricken down, unconscious, dying, would never
need to understand.

"Thank Heaven for that, at least! Thank Heaven!"
he murmured.

Suddenly he stood up, went over to the little shelf — it
was but a step or two away — and took the Bible in his
hand. With it he returned to the hard bunk. After some
seeking he found the Twenty-Third Psalm, the page already
soiled by many a miserable wretch in that steel cage of his.

He read the verse:

Yea, though I walk in the Valley of the Shadow of Death, I
will fear no evil, for Thou art with me. Thy rod and Thy staff,
they comfort me.

All at once it seemed to him he heard his mother's voice,
reading the words of consolation, faith, and trust. Or was
it Enid's? Strangely the thought of those two women
calmed and quieted his fevered soul.

"Yea, though I walk in the Valley of the Shadow of Death —"

he said, and repeated the words with slow insistence.

He put the book up on the shelf again, lay down upon his
bunk, buried his face in both his arms, and let body, mind
and soul relax. The close air was poison to his lungs,
which loved the fresh, pure winds of sea and sky. The
sounds and sights of that great catacomb of human agony
all sickened him. Yet with the thought of his mother and
of Enid strong upon him he could forget — forget, and rest
a while.

Thus the boy lay, thinking, longing, dreaming, wonderfully at peace.

I will fear no evil, for Thou art with me —

"I am with thee, Arthur," echoed his mother's voice.

"I am with thee," he heard Enid's. "With thee — with thee!"

Under his closed lids the tears started; but now they blessed and comforted and soothed.

Soon he slept — slept soundly in that den of tragedy and grief and woe — slept and was blessed by the one greatest boon of all — oblivion.

CHAPTER XVI

WHILE he was still asleep there in the Tombs, Walter Haynes Slayton, his face hard and set, entered the ramshackle old building where Jarboe, the money-shark, laired close up under the roof.

Slayton walked like a man who had business, albeit none of the most pleasant. The creaking elevator bore him slowly aloft, seeming too swift by far. Grimly he stalked down the dusty and untended hallway, paused at the dirt-incrusted glass door that bore the legend:

```
┌─────────────────────────────────┐
│                                 │
│        CHRISTOPHER JARBOE        │
│             LOANS               │
│                                 │
└─────────────────────────────────┘
```

and gave three taps upon the pane, followed by two.

For a moment no sound replied. Slayton stood there, gnawing his nails in a fever of emotion, the dim light through the glass showing his face screwed into a snarl of most extraordinary hate and malevolence.

"Damn the viper!" he muttered. "He can't be out. He surely wouldn't make a definite appointment and then break it."

Again he rapped. This time a chair scraped within. A halting footfall crossed the floor. A chain rattled. A key turned, and the door swung inward, just a crack.

Slayton perceived the old man's bald head, his disfiguring

wen, and a single beady little eye that glittered craftily. Then all at once the door opened wide; and there in the aperture stood the aged Shylock, bowing and scraping and rubbing his hands together with a most malicious politeness.

"Well now! Well, well, well! Bless my soul! This *is* a pleasure!" he wheezed, laughing silently to himself, as was his habit. "Come in, Mr. Slayton! Come into my poor abode! Not much to offer you, sir; but such as it is, such as it is —"

"For God's sake, drop that!" growled the cashier in a low voice, coming in and closing the door, which Jarboe immediately locked and chained after him. "Drop all that infernal mockery of yours and tell me what you want! When I paid up I thought I was through with you and done. But now —"

"Now it appears that you aren't, eh? Is that it?" chuckled the old usurer, hobbling over to his littered desk on the far side of a room indescribable in its dirt, clutter and neglect.

Books, cooking-utensils, broken furniture and old clothing all combined with miscellaneous disorder to figure forth a room more like the vagaries of a nightmare than any human dwelling. At the left a door gave hints of another room — a sleeping-place, perhaps; and if so, then possibly the receptacle of the old man's money; for rumor had it that Jarboe's bed was lined with yellow-backs.

"Yes; it appears that you aren't through with old Jarboe after all, eh?" questioned the wizened patriarch. "Old Jarboe doesn't let his good friends go so easily. No, no, no! Not so easily as all that! Not so easily!"

He fished an old cigar-butt out of the pocket of his dirty, wine-colored dressing-gown, crumbled it in his unwashed palm, and stuffed a clay pipe with it.

"Not so easily, not so easily!" he mumbled toothlessly

as he struck a match and lighted the vile dust of the weed. "No, no, no!"

"See here, you dirty old villain!" blurted Slayton, all his natural suavity and hypocritical smoothness rasped entirely away by his hatred of the miser. "See here now! What do you want? We'll omit all beating round the bush and subterfuge and all that sort of thing. You wrote for me to see you on urgent business. You made a definite appointment. I keep it. What's wanted?"

"Wanted, eh? Oh, nothing, nothing but a little friendly arrangement between you and old Jarboe. That's all; nothing more. Just a little — friendly — arrangement."

He leered hideously, puffing at his pipe.

"Just a little friendly arrangement; nothing more," Jarboe repeated.

"Damn you!" exclaimed Slayton, shaking a fist under his nose. "I want no friendliness with *you!* If you've got business with me, speak out. Come across with it. Otherwise —"

And he motioned toward the door.

"Don't hurry, Mr. Slayton," said the old man dryly. "And please don't shake your fist in my face. That always makes me nervous. It makes old Jarboe nervous, so it does, to have his friends shake their fists at him. Especially when all he wants is a friendly arrangement."

"Arrangement to do what, you Shylock?"

"Oh, to contribute to old Jarboe's income, that's all."

"Contribute to — your —"

"To my income. Certainly! Why not? I'm sure you'll be extremely glad to when you understand my terms!"

"Terms?" echoed Slayton, staring in amazement not untinged with fear. "Why, what terms? What arrangement? I don't owe you a cent, now, you old rip! I paid you in full, principal and interest —"

"The very day after Mackenzie was murdered; yes indeed," interrupted the usurer with an evil glance of cunning.

He sat down in a creaking easy-chair cushioned with ragged carpeting, and waved his hand at another to bid his guest be seated also.

"The very day after he was murdered and the bank touched for one hundred and fifty thousand dollars," the old man went on. "Odd, wasn't it? Very odd coincidence, says old Jarboe. Hmm ! Peculiar, very, that you should come in here and put eighty-four thousand dollars, plus or minus, right down there on that table where that lamp is standing now, the exact day after the night when the murder was done. And what's more peculiar is the fact that the money was all in thousand-dollar bills, and the numbers —"

"What d'you mean, you dog?" cried Slayton, menacing him with clenched fist.

The cashier's face had suddenly gone pasty. His thin lips twitched; his eyes, never firm, now blinked with strange rapidity.

"Mean? What does old Jarboe mean? Oh, nothing, nothing at all. Don't get excited. I was just saying it was peculiar. You'll allow old Jarboe to have an opinion and express it, won't you? Express an opinion to a friend?"

"Confound you! Are you insinuating —?"

Jarboe raised a deprecating hand.

"You asked me that once before," he replied. "That very same question, the day of the murder. I answer you now as then: I'm insinuating nothing. Only I was thinking — yes, yes, yes; old Jarboe was thinking — that if you felt disposed to make a little contribution, say a small sum to begin with, and then from time to time —"

"Blackmail, eh?" snarled the cashier, his white teeth glinting in the lamplight. "So that's your game, is it? Usury and gouging and shylocking in the open, plus blackmail on the side? Well, it won't go with me! Not this time, Jarboe. I'm through with you, for good and all, understand? Done, through, finished! Not a cent, to-day, to-morrow, or any other day. Get *that?*"

The usurer eyed Slayton a moment curiously, noting the pale and writhen face, the swollen veins upon his brow, the look of fear and hate that distorted his face. Then just the vaguest suspicion of a smile curved the old man's lips.

"You interest me," said he quite slowly. "Yes, yes indeed; you interest old Jarboe. Bless my soul, Mr. Slayton, how very — hmmm! — emphatic you seem over a mere trifle.

"If you don't agree with my little plan, why just say '*N-o,*' no. Just give Jarboe the block and stop him on a siding. No harm done. No need to get ugly, is there? Or work yourself into a passion? Or anything of that sort?"

"You skunk!"

"Easy! Easy with old Jarboe!"

And the usurer's eyes glinted with menace.

"Don't abuse the old man. Maybe he knows something and maybe not. No telling. If he should just happen to —"

"What *do* you know, you —?"

"Ah, what, indeed?"

And Jarboe blew a cloud of stale smoke. "Now that's an interesting question. I admit it's mighty interesting. What does old Jarboe know, eh? The whole thing hinges right on that. What does he know? Maybe a lot. Maybe nothing. Maybe —"

"You told me the day I paid you that we were through — that if any skeletons rattled in your closet or mine it was nobody's business! That you —"

"Ah, yes; but I've changed my mind since then, you see. Old Jarboe's changed his mind. He's been thinking things over. His finances have been breaking a bit bad. He's been coming to see that you, with easy access to the kale, would think it a pleasure and a privilege to help the old man out, and —"

"Not a soul!"

"Very well. That settles it. Nothing more to be said; is there? Not a word to say.

"Only, I'm just telling you, if old Jarboe should happen to appear in court when the case is called, and if he should happen to produce certain matters and things, evidence and what-not, and volunteer as a witness, and so forth, and so on, well — don't be surprised, that's all."

The old man leaned back in his chair, pulled at his foul pipe with satisfaction, and smiled horribly, his few discolored teeth showing broken and crooked in his purplish gums.

Slayton gasped and leaned heavily against the table. His face had gone absolutely ashen.

"You — you *wouldn't!*" he exclaimed in a husky whisper.

"Did I say I would? Did old Jarboe state that he would? Emphatically no! He merely remarked that *if* he did you weren't to be astonished. That's all. Nothing more. Why misunderstand me?"

"You couldn't do it!" Slayton exclaimed. "Your record is too rotten. They've got too much on you! You'd never dare appear in court. And then beside, you don't know anything!"

"Well, that remains to be seen. That's your problem to solve. Maybe I know and maybe I don't who really entered the Powhatan Bank that night, and whose hand was inside that glove, and where those gray hairs came from that were found in Mackenzie's fingers next morning. Maybe —"

Slayton sprang at him, to clutch him by the throat; but with extraordinary agility the old man slid down and away, scrambled out of reach behind the table, and stood up, facing him, still with the sneering smile on his lips.

"Don't hurt old Jarboe," he pleaded with mock supplication. "Don't assault the old man or injure him or kill him. Because in that case it would be so very unpleasant, so extremely embarrassing for you. There are papers, you know — writings, documents and so on — that in case old Jarboe were to die might go to District Attorney Ainslow. I'm not threatening you, understand. Old Jarboe never indulges in threats. I'm only warning you like the good friend I am. Warning you — in time."

Slayton, realizing through all his passion that he was caught, groaned in extreme anguish and terror. How much *did* the old sewer-rat know? Nothing, perhaps. Everythings, perhaps. Impossible to tell.

Hopeless to think of risking life on the gamble of this being all a bluff. No, no! A thousand times no! Not that! Not life! Life could not be gambled with, that way.

Slayton, recoiling, lifted a hand to his brow. A cry of utter misery forced itself from his lips. The old man, watching, smiled with satisfaction, nodded, and stroked his chin. The trap, he saw, had caught its victim.

"Well?" he demanded. "Shall we do business? Will you enter negotiations with old Jarboe? All in a nice, quiet, friendly way? Business now?"

Slayton eyed him a minute in silence with a look so baleful, so terrible in its hate, that any other save the aged usurer would have trembled. But Jarboe did not tremble. He only puffed his pipe, smiled a discolored smile, and scratched his wen.

"Business?" he demanded once more.

"Yes."

The answer came in a guttural breath.

"All right. Old Jarboe's ready. Terms reasonable, security and perfect satisfaction guaranteed. As long as you keep your bargain — when we've made it — not a sound will old Jarboe utter. Not a bone of the skeleton will he rattle. Not a breath will he breathe. All you have to do is to meet your just obligations, and —"

"How much? One lump sum?"

"Yes. And then, easy payments," leered the usurer.

"What sum?"

"Twenty-five thousand dollars, cash. And —"

"Twenty-five thou —?"

"Not a cent less."

"But — but I — good God, man, I can't!"

"You can, and will. A man will do much to live in safety and peace. There's lots more where the hundred and fifty thousand came from. A mere trifle, twenty-five thousand. On or before the day of the trial, that's what old Jarboe needs. In cash. Just by way of a little present from a dear old friend, and —"

"Stop! You can gouge and bleed me, you shark, but I draw the line at your sarcasm! Cut that part out, you understand?"

"And then, so much a month, after that," continued the usurer, unmoved. "Just a little monthly present, by way of a good-will offering. Safety-insurance, eh? Old Jarboe's safety-insurance, ha, ha, ha!"

His laughter echoed grim and heart-appalling through the room. Slayton, on the point of collapse, leaned over the table, steadying himself with both palms pressed on its filthy top.

"How much a month?"

"One thousand dollars."

"One — *thousand!* Have mercy! Five hundred, Jarboe — make it five hundred! That's all I can pay — all I can possibly pay!"

"I said one thousand, and that goes. Bottom figure, for the service. Cheap, Slayton; very, very cheap. Sing Sing is so extremely uncomfortable, and they use such tremendously high voltage for the chair, you know, it quite singes a fellow's flesh. Burns it shockingly, I believe. Yes, old Jarboe has heard it shrivels —"

"Stop, stop! Hold on! I give in! My God! I — *I'll pay!*"

"Very good; very good, indeed. I knew you'd be reasonable — reasonable with old Jarboe. It's a life contract, you know. Get that quite clear, Mr. Slayton. As long as old Jarboe lives — and you daren't make way with him, because that would lead to most deplorable results — the little friendly arrangement will last. Is that quite understood?"

Slayton nodded, his face tense with impotent hate and malice.

"Very good, then." The old man smiled with a hideous, oblique leer. "It's all done and settled, you see, quite pleasantly and in good order. Mr. Slayton and old Jarboe are still friends — still the best of friends. One party's got his life insured. The other has a life income, and is positively sure that not a single payment will be allowed to default. What could be more satisfactory?

"So then, no need to detain you longer. You're a busy man, I know. So is old Jarboe. Very, very busy. Let's say good evening, then, and *au revoir!* I needn't detain you. Good night, Mr. Slayton! Good night!"

Slayton eyed him a moment with virulent hate.

"Some day," said he in a low, trembling voice, "I'll get you — get you hard!"

Jarboe made no answer save to request without looking up:

"Please close the door when you go out. Close it, but don't slam it. Good night."

When the cashier, speechless with passion, was gone, the old man chuckled slyly.

"I knew he'd be reasonable with old Jarboe," said he.
"Reasonable and sensible, after all, and willing to do business. As a bluff, my game was surely some bluff. Nothing to go on really except those new thousand-dollar bills, and yet see how he fell for it! If ever a man took a pot on a pair of deuces, that man's old Jarboe. Ha, ha, ha!"

Thus cheered by his reflections, he sat him down again in his easy-chair, took up a list of loans, and, pipe in mouth, once more applied himself to the delightful task of calculating his extensive usuries.

CHAPTER XVII

INDICTED on two charges — grand larceny and murder — by a special grand jury on the last day of November, Arthur was remanded to the Tombs for speedy trial. In view of the atrocity of the crime and the state of public opinion, Governor McIntyre appointed Judge Grossmith to hear the case in Special Sessions. Following the usual order of the court calendar, eighteen months or more might have elapsed before Arthur could have been summoned to the bar. But now, on December 15, he was destined to appear as defendant in the People of the State of New York *vs.* Arthur Mansfield.

The murder charge, of course, obscured the other of grand larceny, with its subsidiary charges. While the robbery, the threat against Slayton, and the assault at the time of arrest would doubtless have their bearing on the case, as factors tending to establish the character of the accused, any specific action on them, or on the admitted theft of the one thousand two hundred and fifty dollars would be held in abeyance till such time as the murder charge should have been heard. Only in the very improbable event of the defendant being acquitted would any of these lesser accusations ever be heard of again.

Every effort made by the police to force Arthur to confess what he had done with the one hundred and fifty thousand dollars they assumed him to have stolen resulted only in more furious denials on his part. For the present, at least, no progress could be made in locating the money.

That Arthur's position was serious in the extreme became
more and more apparent with the passage of the lagging
December days. Though no new evidence against him developed, and though the "third degree," to which he was
brutally subjected, failed to extort any confession, or even
shake his sturdy assertion of "Innocent!", nevertheless
both press and public were now lining up solidly against
him.

Sensationalism rioted with the fact of Enid's support, in
ways appallingly cruel. But Enid neither retracted nor hesitated. Her colors flying from her lance, she still declared
Arthur's innocence. She retained Hosmer & Keene in his
defense — ignoring her father's protests and the world's
cynical amusement — and entered the lists against the power
of the State as militantly bold as ever Jeanne d'Arc rode at
the head of the mailed fighting men of France.

Arthur had only his mother and Sheridan and Enid to
lean upon in his deadly peril. Enid proved the only real
hope. Had it not been for her letters, her flowers, her vis-
its, the messages of cheer she brought him, and the promises of speedy acquittal, Arthur must have sunk, annihilated,
beneath his burden.

The support of ex-teller Sheridan, now that he had re-
signed from the bank, had ceased to have much value. In
some ways it even tended to injure Arthur. Just how it
happened who could say? But means were found by somebody to discredit the former teller to such an extent that
within a few days Hosmer & Keene wrote him, requesting
him to cease all activities on their client's behalf. Thence-
forth he dropped out of the case entirely save as a despairing, miserable spectator.

Arthur's mother, helpless with rheumatism and without
funds, could do nothing save furnish pitiful interviews and
fervent protestations, read with tongue in cheek by a hostile
world. A poor, dazed, impotent old woman, she too sub-

sided into oblivion, crushed by this tragedy as by the death of her husband, which added its burden to her son's bowed shoulders.

After Mr. Mansfield's death, on December 7, from paralysis, unsuspected business delinquencies were immediately discovered which, had he lived, might have sent the old man to the penitentiary. Rumor and innuendo worked overtime — and slander waxed fat. In all Arthur's home town of Millarton not one voice was raised in the boy's favor.

"Like father, like son!" the verdict passed from mouth to mouth; and every nod and look and sneer was caught by quick reporters and magnified through their lenses of exaggeration — caught and flung upon the great white screen of publicity — and witnessed by millions.

None of Arthur's former friends — either in Millarton or in New York — came forward with a single word in his behalf. He was learning now with bitter swiftness how friends fade and fall away in the hour of anguish, need and death!

Yes, and he was learning more, far more — he was learning to know the heart and soul of Enid Chamberlain.

Black and lowering hung the clouds over the boy's bruised and wounded head. Evil vulture-swarms of lies, slanders, griefs and woes attacked him — tore at his heart and beat their wings against his eyes to blind and stun him!

From some source or other, sinister and hidden, full inside details of the crime in all its most sensational features were now and then transmitted by anonymous letter to Manager Gilchrist of the Amalgamated Press. Some of these statements, all strongly damaging to Arthur, were used by that news service. They reached many millions of readers and helped oil the machinery of the law which now was grinding relentlessly on toward conviction.

So positive became public prejudice against the boy that by the 10th of December you might have combed the panel lists of Manhattan County without any real hope of assembling a jury even reasonably impartial.

Thus all the social forces drew together resistlessly with an immense and crushing power to overwhelm him. And against them stood — what? Only a girl, striving against hope. Only a firm of lawyers — keen, clever and resourceful, indeed, yet not themselves convinced of the boy's innocence — and working only for hire.

Thus fate meshed the warp and woof of human destinies, smiling the while in irony at the sorry jest of the poor human drama — Life!

.   .   .   .

"Hear ye! Hear ye! His Honor the Court is now entering!"

Droning and perfunctory, the lifeless, official voice of the court crier uttered the hoary formula, his words hardly audible above the buzz and rustle of the crowded room.

Reluctant silence settled down upon that place of tragedies supreme, close and ill-ventilated under the incandescents' glare — for though the hour was ten of the morning, a leaden December fog-pall strangled the city under its grip of gloom.

Here, there, a court officer with word or frown or nudge silenced some spectator who still persisted in discussion. Without the doors others pushed back the crowding, morbidly eager mob of those who, envying the more fortunate within, sought with craned neck and eager ear to catch some glimpse or sound of the sensational trial now impending.

"Oyez! Oyez!"

A little door at the right swung open silently, and Judge Grossmith appeared. Robed in a loose black gown which with his hooked bill of a nose made a huge, somber, legal raven of him, he walked leisurely toward the bench. Under one arm he carried a couple of law-books. His other hand held a large leather portfolio, whence papers showed their learned-looking edges.

Everybody stood up — District Attorney Ainslow and his staff; Keene, for the defense, and his assistants; jurors, witnesses, reporters, spectators — all. Old Jarboe, dirty as ever and twice as sharp, stood up among the rest, eying Slayton across the room with a sardonic smile that might have furnished forth a painter's inspiration for a face of Beelzebub. Slayton, very pale but quite collected, paid no heed to the usurer's nods and bows and smiles, but kept his eyes fixed on the Court. Chamberlain, standing before the front row of spectators' benches with Enid, did likewise. The girl, her eager eyes intent on Keene, seemed estimating his ability to stem the rushing tides of legalized lynch-spirit which — despite all she could strive for, all she could do — might yet sweep Arthur away, away from her upon its turbulent bosom, away to infamy and death.

Enid! How choice a target for unnumbered staring eyes, for artists' and reporters' pencils, for cameras, for special writers' word-paintings, for innuendo and vapid gossip! How rare a target in her trim gray gown and simple hat; how rare, and how sublime in her indifference to it all! Save for a somewhat heightened color and a dark luster of her eyes — the dilated pupils of which now made them seem quite black — she showed no sign of tension or of stress, but stood quietly, bravely, calmly, waiting the next step of the unfolding drama that meant life itself to her — the battle for the man she loved.

Thus for a moment or two everybody stood there, keyed to attention. Such as had neglected promptly to rise were pointedly adjured by the officers to pay their due respect to the majesty of the law. But now Grossmith slapped his books and papers sharply down, pulled the little chain of his desk-light, and gazed out over the audience before him.

Fixing his glasses on that hawk-nose of his, he blinked

sharp, shrewd eyes at the public. He nodded shortly to
Chamberlain, a client of his in the old days. His glance
rested a second on Enid, but gave no sign of any emotion,
not even curiosity.

It wandered over the witnesses — Mrs. Johansen, Arthur's landlady; Slayton and his wife; Anderson, Ashley,
Roadstrand and Nelson — then flickered across the array
of attorneys, skimmed the jurors in their box, and finally,
having thus appraised the personnel of the approaching
conflict, with a perfectly legalized lack of interest, once more
fell upon the books before him.

A fair, impartial judge, this Grossmith. Even his bit-
terest enemies admitted that. Human sentiment and emotion had long since been dry-rotted out of his soul by the
dust of parchment. A legal machine, he; nothing more.
He would rule on the evidence, the law, the correct procedure, and do no more. As a man, *nil*. As a judge, perfection.

Coughing dryly, he gathered his robes about him and sat
down. Everybody sat down, and a rustling, a whispering,
a murmur of low-voiced conversation began again. Then
all at once as a breeze runs over the tasseled corn, swaying
it in progressive waves, so a new, tense interest moved the
packed audience.

"He's coming now! There he is — look, look! He's
coming!"

"Order!" cried the Court sharply, rapping with his gavel;
but even he could not restrain the fever of excitement that
now possessed the crowd at sight of Arthur, moving slowly
in from the left, flanked by two officers.

"Look, look! There he is!"

The boy was pale, of course, but his head was high — his
head, that still showed marks of the police club. His eyes
met the hostile eyes of the multitude quietly and calmly.
He had recovered from the inertia of the first shock, and

now was neatly dressed and clean-shaven. One might
have thought him merely a spectator who had recently had
an illness, rather than the accused himself, the man at whom
all fingers now were pointing, at whom all tongues were
shouting:

" Murderer ! "

All? No! Not all! If one with God is a majority,
then was the balance in his favor. For one there was looking on him with unshakable love, faith and devotion. One
was smiling bravely. One was sending him the message:

" Hope! Trust in me! For I, Enid, believe in you, and
trust and love you! "

Her eyes and his met for a moment in a message that
thrilled them both. A little smile came to his lips. He
nodded at her, and she smiled, too. Even there under the
shadow of death that ray of sunshine could not be denied
them.

Then Arthur sat down in the chair reserved for him,
looked with unabashed eyes at the "twelve good men and
true " in whose hands his life was soon to be entrusted, and
finally after a glance at the judge turned toward Keene on
his left. Busy pencils already were limning his features or
plunging into descriptive paragraphs. Not an eye in all that
room but focused itself upon his clean-chiseled, pallid face,
with the broad brows, the straight nose, the blue-gray eyes
more fitted for smiles than for sorrow; the lips tight shut,
the chin of contour that promised great strength in later
life — if life indeed were not soon to be reft from his
powerful young body.

Already now the clerk of the court was reading the indictment of the grand jury. Silence fell, so tense that the
ticking of the clock above Judge Grossmith's head could be
distinctly heard. In a mechanical voice, which hardly rose
above the muffled hum of street traffic, without, the old clerk
droned his way through the devious whereases, aforesaids

and herebyes, ending with the charge of murder, against the peace and welfare of the State of New York.

Arthur gave no sign or look of emotion. Calmly he sat there, listening. Enid, too, remained quite calm. Her father, indeed, showed more distress than she. The tragedy was coming close to him at last. On Enid's happiness he had builded high hopes, and now they all seemed crumbling. Each day had put a month of age upon his shoulders — a year, perhaps. Already, as he sat there listening to those terrible words, the man was old, old, old! Senility had all at once laid its chill hand on him, bidding him follow its returnless path.

Now the clerk ceased his droning, and once more sat down.

"What does the defendant plead to this charge?" asked the Court.

Attention once more rose acute. Slayton, leaning forward, forgot to breathe. Jarboe studied him with malice and smiled evilly. Every gaze other than his now fixed itself on Keene, the boy's attorney.

Keene stood up.

"If it please your Honor, not guilty," he answered briefly, and sat down.

A buzz of pleased expectancy filled the room. Obviously the public was happy. Even until that moment a chance had existed that Arthur might plead guilty and throw himself on the clemency of the court. Now, however, it was sure that he was going to fight.

Nothing of course could come of it. He was bound to lose. His plight was precisely similar to that of a rat in a rat-pit with a terrier confronting him. But in no probability now would the door of that pit be opened. The audience was certain of a game and losing fight. Hence its rejoicing. Arthur was now surely to be done to death in its presence.

Amid a tense, expectant silence the judge fixed the date on which the trial was to open.

After days of bitter wrangling, in the course of which the last peremptory challenge of the defense had been exhausted, the jury was finally impaneled. The ponderous mechanism of justice was now ready to winnow out the wheat of truth from the chaff of lies.

Ainslow, the district attorney, arose, faced the judge, and bowed, did the same to the jury, and in a business-like tone outlined the case for the State: That on the night of the 18th of November one Donald Mackenzie, night-watchman at the Powhatan National Bank, had been murdered, and that the State would show the murderer to be the defendant in this action; namely, Arthur Mansfield, now under indictment for the crime.

Keene for the defense outlined the case for his client. He would prove, he said, that the character and habits of the defendant were such as to preclude any possibility of his having committed so atrocious a crime; that on the night and at the hour in question the defendant had been in his own room at the house of one Mrs. Johansen; and finally that, not having had any means of access to the bank, he must be exculpated wholly and the guilt rest with some party or parties unknown.

He sat down, leaving a decided impression of weakness in his case. Against the confident air of the district attorney, and the positive manner in which Ainslow had engaged to prove the facts as alleged by the State, Keene's argument seemed futile in its impotence. Ainslow smiled to himself and cast an appraising eye at the jury as he once more arose.

"Your Honor and gentlemen of the jury," said he, "in proof of the facts alleged in the indictment against this defendant, the State will now proceed to the introduction of testimony to show motive for the crime—the fact of a theft by the defendant of the sum of twelve hundred and fifty dollars from the bank in question, and the strong probability of the theft of one hundred and fifty thousand dollars; the fact that the defendant was possessed of a pistol on the night of the murder and that he threatened human life; the fact that he was out practically all the night of the murder, and that he showed signs of exhaustion and disorder in the morning. The State will also prove that the crimes in the bank were positively committed by an employee of that institution, and that the defendant when accused assaulted the coroner and the consulting physician."

Ainslow next engaged to produce certain material exhibits, all absolutely substantiating the charge in a perfectly irrefutable manner.

He concluded amid suppressed applause, which the officers and the judge's gavel had difficulty in ending. The public already considered Arthur hopelessly lost, and exulted in the fate of a criminal so cold-blooded.

Meanwhile, a strange little underplay had been going on between old Jarboe and Slayton. At the end of Keene's address the usurer had caught Slayton's guilty eye seeking his face with involuntary dread.

How did Jarboe manage to convey his message? Who could have told? Yet Slayton understood it.

Was it a certain look in those crafty, narrow eyes? Was it the smile of malice? Was it the seemingly casual manner in which the old man fingered his scant gray hair — hair that reminded Slayton of the six gray hairs found in the dead hand of Mackenzie? Was it all these or something else?

No telling; but, at any rate, the cashier shuddered, paled and turned away in mortal dread.

He knew now, he understood to the full, that everything lay in that Shylock's crooked hands. He comprehended that a word from Jarboe might free Arthur and seat *him*,

Slayton, in the chair of death. All, absolutely everything,
depended on Jarboe.

Would the usurer keep faith? Having received the blood-
money and the promise of those horrible payments, which
meant to Slayton a life of slavery and continued theft that
could end only in disaster, would Jarboe keep faith?

Slayton's heart turned sick within him. He arose, made
his way to the water-cooler and drank greedily; then once
more sat down, mopping his forehead, wet with the sweat
of so intense an anguish that no human suffering, it seemed
to him, could equal it.

Thus, racked by agony and terror, he watched the opening act of the great drama of life and death. Arthur, the
accused, sat calm and brave and hopeful, sustained by Enid
in his hour of supreme need. Slayton, against whom no
single word had yet been spoken, writhed in torment.

And so now the actual battle of life, of death, began.

CHAPTER XVIII

HENDERSON, Keene's ablest assistant, leaned over to his chief and urgently begged a change of plea.

"For Heaven's sake, Keene," he whispered, "have Mansfield withdraw his 'not guilty' and substitute 'guilty' with a plea for clemency! If he doesn't, they'll send him to the chair, sure as guns!"

Keene nodded approval, pondered a moment, and then conferred with his client. He, too, now believed that in no other way could Arthur escape the chair. But the boy unhesitatingly and indignantly repelled the suggestion.

"I'll either stand or fall on the truth," he whispered back emphatically. "I don't believe a man totally innocent can be convicted of a crime. I'm innocent. Absolutely innocent! I won't perjure myself even to save my life!"

Keene appealed to Enid to get her help in making Arthur change his mind, but all in vain. She took exactly the same ground as he. No argument could shake either of them.

This decision, Keene felt, could have none but a fatal outcome. The testimony of the State was developing terrible strength. Nowhere could the slightest loophole be discovered.

Ainslow first put Anderson, janitor of the bank, on the stand. Anderson told how he had found the body, notified the authorities, and later discovered the pistol behind some ash-barrels in the basement. Nothing of value to the defense was elicited by Keene's cross-examination.

Coroner Roadstrand followed. Under Ainslow's skilled direct examination he narrated his verdict, described the condition of the body, told of Arthur's incriminating appearance on reaching the bank, gave an account of the preliminary medical examination as conducted by himself with Dr. Nelson's assistance, and ended with Arthur's assault in the directors' room. His testimony impressed the jury deeply; it stood firm against all Keene's attacks.

Slayton, nervous, but highly intelligent, gave a coherent narrative. It was noticed that he appeared greatly worn by emotion, and that not once during his testimony did he look at the prisoner. This was favorably commented on as proof of his affection for Mansfield and of his grief at being forced to testify against the boy. A certain well-marked hesitation at times further substantiated this unwillingness.

Twice during his story he was seen to peer at a certain eccentric old money-lender named Jarboe, who sat near by, nodding and smiling, with a few gray hairs twiddling in his gnarled fingers. At these times Slayton appeared to suffer acutely. Only a few persons noted the incidents, and these may have interpreted them to mean that Jarboe was urging him on to testify even more strongly against the boy, which Slayton was obviously unwilling to do.

Slayton's story drove still another nail into Arthur's coffin. His direct testimony about the boy's theft of twelve hundred and fifty dollars, and about the threats that Arthur had made against his life, pistol in hand, damaged the case for the defense almost beyond repair. The cashier's evidence ended with an account of how he had disarmed the accused, had sent him home, had then written Mrs. Slayton, and had gone to bed.

Keene, sensing a certain weakness in this testimony, cross-examined Slayton with searching acuteness; but the cashier met him with admirable skill, and stood the gaff well. The

grueling attacks were all successfully parried. Keene did
no more than bring out a few new details and some trivial
contradictions. Ever since the murder Slayton had been
drilling himself in this story and schooling himself on all its
minutiæ. Now he was able to make it carry with the ring
of truth.

Once he seemed on the point of breaking — one of the
two times when Jarboe caught his eye with a horrible leer.
But he quickly looked away, mustered his nerve again, and
faced the ordeal, pale, but unshakable. The few trivialities
in which Keene succeeded in confusing him did not affect
his story as a whole. It stood.

Mrs. Slayton and Ashley, the Slaytons' neighbor at Oakwood Heights, next testified. Mrs. Slayton read the letter
received by her, mentioning Arthur's criminal conduct.
This letter was placed with other exhibits to be used by the
jury in its deliberations.

Ashley stated that Slayton had walked to the railway station with him at the accustomed hour, the morning after the
murder. Keene briefly cross-examined both without any
results favorable to the defense.

At this point in the trial Slayton became so indisposed
that he had to withdraw to a private room for more than
two hours. The cashier's emotion was extreme. He
seemed to be standing on the edge of a complete breakdown.
Everybody commented favorably on his grief for Arthur,
and on the evident reluctance with which he had testified
against the boy.

President Chamberlain, of the bank, stated the amount
of the financial loss: twelve hundred and fifty dollars in the
first instance, acknowledged by the defendant to have been
taken by him, and one hundred and fifty thousand dollars
in the second instance, denied by him. Led along by Ainslow, the witness also described how the safe had been
opened by means of the combination, told of the destruction

of the pages in the ledger containing records of the thousand-dollar bills, and ended by a gratuitous plea for clemency, which was suppressed by Judge Grossmith with some severity.

Keene's cross-examination for the defense did not change this story a hair's breadth. Recess now intervened, leaving the State, so far, undisputed master of the field.

Dr. Nelson's expert medical testimony, after recess, completed the case for the State.

It held the fagged audience spellbound, furnished fresh thrills to the wearied newspapermen and sensation-seekers, and put the final touch of gruesome tension to the already overwrought drama.

His story fell like lead on Arthur's sinking hopes, and Enid's. He spoke in a cold, impersonal manner, wholly devoid of rhetoric and without the slightest possible animus against the defendant. Calmly he instructed the jurors as to the basic principles of medical proof, and thereafter exhibited the grisly evidences of the boy's blood-guilt.

"Gentlemen," said he, "these are not matters of sentiment, but of science. Science knows neither good nor evil. She knows only facts.

"No criminal has yet been able to commit a crime without leaving certain traces which the eye of science can detect. The old saying, 'Dead men tell no tales,' has become false. He who depends on it in murdering depends on a fallacy.

"To-day the murderer has to reckon with the chemist, the physicist, the Roentgenologist, and other scientists, including the Bertillon-measurement expert, the finger-print analyst, the expert blood-tester and many others. Between them, the way of the transgressor has become hard indeed."

A breathless silence held the room. Spectators, jurors, all gazed intently at this bald, little man, whose keen eyes peered so impassively through those round shell glasses of his. Enid, clasping her hands with more nervousness than she had yet exhibited, watched him intently with parted lips and fading color. Arthur, his eyes for the first time expressing a doubt, a fear, listened to every word with terrible eagerness. Nelson, paying Mansfield no more heed than as if this man whose life he was about to take away had been a block of stone, continued calmly:

" A case took place in France, in 1913, in which a man was found walking quickly away from a place where a murdered man was lying. The former was known to be a bitter enemy of the latter, and had, moreover, a blood-stained knife in his possession and blood-stains on his clothing. On the point of conviction, the methods of Professors E. T. Reichert and A. P. Brown — which methods can identify the kind of blood, human, animal, or reptilian, its age, race, and even the length of time since it was shed — proved this blood to be that of a rabbit, and the prisoner was acquitted."

A more hopeful look came into Arthur's face. Enid glanced at him with loving encouragement; but Keene, wise in the methods of this impersonal machine of a man, frowned slightly.

" I could tell you other cases, gentlemen," continued Nelson, " in which blood claimed to be that of rabbits, fowls, or pigs has been proved to be that of human beings, and men have been caught and hanged thereby for murder. Lechanarzo, the Italian expert, can tell you when any particular specimen of blood was spilled; and his method has saved many innocent men and condemned many guilty ones.

" Mutilations of a body often betray the criminal by the skilled or unskilled nature of the cuts. Occupational deformities or diseases have their story to tell in evidence. Let me cite you a peculiar case. A man recently murdered his father and cut him into more than a hundred pieces.

He buried these pieces, confident that even if any of them were found the mutilation was so complete that identification could not be made. Daily he expressed surprise that his father did not return home.

"Six months after the deed a farmer dug up a human hand. This apparently gave no clue. It might be anybody's hand. But an expert criminologist noticed certain callosities on the palm, of a peculiar nature. He begged the old man's walking-stick from the grieving son as a keepsake. The curiously carved knob of the stick fitted the calloused hand, and — the son was hanged."

The pause he made so simply was dramatic in the extreme. A sigh of intense emotion rose from the stifling, fetid room. Two or three of the jurymen leaned forward. Evidently Nelson was leading up to something of great moment.

Keene suddenly arose.

"Your Honor," said he, "I object. This discussion is not relevant, and tends to prejudice the minds of the jurors against my client."

"Objection overruled," answered Grossmith. "In the opinion of the court, matters tending to enlighten the jurors on the scope and function of evidence are apposite to the case."

Keene, disgruntled, subsided, and Nelson continued:

"If a man is found dead, shot through the head and with a pistol in his hand, gentlemen," he went on evenly, "what is more rational than a verdict of suicide? But in real suicide the weapon is held so firmly that force is required to dislodge it. I refer you to an article by Davina Watterson, in the *Alienist and Neurologist,* for full facts in such cases. The muscular spasm persists until *rigor mortis* sets in. It is impossible to make the hand of a corpse grip a weapon that was not in it at the moment of death. This fact has often opened the door to detection.

" Simulated suicides by hanging, drowning, poisons or other means always leave their traces, to be read by the scientist. The action of fire on a body often tells the tale of murder. A man recently rushed frantically to a doctor, summoning aid. His wife, he said, had just been burned to death. The doctor observed that burns made before death contain serum, and in this case there were none. The man confessed to having strangled his wife before burning the body.

" To quote my authority, gentlemen of the jury:

" ' Lynx-eyed science is rendering it ever more difficult to dispose of a body or hide the crime of murder. Human hair and blood and bones have characteristics distinctly their own. The gory knife of melodrama is no longer sufficient to fix a crime; and even if the penny novelist should kill his hero with radium, the physicist would come along with the electroscope and with it absolutely refute or confirm the accusation.' "

The doctor turned now, amid universal silence, to the attorneys' table, took up a box, and once more faced the jurors.

" All this," said he, " leads up to the statement that science, taking no cognizance of morals, of right, of wrong, can infallibly be depended on to protect all those human concepts. Her proofs, gentlemen, are indisputable. She cannot lie. Her truth is absolute. On it, in this case, you must base your judgment in the forthcoming verdict."

He next took from the box the pistol that had done the murder, held it up, showed it to judge and jurymen, and turned to Grossmith again.

" This is the weapon that killed Mackenzie," said he calmly.

He passed it to the jurymen, and followed it with the bullet, which they likewise inspected. Quietly he lectured them on the effects of the shot, the distance whence it had been fired, and the manner in which it had been recovered.

Next he exhibited the broken letter-opener and the point that had been severed from it, and expounded how it had been used to open Slayton's desk.

The burned glove-snaps followed, and the intact glove with the blood-marks, identified under the microscope and chemically as Mackenzie's blood.

Then came the bits of paper bearing the carbon-copied letters and figures of the combination. After this, a statement from the doctor that the button he now showed had been found close by the body. Arthur's coat was produced, and the jury were shown how the button matched, and where it had fallen off from the sleeve.

"This, gentlemen, completes the exhibits," concluded Nelson gravely, "with the exception of one bit of evidence which we have not been able to correlate with anything else in the case. I refer to these half-dozen gray hairs found in the dead hand of Mackenzie."

He held them up for inspection, wrapped with a thread and sewn to a stiff card.

"These, gentlemen, are not human hairs at all. They constitute a most peculiar factor in the case. We have no hypothesis to explain them. They may mean nothing, and they may mean everything. In your deliberations give them due weight. I have no more to offer, and I thank you for your kind attention."

Nelson sat down, took off his glasses and wiped his brow. Again the buzz and hum of voices sounded through the room. Enid, now deathly pale, her large eyes fixed on Arthur, seemed lost in despair.

For the first time her optimism had deserted her. Her look met Arthur's and she tried to smile, but miserably failed. Tears blurred her vision, but still she looked upon the man she loved, now wan and worn and suffering.

Keene exerted himself to the full in the cross-examination of the doctor, but made no progress. He dared not question the identity or ownership of the pistol, the letter-opener, the glove or any of the exhibits — a point that told heavily against him.

Though he tried to make capital out of the finding of the gray hairs, he failed to reach any conclusion, since he had no hypothesis to work on in this enigma. Nobody short of a Sherlock Holmes could indeed have deduced anything from that seemingly insoluble mystery. Nobody knew what those hairs meant, or could guess — nobody but the absent Slayton, who had crept away to seclusion, unable longer to endure the presence and the menace of old Jarboe.

After forty-five minutes of cross-questioning, together with some re-direct and a little re-cross-examination, Keene found his case no better than before. Against that stone wall of evidence no power at his disposal could make one inch of progress.

The State's case now being concluded, Keene made the usual formal motion for a dismissal of the indictment. Grossmith denied this with equal formality, and witnesses for the defense were now called.

The testimony for the defense, pitiably weak, took no great time. Keene had decided to withdraw any general evidence as to Arthur's previous good character, as now being valueless. It might, his legal wisdom told him, even prejudice the jury by making them think the boy a hypocritical and underhanded villain. Practically the whole defense rested with Mrs. Johansen's statement and the boy's own story; for Arthur had insisted on taking the stand in his own behalf.

Mrs. Johansen testified that on the night of the murder Arthur had been in his room. At just what hour he had come in, she could not swear; she thought it was about 3 A. M. Under Keene's gentle leading — for she was a simple soul and much abashed — she told her tale, ending with a little exordium on Arthur's being " the best boy in the world, your Honor, and so kind to me I just *know* he couldn't ha' done it!"

Ainslow smiled contemptuously and proceeded to entangle her to such an extent that she finally went to pieces and could not be sure of anything. She had not seen Arthur at all, it developed, but had only heard somebody in the room at an uncertain hour.

" That will be all, thank you," smiled the district attorney, dismissing her while the effect of this admission was still fresh upon the jury. Keene's re-direct examination failed to brace her testimony into anything like coherent strength.

Arthur himself now took the stand, bloodless but very cool; and, being sworn, told a straight story. Interest became breathless. Enid in particular hung on every word with intense eagerness.

Every look, every gesture of hers spoke absolute faith in him. Twice or thrice their eyes met with a calm look of mutual love and trust and faith.

The boy narrated everything without evasion, subterfuge or exaggeration: his misstep in having stolen the one thousand two hundred and fifty dollars, his desperation, and his visit to Slayton.

" Yes, I admit I stole," said he. " You all know why now. It was to protect my father and keep him out of the penitentiary. He's dead now, and everything about his — mistake — is known. I didn't manage to help him much, and I got into this trouble trying to. It doesn't matter that I'd have returned the money. This murder-charge is all that matters now.

" I never did it, gentlemen. Never in this world. I'm absolutely innocent! "

He spoke in a level, distinct tone that trembled hardly at all. His hands gripped the rail before him very tightly, but his look was clear and honest, his bearing manly and strong. The impression he created was favorable; and many a whispered word passed through the room, words of wonder that so black a murderer could seem so guiltless, words of pity that so splendid a young chap must shortly face the chair.

"My trip to Mr. Slayton's house at Oakwood Heights was for the purpose of borrowing money to make good my theft," he continued. "It is true I took that gun with me. That was because if Mr. Slayton refused to help me I was going to kill myself.

"Mr. Slayton received me kindly. He promised to lend me enough to clear myself, and told me to see him at nine next morning and take an envelope he would hand me.

"Before I understood his exact meaning I thought he was going to refuse me, and I drew the pistol. He took it away from me and put it in his desk-drawer. That's the last I ever saw of it until it was just now shown me here in this room again."

Looks and murmurs of incredulity passed between the jurymen and through the audience. A peculiar situation had arisen, in which all the perjuries being told seemed gospel truth, and the only truth bore every indication of being perjury. So absurdly false did Arthur's words appear that, save for Enid, not one person in all that room gave them the slightest faith or credence whatsoever. Yes, there was one other — Jarboe!

The old man, smirking, nodding, scratching his wen and otherwise manifesting every sign of intense satisfaction, sat there drinking in every word.

He knew Arthur was telling the truth; *he* knew the boy was innocent. In three minutes he could have demanded to testify, have been sworn, and given facts that would inevitably have cleared Arthur and landed Slayton behind bars. But still he sat there saying nothing, volunteering no word or sign, listening or chuckling with Satan's own delight.

Aye, delight and high rejoicing. For in Arthur's conviction and the lash of terror Jarboe could hold over Slayton, still at liberty, lay a clear thousand dollars income every month he clung to his sordid, unclean, greedy life.

Dollars, dollars, dollars! For dollars old Jarboe kept his mouth shut. For dollars the one and only witness who could have saved the boy sat there with sealed lips, and, leering and mumbling to himself, watched a human life go down into the shadows, innocent yet convicted.

Arthur glanced at the girl, took courage from her look of faith, and continued:

"I went back to the city on the midnight train. When I got to South Ferry I took the subway to One Hundred and Tenth Street and walked straight to Mrs. Johansen's. I let myself in and spent the rest of the night in my room. It was about 3 A. M. when I got there. I was so upset and troubled that I couldn't sleep, but walked the floor. About four o'clock I lay down, dressed, on my bed, and after a while fell asleep.

"I didn't wake up till eight. I remembered that Mr. Slayton had told me to see him at nine sharp. My time was mighty short, I saw. I didn't wait for anything, not even for breakfast, but hurried down-town. That accounts for my appearance being unnatural. I was hungry and tired, and I hadn't slept enough, and, of course, I was worried, too.

"The first thing I knew about the murder was when I bought a paper in the subway. Of course I knew then that all my plans and hopes of making good had been upset. I saw I was sure to be ruined. You can imagine my state of mind."

Arthur paused a minute, drew a deep breath and glanced about the court-room, seeking a friendly face, perhaps, and finding not one — not one save Enid's.

"The rest of it," he continued, "is as the coroner has al-

ready told you, except that I didn't attack Mr. Slayton with
any murderous motive in the directors' room. When I realized how he had deceived me and accused me falsely, I
couldn't control myself. I struck him, gentlemen. It was
wrong, I admit, but it was human. A man can endure only
about so much.

"I am guilty of some things, but not of the greatest thing;
not of the thing I'm on trial for now. I have stolen and I
have committed an assault. For these offenses I am willing
and glad to pay. But not for a crime I swear to you I
never even thought of committing! Not for a crime I never
came within a thousand miles of committing!"

His voice, strengthening, began to ring with challenge.
His eyes brightened. Into his cheek a little tinge of color
once more crept back. Enid, gazing at him with terrible
eagerness, smiled slightly — a hopeful smile, a smile of confidence and trust. Her soul was vibrating with his every
word. Surely when her boy was speaking truth, God's own
truth, the very truth of truths, they must believe him!

"Gentlemen," said Arthur slowly, "this is all I have to
tell you. You have my story. It is true from end to end.
That night I never even approached the bank. Had I gone
there I couldn't have got in without a key, and I had none.
At the hour of the murder I was in my room.

"I know perfectly well you have seen and heard a tremendous mass of testimony against me. I know the circumstances seem overwhelmingly against me. But still, truth
is mighty. And the truth is that I am innocent.

"All these things you have seen "— and he motioned to the
exhibits now lying on the attorneys' table —"are only
'plants,' gentlemen. They form part of a cleverly laid plot
to convict me. As there is a heaven, I swear to you this is
the living truth!

"The hands I hold out to you, appealing for justice, are
free of human blood! There is no guilt of murder on them.

I ask you, gentlemen, to do me justice and to free me of this false and terrible charge!

" If you convict me here and now you will be convicting an innocent man! "

CHAPTER XIX

PALLID and trembling with the vehemence of his supreme appeal, Arthur now had to face the cynical smile and coldly dangerous incisiveness of Ainslow's cross-examination. True though his story was, inside of five minutes Ainslow had forced him into several contradictions, on which the district attorney dilated with telling effect.

Before this attack Arthur's narrative soon was riddled. Ainslow added to the force of his assault by making it short. His air said plainly:

" Gentlemen, there is no use in wasting your time on trivialities such as these!"

The way in which he dismissed the boy with a " That's quite enough, thank you," and the grim smile on his lips, spoke volumes.

Keene subjected Arthur to a few minutes of re-direct examination, with the hope of strengthening the defense. To this Ainslow did not even deign to reply with any re-cross-examination. This created a favorable impression for the State, and damaged Arthur considerably.

Quite exhausted, Arthur stepped down from the witness-stand and resumed his seat beside his counsel. Keene nodded reassuringly to him, but it was plain to see the lawyer felt that his client had not driven the truth of the story home. Arthur had had his chance and had failed to make good. Against the mass of evidence condemning him his story had fallen as ineffective as a broadside of peas against a dreadnought.

Yet Enid seemed to think the case won. Her dark eyes,

going from Arthur's face to the stern, set faces of the
twelve men in whose hands now lay her boy's life, no longer
pleaded. They commanded, rather. They seemed to say:
"Now you have heard the truth, set him free!"

Keene, tired-looking and worn out, failed even to hold
the attention of the jury in the final summing-up for the
defense. Anybody with half an eye could see that the verdict was already formulated in the minds of these twelve
men, and that the only problem now remaining was:
"What degree?"

The audience began manifesting impatience. Some disturbance, as two or three men tried to leave the room, further destroyed whatever effect Keene's words might have
had. The jurors, tired out and hungering for nicotine, fid-
geted as he addressed them. Plainly they were longing to
get up and stretch their legs; to leave the stifling, crowded
place and reach the comparative freedom of the jury-room;
to light tobacco, free their tongues in discussion, and come
down to the business of Life vs. Death.

Keene, noting all this, cut his address short, but threw
into it all the power now left in him.

"Gentlemen, I solemnly adjure you," he concluded, "not
to throw away or jeopard a human life merely because of
prejudice or indolence of thought or through circumstantial
evidence. Legal history is crammed with cases of innocent
men done to death on circumstantial evidence. Beware of
trusting to its fallacies!"

Here Juror Ellis yawned and Foreman Crowther glanced
impatiently at the clock.

"Gentlemen! The evidence has demonstrated that my
client did not even approach the bank on the night of the
crime; that he spent the hours in question in his room; and
that the real criminal, by juggling certain matters, has managed to lay the blame upon a man innocent as you, or you,
or I!

" Not one scintilla of real proof exists against the defendant. One of the most vital pieces of evidence, the white hairs found in the victim's grasp, has never been explained by the State. No theory has been advanced to account for this fact, which would infallibly give us the real clue to the murderer."

" The real clue! Aye, the real clue!" muttered Jarboe, fixing malevolent eyes on Slayton under the glare of the incandescents. " The real clue! Hear, hear!"

Slayton, seeming to sense his gibe, turned fearful eyes toward the filthy little Shylock. Despite every effort the cashier was sweating and shivering. It was not yet too late for Jarboe to spring a coup — not yet, not yet!

" Gentlemen!" cried Keene in peroration. " The defendant is innocent under the law until proven guilty. You understand? Not assumed guilty, but *proven!* I solemnly call you to witness the fact that no adequate proof has been adduced. You have heard assumption and inference, but no proof. All the proof in this case lies on the side of the defendant. He is an innocent man, and I adjure you to acquit him. Truth is mighty and will prevail!"

He finished with an assumption of intense emotion — mercenary emotion, wholly unreal and quite incapable of touching men's hearts, even were those men not restless and impatient like the jurors. But to Enid his words were balm and manna. They cried to her:

" Salvation!"

Her spirits had quickly revived under their stimulus; and now she could almost find heart to smile through all her grief and fear.

Again her eyes met Arthur's. The boy's lips silently formed three words:

" I am innocent!"

Hers answered:

" I know it!"

And their look, each at each, pledged faith and trust and love in whatever joy or pain still awaited its fulfillment, even "the narrow Gates of Darkness through."

Ainslow now rose to sum up for the State. This he did with less than his usual energy. His voice, look and manner all asked with supremely effective art:

"Why waste strength on a case already won?"

Clearly, but with rather perfunctory brevity, he restated the facts already made known and proved. He admitted the circumstantial character of most of the evidence, but remarked that in some cases such evidence amounted to a positive certainty. He ridiculed Keene's assertion that the boy could not have entered the bank.

"A criminal, gentlemen of the jury," said he, "who could show sufficient foresight, skill and coolness to conduct an affair like this — even in the wearing of gloves, the attempted planting of evidence on a fellow clerk, the manner in which he brought a chair and sat down by the body to study out his plan of escape —"

"It's a lie!" shouted Arthur, springing up, unable to control himself. "A lie, I tell you! I never even —"

Grossmith pounded furiously with his gavel.

"Order! Order in this court!" he commanded.

Arthur subsided under this command and Keene's vehement admonitions. Presently, when quiet had been restored, Ainslow resumed:

"Even in the manner in which he destroyed the pages of the ledger, bearing records of the thousand-dollar bills stolen, he showed himself a shrewd, clever criminal. He went so far, gentlemen, as to put on rubbers, lest his footprints might betray him. He attacked and killed a feeble, harmless and unarmed old man in the discharge of his duty. This crime, as I have reconstructed it for you, proves the defendant to have been a most conscienceless, astute and calculating murderer."

He leveled his forefinger at Arthur.

"Most conscienceless, astute and calculating," he repeated impressively. "And yet he and his counsel ask you to believe he could — not — have — entered — the — bank!"

Snapping his fingers, he dismissed the idea as an absurdity. One or two jurors nodded. Evidently the point had gone home.

Ainslow then tore to shreds the feeble alibi Arthur had attempted to establish. It rested only on his own testimony and that of an infirm landlady, none too intelligent. When the district attorney had finished with it only a sorry rag remained, not enough to protect Arthur for an instant from the chill winds of fate now blowing keen against his defenselessness.

The approving public smiled and nodded, looking hate, scorn and vengeance against the boy. Slayton, blue about the mouth, kept a stony impassiveness. Old Jarboe rubbed his hands and chuckled. Chamberlain sat there erect and grim, stoic in his coolness. To his arm clung Enid. With all her confidence and hope now torn away, wide-eyed and anguished, she watched this man Ainslow murdering her boy's hopes as if he had been dipping his hands veritably in Arthur's blood.

"I ask you, gentlemen of the jury, for justice," concluded Ainslow. "Not vengeance, but impartial, even-handed justice. You have the facts. They are absolutely conclusive. We are not persecuting this man. We are merely protecting society. We are impartially meting out that which should and must be meted out.

"*Fiat justitia, ruat coelum!* Let justice be done, though the heavens fall!"

He kept a moment's impressive silence, looking the jurymen fair in the face, his eyes going from one to another as if driving home the imperative demand. Then, bowing, he

sat down, his work at an end. And Judge Grossmith's
gavel, backed by all the available court officers, hardly more
than sufficed to quell the applause.

When he had restored order, Grossmith fixed his spectacled gaze on the jury, and began delivering his charge.

He dwelt at some length on the nature and value of evidence, direct and circumstantial; described the various degrees of murder and warned the jurors of the solemnity of
their duty. Having covered all the necessary points of law,
he ended with:

" You have now heard all the evidence *pro* and *contra*.
On this, and on nothing else whatever, you must bring in
your verdict. Remember, gentlemen, you can acquit or you
can convict of murder in the first, second, or third degree.

" Remember also, first degree involves premeditation —
an act done in cold blood without the extenuation of self-
defense or sudden passion. Take this into consideration
in your verdict, and also the fact that the evidence is almost
wholly circumstantial.

" Let your verdict express your firm conviction, not
reached in the heat of argument and strife, but calmly, deliberately and dispassionately, in a spirit of complete, impartial and immutable justice.

" Gentlemen, you will now retire for deliberation."

The jury, thus dismissed, withdrew, taking with them the
grim exhibits, relics of the crime. Arthur, with one last
look at Enid, was led away by two officers to his cell, there
to suffer the racking torments of suspense — anguish beyond
all words — anguish which Enid, too, was destined to endure, waiting with her father in Grossmith's private chambers as the judge's guest.

The audience now thinned out; the corridors emptied
themselves; the reporters and artists took themselves off to

work their material into shape. A few spectators still lingered wearily on the benches, determined to make an all-night session of it if need were.

Among these was old Jarboe. Though Slayton had departed, obviously quite at the end of all his strength, the unclean, usurious bird of prey sat there buzzard-like. Mumbling to himself, brooding, pondering, he remained on watch. Ominous and enigmatic, he waited.

What meant that glitter in his eye? What was the old man thinking now? What was he planning?

Nine o'clock came and went, and ten, and eleven. Still no verdict.

What was taking place there inside that locked door of inviolable secrets? What battles of circumstantial evidence, of reasonable doubt, of mercy, of prejudice, of vindictiveness, were being fought out there with bitter argument amid tobacco-smoke, excited words, the waving of fists, and all the most violent passions of men in strife of principle and strong determination?

What ballots had been taken and were being taken? How was the tide of conflict turning? None outside knew; none might ever know any but the one final, vital, crucial thing — the verdict!

Thus passed the hours of that night — anguishing, soul-destroying hours, hours of agony for Enid and the boy, hours of torment.

And suddenly, at eleven forty-two, word came out of that sealed place — word of decision — word of terrible hope and fear — word of supremest tension: *We have reached a verdict!*

Interest and excitement quickly revived. The benches began to fill again. The opposing lawyers returned. Telephone messages began to draw crowds of spectators and reporters, each newspaperman eager to get the verdict first to his own waiting sheet. A buzz and hum of life once more filled the corridors and the sad room of human hopes and fears.

The jury now entered. Grimly and in silence the twelve men filed into the box, knowing the secret of the boy's fate, which they had sealed and now held in their hands. Judge Grossmith came in from his chambers, still robed and gravely impassive.

Chamberlain supported Enid, who clung to his arm, plainly on the ragged edge of collapse. Her pallor was extreme. Her big, dark eyes were undershadowed by marks that seemed bruises on the white flesh.

Now Arthur appeared, led in by two officers as the jurymen and judge sat down. He, too, was very pale; but his eyes looked bravely at the girl, and on his bloodless lips a smile managed to hold itself — a smile she tried to give him back, and failed.

Arthur sat down near Keene, a guard on either hand. The clerk of the court, who had entered before Grossmith and had been fumbling over some loose papers, turned toward the jury-box. He fixed his eyes on the face of Crowther, foreman of the jury.

Listening with intense eagerness, old Jarboe leaned a little forward and gnawed at his crooked fingers, his eyes strangely gleaming. Still there remained time for him to speak. At this last moment, on the verge of Fate, what might he not still do?

Enid, trembling violently, hid her face in both hands and shuddered against her father's breast. The old man soothingly drew his arm about her, patting her shoulder as if she had been only a little child.

The clerk coughed slightly.

" Gentlemen of the jury," said he, " have you reached a verdict ? "

Crowther nodded as he stood up.

" We have," he answered in a tense, hoarse voice.

The pause that followed, though but a second, seemed an eternity to Enid and the prisoner.

"Prisoner at the bar," said the clerk, "stand up and look upon the jurors."

Arthur arose and stared at the foreman with terrible intensity, both hands clenched, jaw set hard, holding himself together by sheer force of will. Old Chamberlain's arm tightened about his daughter. A rigid tension of silence held the room.

The clerk asked:

"What is your verdict, gentlemen?"

All the jurors stood up. Their faces for the most part showed pitiless and hard. One or two, however, glanced compassionately at the boy.

"What is your verdict?"

"Your Honor," answered Crowther, the foreman, addressing the Court, "we find the prisoner guilty of murder in the second degree."

Jarboe's blinking eyes never for a second quitted Crowther's face. His lips moved slightly. He seemed preparing to speak. On him Slayton fixed a gaze of shrinking, appealing terror, which the old man did not notice.

CHAPTER XX

"MURDER in the second degree!"

As the words died to silence in the musty court-room Judge Grossmith struck the bench with his knuckles.

"Remanded for sentence January 4," said he. "Gentlemen, you are hereby discharged. Accept the thanks of the Court."

Jarboe nodded grimly and leered at Slayton, who sank back deathly pale with a gasp of relief. Enid, crying, "Arthur! Arthur!" tried to struggle up, but her father's arm restrained her.

"No, no, Enid!" he implored in a whisper. "No scene here — no scene!"

"Come on, you!" ordered one of the guards, clapping a hand on Arthur's shoulder as the boy sat there too dazed even to stand up. "Come along, now!"

Arthur's eyes met the girl's a moment; but they seemed to see nothing, to understand nothing. Enid through all her anguish felt a numbing chill. Already the impassable gulf was yawning between them. Already the shadows of the penitentiary, now opening for this man — a living tomb that nevermore might let him go — had irrevocably fallen on them both.

The court-room seemed to whirl, to circle round and round her. Everything looked black and spinning. Where was Arthur? What were they doing to her boy?

"Arthur!" she cried again. "Arthur!"

She saw him now. The clerk had taken his pedigree, and the officers were leading him away. He did not look back, but shuffled between his guards, one of whom dangled hand-cuffs. Bright high-lights glinted from the steel of those handcuffs. She saw them dance and waver fancifully.

Unsteadily she put out her hand.

"Father!" she pleaded. "It's a lie — a lie!"

He gathered her close.

"S-h-h-h-h, Enid! There, there, there!"

A door closed with hollow echoings. Arthur was gone.

Already as the jurors were filing out of their box, Keene had risen to his feet, a sheaf of papers in hand.

"Your Honor," he exclaimed, raising a long forefinger at Grossmith, now already preparing to leave the bench, "I apply for a writ of error *in re* the —"

"The motion will be heard on December 24."

Keene nodded, the judge withdrew, and the spectators began to disperse. Jurors and all, relieved, hunched on their overcoats, put on their hats, and scattered down the corridor, where fragmentary conversations formed and dissolved and drifted away in scraps of comment, speculation, criticism or approval.

Reporters hastened to telephone-booths, eager to rush the news to their papers. One or two bolder spirits among them, essaying to pick a little forbidden fruit by interviewing jurors, and hoping for some information on the wrangle that had taken place in the jury-room, were driven away by officers. In a few minutes the verdict would be whirling through the rotary presses of huge newspapers; and in the morning all New York, all the world, would know that Arthur Mansfield, *fiancé* of Banker Chamberlain's daughter, had been duly convicted of murder in the second degree for having killed Watchman Mackenzie.

The most sensational murder trial of the year was at an end.

Keene, the head of Mansfield's staff of counsel, stuffed law-books, briefs and papers into his green baize bag and pulled the tape. Then he turned to Chamberlain. The look that passed between the two men, and the gesture of helplessness the lawyer made, spoke volumes.

"If I'd had anything — anything at all to go on," said Keene in a low voice —"anything at all, you know —"

"I understand completely," answered the banker, nodding.

"Impossible situation," added Keene.

Slayton, hesitating, approached the group; then felt his nerve desert him and retreated into the corridor, followed by old Jarboe, who was chuckling and rubbing his hands together.

"Quite impossible," Keene went on. "Of course, I'll take all possible legal steps to secure a new trial; but —"

Enid looked up at him. She had grown calm again. The temporary weakness had passed.

"Next time you'll win," she declared with splendid optimism. "You'll win, and he'll go free. They can't, can't, *can't* give an innocent man a life sentence and make him serve it!"

Keene bowed, deftly avoiding any possibility of argument.

"My dear Miss Chamberlain," he answered, "believe me when I say every possible means will be employed to have this verdict reversed. But I must warn you not to entertain any false hopes. All that can be done shall be. But still you mustn't build any air-castles just yet."

She managed to smile wanly with a supreme and unshakable faith.

"I'm not afraid," she declared. "Arthur's an innocent man, and justice shall be done some day."

An electric switch snapped. . Some of the lights in the

court room died. An attendant was clearing the room of the last few idlers and curiosity-seekers.

"Come, Enid," bade her father. "There's nothing to be gained now by staying here any longer. It's long past midnight. Let's go home."

Together all three left the building. A few minutes later father and daughter were whirling up-town in their limousine. Sunk far back in a corner of the cushions, Enid kept silence. Arthur's stunned and uncomprehending face rose constantly before her. A fine, sifting snow had begun to fall, shimmering in moving whiteness round the electric lights of the car and the street-lamps that swiftly flitted backward and away. Its swirls seemed to be weaving a cold white veil between that face and her.

On the 24th of December at 10.30 A. M. Keene's writ of error, asking a new trial, was heard by Judge Grossmith. His Honor carefully and honestly examined into the matter with perfect impartiality and no bias whatsoever, viewing merely the legal aspects of the case.

After due consideration he decided that all had been done quite regularly and in order, according to the strictest interpretation of the law, and that no error whatsoever existed at any point of the procedure. He, therefore, denied the writ.

Enid, apprised of this fact, smiled bravely and bade Keene go on fighting, at all expense. The girl had grown notably thinner; she had lost her fine, vigorous color; but her blue-black eyes still held true and steady with brave confidence. A thoroughbred, she had not yet even begun to fight. None of her father's pleadings had yet been able to make her leave the city, go South, West, anywhere to get away from the case.

"No," she would always answer. "Arthur needs me here. Without me he'd be lost. Do you think Edward

Chamberlain's daughter could be happy at Palm Beach or Santa Monica, or even at Nice or Cannes, while he sits all alone under the shadow? "

Sentence was passed on Arthur the morning of Thursday, January 4. Only a few reporters and casual visitors were present to hear the words of doom pronounced against him. Convicted and disposed of, Arthur had ceased to be even a good news-feature.

Enid was not there. At Arthur's urgent plea she absented herself. This ordeal, useless from any standpoint, was spared her. Alone at home she spent a day of shuddering prostration, her imagination making the scene a hundredfold more terrible to her than the reality.

Arthur came up with a batch of eight others who were slated for sentence on various convictions. Except Keene, he had no support through this terrible hour. Slayton's lantern-jawed face was to be seen, eager and furtive, as the cashier listened with terrible intensity on one of the back benches; but Arthur, after one look at this hated visage, steadfastly kept his eyes away from it.

The whole affair was businesslike, and took only a little time, that dark and misty winter morning. Three others were sentenced before Arthur himself.

This helped break the shock of it a little. Nevertheless, when the clerk called " Arthur Mansfield! " in a toneless voice and the boy knew his hour had struck, a sinking weakness possessed his body. He could barely manage to stand up and face the raven-like countenance of Grossmith on the bench.

Arthur had grown emaciated already. His face had begun to assume the sallow, unhealthy pallor that always follows the most barbarous of all human inventions — the confinement of a human being in a cage of steel.

Judge Grossmith peered sharply through his spectacles

at the boy, standing there with both hands on the railing in front of the bench.

"Have you anything to say why sentence should not be pronounced upon you?" asked the judge in routine form.

"No, your Honor," the boy managed to answer huskily. His lips and tongue were parched as with a fever.

In this reply he was acting under Keene's instructions. It would be worse than useless now for him to speak or plead his cause. Whatever could be done would be in due legal course.

The judge coughed dryly, glanced at his memoranda to refresh his memory of the case — for really he heard so very, very many — and then raised his eyes to Arthur's face.

"Mansfield," said he, "this crime of which you stand convicted seems to be one of particular atrociousness. The fact that the evidence was all circumstantial defeated the rendering of a verdict of murder in the first degree, whereby the ends of justice would have been better served. The verdict is of murder in the second degree, and the penalty is mandatory. I regret that I cannot exceed its provisions.

"It is now here by this court ordered, and the sentence of the court is, that you be imprisoned at hard labor in the penitentiary of the State of New York at Sing Sing for the term of your natural life."

The judge ceased with a severe contraction of the lips. Arthur made no sound, no sign, no move. His hands tightened a little on the rail, perhaps; but he still stood there firmly enough. His eyes, however, seemed to behold nothing; nor did he sit down again as he should. One of the officers had to tap him on the shoulder and motion him to a chair.

He sat down then, mechanically and stiffly, licked his lips once or twice, and then stared straight in front of him, almost indifferently. Those who had perhaps expected acute emotions in the boy, a heart-rending appeal, a dramatic scene to furnish forth a write-up, were disappointed. Arthur had proved undeniably tame.

The clerk entered the sentence in due and proper form, and the next prisoner stood up to hear his words of fate. Arthur sat there quietly until summoned to return to his cell. The world already was retreating from him — the living world of men and women, the world of freedom, light, and life. He stood now on the portals of a world of shadows, steel-barred; of gray, dim, silent figures; of endless drudgery and pain eternal.

Soon he must pass that portal, over which Dante's " All hope abandon, ye who enter here " should be graven for so many. Soon, with only the backward look of yearnings that availed not, he must leave the real world, where sunlight was and love and laughter; where men labored for reward and found rest sweet; where achievement beckoned and the promises of better things lightened the burdens of the way. He must leave that world — not through swift and merciful death, but through the clangor of steel barriers in a place of horror where

> Never a human voice comes near
> To speak a gentle word,
> And the eye that watches through the door
> Is pitiless and hard,
> And by all forgot, men rot and rot,
> With soul and body marred.

That same afternoon at four-fifteen Arthur bade New York good-by. His going was a horrible and shameful thing. Clean, strong, innocent, they hauled him through the streets in a black, barred motor-van with eleven other wretched men — hauled him through some of the very highways where only a few weeks ago Enid and he had ridden in Chamberlain's " Lormont Six." Handcuffed to a swart Portuguese wife-murderer, they herded him through the Grand Central to the train.

Even though he was spared the anguish of passing through the spacious waiting-room and the concourse, the ordeal of undergoing public observation in the side entrance and along the platform to the smoker left him sick and shaken. Keene appeared before the train left, and with perfunctory words of hope said good-by to him.

But even the privilege of a handclasp was forbidden now. The State had laid its penalty upon him. It dared not risk the danger that some kinder agency might put the nepenthe of a merciful poison in his grasp.

Huddled in the seat with the wife-murderer, Arthur made the horrible trip up the river, numbed with the ghastliness of this thing which must be a nightmare, which could not be real, could not be truly happening to him.

River and Palisades, white sail and plowing steamer, forest and town and sky all beckoned:

"*Come away, come away!*"

The roaring car-wheels clattered their antiphony:

"*Never, never, never any more! Any more, any more, any more! Never any more!*"

Though thoughts and love of Enid strove for entrance in his soul, he put them all away from him, for now the anguish of them passed the limit of his strength. Never any more such happiness for him! All things, save frightful things, were fading from him wholly. All that makes glad the soul of man, all that blesses, all that strengthens through the very stress and toil of attainment, all, everything had vanished in a phantasmagoria of hideous woes.

"At hard labor for the term of your natural life!"

It stunned, deadened, killed.

Night found him nameless, caged, crushed. At last the ultimate blow of fate had fallen. He was a "lifer" in

Sing Sing. He had become only a numbered thing — a man no longer, but just " 3265 "— with shaven head, with horrible striped garb of black and gray, with felt slippers noiseless on the chill cement.

A shelf, a greasy bunk, walls of rough stone, a steel-barred door, to which was chained a rusty tin cup — behold now his home till death. A cage in the cell-house, not even windowed through an outer wall, so that he might sometimes see " the little tent of blue which prisoners call the sky," but a cell facing a solid stone wall eight feet away, where in all the ninety years of the prison's existence the sun had never entered; a cell where madness might attack and death release him, but from which, alive and sound, he should be freed now nevermore.

Life was done. Love was past and gone. It must be put away and quite forgotten. What had they, or thoughts of liberty, to do in that pestilential hole?

The first night of his death-in-life, his living burial in the tomb " where some grow mad and all grow bad, and none a word may say," he huddled upon his foul-smelling bunk, listening to the melancholy prison sounds — hollow footsteps of warders, vague echoings of meaningless words, clankings of metal — and knew that something was gone from him that never could return — trust in the majesty and righteousness of Law.

A little gleam of hope burned, flickering, vaguely in the prison night — hope that, perhaps, somehow, some time, appeals might yet avail and justice be done. But this gleam proved transitory. Arthur was still too sane for any further self-delusion. Having once felt the annihilating fist of " Justice," and staggered beneath its blow, he could no longer count on any reversal of the verdict.

And if pardoned, what then? Freedom — with that hideous blot upon his name? Freedom — with that guilt still branded on his brow?

No! Not freedom! Better a thousand times the stifling seclusion of the cell than that. • The Law had pressed the brand upon his forehead. Nothing could ever make him whole again.

He thought of Enid and his mother then in those first hours, bitterer far than death; and his soul was calling out to them, even though his body lay upon the prison bunk, in the cell malodorous of stived breath and sweat and carbolic.

There he lay, his wan face buried in his crossed arms, his fingers clutching the coarse gray blanket, his shaven head grotesque and hideous in the dim light from the gallery. Twice as he lay so, a silent-footed warder peered through the grated door at him, but spoke no word and made no sign.

Nothing now outwardly distinguished the boy from the seventeen hundred other wretches crowding that sad place. The unusual strength and fineness of his body had quite vanished, swallowed by that horrible prison dress. A convict among convicts he had become, stamped already with the marks of that vile servitude wherewith man, " reforming " his brother, first degrades and brutalizes him.

After a certain while he grew more calm. Then it seemed to him — as in the Tombs — that Enid, the faithful, was with him, saying:

" I will believe you, Arthur; always believe and trust you — and I will be true! "

And then his mother stood beside him, her hand upon his striped, degraded shoulder, saying:

" Yea, though I walk in the Valley of the Shadow of Death, I will fear no evil! "

Thus, sleeping not, Arthur lay that night, keeping vigil with his soul.

CHAPTER XXI

THE Appellate Division of the Supreme Court up-held the verdict on February 10. One month later the Court of Appeals at Albany refused to grant a new trial. On June 6 a petition for a pardon was presented to Governor McIntyre and the Board of Pardons. A fortnight later, after due consideration, it was rejected.

Everything had now been done that could be done. Every means had been exhausted. The ultimate expedient at large cost had been tried and had failed. The sentence stood irrevocably confirmed.

Arthur's fate had now been definitely pronounced:

"Imprisonment at hard labor for life in Sing Sing."

Only one vague hope still lingered. With the induction of a new governor in eight months a new petition could be presented. Should this fail it could be handed every two years to each new governor. Tenuous and tedious as this hope might be, nothing else remained.

Buried alive, "mugged," and Bertillioned, Number 3265 — a human being whose personality had been lost in four figures — took his place as one cog in the vast factory of woe up the Hudson. They set him to making shoes with some scores of silent, morose and broken men with clipped heads and furtive eyes. His respectful request for clerical work they refused. Already they had too many convicts on such jobs. Later, perhaps, if he proved trustworthy —

Number 3265 pondered constantly. He thought as never before. Day by day and week by week he reviewed the past, analyzed the present and tried to organize his plans for the future — a future that never for one moment lost sight of Enid Chamberlain.

After a short period of absolute, numb despair, which rejected food and sleep and everything, the natural buoyancy of youth and strength began to reassert itself. Hope revived. Sanity returned, and purpose and some degree of calm. The boy realized that health must first of all be preserved. Without it all would be lost.

He must keep as strong and clean as it was possible to keep. He must not smoke the vile prison weed. He must resist all temptations to lighten his pain with dope, as so high a percentage of the convicts did. He must avoid the vices common to all prisons and make the best of the vile prison fare. Penned in his cell — three feet four inches by six feet seven — he must invent and keep to a hard, regular system of calisthenics.

So long as life remained there might still be some chance of rehabilitation. With admirable wisdom and strength of purpose Arthur undertook every measure possible for his welfare.

His mind, too, he realized, must be looked after. He began taking from the prison library the best books it afforded, and started systematic reading. Two hours every evening until the lights went out in the cells he devoted to extending his education. He began writing for *The Star of Hope,* and volunteered for every entertainment. The outlet of a minstrel-show or a little play afforded him infinite relief.

Though not of a religious turn of mind, he enjoyed chapel. With hundreds of others, all in sad gray and black, all with shaven heads, he bawled hymns at the top of his lungs, and found great physical and mental comfort therein. To be allowed to make a noise, even if only in chapel, was a stupendous privilege.

Up to the limit of his allowance he wrote to his mother —

now totally bedridden — to Enid, and to Sheridan, the ex-
teller of the bank, who always had believed in his innocence,
and received letters from them. The correspondence had
to undergo the strictest censorship, but still it infinitely comforted him.

Poor Sheridan had only bad news to send. His stand
in the case had practically blacklisted him. The best work
he could find now was book-canvassing, and even that job
was precarious. Arthur's heart ached at thought of the
man's brave but wholly useless self-sacrifice for him. The
mother's letters, and Enid's, brought love and cheer and
hope. Neither woman doubted his innocence for a second;
neither one despaired of triumph and of liberty some time.

Bit by bit through long nights of occasional insomnia, or
bent over his " nigger-heel " in the shoe-shop, Arthur began to piece together something of the truth in the case.
Slayton occupied his mind extensively. Living the tragedy
all over and over again, unnumbered times, he found the
cashier looming ever larger as the one most sinister figure
in the ghastly mock of justice that had forced this martyr-
dom upon him.

As yet he could not see the whole sequence clearly; but
here an indication, there a hint, farther on a tiny gleam of
probability all kept combining with more and ever more evidence to build a mass of wondering suspicion. As twigs
and refuse collect above a dam, eventually spreading into
a wide expanse of floating detritus, so now on the moving
current of Number 3265's mind, checked by the barrier of
that crime, the drifting indications one by one came to rest.

Gradually conviction forced itself upon the boy. Gradually he seemed to understand the truth of that black deed,
the essence of that frame-up, the general outlines of that
plot which with incredible villainy had flung him here to
agonize, to rot, to die.

He saw again that room in Slayton's house at Oakwood

Heights and heard the promise spoken there. He recalled the treachery of the next morning, Slayton's false witnessing, and all the damning evidence heaped up against him — by whose hand?

Reason answered:

Slayton's!

Analysis clarified all. Bit by bit Arthur patched everything together; and as conviction grew in him that Slayton was indeed the murderer — a murderer who with fiendish skill and malice had flung the guilt upon his shoulders — so hate grew likewise.

Bit by bit he pieced together odds and ends of prison gossip and underworld information that in different ways filtered through to him; and so he came to know the name of Jarboe and to garner in vague, ill-defined rumors that this loan-shark had got a grip on Slayton as on so many more; and this uncertain knowledge, too, helped the hypothesis his active brain was formulating.

A wide clarity of understanding came to open out before the mind of Number 3265. An understanding that totaled positive certainty lighted the black horizons of his soul. The whole infernal villainy unrolled before him. He saw; and, seeing, comprehended.

At night sometimes he would give his poisoned soul over to loathing and to hate of this man, now safe from all accusation, all danger, all attack — safe forever as Arthur thought with terrible despair. In the dusk of his cell, with face passion-distorted in a snarl of hatred, he would clutch his blanket with fingers that lusted to be at Slayton's throat, tearing the very life from that cold, false, murderous being.

And new ambitions dawned in him, new desires to live, fresh hopes that fanned the flame of his passion for freedom. One hope he came to cherish in particular above all others — the hope that he might some time go free and live to settle this foul score once and forever, to pay this debt in full, to wipe it out, and look on the dead face of Walter Slayton — and laugh.

Shortly after the Governor had refused the petition for a pardon, Slayton's supreme insolence led him to visit his victim in the sad place where

> Each day is like a year —
> A year whose days are long.

Slayton's purpose in making this trip — like everything he did — was well and cautiously calculated. He figured that the act would redound to his credit. Arthur had accused and assaulted him. He would do his Christian duty, that duty he was so fond of talking about, by returning good for evil and by heaping coals of fire on the head of this wayward boy.

Then, too, a kind of morbid curiosity possessed him to see the horrible place where — save for his own quick wits and diabolic skill — he himself would now be awaiting death. He wanted to behold the vicarious sacrifice, Arthur, paying the bitter price for the crime of hands still free.

Last of all the cashier figured that Arthur might do or say something which could be heralded abroad with the effect of still further proving his guilt, and thus rendering Slayton's own position safer still. All this time the menace of old Jarboe had been gnawing at Slayton's withered soul as rats gnaw a moldy cheese. One look at the cashier's face revealed the wasting effects of that menace.

Several times already he had paid the thousand-dollar "insurance premium"— as the repulsive Shylock insisted on calling it with cackling mirth that harrowed his being to its roots. He knew perfectly well now that Jarboe was in deadly earnest, and that a single defaulting of those payments would mean accusation, scandal, perhaps fatal results. If by any possible means Slayton could more thoroughly discredit the boy, more deeply involve him or ruin him more totally, the inevitable risks of the visit would be well worth while.

A coward at heart, he assured himself no real danger could attach to the interview. Arthur behind bars could not possibly injure him. It would all be as safe as for a cat to watch a caged mouse. His ostensible motive would be to beg some confession about what Arthur had done with the stolen one hundred and fifty thousand dollars — a motive that Chamberlain very strongly approved.

" By all means, my dear Slayton, do try to get some information from him on this point," old Chamberlain had said to him when he had mentioned his plan at the bank.

The bank, by the way, had long since fallen into all its old ruts of quietude and peace. New tiles now replaced the blood-stained ones where Mackenzie — already in process of being forgotten — had fallen. A new clerk occupied Arthur's desk. Already the crime was retreating into the background, becoming a tradition in the history of the institution.

" Do by all means add your efforts to all that has been done to get some trace of those missing funds," repeated Chamberlain. " So far, as you know, not the slightest clue has been discovered."

" Nothing whatever," answered the cashier, whose salary, by the way, had been materially increased because of his courage and his services to the bank at the time of the murder. " Nothing whatsoever, Mr. Chamberlain. Perhaps I may have better luck than the — professional investigators. At any rate, even though I fail, it is my manifest duty to try."

" Quite so," assented Chamberlain. " I must admit I'm badly disappointed in the Securitas Agency. It seems to have signally failed in this case."

" It does, indeed. I'm frank in telling you, Mr. Chamberlain, that I don't believe the money will ever be recovered unless Mansfield himself can be induced to reveal its whereabouts. Sharp, that boy was. Sharp, keen and clever. He must have hidden it somewhere in some extraordinarily secure place with the idea that he might yet escape and get it, or at least use it to buy some special favors — to have the case reopened or something of that sort."

"Very likely, very likely," muttered the old banker wearily. "A sad, bad affair all through. Well, do the best you can, Slayton. Do the very best you can. I know you will, without being told. Your duty and devotion to the bank have been beyond all criticism. Some day, I hope, the institution may suitably reward you."

He shook his head with dejection, while the cashier, his crafty eyes blinking behind his glasses, eyed him with great satisfaction. It seemed hard to believe Chamberlain could have aged so rapidly in a few short months. The loss to the bank, his grief at Arthur's crime, and worry over Enid's prostration had brought him low indeed.

"Go, by all means," reiterated the president, turning to his desk with a tired gesture. "Go, visit the unfortunate young man. Perhaps you can discover something. Point out to him that concealment can do him no good now, and that he can't expect to buy any favors whatever by offering the money as a bribe. Show him how the withholding of the sum in question is hampering the bank to a certain extent, and must, therefore, indirectly react upon Enid. Appeal to his sense of honor —"

Slayton laughed ironically.

"If he has any left," the old man continued. "Appeal to his regard for Enid, though I hate to think of her name being mentioned to him again and spoken in that terrible place. Try to reach him in some way.

"There must be something good left in the boy. God puts a little spark of the divine even in the most criminal

breast. You can possibly find it and kindle it to do a little
right after so much wrong. Go, do your best with him!"

He dismissed Slayton with a nod. The cashier, saying
no more, returned to his work. Next day he visited Sing
Sing.

CHAPTER XXII

IT was on Sunday, July 3, that Walter Slayton with guile and malice in his heart repaired to the huge gray place of pain beside the smiling river. A hundred millions of Americans that day were preparing to celebrate Liberty. Slayton, worn and fearful as he was, with boding thoughts of Jarboe ever in the background of his mind, none the less felt a real elation as he made ready to celebrate Servitude.

The thought of his victim, hived there in the vast, barren caravansary of anguish, brought a smile to his thin, straight lips as he came up the boardwalk near the prison. The grim entrance of the penitentiary filled him with exultation. Its very massiveness and all the ingenious safeguards thrown about the unhappy victims of an insane social system spoke to him of his own safety. Should Arthur ever go free, new and terrible perils would confront the cashier. But Arthur could never go free, and Jarboe was old — old — old! Arthur would remain buried alive, and Jarboe would die some time. In a few years at most all peril would be done forever. Patience and fortitude would win in spite of all.

Self-congratulations mingled in the cashier's mind with brutal anticipation at the prospect of being able to triumph over the boy, and subtly sneer at him and torture him from a safe vantage-point outside steel bars. Like all cowards, this man possessed vast depths of cruelty. His soul lusted for the joy of taking vengeance on the man he had immolated — vengeance for the attack there in the directors' room at the bank. Slayton had not forgotten that moment. He had not forgotten the strength and precision of Arthur's blow, and never would he forget.

Thus a baleful joy came into his eyes as he stopped a minute in the clear July sunshine, peered up squintingly at the gigantic steel-and-granite pile, and realized that one peril at last was buried forever and forever without end.

The sun sparkled on his patent-leather boots and on the silk top-hat he wore as he climbed the prison steps. It brought out the fine quality of his broadcloth coat and brightened the carnation in his buttonhole — the blossom whose fresh color contrasted so painfully with his claylike skin and lantern jaw.

Since the crime Slayton's outward aspect had improved — so far as dress could improve it. Despite his obvious falling off in health, he had now assumed a new importance. His prestige and his prospects, both increasing, had raised his social status. Could he be grooming for the presidency of the bank?

Thinner than ever though he now was and somewhat aged in aspect, as some said his grief over the boy's misconduct had made him, the cashier none the less presented a fine, dignified figure of a man as he entered the office of the Pen.

An automaton in uniform, to whom he stated his errand, respectfully asked him to sign the register and to be seated with some other visitors, all strained-looking and hushed and nervous. Two or three of that sad company on the benches were weeping, or had been. Nobody spoke a word. Presently a warder came in, dangling a ring with many keys, and nodded to Slayton. The cashier rose and followed.

Steel doors creaked to admit him to inner places that were reached only by dint of much unlocking. Slayton, hat in hand, blinked with real interest at the cement floor, the

stone walls, the guarding bars of steel — the kind of interest we all feel in prisons — the morbidity that whispers:

"What if *I* were here?"

Presently the warder ushered him into a reception-room
provided with a double grating down the middle. The
grills were six feet apart. A momentary illusion came
upon the cashier. He seemed to stand again in that grilled
corridor in the bank. Gloom shrouded everything. Before
him lay a prostrate and distorted figure — a figure whose
bleared, dead eyes stared up at him.

Swearing beneath his breath, Slayton recoiled. He felt
a touch upon his arm, whirled round, and clenched his fist.
The warder, saluting, looked at him with astonishment.

"What's the matter, sir?" he demanded.

"Oh, nothing, nothing! Here — thanks ever so much!"
And the cashier slid a " V " into the official's hand.

"I — I'm a bit agitated, that's all. Dear friend of mine,
very. He's coming soon?"

"Right here now, sir. Thank you, sir!"

He motioned toward the other side of the double grill.
Slayton, still badly shaken, peered through the cage. He
felt a certain tightening of the heart. His breath caught;
both hands clutched the steel netting.

Within, a convict was standing. A convict — *the* convict. The boy that he himself, Walter Slayton, had put
there for the term of his natural life.

At first Slayton could hardly recognize him. The clipped
head, the formless striped clothing, the wan and yellowed
face — already tinged with the unmistakable marks of prison
pallor — had changed Arthur almost beyond recognition.
Mental anguish, wretched food, lack of exercise, and the
deprivation of light and air had all taken their toll of him.

But his shoulders were still erect and strong. The fine,
broad brows had not altered. The wide-set eyes, though
sunken, were still the same. No, not quite — for now as

they peered out at Slayton, standing there immaculate and trim, they glowered with a light the cashier never yet had seen there — a smoldering flame eloquent of hate that nothing short of death could ever satisfy.

For a pregnant moment the two men gazed at each other, while the guard looked on with only an indifferent interest. Life for him held far too many such scenes for them to possess any meaning. The very air he breathed was blended with human tragedies and sorrows past all telling.

Arthur gave no sign and made no sound. He simply stood there at the inner grill, did Number 3265, his fingers hooked over the wires, peering out at Slayton with silent hate. Slayton coughed nervously and glanced about him. His eyes could not meet Arthur's.

"What do you want here?" asked the boy suddenly, his voice trembling a little.

"My duty — compels me —"

"Your — *Christian* duty, I suppose?"

"My duty to my fellow man, my brother in distress."

Arthur turned toward the warder.

"Have I got to listen to him?" he demanded. "On top of all I have to suffer here, have I got to see this fellow and hear his damnable hypocrisy?"

The guard shot him an ugly look. The "V" Slayton had so wisely slipped to him was potent.

"Cut it, cut it!" he retorted. "*You* ain't such a much to throw up a holler against nobody, much less him!"

Number 3265 made no answer, because he knew that nothing he could say would possess any weight. Once more he peered out at Slayton silently. There fell a strange, tense quietude between these enemies, now so unequally matched.

Slayton broke it.

"Arthur," said he in his most unctuous tones, "this is a most painful occasion, but highly necessary. It grieves me to the heart to see you here. But duty demands it. Where duty leads I follow. I am here to speak to you without animus or ill feeling.

"I cannot forgive you your crime. Only God can do that. But whatever wrong you have done me personally, whatever accusations you have made, and whatever violence you have inflicted on me, I can and do forgive."

Arthur laughed — a shuddering and terrible laugh.

"*You* — forgive — *me?*" he asked.

"I do," answered Slayton, feeling the sweat start on his forehead, though the air of that pest-hole hung dank and chilly despite the heat without. "Fully and freely I forgive you. But that's not what I've come to talk with you about, Arthur. I'm here to ask you reasonably and honestly to repair what damage you can, and to make good whatever can be made good now."

"What do you mean, Judas?" demanded Number 3265.

Slayton blinked angrily, as if about to repel the epithet, but thought better of it and made no retort. Instead, adopting a meek, conciliatory tone, he answered:

"I mean just this, Arthur: give back the money!"

"The — money?"

"Yes; the one hundred and fifty thousand dollars. You can't restore poor old Mackenzie to life again, but you can make restitution of the stolen funds. The bank has felt the loss, Arthur; no denying that. In spite of it," he could not refrain from adding, "the directors have materially increased my salary and bettered my prospects. I am grateful, naturally, for this recognition of my services at the time of the — er — tragedy. I want to do my duty by the institution. I owe the bank a great deal, Arthur; a very great deal —"

"You're damned well right you do! You owe it one hundred and fifty thousand dollars!"

Swiftly the words shot at him across the grilled space, winged bolts of hatred.

"Eh? What?" stammered Slayton, his lean face puckering strangely.

"I said," repeated Arthur, "that you owe the Powhatan National Bank one hundred and fifty thousand dollars. And I add that the man who killed Mackenzie with my gun is standing in front of me now. And on top of that, Slayton, I will tell you that, as God lives, I'm going to get out of here some day; and when I do — when I do — *look out!*"

Slayton, gasping, turned toward the warder.

"You hear him?" he demanded.

"Sure I hear him! He's woody — bugs, you know! Must be, to throw that kind o' bull. Maybe a touch o' the cooler might bring him out of it. He's liable to get it, all right."

Arthur laughed again.

"Put me in the cooler all you damned please," he retorted. "I'm giving you facts."

"Arthur!" cried Slayton, strangely shaken. "Your conduct surpasses every limit of tolerance. Mr. Chamberlain had intended to interest himself in your behalf, and so had I; but now —"

"Now you know that I know all about the inwardness of the case," interrupted the boy. "I've got the whole thing on you, Slayton. You got away with the money, you killed the old man, you framed me, and sent me up for life!

"Safe now, aren't you? Safe, with me 'buried'? Guess again! The story's not finished, Slayton. It's not done yet. There's going to be another chapter some of these days, and the ending will be different from anything you've doped out.

"I'll wait for it, Slayton! God! I'd wait fifty years to get my fingers on your windpipe! So now you know what's coming. I've said all I'm going to. Get out, and let me alone!"

The cashier, holding on to the outer grill to steady himself, made no immediate answer; but stood there, paler even than his victim, with a strange look in his eyes — those blinking eyes that never held true.

"Arthur," he managed to say at length, while the boy still fixed a look of most intense malignity upon him —" Arthur, my duty forces me to forgive you these slanders and overlook these threats. Nothing that you can say about me can matter in the least. Your idle vaporings are impotent to harm me. My only concern now is the recovery of those funds.

"I know your better judgment will not wish to see the bank hampered in any way, which must react upon — upon —"

"Not a word about her! Don't you dare to speak her name, you skunk!"

"— Upon Miss Chamberlain — Enid — as I was saying," persisted the cashier, smiling with cold malice. "Therefore, I beg you again, my dear boy, let us have the truth. Nothing can matter to you now. You are here, unfortunately, for life. You have done much evil. Do what good you can now; tell me where that money is."

Arthur pondered a moment, pressing his forehead to the grill. Slayton, meanwhile, regarded him with cold and cruel pleasure.

Suddenly the boy raised his head again.

"All right, Slayton! I'll tell you," he exclaimed, "if you'll promise to go then and get out of my sight — and not come back. Never come back here again; you understand?"

"You — you'll tell me?" demanded the cashier, surprised. "Ah, that's fine, my boy — that's fine! I knew you'd be reasonable. I knew you'd listen to argument!"

He smiled with a glint of teeth. Things were breaking well for him that day. Against all expectation Arthur was about to make a statement which would absolutely clinch the case and make Slayton's position forever secure. Just to get rid of him, thought the murderer, Arthur was willing to tell any falsehood, no matter how damaging to himself. Desperate and hopeless, he was about to drive the last nail in his own coffin.

"Where *is* the money, Arthur!" queried Slayton eagerly. "Where?"

"I don't know where *all* of it is," answered the boy in a peculiar, strained voice that shook a little, as if by main force he were holding it back from a raging outburst of passion. "I can't tell you where it *all* is. But I know about a part of it."

"Part will be better than none, Arthur. Tell me! Where is it?"

"Well," said Arthur slowly, "some of it has gone into those smart new clothes of yours, Slayton. Some of it is in your pocketbook there, I guess," and he jabbed a forefinger at the cashier. "Some you've probably salted away. And the rest has most likely gone to square up money-sharks and others that you must have got mixed up with before you made the break.

"Now you've got it, Slayton. You've got the answer. Keep your promise and get out of my sight! *Get — out!*"

Dazed by this smashing right-and-left attack, which crashed home on him with shattering force, Slayton stared for a long, silent minute at the boy's pallid face which showed through the grill, contracted in a grimace of hate and loathing.

Then, shaking his head, he turned to the guard.

"You hear that?" he queried. "No use talking to this man. He must be crazy!"

"Crazy is right! We'll soon cool him off, believe me!"

"No violence, I beg. The poor fellow's mind is affected. He needs kindness and attention."

The guard grinned significantly.

"That's our only treatment here, sir," he answered. "Kindness an' attention is Sing Sing's middle names!"

"Take me out, please. I've had enough."

"All right, sir. This way, please."

As the door of the reception-room opened to let Slayton out, the voice of Arthur snarled after him:

"Don't forget! You owe me something — something that I'm coming to collect, some day!"

CHAPTER XXIII

RIVERSIDE DRIVE AND SING SING

CHAMBERLAIN heard Slayton's report on the interview that evening with infinite sadness and regret. The cashier, greatly shaken by the clairvoyant precision of Arthur's accusations — most dangerous in their possibilities, even though as yet believed by nobody — and by the threat he well knew Arthur would try to carry out if ever the boy recovered liberty, returned to New York in a state of extreme depression. Only one thing stood clearly forth: Arthur must at all hazards be kept behind bars. Every attempt to win a pardon, now or in the distant future, must be undermined, combated and overthrown.

"You mean to say he refused to give any information concerning the stolen funds?" asked Chamberlain when he and the cashier had seated themselves with tobacco in the library of the president's house on Riverside Drive. "He wouldn't tell you anything?"

"Not a word; not a word."

"Hmmm! That's bad, very, very bad. I'm afraid the loss is going to be total. I was hoping he might be willing to make some partial atonement for his crime by restoring at least a part of the money."

"He isn't, and probably never will be willing to say a word. Perhaps it was a mistake to have me see him at all. He seems to entertain the most deep-seated antipathy to me. If you'd been able to go, perhaps —"

"No, no, no!"

And Chamberlain raised a negative hand.

"I'm sure I couldn't have done a thing with him. He knows I believe him guilty. He's probably figured that I've tried to turn Enid against him — which is perfectly true. I know he'd never talk to me. You, Slayton, have consistently befriended him. He owes you a debt of deepest gratitude. If he won't tell *you,* then the money's gone forever."

"I'm afraid you're right, Mr. Chamberlain. Very, very much afraid you're right. But don't, I beg you, talk of gratitude in connection with that fellow. He doesn't know the meaning of the word. Instead of being grateful to me he'd like to kill me if he could. I tell you, sir, there's a hard, vicious type for you. An old, evil head on young shoulders.

"If ever a man got what he deserved it's Mansfield. Nothing saved me from assault and probably murder to-day except a steel grill-work between us. You know how he struck me down at the bank. Well, he'd have killed me this morning right there in the prison if he could have got at me. There's the man you used to receive into your home, Mr. Chamberlain. There's the man your daughter's still defending!"

"Dear, dear, dear!" exclaimed the banker, much agitated. "How very distressing! You say he threatened you?"

"Absolutely! He swore to kill me if he ever could manage to get out."

"What? You don't say!"

"I *do* say! I can prove every word of it by the guard who stood beside me during the whole interview. The fellow got so abusive I had to withdraw."

"*Ts, ts, ts!*" chuckled Chamberlain with his tongue. "This certainly puts a still worse light on the whole matter."

He drew at his cigar and gazed on the cashier with wrinkled brows.

"Hmmm! What a viper I did cherish in my bosom, so to

speak! I'm afraid we've all been very grievously deceived in Mansfield from the very beginning."

"Deceived isn't the word for it, Mr. Chamberlain. The man is a criminal from the word go. His father was a crook before him. He's of bad stock. Rotten, clean through."

"Yes, yes; of course. Odd, though, how clean and fine he managed to appear."

"A finished criminal; very smooth, that's all," said Slayton. "One of the slickest propositions alive. In a way perhaps you got out of it cheaply. If he hadn't made this break and got caught he'd have gone on and on deceiving you. He'd have inevitably continued hoodwinking your daughter. He'd have induced her to marry him.

"Then he'd have entangled you in ways too vast for imagination. He might have entirely wrecked the bank and got away with a million or two. And if you'd stood in his way he'd have shot you down like a dog — or maybe given you the more subtle treatment of a slow poison in your own house."

"Quite likely," assented the banker. "Well, Slayton, there's a silver lining in every cloud. There's good in every evil. Perhaps this tragedy, after all, is for the best. Maybe it's saved the bank from destruction, spared my life and rescued Enid from a life of anguish and appalling disgrace."

"I'm sure of it," said the cashier, gazing at the smoke of his cigar. "It's all for the best. It's shown us the duplicity of human nature. It's given us a chance to do our Christian duty. Hard as it's been for all of us, especially you —"

"It has been hard, Slayton!" interrupted the president, his eyes watering with sudden emotion — for senility was creeping fast upon him. "This affair has taken hold more deeply on me than I can possibly tell you. Especially Enid's sorrow and her uncompromising attitude of blind faith in that scoundrel. Her —"

"You don't mean to tell me she still clings to him?" demanded Slayton, leaning forward with mock surprise.

The fact was perfectly well known to him; but it suited his purpose to pretend ignorance thereof.

"I'm afraid she does," admitted Chamberlain.

"In spite of everything? All these oceans of proof?"

"In spite of everything. Nothing has had the slightest weight with her. Not even what you've just told me would have any effect, I'm sure. She's formed a certain heroic concept of him that nothing can change — nothing whatsoever. Looks upon him as a martyr, a victim of some kind of a plot; has all kinds of fantastical vapors and ideas, you know."

He spread his trembling hands, palms outward, in despair.

"You don't tell me!" wondered Slayton with arch-hypocrisy.

"Yes, yes; it's the truth. Women are like that, you know, at times. They get an idea and worry it to death; hang on like a bulldog; nothing can ever make them let go. Enid is absolutely obsessed by her belief in Mansfield.

"And what can I do about it? Nothing, sir; absolutely nothing. She's of age; has her own independent fortune; is a free agent. I can advise, plead, appeal; but beyond that — nothing."

"Very unfortunate, I'm sure," agreed the cashier. "Too bad she's not a minor."

"Too bad, indeed. But she isn't, and I'm helpless."

The old man looked it indeed as he sat there in the huge leather chair, sucking feebly at his cigar.

"I've tried to get her to go South or West or over to Europe, but she won't stir. In spite of the fact that she's got downright nervous prostration and is a sick woman she still remains here. Clings to some sort of idea that somehow in one way or another something may yet turn up to free Mansfield. And —"

"God forbid!" exclaimed Slayton, starting.

"Claims the 'conspiracy' will yet break down, and — and all kinds of notions of that sort, you understand. I don't know, Slayton; I don't know what to do, indeed I don't."

He relapsed into silence. For a moment or two the men smoked, vis-à-vis across the library table, each peering at the other. Old Chamberlain shook his white mane despondently. His face, now much more deeply wrinkled than it had been six months before, drooped impotently. Slayton enjoyed the glister of tears in the old man's eyes. A keen, hard, malicious look of calculation came into his own.

He was thinking:

"Chamberlain can't last long at this rate: Even if he doesn't die he'll have to retire. I don't give him five years more at the outside. And then — a new president! Why not Walter Haynes Slayton?"

Slayton's terror of old Jarboe had probably caused him more acute suffering than any Chamberlain had experienced. Then, too, the cashier's continued thefts to meet the Shylock's demands had given him many a sleepless night, taken flesh from his bones, and put wrinkles in his face. Yet after all Slayton was a young man and could stand the gaff infinitely better than Chamberlain.

Fate might yet be kind. It might strike down Chamberlain and exalt Slayton. And once in the president's chair, Jarboe's leechings would no longer be serious — unless, indeed (the chill dread sometimes came upon Slayton), the blackmailer should raise his "insurance-rates" to meet the rise in salary.

All this and more passed through his mind as he sat facing the old man, smoking there in the library. And again the thought recurred:

"Jarboe is very old. Jarboe will die before long. The real and vital danger is Mansfield!"

Mansfield, at all hazards, must be kept in durance. Only through one agency might he ever be set free — and that was Enid.

Enid, then, at last analysis constituted Slayton's greatest peril. His prehensile mind, grasping this fact, turned it and analyzed it with a precision. Something must be done at once to forestall any continued action on the girl's part in Arthur's behalf. In some way, at all hazards, her mind must be poisoned against him.

But how?

The answer came to him not half a second later than the question. Through Dr. Nelson the thing could be accomplished — Nelson, the medical assistant who had helped Coroner Roadstrand make the preliminary examination of Mackenzie's body; Nelson, whose cold, unimpassioned, scientific testimony had sealed the boy's fate.

Dr. Nelson, if anybody in the world could do it, would be able to convince Enid that Arthur was a murderer. Not in an hour, not in a day or a week or a month perhaps; but eventually. Once he could be brought in contact with her as her physician, the result was bound to follow.

The solution of the problem dawned on the cashier like a veritable inspiration. Involuntarily he slapped his lean hand on his knee.

Startled, Chamberlain looked up.

"Eh, what?" he asked.

"The consummate villain!" ejaculated Slayton indignantly. "If he had his just deserts he'd have gone to the electric chair!"

The old man nodded melancholy assent. Gradually a new conversation knit itself between them sporadically, Slayton leading Chamberlain deftly whither he would. It lasted more than an hour before Slayton — having even more securely fortified his position and improved his prospects — sensed that Chamberlain was growing weary, and took his leave.

Bit by bit he knew the old man was coming to lean more and more upon him. Bit by bit he knew his power was extending itself, increasing, deepening. And inwardly he smiled with evil satisfaction.

Many things he knew; but one thing he did not know — that Enid, standing tense and eager behind the brocaded portière between the library and the music-room, had keenly followed every word of the long conversation, and that new thoughts had come to her, fresh hopes been born, new suspicions wakened in her loyal and untiring heart.

Summer faded into fall, and fall died into winter; and a year had worn itself away since Grossmith's words of judgment had fallen on the ears of Arthur Mansfield, now metamorphosed into Number 3265.

Far worse, now, his condition had grown than it had been in the beginning. At first he had at least occupied a cell by himself in the cell-house, a huge stone building five hundred feet long and forty-four wide, with walls three feet thick. These walls pierced only by tiny windows and by iron gratings twenty-five feet apart, were always beaded with moisture. The place was a Gehenna; and yet the luxury of having a separate cell had at first been Mansfield's. In the Pit, even a slight cessation of anguish seems a pleasure.

The cell-block itself, built inside the cell-house — a vast series of 1200 cages, back to back in tiers of two hundred each — was wholly deprived of fresh air or sunlight. The ground-floor cells opened onto a flagstone corridor; those on the five upper tiers gave onto narrow wooden galleries. Everything was dank, wet and malodorous. As a prison, Arthur soon discovered that Sing Sing justified the common saying: "A joke by day and a Hell by night."

Some hidden, malign influence emanating from Slayton had got him assigned to a cell on "the flats," as the lowest tier was known in the prison slang. Here germ-infested dust from sweeping, above, sifted down; and the dampness was far worse than in the higher tiers. The cell-house was built very low, directly on the ground near the river — the River of All Hopes — and its walls showed a distinct water-mark, four feet from the floor. To that height the moisture had been absorbed by the old building, which in all its lower parts was slimy and mouldering. Rheumatism therefore came to nearly all the convicts, as a free gift from the State — together with some other maladies far less desirable.

None the less, as I have said, Number 3265 at first en-joyed the unusual luxury of a cell all alone. The tiny cubi-cle of undressed stone, so damp that he could wet his hand at any time by drawing it over the surface, was at least all his. Through the forty-two small openings in the grated door very little air filtered, and such as came in was fetid as that in a charnel-house; yet for a time, all of it was his. The small circular vent at the rear of the cell, supposed to communicate through a chimney arrangement with the attic of the cell-house for ventilating purposes, but really almost clogged with dust and serving mostly as a breeding-place for vermin, drew little or no foul air from the cell; but at any rate Number 3265 in the beginning got all the slight benefit of this arrangement. The little bucket of stale water, the grimy drinking-cup, the dust-impregnated vege-table-fibre mattress on its gas-pipe frame all were his; and he could read, undisturbed, could move about a little, and could write without interruption.

Toward the middle of January, however, his windowless "hole-in-the-wall," unfit for an animal to lair in, was in-vaded by a square-headed blue-jawed "gopher-man" or yegg. This convict, having killed a man in his last "crush," had (like Number 3265) got "track 13 and a washout," that is to say, a life-sentence. The Warden had assigned him to Cell 46, with Number 3265. Arthur Mansfield, loving everything clean, had now become one of the 1300 unfortunates forced to "double up" at Sing Sing. His real torture now began in earnest.

They let down the upper bunk, only thirty inches above Arthur's, and they installed the big-jawed beast with him. Thereafter there was no slightest measure of privacy, peace, comfort, decency. Arthur's ears had to hear every conceivable atrocity of crime and vice, every vile suggestion, every revolting and degrading thing the murderer's bestial mind could conceive. After some days of this it was that he determined he would die rather than submit to such a life. They could kill him, if they would, but he would get away — living or dead — from contact with that monstrous degenerate.

The new-comer was not only a "coker"— a cocaine-victim — of the worst type, but was also afflicted with tuberculosis, which Arthur knew he was bound to contract in time, despite his greatest care. Yes, they had shut a man with T.B. into that narrow, unventilated place with him, and had not even given him a separate cup or water-pail. Arthur's very soul sickened. His underfed body, too, would sicken soon, no matter how hard he might work to keep his health.

The yegg soon proved to be a "rat," as well; that is to say, an informer who for dope or other favors, or possibly with the ultimate hope of a "life-boat" (a pardon), was eager to curry favor with the "screws" by snitching.

Arthur's every word of protest was transformed by him into mutiny; his every aspiration was metamorphosed into stiff-necked insubordination; his every hope changed to conspiracies and plottings.

Thus three weeks passed, and Arthur felt a berserker rage gaining possession of him. Sometime, he knew, if that animal were kept with him, he would really do murder — an act of virtue, if ever one were virtuous in this world. Sometime, with some rude weapon he could fashion, or with his naked hands, he would slay the degraded moron whom the authorities had forced upon him.

And then they would electrocute him. The convicts would all be locked in their cells that day. None would find the consolation of toil. None would " do their separates," as exercise was called. Those in authority would shut him up in the death-house, amid all that human agony; and at an hour of silence through all the hideous place, when even the most hardened would weep and pray, crouching on the flagged floor, they would march him through the little door — to liberty!

The "wail of impotent despair" that would swell from near two thousand throats would be his requiem, as his soul was seared from the crackling flesh. At last he would be free!

The scene came to dwell insistently with him. Only a week or so before, three men — two whites and a " Jap," as the underworld calls a negro — had gone " up the escape," and Number 3265 had heard that wail. Silent, he too had prayed; though why, he could not have told. In a way he found satisfaction in dwelling on the electric chair. At last resort, *there* was a way out. Had it not been for his mother, for Enid, and — now coming to be terribly potent — the hope of sometime feeling his fingers close on Slayton's throat, he might perhaps have chosen that way.

But desperation had not yet reached its limit. Unwisely, Number 3265 decided to apply for a change of cell. He might possibly get one by himself again. At any rate, even should the new one have an inmate, he could not possibly be so foul as the yegg.

The " flats," Arthur knew, were largely reserved for what in Sing Sing are called " bad actors," or cripples who cannot climb the ladder steps leading from one tier to another.

Number 3265 was still strong and active. With some show of excuse he might make bold to apply for a cell on the extreme upper tier, more free from dust and moisture. This, then, he finally decided to do.

His application was made on February 16th, respectfully and in proper form. Its results were immediate, and twofold. First, it was refused. Second, Number 3265 was "stood out."

"Stood out" means punished. Arthur had now marked himself for retribution. Never having snitched or bribed the screws, he had become a *persona non grata*. The yegg, his cell-mate, had also fastened an evil reputation on him — the most evil of all prison-reputations: that of refusing to toady, to spy, to sink to the beast-level of the lowest.

Then, too, Arthur's threats against Slayton, in the reception-room, had been laid up against him. Those threats had at the time brought him only a warning. He had been spared the "cooler." Now, this punishment was upon him.

Arthur was locked in his cell next morning and kept from the shoe-shop. At ten o'clock he was taken to the warden's office to be judged by the warden's court, consisting of the warden, the chief keeper and the doctor. Charges of insubordination were read to him and he was asked to reply. Two minutes later he was furiously bidden to "shut his damned mouth." Sentence of the cooler was passed upon him and he was led away to torture.

Do you know what the cooler is, at Sing Sing? If not, hearken.

The cooler is a dungeon into which sunlight never penetrates. It has two doors, tight-fitting lest light and air reach the victim. The inner door is steel, the outer wood. Absolute darkness reigns in that fetid, damp and stenchful oubliette. Through the wooden door two covered slits are pierced, to let in just enough air so that the victim shall not stifle to death.

Into this place, then, they flung Arthur Mansfield, and there for three days they kept him, one of eight men similarly punished. Sing Sing has eight coolers; they are almost always full. Night ceases to exist there, as distinguished from day. Arthur slept, woke and slept again, but with no idea of time. His only bed was the cold stone flagging, damp and foul with nameless filth. His only food was handed in once a day: a slice of stale bread weighing ten ounces, and about three-quarters of a glass of water. This just sufficed to keep the boy alive and at the same time produced the most exquisite suffering from thirst.

Numbers of men have gone insane in the cooler, and some have attempted suicide. A normal man requires fifty ounces of water a day. The victims of the cooler get a scant eight ounces. Not a few cases of death have been recorded from this kind of reformation given by the Empire State to its unfortunates or its criminals.

Arthur did not die, attempt suicide or go insane. He emerged from the oubliette far thinner, weaker — and wiser. He returned to his cell, to the " coker," to silence.

Whatever might happen, now, he would never open his lips again. He had learned the prime lesson that no convict, no matter how deeply wronged, has any rights that any prison-guard or officer, trusty or stool-pigeon, no matter how debased, need respect.

He had long since lost all hope of justice being done him. Every legal means for obtaining his release had been tried by his friends. There remained only extra-legal means. These Arthur meant to try by himself.

In his soul was burning, burning more brightly than ever, the one consuming flame, the passion for escape.

Escape — either in the flesh or in the spirit. Either out of that Hell, alive, or out of it dead.

The end was drawing close. Number 3265 had deter-

mined to go free. For he knew now — and, knowing,
would not tolerate it longer —

> That every prison that men build
> Is built with bricks of shame,
> And bound with bars, lest Christ should see
> How men their brothers maim.
>
> The vilest deeds, like poison weeds,
> Bloom well in prison air.
> It is only what is good in man
> That wastes and withers there,
> Pale Anguish keeps the heavy gates,
> And the Warder is Despair.
>
> With bars they blur the gracious moon
> ' And blind the goodly sun,
> And they do well to hide their hell,
> For in it things are done
> That Son of God nor son of man
> Ever should look upon!

CHAPTER XXIV

THE GETAWAY

NOVEMBER once again. Just such another night once more as that frosty, moonlit one, two years before, when Mansfield had sought the Judas help and friendship of Walter Slayton and when old man Mackenzie had fallen with Slayton's bullet in his brain.

Just such another night; and yet how much had come to pass since then! How very much was coming to fulfilment in the swift spate of events!

The minotaur bellowing of the penitentiary siren, hurling its echoes against the high banks of the railway-cutting to eastward and far to the west over the sliding floor of the Hudson's big waters, screamed its warning and its menace to the whole countryside. It startled the slumbers of many a sleeping village up and down the river. Timid people shuddered in their beds or made doubly sure all doors and windows were carefully locked.

Already the news was spreading everywhere by telephone and telegraph. Already the net was reaching out. But the siren gave the alarm vocal expression, flung it to the winds, and shrieked into the November night:

"*Convict escaped!*"

Just where the river narrows somewhat opposite the stern gray walls of the penitentiary, a man was dragging himself more dead than alive out of the chill black waters that sparkled so eerily in the moonlight.

As his numb, bare feet touched the pebbled bottom of the

west bank he staggered forward, fell splashing on hands and knees, and then sank exhausted with only his head out of the water. There he lay a few minutes, panting. Just his white face showed, ghostly in the wan, changing light that waxed, that waned, as scudding clouds revealed and then obscured the burnished disk of silver in the black and frosty sky.

Presently, with reviving strength, he made another effort and succeeded in dragging himself up over the boulders, through the alders that fringed the stream, and so into a clump of bushes, where he once more fell inert and nerveless.

There he lay shivering, absolutely spent, but free, free, free! Coatless and bareheaded he lay, clad only in striped gray-and-black trousers and a woolen shirt. Around his neck, held by their knotted cords, hung a pair of coarse, heavy prison shoes. Sodden with drizzling water, shaken by agonizing chills, he could make no further effort for a while. To be still alive, alive and outside the walls of Sing Sing — that was enough.

After a certain time the man roused up a little and began to take note of his environment. He peered about him in the cold, hard moonlight that filtered down through the network of leafless branches all about and over him.

" Made it, by God! didn't I? " he muttered.

As if reaching out to lash him back into servitude and horror, the flails of the siren struck his senses. He smiled bitterly and spat toward the far prison.

" Blow and be damned to you! " he gibed. " You can burst your boilers blowing, but you'll never get me back there alive! "

Arthur Mansfield, heartened by this thought, found that in spite of his extreme exhaustion and the biting chill in the air his forces were returning. His body was still hard and strong. No excesses had ever sapped his great natural vigor. Though far below his normal condition he still had reserves of latent strength to call on. Even after the terrific struggle that had landed him on the west bank of the river a mile down-stream from the Pen, he felt he still had force to get up again soon and fight his way along.

Peering through the bushes, he carefully observed the river and the eastern shore, took note of his surroundings, and began laying plans for the next step toward complete liberty.

Far across the liquid barrier glimmered the lights of Ossining. Dominating them a searchlight whipped impatiently across the flood. A few little sparks were moving on the black waters. Mansfield smiled contemptuously. Not with search-lights or with motor-boats would they ever find him now!

The first step, the hardest step of all, had successfully been taken. It had come sooner than he had quite expected, but he had recognized the opportunity and had grasped it; nothing simpler.

He smiled at thought of all the excitement that had exploded in the penitentiary when the ash-gang had been locked in. Eighteen men in stripes had loaded the scow. Only seventeen had gone back from the wharf. The eighteenth had seen the moment's chance, had slid noiselessly into the water, crawled under the piling, and there had left his hampering coat of woolen stuff. The early winter dark had favored him.

Before the alarm had been given he had been half way across, swimming strongly with his shoes slung about his neck. The simplicity of the thing had given him tremendous satisfaction, to add to the wild, maddening exultation of being once more — at last! — outside the numbing walls of granite, free, free, free!

That had been a fearful swim; the latter part of it a frantic fight for life itself in the inky, freezing waters, which he had lashed to foam with gasping struggles to keep the pin-pricked stars and sliding moon in sight.   Toward the end desperation alone had sustained him.   He had given himself up for lost; but even in that supreme moment the dominant thought had been:

"Liberty!"

Enid had come as a transitory image; and his mother too —now dead a year and resting from her sorrows; but neither of these had usurped that one wild surge of exulta-tion:

"*Liberty!*"

Let death come now if come it must.   It would not at any rate find him in prison walls.   It would be out there under the sky, out in the free wind and water, merciful and well-beloved.

Then he had sunk — had struggled up again and thrashed his way along blindly, gasping and choking but game to the end — and all at once his feet had touched the boulders of the shelving shore.

Arthur dismissed the struggle from his mind, and put the prison all away as though beneath contempt.   He peered about him, rising on hands and knees to make reconnaissance of his present situation.   So far as he could see, no sign of human life or habitation was visible on the west shore. His entire prospect on the landward side of his clump of bushes was a sparse tract of woodland — birches, maples, and a few poplars, sloping gradually up away from the river.

No sign of man.   And yet Arthur understood perfectly well that he was now in a rather densely populated section of New York State, networked with roads and wires, dotted with towns, villages and hamlets, highly organized for the pursuit and capture of just such fugitives as he — a dan-gerous locality, in short, far more perilous in all its seeming wildness than the crowded thoroughfares of New York City.

Arthur took counsel with himself. His plan so far had been successful. What next? Having reached the west shore of the river somewhere in the vicinity of Rockland Lake, what must yet be done to bring him to Staten Island, to Oakwood Heights, to the house of Walter Slayton, to the payment of the one great debt that he had sworn must and should be paid at once — at once, before any evil chance might possibly take from him all hopes of ever being able to pay it?

What was to be done?

Arthur pondered. His present equipment was most inadequate for traveling. In those striped trousers and that flannel shirt he could not hope to reach his goal. Wet through and chilled to the bone, cold alone would defeat him even did not arrest threaten him at every point.

And yet he had no change of clothing. No accomplice outside of the prison had cached a handy bundle of raiment, as in the story-books. Such things always happened most conveniently in novels; but this was stern reality.

Arthur Mansfield now found himself shivering and freezing in a thicket by the river-bank, on a frosty night of late November. The prospect was appalling. Yet his plan stood firm. His overmastering passion — revenge on Slayton — did not waver for a second. Long ago he had given up every hope of rehabilitating himself, of ever seeing Enid again, of ever reëntering the ranks of society as a normal man. Even to approach the girl would now be fatal. Identified, he would be instantly seized and rushed back to that living death, that Inferno whose lights now flailed the river, searching for him. Reincarcerated, terrible punishments would be meted out to him. He would be placed under special restraints and forever lose all hope either of pardon or escape again.

No! Come what might he must remain for all time a hidden, lurking, fleeing creature. Never again could he re-appear as Arthur Mansfield. Disguises, ruses, flight might save him. Sufficient ingenuity and skill might keep him free. But it must be only as a vagabond, a hunted thing. Arthur Mansfield was dead. Another man was born in his place — another man: Number 3265, Escaped.

That man would live and die in the open. Living, he would never reënter Sing Sing. With an oath Mansfield once more affirmed that determination. It steeled him against all contingencies. And beside it stood another — Slayton's death. That too was fully determined. Now that he was a fleeing fugitive, with "Murderer" written against his name, nothing remained to deter him from ex-acting with his own hands the justice that society had de-nied him. Swiftly he would take full payment for old Mackenzie's death and for the irreparable wrong Slayton had wrought on him.

Arthur put on his shoes, stood up, and peered about him, still shivering. He saw nothing but woods to westward. Yet there, he knew, ran the West Shore Railroad, not very far away, his only hope of reaching Jersey City, Elizabeth and Staten Island. His location was quite clear to him. Under a guise of studying geography in the prison he had long pored over maps of New York State and New Jersey; and as if photographed on his mind he could behold the exact lay of the land.

To east of him spread the reaches of Tappan See. Two miles to westward was the railroad. But no station on that line lay nearer than Haverstraw, ten miles north, or Or-angeburg, twelve miles south. Between stations he could not hope to jump a freight. So far as the main line was concerned there was "nothing doing."

On the Nyack branch, however, Nyack itself — the ter-minus — lay only three miles down the river. The place would certainly be warned and watch would be kept for him; but it was his only opportunity. By holding through the woods or striking into the road he knew must be a little distance west of him, he could not miss the town. Darkness favoring, he might possibly raid some house or store for clothing and find the friendly shelter of a box-car. A desperate chance indeed — but his only one.

Arthur, peering intently, advanced slowly through the thicket down-stream. Everything spoke of calm, peace and quietude — everything save that infernal bellowing of the siren, echoing across the bosom of the river. No breeze stirred the black and leafless twigs and branches of the wood. A little crisp snow crunched here and there underfoot. The moon, more obscured by thickening clouds, now showed only as a bright blur in the heavens, once and again glimpsing forth only to be quickly hidden by the drifting vapors that, moved by some current high in air, lagged toward the open sea. A light or two moved silently on the waters; and far away, mirrored in long lines, other lights from the habitations of men at peace, men unafraid, not hunted like wild animals, vaguely streaked the surface.

A far whistle caught Arthur's ear. He stopped, looked, saw a speeding string of little bright dots — a train, rushing down the east shore to New York.

"That'll be in New York in an hour or less," he pondered with bitterness. "I wonder if I'll ever be?"

The thought infused fresh energy into his shaking body and chilled heart. Yes, by Heaven! He *would* make his goal — Staten Island — if it cost him his life! With new strength and courage, though with the most extreme caution, he once more crept forward.

Some few minutes he thus made his way through the forest. Still nothing threatened. At this rate, he felt, inside of an hour he would come upon the cleared land, the farms, the outlying suburbs he knew must fringe the town.

By seeking a road to westward he could advance much
faster; but caution held him to the woods. Every country
road and lane might already be guarded. They were all
bound to present greater dangers than the forest. Lacking
any confederate to pick him up in a motor-car or in a launch
and hurry him away to safety, he must depend on his own
wits and energy.

He still had many hours of night ahead of him. The cold
was numbing his very heart, but somehow he did not mind
it much. The fires of his purpose and his hate kept him
warm. And the intensity of his listening, peering through
the gloom, watching for every sound or sign of discovery,
prevented him from dwelling on his physical distress.

Thus Arthur advanced. Twenty minutes passed — half
an hour perhaps. Silence reigned. The blaring of the
prison siren had stopped, its cessation seeming to leave a
vast, grateful emptiness in the night.

Arthur felt much stronger now, and more confident.
Even the moderate exercise of moving through the wood
had warmed his chilled blood. Hope of success began to
loom big in front of him. Yes, surely he would make
Staten Island; he would come to grips with Slayton; he
would drink his fill of justice. After that — what could
anything matter?

Suddenly he stopped. Ahead of him, vague, dim and
black, loomed something through the trees.

A house, was it? Yes; certainly a house.

Inhabited? No telling. Arthur crouched down amid the
bushes, peering, listening, spying. Not a sound, No light.
No sign of any life.

After a while the fugitive crawled forward slowly on
hands and knees through the snow, through the dead, dried
ferns and crackling weeds and bushes. Every few feet he
stopped to harken and to watch. But still nothing seemed
to threaten. And thus, after a pretty long time, he came

close up to the building and recognized quite surely that it was abandoned of men.

Cautiously he crept about it, inspecting it from all sides by the uncertain light of the moon, now very wan and dim. It seemed a kind of rough shack somewhat in disrepair, set down in the woods about two hundred yards from the river. In front of it the trees had been cleared away. At the rear a path led to westward, probably to a, road. The windows were all closely shuttered; but on one side one of these shutters had been pried loose, as if the place had been entered through the window.

Arthur pondered.

"This place is evidently some kind of a hunting or fishing-camp," thought he. "Probably it hasn't been used for a good while. Surely there can be no danger here. Things seem to be coming my way."

A few minutes later, he was inside the shack. The place smelled damp and musty. A penetrating chill pervaded it, worse even than the cold of the open air. Save for a dim gray rectangle where the blind had been thrown back, absolute darkness shrouded the room in which Arthur stood.

Groping, he explored. His heart beat rather fast; he breathed through his mouth as men will do under stress; his eyes, opened wide, sought to pierce the gloom. No telling what peril might at any moment face him, unarmed as he was, and alone.

The place contained little save some common furniture, a stove and a shelf with tin dishes. One, knocked down by his hand, clattered terribly on the floor, giving him a terrific start. For some time afterward he dared not move or even breathe deeply; but no harm had been done. Nothing happened. Nobody had heard the noise out there in the woods. Arthur, realizing the isolation of the place, felt vastly relieved and now proceeded with greater confidence.

Could he find food there? Clothes? Anything of value?

He would have given a great deal for even one match; but matches there were none to be found. A tin lamp without a chimney stood on the shelf with the dishes, and this, he found by shaking it, was half full of oil; but it only mocked him. Arthur, shivering there in the dark and cold, cursed the lamp and set it back on the shelf.

He explored everything for eatables, but discovered nothing. There were, however, some dirty dishes on the table, a carving-knife with a nicked blade and a kettle on the stove with the remnants of some kind of porridge dried on to the bottom. Evidently food had been prepared and eaten here by somebody who had not taken the trouble to clean up afterward.

Mansfield made another round of the shack. On the walls he discovered fishpoles and tackle, supported by nails. He came upon a door, opened it, and found another and even darker room. This on examination by his only possible means — his hands — turned out to be a sleeping-place. Two cots stood here with tumbled bedding half on the floor. Arthur's hopes revived. There might be clothing here, after all!

Eagerly he investigated. He presently found a row of nails driven into the wall, but they were bare. His heart sank. Ill luck was surely dogging him. The tenth-rate sportsmen who evidently had used this place might at least have left some old clothes for him. He included them in the malediction he had cast upon the lamp.

Moving away from these disappointing nails, he trod on something soft. He stooped, picked up the thing, and felt of it with intense eagerness. His joy in recognizing the object surpassed almost any in his entire life. It was a coat!

Shaking with eagerness and shivering with cold, he returned to the window of the other room, and by the dim light from without examined the coat. It was a wreck, a ruin, tattered and torn; but still it was a coat! Arthur praised "whatever gods there be," and slipped the welcome rags upon his back. Then he hurried into the other room for more — if more there were.

Again Fortune favored him. In a corner he found a pair of trousers. Groping on hands and knees, he discovered this priceless boon. The trousers were worse than the coat; but at any rate they were not striped with the black and gray of penal servitude. Lying close beside them was a greasy derby with liberal ventilation through the crown. Arthur crammed it upon his clipped head and laughed for joy.

He understood now the pried-open shutter, the remnants of mush in the kettle, the cast-off clothes and the absence of any better ones.

"God bless the hobo that camped here!" he exclaimed with inexpressible gratitude.

CHAPTER XXV

FOUR-AND-TWENTY hours later, in the library of Walter Slayton's house at Oakwood Heights, Staten Island, the last act in the cashier's life was coming to its culmination.

Seated at his desk, haggard, wan, and grim, the man was writing. A great silence reigned. No sound was audible save the ticking of the clock upon the mantel and the scratching of the nervous pen.

In front of him lay a tin box containing the gray wig he had worn when he had murdered old Mackenzie, and an automatic pistol. A close observer would have seen it was the very same weapon which, two years before, had sent the bullet crashing through Mackenzie's skull. Dr. Nelson after the trial had kept it as a gift from Roadstrand. Slayton had been instrumental in having Nelson called in consultation on the case of Enid Chamberlain. The case had proved most lucrative. Nothing more natural, then, than that the doctor had been willing to grant so slight a request as that of Slayton when he had asked for the automatic. Now there it lay in front of him on the desk, blunt, competent and businesslike.

Slayton eyed it from time to time in pauses of his writing. Once he smiled. The sight of it seemed good in his sunken eyes. Maybe it brought him thoughts of rest and peace after two years of torture so acute that nothing in Hell's pit could equal it — who knows?

" Midnight," said he, nodding. " Midnight will be the

time. I've got half an hour yet.   Time enough to finish!
Time enough!"

Then he went on writing.   Carefully he wrote and well,
weighing his words, making here a change, there an erasure.
Under the vertical light from the hooded incandescent the
ravages that fear and evil-doing had wrought in his face
became terribly apparent.   For months now, every time
darkness had surrounded him, the dead eyes of old man
Mackenzie had seemed to stare at him, half open, glazed,
hideous as he had seen them there that night in the bank by
the light of the little electric flash-lamp that had fallen from
the dead man's hand.

For months he had not dared sleep in a dark room.
Feigning the nervous affliction known as *skiaphobia,* in
which a patient dreads the dark, he had had a tiny incandescent night-light installed beside his bed; and always its
burning filament had banished the fishy eyes of Mackenzie.

Almost always — not quite.   A few times those eyes had
looked at him even in the light.   They were most apt to
lurk in corners, in dim corridors, in unexpected places, suddenly appearing — not reproachful, not angry, merely looking at him.

Slayton had been obliged to avoid going out at night on
account of them.   He had come to dread the walk from the
station to his home of an evening.   Certain peculiarities of
his conduct, forced upon him by those eyes, had even
started a bit of gossip going; not much, but still a little.
Slayton was coming to be known as eccentric.   Nobody
understood it but himself.   Nobody else knew the truth —
incipient madness.

Those eyes and old Jarboe's houndings — had they not
been enough to drive any man mad ten times over?   No,
it was not conscience that had ravaged Slayton in those two
years.   He felt no very deep pangs of regret.   A little, but
not much.

The determining factor was and had always been fear — fear of exposure, fear of Jarboe's increasing extortions, fear of the Shylock's threats, fear of consequences in a few years at the outside in case Jarboe should not die and Slayton's continued thefts should be — must be — discovered. Fear of all these and other things; and, above all, fear of the dead man's eyes.

Slayton smiled grimly, nodding as he read what he had written. Something in his nature, some latent vanity perhaps, certainly a cynical quality of mind, perceived the tremendous sensation he was about to produce. The fact that he had misled and deceived a whole community, a State, one might almost say a nation — for the case had attained some national prominence — and that he had set law and justice by the ears, hoodwinked authority and conceived and carried out one of the most plausible hoaxes ever known, gave him a certain desperate satisfaction. Now, even in the face of death, he smiled.

" It was a big game while it lasted," he muttered. " And, now it's done, it's going to make a damned big sensation ! "

Everything had befallen as he had planned it — everything save Jarboe's interference. Except for the accident of the wig, even that would not have come to pass. Well, that had been a scurvy jest of fate. Those six gray hairs clutched in Mackenzie's dead hand had beaten him after all — those, and Jarboe's infernal intelligence.

He had played the game hard. He had found it not worth the candle. Sooner or later, he knew, he must go quite insane under the various stresses. That would mean loss of mastery of the situation. Slayton intended to be master at all hazards.

There was only one way out, and he would take it. For that purpose he had sent his wife away. For that he had written the pages there before him on the desk. For that he had taken the automatic from its place in the top drawer of his chiffonier.

Despite all his cynicism, and all the cold-blooded, unemotional aplomb which constituted the keynote of his whole character, he could not now in this supreme moment put away the sick and gnawing fear that moment by moment was besieging his soul. His eyes, hollow and blinking, followed the closely written lines of the letter — the last he ever was to write. Even with the end of everything at hand, his methodical mind reasserted itself. Here he crossed a " t," there dotted an " i." He was winding up his affairs and ending his life with well-calculated good order, just as he had always lived it.

The letter was to his wife. It said:

NOVEMBER 15.

MY DEAR JANICE:

This is my last letter to you, my confession and my statement of the very good reasons why I find life impossible. My death will not only free me, but will also set another sufferer at liberty. I refer to Arthur Mansfield, unjustly sentenced to life imprisonment through my activities following a crime committed by myself.

The case from beginning to end was a " plant," arranged by me and taken at its face value by all concerned. Mansfield's story was the absolute truth. That of the prosecution, based on materials arranged by me, was absolute falsehood.

Mansfield is innocent of that murder as a babe unborn. I killed Mackenzie, and by the time you read this I shall have paid for it with my life.

Five years ago I got into the clutches of a loan-shark, Christopher Jarboe. You can easily locate him and force him by legal means to testify to the truth of much of my story. He has known of my crime from the first. If this letter will not free Mansfield, Jarboe's evidence can; and I entreat you to have the State make use of it in doing justice to the unfortunate young man now in Sing Sing.

Jarboe entangled me to such an extent that I was forced two years ago to rob the bank of one hundred and fifty thousand dollars in order to keep him from exposing my speculations and ruining

me. Mansfield's bad luck brought him to our house that same
night. You recall his story, so improbable and yet perfectly true.
During the commission of the robbery, Mackenzie discovered me
— or would have, had I not shot him. Following the crime, I
arranged all the evidence to point to Mansfield.

Slayton paused in his reading to add a few more words
of explanation in the margin. These did not satisfy him.
He took another sheet of paper, and with great detail described exactly how he had planted all the evidence. This,
he knew, would have the greatest weight in any action to
free Mansfield.

When he had completed this and pinned the sheet to the
letter, he continued reading:

Only one piece of evidence confused the State, and that was the
few white hairs found in Mackenzie's dead fingers. These constituted a grave peril to me. Let me now explain the mystery.

I wore a disguise for the robbery. Part of it was a gray wig —
the wig that went with my costume for the Rosemount Club theatricals in 1913. In the bank I accidentally dropped that wig on the
floor. Mackenzie picked it up. I shot him while he still held it in
his hand. In pulling it away from him I unknowingly left a few hairs
in his grasp. The puzzle that so vexed Dr. Nelson and Coroner
Roadstrand is now clear.

In addition to all this I must explain that I discredited and ruined
Sheridan, who was trying to defend Mansfield. I also wrote those
anonymous letters to the Amalgamated Press, which helped turn
public opinion against the victim. In fact, I engineered the whole
thing. Through me a totally innocent man has been subjected to
frightful punishment and anguish. In dying the least that I can do
is to clear his name.

My dear Janice, I have wronged so many people — you, first of all,
and Mansfield and his mother, Chamberlain and his daughter, Sheridan, and others — in addition to having murder on my soul and the
lesser crime of grand larceny — that I spare myself the futility of
any plea for pity or forgiveness. I imagine the only person really
sorry to have me die will be old Jarboe, who has been royally black-
mailing me for two years, forcing me to still further thefts and
gradually driving me to a state of absolute desperation.

The change in my health and conduct you have noticed has not been physical but mental. In dying I will try to be honest. Jarboe's exactions, thoughts of Mansfield, and persistent hallucinations concerning the murdered man have combined to make life intolerable. I am glad and happy to be free.

Thank Heaven we have no children to labor under this burden of disgrace. It will be hard for you to bear, but less hard than to have me living and disgraced, imprisoned, maybe electrocuted.

Yes, almost surely electrocuted. Exposure was bound to come some time. I am only forestalling the executioner by taking matters into my own hands. In a way I am sparing you the greatest disgrace of all — that of being the widow of an executed murderer.

What I have been able to do for you financially I have done. My insurance policies are all paid up, and none can be invalidated by suicide, as the time-limit on all has passed. They will bring you approximately $24,500.

You must keep this money. Do not let a misguided sense of honor induce you to give it to the bank. I now owe the bank $217,586. Your mite would be only a drop in the bucket. In dying I pay my debt. If you choose you can liquidate Mansfield's debt of $1,250, but I beg of you do no more.

My last request is that you put this letter at once into the hands of the district attorney and insist on immediate action being taken to free Mansfield. I have no more to say. I am not skilled in literary effects, and shall omit them. All I want is to make my meaning clear.

I am the murderer. Mansfield is entirely innocent. In dying by my own hand I am paying my debt to you, to him, and to the bank as fully as possible. Let me atone in death for at least a part of the great wrong I have done in life.

Good–by.

Your husband,

WALTER.

The letter all revised and amended, Slayton put it into a long envelope, addressed it " To My Wife," and sealed it with care. The time was now growing short. Only a few minutes remained before midnight, the hour when Slayton had determined to pay his debt.

He felt it must be then or not at all. Having made up his mind to this one fact, he sensed that, should the hour pass and find him still alive, he could not muster courage again to fire the shot. So he must act at once, leaving no time for thought, for analysis, for fear, for hope.

Where should he put the letter now that it was written? At first the obvious answer was: on the desk. But this did not meet his approval. Mrs. Slayton would not return till the morning of the 17th. Meantime, somebody else might investigate. The letter would then inevitably fall into other hands than hers.

It might miscarry of its purpose. The thought occurred to him that he could mail it to her; but here two objections intervened. One, a slight chance existed that it might get lost. The other, it would give her a frightful shock away from home, and subject her to a large variety of disagreeable experiences while among strangers. Together, these objections decided him not to mail it.

Then again, once he should leave the house and breathe the fresh night air, his determination might desert him. He might delay, postpone the deed, never again find nerve to do it. No, no! Decidedly he would not mail the letter. But where then should he put it?

He thought a minute, and then nodded. Yes, that was a good idea. He arose, took off his coat, slid the letter into the inside pocket, and, going out into the hall, hung the coat in the little closet under the stairs — the very same place whence he had taken the old clothes for his disguise on the night of the murder.

Here, he knew, Janice would be positive to find it, and here it would probably be safe from other hands than hers. The arrangement was not perfect, but it would do.

Satisfied, he returned to the library and to his desk, where lay the black, ugly automatic.

At this same hour and minute a hungry and shivering but most determined tramp was making the last lap of the distance down the country road from the Oakwood Heights station to the cashier's house. Both hands were thrust deep in his pockets. The right gripped the handle of a knife there — a carving-knife with a nicked and rusted blade.

A coarse woolen shirt, a ragged coat, and trousers grotesquely tattered did their best to keep him warm, but failed. Pulled tight down on his head, a thoroughly ventilated old " dip " gave but mediocre shelter to a head otherwise unprotected; for this tramp's head had been lately clipped close, and now only a bristly stubble of hair covered its fine proportions.

In some ways the tramp seemed but an ordinary vagabond — one of the miserable bits of social flotsam cast up by the tides of civilization. In others, however, he seemed not true to type. His blue eyes, his high and, well-modeled forehead, the straightness of his nose and the firm contour of his unshaven, bristling chin might have made an observer wonder how such a man, obviously well built and of unusual strength, should have come to take his furtive place in the army of the unemployed.

Fortunately for the tramp's peace of mind, there were no observers at that hour and on that road. All the day before he had lain hidden — still fasting — in a deserted waterman's hut out on the Hackensack marshes near Leonia, where at daybreak an irate Erie brakeman had ejected him from a " gondola " at eighteen miles an hour. At nightfall he had ventured forth from his lair, had managed to jump another train — blind baggage on a passenger this time — and had struck Jersey City not long after.

He had left this train in the dusk under a big bridge where it had been held up by adverse signals. Sheltered by the bridge embankment, he had found a couple of knights of the road engaged in warming their numb fingers over a little fire of tie-chips and other refuse. Admitted to their society by virtue of his rags and greater poverty than theirs, he had presently come into possession of half a frankfurter and a piece of biscuit — the first food to pass his lips since he had taken such unceremonious leave of his gray granite boarding-place far away up the Rhine of America.

More valuable even than this largesse had been the discovery that the railway on the bridge was a through line to Elizabeth, and that in half an hour a freight would halt a mile to westward at a crossover. The tramp had thanked his new comrades and had departed toward that spot, eager to be on hand for the freight.

This train had landed him in Elizabeth about quarter past eight. He had left it in the outskirts of the town, and by making judicious inquiries — always of children — had managed to find his shivering way to Elizabethport, and later to Bayway, where the tracks cross on the long trestle over to Staten Island.

Once *en route,* he had seen a newstand with a copy of the *News-Clarion* displaying his picture with big headlines; but he had not paused to read, and penny he had none to purchase the paper. Several times he might have snatched food from shops, but not once had he risked any such attempt; nor had he begged.

Famished though he was and racked with cold, he was determined to risk nothing till he had settled with Walter Slayton. The slightest mischance now might baffle him and forever lose him the chance for which his soul lusted.

After the account had been squared, there would be time for everything else. Till then his one consuming passion had been to press on — footsore, shivering, starving — to the goal.

With a supreme rallying of all his forces he had made the distance, tramping straight across the island from Port Ivory to New Dorp and thence to Oakwood Heights.

Fatigue he had not felt. The raw blisters on his sockless

feet he had never even heeded for an instant. The piercings of the cold, the gnawings of famine had been powerless to stay or hinder him.

For now the village of the Heights lay behind him, and he was plodding down the outlying road where dwelt the man he sought. Now the burning dream of many terrible months was about to be realized.

Now already he had won within striking distance of his arch-enemy, Walter Slayton.

CHAPTER XXVI

THE DISCOVERY

KEENLY Mansfield observed the scattering houses of Oakwood Heights, strung out along the road at considerable distance from each other. Slayton's, he well remembered, was the last one before the roadway turned toward the distant salt-marshes and became a mere trail to the timber-littered beach.

As he beheld the vague bulk of this house afar off, isolated from its nearest neighbor by three or four hundred feet, a curse mounted to his lips. The moon broke through a rift and cast a pale illumination on its gables. It made black shadows beneath its porch, and glinted from its upper windows.

Mansfield halted a moment with lips drawn back and teeth showing. His face was changed to that of a brute. His right hand clinched the handle of the carving-knife in his pocket with ferocious energy.

Cautiously he peered up and down the road, saw nobody, and once more came on. At that late hour and in that scattering suburban community the chances of detection were slight. He thrilled with hate and exulted with confidence. Once he could effect entrance into that house he knew he could take vengeance on the coward and the monster who had wrung him dry and flung him into Hell.

Now the house lay hardly a quarter-mile down the road from him. Only a single light was showing in it — a crack of light at the front window — the library window — the very room where two years ago Slayton had falsely promised him aid and had thus lured him on to ruin.

Mansfield's heart leaped with savage joy. Slayton, he felt, was probably all alone in that room — reading, no doubt; enjoying the luxury resulting from his crimes, thinking himself safe in the security he had bought by having sent his victim to a living death in Sing Sing.

"Just a window-pane now between him and this eight-inch knife!" muttered the fugitive, creeping down the road under the shadow of the trees.

Suddenly he stopped. The light in the library had all at once gone out.

Mansfield pondered a moment, then came on again. A moment later he thought he heard a distant, faint detonation, hardly audible; but to this he paid no heed.

Drawing the knife from his pocket, he slid along the road, silent and ominous. A smile parted his lips — the first smile in weeks. For now close before him stood the house of Slayton, goal of all his hopes and dreams, reward of all his agony and toil.

The cashier, firmly determined on death by his own hand, returned from the hall to the library, after having hung up his coat in the closet, with the confession of his crime in the pocket.

A glance at the clock showed him he had only three minutes to live. Though extremely pale, he was holding his nerve. A certain unnatural calm after the storm of terror and indecision now possessed him. After all, it would soon be over and done with. When life is no longer possible, death becomes a blessed refuge.

Slayton sat down at his desk, took the pistol in his hand, and glanced about him for the last time, saying farewell to the familiar room, the books, the desk, the telephone, the lamp — all the commonplace little things of life that through long years of use become, as it were, part of ourselves.

He reached out with his free hand, took up a silver frame containing a small photograph of Janice, his wife, kissed it twice, and put it back methodically in its place. Curiously he turned the black gun to and fro, peering with a kind of eager wonder at the round, ugly muzzle whence two years ago he had sent death to another, and whence he now planned to give it to himself.

Nervously he blinked, as was his habit, took off his glasses and laid them on his desk, and then pulled the little chain that controlled the incandescent.

"Damn it!" he muttered. "I can't do it in the light, anyhow. That's too much — too much!"

The clock on the mantel gave its little premonitory *click* that told it was about to strike the hour.

Slayton swallowed thickly and wiped his left hand across his forehead, where the sweat was beaded heavily. His lips twitched unsteadily; a kind of shuddering quiver trembled through his whole body.

None the less, with considerable coolness he raised the automatic to his head. He brought the muzzle round to his right ear and just behind it, to that most vital spot where a bullet infallibly brings instant death — the same identical spot where he had shot old man Mackenzie.

Now that the electric lamp was out, a ribbon of pale moonlight fell across the floor from above the window-shade which fitted imperfectly. Slayton fixed his eyes upon this ribbon, the last light he ever should gaze upon. It was just such moonlight as that when he had done the murder — and just such a night.

A sudden, hot impatience swept over him.

"Why the devil doesn't that clock strike?" thought he desperately, angrily.

As if in answer to his question, the first of its twelve little chiming strokes broke the stillness.

Motionless, the cashier waited till the sixth had sounded,

his hand tightening on the butt of the automatic, his finger squeezing the trigger with cumulative force.

Then just as the seventh stroke came, making the exact beginning of the new day, that finger swiftly tensed.

A hard report shattered away the silvery striking of the clock. Slayton pitched forward on his desk, knocking the telephone over. He slid from it, collapsed on the floor, and lay there motionless, the pistol still in his right hand.

He had just done the only courageous act of his whole existence.

So far as he could ever pay, his debt was paid.

Over the dead man's face the ribbon of moonlight streamed, cold, wan, ghostly. It alone, it and the busy little pendulum of the gilt clock above the fireplace, now moved in that quiet room. Save for the moonlight and the clock, all was motionless and still.

Thus a few minutes passed. And now the moonlight faded. Some vagrant cloud had drifted athwart the moon. A velvet gloom shrouded the library. But still the garrulous clock kept telling its story of time to ears that heard not — heard not, for time had ceased for them, and eternity begun.

All at once a plank creaked somewhere beneath a cautious, furtive tread. Where was it? Hard to tell. It seemed, however, to have sounded on the porch. Yes! Surely it must have been on the porch.

It was but a momentary sound. Silence followed. Silence that lasted now full five minutes.

Then, slightly scratching, a little noise — all but inaudible — began to develop at the front window. It came, ceased, began again — a sound as of some implement being cautiously forced in between the two sashes near the window-catch.

Now it paused two or three minutes, as though somebody were listening there outside. Whoever the intruder might be, he heard no disquieting sound; and presently the blade of a long, rust-bitten carving-knife exerted a strong, steady pressure on the catch, forcing it back.

This manœuvre produced a slight squeak, which was followed by another period of profound quiet. When the man outside had obviously satisfied himself he had not been heard, he once more began his labors.

Almost noiselessly the lower sash of the window began to rise, an inch at a time. Soon it was fully open. A hand now grasped the bottom of the shade, and after two or three attempts raised this also without any very appreciable noise.

In the aperture, vaguely grayed by a dim ghost of moonlight filtering through cloud-banks high and chill, the form of a man became dimly visible there at the window.

Crouching, he stood there, listening intently. One hand gripped the window-sill. The other held a long, slim object — an eight-inch blade set in a hardwood handle.

Still no sign, sound or hint of detection, opposition or danger reached the straining ears of the intruder. Cautiously now, moving with the utmost deliberation, he raised one leg and put it over the sill, feeling for the floor within with his foot.

He found it, rested his weight on the advanced foot, and — holding to the window-jambs — clambered silently into the library. There, now fully inside the house of the man he hated with a hate unspeakable in its virulence, Arthur Mansfield remained perfectly motionless for at least two minutes, listening for any possible sounds from above-stairs.

Slayton, he figured, had turned out his light and gone to bed. Very well. Either he would seek and find the cashier up-stairs, or he would lure him down. In either case the end would be the same.

But where was Slayton? Mansfield could not yet be

sure. At all events, it seemed certain the entrance into
the house had passed unnoticed. Turning with meticulous
care, Arthur lowered the window again and slowly pulled
down the shade. This done, he smiled grimly with savage
exultation. The long-hoped, eagerly-desired moment now
lay close at hand — the moment when he could feel Slayton's life spilled out by his hand — the moment when, if
only for a second, he could gaze upon that Judas corpse
and spit on it and laugh.

Cautiously now, moving with extended hands, Arthur
advanced across the library floor. The hardwood strips
were solid and the rugs thick. No plank creaked. Arthur
bitterly contrasted this warmth and comfort with the foul
cage into which Slayton had flung him — as the cashier
had hoped, for life. And a vast, overwhelming joy blazed
up in him now to be here in this very room where the initial
treason had been wrought on him — to be about to deal
out justice, swift and sure, by his own hand in this same
room to that traitor, coward and wrecker of his whole
life.

No thought now of mercy could find entrance into that
inflamed and raging soul. If any memory of Enid, inclining
him to stay his hand, sought to gain entrance he put it violently away. Obsessed by this one idea, indifferent to past,
present and future save as these bore on this one thing, he
stalked his prey.

A moment he advanced in darkness, but only a moment.

All at once, moving with extreme caution, he felt his
right foot strike some heavy and inert thing lying in his
path.

This thing was soft and strange. It gave slightly under
pressure, but made no sound. Puzzled, Arthur stirred it
with his foot, and wondered what the thing might be.

Then he stooped to touch it.

Just at that moment the moon slid from her veiling bank

of cloud. A pallid band of light drew itself across the floor
— across the floor and over the peculiar object of his won-
derment.

Arthur beheld a black something lying there; then he saw
white — white and red.

Blinking, perfectly unable to grasp the slightest idea of
what he so imperfectly saw, he crouched closer, extended
his hand — and touched a human face.

The band of moonlight all at once revealed to him, as he
moved slightly and let it shine full on this face, a glazed,
unmoving eye that with dull fixity seemed to be regarding
him. Just that he saw — the vague black-and-white object; the face with the strange red blotch upon it; the filmed
eye.

A quiver of panic twitched through all his limbs. Again
he groped for the thing. He drew his hand back, back into
the ribbon of misty light.

His fingers were smeared with red.

The light strengthened. Now he recognized the face,
the dead and lusterless eye so cynically fixed upon him.

"*Slayton? Dead?*" he stammered, recoiling.

CHAPTER XXVII

HARDENED against fear though Arthur had become in the two frightful years of his imprisonment, and proofed against all weaknesses of nerve or sensibility, yet the dawning horror of that apparition lying there before him, dead and blood-drenched on the library floor, came nigh to shattering his self-control.

He barely stifled a harsh cry. Stumbling back and away from the body, he collided with a chair, half fell into it, and subsided, quivering. His hands clutched the chair-arms. Shaking and horror-stricken, staring at the motionless thing there in the moonlit ribbon, he sat there stunned.

This first spasm of unreasoning horror lasted only a brief moment. No longer was Arthur the ingenuous, impressionable boy of other days. He had grown wise, resourceful, strong. Almost as the terror came upon him, strangling him in its grip, he fought it off again. Once more he mastered himself, and with quick aptitude began formulating plans for action under these dazingly unexpected conditions.

A thousand questions assailed him.

What had happened? Who had done this murder, and why? Where was the murderer now, and who might he be? Was he still in the house?

And Mrs. Slayton, what of her? Was she still living — or had she, too, met the same fate? Had the alarm been given? Was urgent peril near?

Useless to outline a hundredth part of the overwhelming problems now confronting him. Arthur faced them, reeling, yet full of fight. All he could be sure of now was just this: The fact that through some jest of fate — just such another ugly trick as the one which had first branded him a murderer and flung him into servitude — he had now been not only cheated of his heart's desire, revenge, but also stood in utmost peril of a fresh accusation which this time must inevitably land him in the electric chair.

Arthur realized there was no moment to be lost. Slayton had escaped him. By a few minutes he had lost that for which his heart and soul had lusted. Now nothing more remained to be done. The only matter of importance was his own safety.

He advanced to the body, the knife still in his right hand, his left blood-stained. A swift vision of his plight brought a grim smile to his lips.

"No alibi possible *this* time if I'm caught here," he muttered. "As a situation, some situation!"

Again he stirred the body curiously with his foot. The face moved slightly in the moonlight; the eye seemed to be looking at him. Yes, there lay Slayton dead before him; but now he had lost all desire to spit on the Iscariot. Death even in that form had suddenly invested the creature with a certain inviolable dignity. The helplessness of the arch-enemy — traitor, perjurer and murderer though he was — formed the supreme appeal. Arthur shook his head.

"You win, damn you!" he said with a consuming bitterness.

He sensed the wetness of his fingers, and instinctively was about to wipe them on his rags, when caution stayed his hand. No; he was wiser now than once. Instead he stooped over and cleaned his fingers on the dead man's coat.

No alarm as yet had been given. There might be a few moments' time yet for him to get his bearings. Nothing could be more ill-advised than for him to depart in haste without plans, ignorant of just what had taken place here. By all means he must wait a minute or two before retreating.

The moonlight died again. Arthur now found himself in the dark with his dead enemy. This fact did not disconcert him. He felt neither repulsion nor fear, but only annoyance.

Taking his bearings as best he could, he felt for and reached the desk, found the incandescent — still just as it had been two years ago — and turned it on. Some risks had to be assumed, and this was one of them. The fact that every curtain was close drawn, and that a profound silence reigned throughout the house and over all the neighborhood, was reassuring.

Swiftly Arthur now surveyed the room, taking in every detail with the quick precision that his watchful prison habits had taught him. Nothing had been disturbed in the library. No signs of a struggle were visible. Slayton lay between the desk and the center-table, his head toward the desk and near the legs of the desk-chair, as though he had slid down from it and fallen there by his own weight.

In his right hand he still clutched a pistol, black and grim. Back of his ear an ugly wound showed whence life had fled.

"Suicide," judged Arthur at once. "Nothing to it but that!"

He knew by all the signs, and most particularly by the manner in which the gun was held, that Slayton had come to death by his own hand. Dr. Nelson's testimony still remained clearly graven on his mind. It was most useful now, was it not?

With a start he recognized the weapon. He slid the carving-knife into his pocket, crouched down beside the body, and examined the automatic. Yes, it surely was his own, the very gun wherewith he had thought to end his life two years ago, the gun that had played so large a part in convicting him.

Should he take it or leave it there? Quickly he debated the question. The gun might be dangerous to him if left. His threat against Slayton was known. His escape had happened to coincide with the hour when Slayton had killed himself. Would the gun clear him or would it not?

The fact that it had belonged to him and that it had his initials, "A. M.," cut into the hard-rubber butt, might be very prejudicial to him. Popular opinion, the press and all would raise a terrible hue and cry against him on that account.

Even though it could be shown that Slayton had probably committed suicide, that would not matter. If Arthur were ever tried for this crime the State would show that he had simulated the cashier's suicide and that a real murder had taken place.

Arthur shuddered, glanced warily about and listened for possible danger. The electric chair this time and nothing less was looming before him now. On just this one decision might hang life or death for him.

"I'll take the gun!" he suddenly exclaimed, and reached for it.

At all hazards he must have it. Not only might it be of tremendous value to him in case of pursuit, but it must not be left there. The accusing story that could be framed, how he had returned to the cashier's house, broken in, found the gun and with it murdered Slayton, then put the weapon in the dead man's fingers — despite all the denials of medical science — and fled, avenged, would be too utterly damning.

The gun must go with him.

Quickly he loosened the dead man's hand. The body was still warm. Though the tensed fingers resisted, Arthur forced them open and slid the pistol into his pocket.

Now what next?

Again he listened, but all was silent as the grave. He tiptoed over to the library windows, first one and then the other, and cautiously peeped out around the edge of the shades. Nothing could be seen. Night brooded undisturbed over the suburban quietude.

Reassured, he came back to the body and once more studied it. Probably there would be time enough for all he needed to do. As he pondered, looking down at Slayton, he smiled. The poetic justice of that death-wound did not escape him. He grasped the significance of the fact that the cashier had shot himself in precisely the same place where he had dealt death to old Mackenzie. With a kind of grim approval he nodded.

There was, however, scant time for introspection. Much had to be done at once. Arthur's forces were now well-nigh spent. He must eat, change his clothes and make his getaway immediately.

He felt positive nobody could be upstairs. Had there been, that person must inevitably have come down, at sound of the shot. Without any question Slayton had been alone in the house when he had killed himself. Arthur, therefore, felt safe to proceed with his task of recuperation and flight.

Taking his bearings, he swept a glance about the room. Through a door at the rear he caught a glimpse of a polished oak dining-table, and beyond it of a sideboard with cut-glass and silver, dimly visible by the light reflected from the hooded desk-lamp.

Cautiously he proceeded into the dining-room. His nerve had now returned. He felt cool, unshaken, confident. Constantly he listened for any suspicious sound outside or up-stairs. Hearing nothing, he made his way to the kitchen. Here he pulled down all the shades and turned on one incandescent. Next he carefully washed his hands at the sink, wiped them on a dish-towel, and was about to hang this up again when he paused, struck by a thought. He pocketed the towel, smiling. Experience had taught him much. No more evidence of any kind was to be left behind, this time.

Arthur now routed out an abundance of provision — half a leg of mutton, some cold baked potatoes, bread, cheese and cake. A case of beer, half full, stood near the refrigerator, in which were half a dozen bottles on ice. Arthur found them there when he opened the little door, using the flap of his ragged coat to turn the handle with.

" No finger-prints ! " thought he. " And no beer ! "

Plain water from the faucet — also turned without the contact of his fingers — better suited his need of keeping a clear head and steady wits. He ate ravenously, wolfing the food in huge bites as he walked to and fro in the kitchen. He drank from the running stream at the faucet. This avoided the danger of touching a glass with greasy fingers.

Satisfied in part, he next proceeded to hunt for clothing. The front hall, when illuminated by an incandescent, revealed many possibilities. A variety of hats and overcoats were hanging on the rack. Arthur chose an ulster and a soft black felt. The proximity of the dead man now disturbed him not a whit. He worked as calmly and methodically as if the house were his own, and he were all alone there.

So far so good. But he needed much more. The half-open clothes-closet under the stairway attracted his attention. He investigated and found splendid possibilities.

Quickly he routed out shoes, rubbers and a coat, together with a waistcoat and trousers. He thrust his hand into the pockets of the coat. It touched a wallet and a folded paper in the inside breast-pocket. For one second of time Arthur's hand rested on Slayton's confession. Then the wallet attracted his attention and he forgot the paper.

The wallet felt plump. Arthur smiled but did not investigate. Time enough for that later. Whatever it might contain would help in this emergency. Slayton owed it to him a thousand times over.

Arthur laid all his plunder on the seat of the hat-rack and scouted up-stairs for accessories. His fear of interruption had now largely disappeared. He now knew that nobody was at home. Nobody was coming, he felt sure, from outside. Doubtless the whole night lay ahead of him to do with as he pleased. He had time enough, yet none to lose. The quicker he could be out of there and away the better.

The upper story fully supplied him. Fifteen minutes later, completely clad in the dead man's clothing, from socks to tie and from boots to felt hat, Arthur made his way back into the library.

In his hand he carried a bundle — every article of clothing he had taken off: prison shoes and underwear, tramp's rags, greasy "dip" and all. These things he intended to destroy. Not a trace of him must be left in the house.

But first he felt the inclination to gaze once more on Slayton. The body gave him a certain satisfaction as he stood there looking down at it; yet after all he felt less exultant than he had dreamed of feeling. For many months he had lusted after this moment, and now that it had come the effect was anticlimactic.

Slayton was dead and he regretted it. He realized now that what he had desired had not been Slayton dead, but Slayton dying. He had not really longed to have his enemy destroyed; he had burned with passion to sense the act of destruction.

And that pleasure had been denied him. The throat between his fingers had not been given him to feel. Not his to witness the spectacle of death.

With an exceeding bitterness he turned away. Even in
this he had been outwitted and rebuffed.

" Cheated, even here! " said he.

His eye swept the desk. It noted the disorder there —
the blood-spattered papers where Slayton's head had fallen,
the upset telephone, the spilled clips and pins, always neatly
kept by the dead man.

He reached for the telephone and stood it up again, replacing the receiver on the hook. A frown creased his
brow. Vaguely he sensed a certain uneasiness.

That telephone — how long had it been lying thus? Obviously since the moment the shot had been fired.

But then might it not have given the alarm? Might not
some investigator even now be on his way to the house to
see what the trouble might be?

" Damn it! Just my luck! " growled Arthur. " He
couldn't even kill himself without making a rumpus about
it! "

No use, however, in execrating this evil fortune. It
merely spurred him on to quicker action.

Was there anything else on that desk that he should
know about? Swiftly he looked it over.

A black tin box caught his attention. He flung up the
cover. Inside he saw something which at first he could not
identify — something gray, like fur.

He dropped his bundle of discarded clothing beside the
desk and raked out the contents of the box. In his hands
he found a wig and a false beard.

What the deuce could these be? And why should they
be there, on Slayton's desk?

Holding them in both hands, he studied them intently
under the plunging light of the incandescent. All at once
it seemed as if a flash of understanding dawned on him with
swift clarity. The look and feel of those gray hairs recalled something to his fevered mind — but what?

A moment he stood there, wrestling with himself to wrench this half-knowledge out into complete consciousness. Then all at once he knew:

"Those gray hairs in Mackenzie's hand — came — from here!" he cried exultantly.

His eyes blazed with a wild joy. His face, wan with prison pallor, twitched in excitement. He understood the truth at last. He knew! He knew!

Trembling, he stuffed the wig and the rest of the make-up into the capacious pocket of his overcoat and flung the black tin box back whence it had come. Not yet could he fully grasp the entire possibilities of his discovery, but he understood that here perhaps he held a clue of marvelous scope.

If this belief of his could be proved, what might not result?

But now he had no time for further thought. He must be off and away. He picked up his bundle of rags again, turned off the light, and without another look at Slayton went back to the kitchen by way of the hall, where too he left all in darkness.

Nothing now remained for him to do save get rid of the telltale bundle of clothing and then escape from the locality. The little tin alarm-clock on the kitchen shelf marked 1.10. He had spent only an hour in this house of death. It seemed an eternity.

Ahead of him he still had four or five hours of darkness in which to reach New York and go into hiding there in some obscure nook or corner. Now that he had clothes and funds he could escape. And the city would prove safer far than any country place.

Arthur's two years' association with men of the underworld had taught him many things. Now, a fugitive, he recalled the evil wisdom of the crook, the cunning of the criminal, and knew the city would receive and hide him in some "kip" or "ink-pot" till the storm should have blown over. The name and place of more than one such thieves' haven he knew.

Before having found Slayton, he had thought only of revenge, with no care for the aftermath. Now the desire for life, for freedom in itself, lay strong upon him. To win he must act quickly. He must be on his way.

He took matches and, bundle in hand, descended into the cellar. Here he peered about by the feeble flame of a match till he discovered an incandescent. He went to the furnace, opened the door, and peered in. Only a dull glow of coals was to be seen. Surely there was not fire enough to make certain that all the clothing, the boots — everything — would be destroyed.

He must have wood. By piling the furnace full of wood he could insure the destruction of the evidence that he, Number 3265, Escaped, had been in that house. At his left he saw a bin half filled with pine-slab kindling. To this he went, stooped, and gathered an armful, threw it into the furnace and jammed the bundle of clothes in after it.

Then he returned for more.

He stooped again. As he raised another load, the folded paper and the wallet in the breast-pocket of his loose-swinging coat fell out upon the kindling, which slid across them.

Mansfield perceived this. He hesitated, uncertain whether or not to drop the kindling and recover the things at once. Chance decided him to wait, a moment. Quickly he turned to the furnace and shoved in the second armful.

A few pieces of pine fell to the cement floor. These he picked up and tossed in. He squinted into the furnace, made sure the coals were hot enough to ignite the wood, and then closed the door. That job at last was done.

With both hands he brushed his coat and turned back toward the kindling-bin to recover the things he had dropped. But on the instant he froze to motionless attention, every sense alert and quivering.

Outside, a footfall had just become audible. Through the half-open cellar-window he heard it plainly, falling with staccato resonance on the walk in front of the house. And now he heard another — then a voice speaking, and another answering.

Listening, Arthur stood motionless, alert and tense. Would the men pass the house or were they coming in? On this question everything depended. He cursed the glaring incandescent in the basement. Its rays, he knew, must be visible through the little cellar-window — not the open one — at the front of the house. And he too would be visible to anybody coming over the lawn and peering in there. The fact that the upper part of the house was all dark and that only in the cellar was there any light might excite suspicion.

Bitterly execrating his evil luck, he remained there a moment, undecided, at a complete loss what to do. His hand, however, slid into his pocket and felt the butt of the automatic, and was comforted thereby.

Louder now the footsteps had become, and nearer. They were rapidly nearing the house. The voices had fallen quiet. Listening intently, Arthur knew the men had turned in at the gate and were coming up the walk to the porch.

Desperately he tried to collect his nerve and rally his stampeded wits, but for the moment failed pitiably. A kind of horrible stage-fright assailed and gripped him, numbing his limbs as in a nightmare.

The situation exceeded the limits of the appalling. Somebody was about to visit the house — the house where Walter Slayton lay newly dead. And he, Number 3265, was skulking in the cellar with the dead man's clothes upon his body and the dead man's pistol in his hand!

All at once the steps leading up to the porch echoed beneath rapid footfalls; but these were the footfalls of only one man. The other — where might he be, and who? The porch itself thudded hollowly under the tread of the visitor. Now already he had reached the front door.

Arthur gulped with paralyzing terror. His eyes shifted wildly, their pupils dilated by fear till they looked quite black by the light of the electric lamp that swung near the furnace. He would have put that light out now, had he dared; but he did not dare. That act might have betrayed his presence there. But before long, if these men entered the house, they would inevitably come down into the cellar.

Could he find a hiding-place there and hope to escape later? If not, could he shoot them as they came down hunting him? Could he fight his way to freedom? What was to be done?

A sudden passionate hate of the telephone flared up in him, irrational and wild. That accursed thing, he knew, had given the alarm. Tipped over by Slayton at the moment of death, it had cried, "Trouble!" to the Oakwood Heights exchange; and now investigation was at hand.

Investigation — and that could have only one end for him. Investigation — and he was trapped like a rat in the basement of the house where suicide would surely be spelled murder, and where the murderer would inevitably be named Number 3265, Escaped!

CHAPTER XXVIII

A VOICE IN THE NIGHT

SUDDENLY the electric door-bell, trilling again upstairs, energized him into action. Whatever might happen he must not stand there inert, exposed to observation through the cellar-window, and supinely await capture.

He who had suffered so terribly for no crime, he who had dared so much for vengeance now forever frustrated, would not at any rate throw down his cards at the last moment and cry quits.

At all hazards he would make an effort to go clear. Before it should be eternally too late he would strike out for the free air, the open road, the way toward New York and a chance to hide from the merciless hounding of the law.

Arthur's wits were coming back to him again, and his strength and coolness. He had not passed two years in Sing Sing only to lose his nerve now at the first touch of peril.

Noiselessly and quickly he tiptoed to the bin where he had dropped the wallet. Money at all events he must have. Without that he would be lost. Quickly he took away the pieces of wood that had fallen over the wallet and laid them down; and all this time, intermittent, strident, loud, the hall-bell above-stairs continued to racket through the darkness.

Now Arthur could see the pocketbook. Now he laid hold of it and drew it out from under the last retaining slabs of pine. He crammed it into his pocket and stood up,

leaving the folded paper — that all-precious paper, Slayton's full confession — still lying hidden.

He had small time or thought now for a sheet of paper.
In his hand he held what seemed to him the one essential —
cash. Now he was armed for all contingencies. A full
wallet and a loaded automatic may carry a man far.

Silently he returned to the furnace, while the bell still
made its futile clamor, to which a vigorous knocking with
fists and kicking with boots now furnished a contra-bass.
He slid open the furnace-door, noting with satisfaction that
the kindling was smoking vigorously and would surely
flame in a few moments, consuming his discarded clothes.
Then he closed the door again and took his bearings.

Almost in front of him he saw the stairs leading up into
the kitchen. For a moment he was half-tempted to take
that chance, go back to the kitchen and flee by the door;
but second thought deterred him.

The bell had ceased ringing all at once, and the voices
were sounding again. He heard a heavy step on the porch,
then a *crack!* as of breaking metal, and the squeaking of a
window being raised.

Swiftly he interpreted the sounds. They meant that a
policeman, armed with authority, was breaking into the
house — into the very library, there at the front, where
Slayton's body lay. And Arthur's nerve for a moment for-
sook him again.

He simply could not climb those stairs up to that kitchen.
Once there he would have to fumble in the dark for the
door. The lock might baffle him. He might knock something over. Most easily he might be trapped there. No;
not that way did he dare escape.

There remained then only the cellar-window. Already
guarded, perhaps? He could not tell. At any rate nothing
else was left to try. Observing its position, he caught up
an empty wooden box that was standing by the chimney

and advanced toward the window. One twist of his wrist, and the incandescent died.

Now utter darkness shrouded him. Even though this might give warning of his presence in the cellar, it would prevent his being an easy target from without as he should clamber through the narrow space.

Setting the box beneath the window, he stepped upon it, caught the sill, and pulled himself through. The task was hard to force his way out in silence, but he succeeded. A minute later, laced with cobwebs and grimed with coal-dust, he crawled free upon a narrow strip of turf between the house and the driveway that led to Slayton's garage. Here for a second or two he paused to listen.

Crouching, he gave ear. Outside, all held calm. The moon, shrouded again, shed only a ghostly dimness across the sky. The vague outlines of a quickset hedge vaguely appeared in front of him across the drive. Beyond that all was uncertain; but the fugitive sensed that out on that expanse of salt marsh, traversed by paths that led to the inchoate jumble of summer-camps and shacks along the beach, he might find safety for a while.

Yes, if he could only reach that deserted settlement half a mile away to eastward on the edge of New York Bay, everything might yet be well with him.

But could he?

Already within the house, sounds of excitement told him that the body had been discovered. A light now shone out through the hall-window above his head, casting a pale yellow band across the drive. This light, he knew, must come from the library, through the hall-door, and so out this window at the side of the house where he now was. He heard vaguely from within quick and interrupted exclamations, an oath or two, then staccato sentences that indicated somebody was telephoning.

Not a second was to be wasted now, if ever he were to

hope for freedom or for life. To be caught now meant worse than a return to Sing Sing for life; it meant the death-house, the electric chair, the dissecting-table and the unmarked grave. Every fraction of time hung heavy with supreme value.

Half-rising from his hands and knees, he crept with extreme caution across the graveled drive to the hedge. Here he paused again, panting heavily, undecided whether to try for the end of it or to break through. The former way would take a little time and risk exposure. The latter might make a bit of noise and leave damaging clues.

A sudden opening of the front door and a hasty step on the porch decided him. At all hazards he must get that hedge between himself and the house. He dropped on all fours and pushed through, knowing not what might lie on the other side.

"Hello! Who's there?" cried a voice, harsh and angry.

Arthur knew he had been heard. Crouching, he ran along the side of the hedge away from the street. The automatic in his pocket thumped against his body. He gripped it and drew it out. Pursued, he would kill.

"Stop or I'll shoot!" shouted the man on the porch.

Arthur heard him running. Then came a thud on the gravel. The man had leaped over the rail.

Panting a little, the fugitive quickened his pace. He stumbled over a pail of ashes or something of that sort, and fell sprawling onto a rubbish-heap that cut his hands with broken bottles and tore the knees of his trousers; but still he held on to the pistol. Up he scrambled, and now with the unseen challenger — a patrolman whom the telephone-man had met on the way to the house — in full cry after him, ran at his best speed down a long, vague path toward the beach.

Three crackling concussions and three little spits of fire from the patrolman's gun told him the officer meant to kill.

Close past him zooned the bullets; but by that dim light the pursuer's aim could not hold true.

Arthur halted a second, wheeled and sent a volley back in answer. He heard a curse from the vague figure there some two hundred yards behind him. And all at once the figure ceased running and began to hobble, futilely banging away.

The fugitive laughed with harsh merriment.

"You're winged now, and you can't catch me!" he shouted in defiance. "I've got plenty of ammunition here. Now if you want me, come along."

No answer. The policeman fired a few more shots, all wild, and then limped back toward the house. Arthur laughed again.

"Good night!" he called, then turned once more and at a brisk trot set off for the beach settlement.

As he ran he thought. For the moment he knew he was safe from interference. The officer could not pursue, and the other man would never risk it. The best they could do would be to telephone for help. Reënforcements could hardly reach them inside of half an hour. Perhaps an hour might elapse before others would take up his trail. Arthur blessed the lucky-chance shot and jogged along, peering keenly in the gloom.

A few minutes and he had come out through the nexus of pools, canals, muddy brooks and rush-grown swamps to the long dunes edging the sea. The edge of the beach was sharply defined. Here, salt marsh. Six feet farther, beach. Arthur's feet now sank far into the white, dry sand. He nodded approvingly. Few men, he knew, could ever track him through a shifting trail like that.

Planless save for the general idea that he would make his getaway to the city by some means or other, he trudged northward along the edge of the beach, fringed by tall grasses and coarse weeds. The place spoke to him of lib-

erty. Even though this should be his last hour of life, it
was a free hour.

Behind him and at his left, nothing save the marshes and
a far-off light that meant the house of Slayton — just a
vague glimmer across the waste land. Over him a clouded
November sky with a moon impotent to pierce the veil.
At his right hand the solemn, moving mystery of the
sea.

He could hear it murmuring with vague complaint along
the sands. The wild, free smell of it was perfume to his
nostrils, long used to the fetid prison air of Sing Sing.
Vaguely the deserted buildings loomed along the lip of the
sea. The fugitive laughed with an abandon of joy, kicked
the sand in big jets, ran along the beach and breathed his
lungs full of ozone. Not a soul anywhere near to spy on
him or to pursue — as yet. He was all, all alone with the
night, the sands, the moving clouds, the moon, the ceaseless
creaming murmur of the surf.

Presently Arthur's exultant mood passed. Even though
not one human being was in sight, nor any light nearer
than the dull-green starboard-light of some vague schooner
beating out to sea not far offshore, yet he realized he was
still within the boundaries of Greater New York, and that
ere long thousands of police, detectives and private indi-
viduals would be keenly watching for him.

This seeming liberty of his was merely illusory. He
might run and shout and gambol never so much along the
dark sands by the Lower Bay; yet still about him the iron
ring was closing and the vast net being flung.

Every exit from Staten Island, he knew, would soon be
closely guarded. The whole area of it would be combed
for him. If he remained there, no matter how carefully
he might hide, a day or two — a week, at the outside —
would find him in the clutch of the law once more. And
after that —

Shuddering, he seemed to awaken from his illusion of freedom. He paused now, faced the sea, and thought:
" What next? "

Many things now stood in his favor, which two hours before he had not possessed. Then he had been starving, unarmed and in rags, without a cent in his pocket or a thought in his heart save one — Slayton's death. Now he was full-fed, warmly and finely dressed, with a formidable gun and with new-born ambitions for liberty *per se,* not as an end to vengeance. A new thought had been born to him — the possibility of getting clean away at last; of beginning life again somewhere; of really being once more a man.

He raised his left hand and struck his right fist into the palm of it with violence.

" By God, I will! " cried he.

His back had straightened now, and into his eyes a new look had come — something almost of the old, brave, honest look that Enid had so loved. Through his fresh consciousness of possibilities of life perhaps still ahead of him did there flit some thought of the girl, some hope, some prayer? Who shall say?

Severed as he was from her, and standing under the shadow of death, still in his heart he knew his innocence. He knew the goad that had driven him to lust after the death of Slayton. Had he not sought to turn on that Judas, he had not been a man. In his own soul he found his judgment:

" Not guilty! "

And as he faced the sea he raised his eyes to the vast moving wonder of it, and once more cried:

" I will! "

This mood of exaltation passed, and now he began taking definite steps toward safety. His calculating shrewdness returned. He forgot to be thrilled now by night and sea.

He put away aspiring, visionary thoughts of Enid, and began figuring ways and means.

Calculatingly he observed the prospect. For a getaway
it was not encouraging. Far across the Bay a long neck-
lace of shining beads marked the lights of Coney. Away
off to southeast the intermittent stab of Sandy Hook Light
pierced the night.

The sea attracted him. More dangerous than the land in
its own being, it now had become far safer as regarded
mankind. Untracked, if he could find a boat, he could
escape from the Island. The risk of being swamped, carried out to sea, or run down by some big craft was dwarfed
by the certainty of capture on the Island.

With an appraising glance he observed the lights of Coney.
The distance, he knew, could not be more than ten miles.
With fair luck in a reasonably decent boat he ought to
make it in three hours. He could land anywhere along
the beach, make his way to some car-line, and reach Manhattan before daybreak. Surely the police would hardly
watch the trains from Coney Island for him. Once he
could cross the Bay he knew that a vast step would be taken
toward the longed-for goal, liberty.

Huge difficulties still confronted him, he knew; but at
least a chance of success existed. He wanted no more than
that — a fighting chance.

With a definite purpose in view he once more advanced.
A boat! He must have a boat!

But where was a boat to be found? Along the beach
perhaps, drawn up in front of or between the shacks. Yes,
a bare possibility existed that one might be discovered
there.

But even so, Arthur reflected, the season was long past,
and any boat here would probably have been many weeks
out of the water. It might leak badly. No matter!
Leaky or not, if once he could discover a boat, into the surf

it would go, and away with him on the dubious night-journey across the Lower Bay.

Arthur turned toward the line of shacks. He stumbled upon a rough sidewalk built of rotten planks and ships' timbers cast up by the sea. Along it he plodded, peering everywhere for the longed-for sight of a hull.

Not a single light was visible anywhere among the camps and shacks. Rough-built structures they were, framed of much the same materials as the sidewalk that did common service for the whole irregular community. Every possible degree of rudeness and ugliness could have been seen there, had the light sufficed. There they stood, a mournful file, ragged and unclean, with the salt marsh behind them and the refuse-littered beach in front. Arthur, straining his eyes by the vague whitish glimmer of the shrouded moon, thought that in all his life he never had beheld so ugly or so strange a settlement.

Humming to himself, peering everywhere as he advanced, he kept along the sidewalk. A growing anxiety was beginning to possess him.

What if after all no boat was to be found? What then?

The prospect was not one to be faced with equanimity. He would not admit it as a possible event. Surely in a place like this at least one boat must have been left!

All at once Arthur stopped short, a curious tightening at his heart.

He had thought himself a mile at least from any human being; and yet suddenly the unmistakable smell of burning tobacco had been wafted to his nostrils.

Standing motionless and alert, unable to believe his senses, he sniffed the breeze. Yes! There could be no mistaking the smell — it was tobacco!

A quick wave of fear ran over him.

Who could be there? Had he been seen? Could he still retreat unobserved?

Wild-eyed, he peered ahead at the shacks. At first he could perceive no sign of life, even though the tobacco-smell persisted and strengthened. Then suddenly he observed a dull reddish glow in a doorway just beyond the shack where he had stopped.

This glow waxed and waned. No doubt about it; a dottel of tobacco was burning in a pipe.

Arthur's presence of mind reasserted itself. Perhaps he had not yet been noticed. Quickly he dropped on hands and knees, slid off the walk on the landward side, and started creeping through the sand with the hope of putting the shack between himself and the unseen smoker.

Forgotten now for the moment was the campaign in quest of a boat. Forgotten all his plans. Forgotten everything save just the one supreme hope of escaping detection in the deserted village where he had thought no living creature still remained.

Ten feet he crept — fifteen — twenty. Already he thought himself safe. Already the bulk of the shack was near to hiding that little, sullen glow of red.

In a minute more Arthur knew that he could rise and steal away soundlessly through the sand — away around the building at his left — down the beach again — any-where, just so it should be away from that unseen and unknown man.

At that very instant, however, the red blur of the pipe described an arc in the gloom, indicating that its owner had removed it from his mouth.

Then, harsh above the murmur of the surf upon the beach, hoarse, raw and repellant, a voice came through the night to him:

" Hey, there! Who the Hell are you? An' what you doin' round here? "

CHAPTER XXIX

IN THE BEACH-COMBER'S SHACK

STRUCK motionless by this direct challenge, Arthur remained where he was, unable to speak or move. A terrible anguish assailed him. At one blow his plans had all been shattered. Now in the very hour of probable success he was confronted by failure, ruin and destruction. The moment was bitter with the gall of defeat.

Again the harsh voice sounded:

"Come along out o' that, you! Come along or I'll bring yuh!"

Arthur realized that evasion or attempted flight would now be worse than useless. He must face this unknown man, and bluff or bribe his way through. With quick wits and a fat wallet he might still travel far, despite everything.

And at the last resort he had the automatic.

On the instant all the softening, refining and ennobling influences of freedom, of night, of memories and hopes had once more vanished. All thoughts of Enid had taken swift flight. Now the cunning and the wiles of the hunted prison-animal had dominantly surged back. At that hail, good had quitted the boy, and evil had once more laid its blighting, withering clutch upon him.

Arthur stood up, faced the unseen man with the pipe, and advanced toward him through the loose sand.

"Who are *you* anyhow?" he demanded boldly.

The other ripped off a string of oaths.

"Say, you cert'nly got some nerve, you," he retorted,

"to be askin' *me* who *I* am! Come on out o' that, now! I won't have no sneak-thieves nor rummies hangin' round my place this time o' the mornin'!"

"Who's a thief and rummy?" demanded Arthur angrily. "You be careful!"

The smoker laughed sneeringly.

"Come here! Come here!" he reiterated. "Let's have a slant at you."

He rose from where he was sitting, advanced to Arthur and suddenly flashed an electric beam in his face. Startled, the fugitive blinked and stepped back a pace. The other laughed again.

"Got your goat; hey, kid?" he jested clumsily. "Well, who are you an' what you doin' here?"

By the vague reflection of the beam Arthur sensed that the fellow was a hulking, big-shouldered brute with an evil countenance. The rank pipe still between his jaws emitted noxious fumes. The fugitive felt a strong impulse to draw his gun and shoot the ruffian down — some beach-combing tough, scoured off the city's dives and slums, no doubt. But he restrained himself. Even though this man stood squarely in his path to liberty he would not kill — yet.

"Who are you?" once more demanded the beach-comber. "Strike me blind! Spit it out!"

Swiftly Arthur thought. To frame any kind of passable story, he knew, would be totally impossible. This type of man, shrewd and evil, would fathom any lie that he could tell. The only possible course must be the frontal attack of bribery.

"What's that to you who I am?" he therefore parried.

"What's it to me? A lot! This here's my property, see?"

He jerked a thumb at the shack behind him.

"I won't have no —"

"Oh, forget it!" interrupted Arthur. "Your whole

damned place isn't worth a minute of my time. I could buy out the whole strip of dumps here, and then some, and never feel it. If a man happens to have business out here and then happens to want to get back to the city, do you kick? Are you a wise guy or not?"

Silence a moment. The electric beam went out, and the pipe glowed strongly. The man was pondering.

"Say! What you givin' us, anyhow?" he suddenly demanded.

But though the words were hostile, Arthur sensed the change in tone. Already he had succeeded in establishing a line of communication.

"What d'yuh mean?" the tough challenged.

"That's nothing to you what I mean," Arthur replied, lowering his voice. "Anybody else round these diggings? Anybody rubbering?"

"Nope. Why?"

"D'you want a bundle of kale?"

The question, point-blank, struck the ruffian a heavy blow. The blow went home right enough.

"Kale?" he demanded eagerly.

"Kale is right. I've got enough for us both."

"What for?"

"What do you mean, what for?"

"What do you want o' me?"

"A boat."

"A boat, hey? Getaway? Is that it?"

"You've got me right. How about it?"

The smoker pondered again, then nodded toward the doorway of his shack.

"Come along up an' we'll chew this thing out, kid," he answered.

His tone had greatly moderated now. Perfectly well he understood — or thought he understood — that he was dealing with some crook or dweller of the underworld. From

that very moment his hostility was beginning to melt. A
kindred spirit was developing. Arthur's line of action had
been unerringly correct; the only possible one at all under
the circumstances. The instinct developed by his weary
months in Sing Sing could not fail him now.

Well-pleased, he followed the man up to the rough porch
of the ramshackle building perched on the dune. Already
he felt that the situation was well in hand. How much.
money he had in the wallet he did, not know, but whatever
the sum might be, he would give it all if need were for escape. He felt it must surely be enough — more than enough
for this emergency.

"Sit down an' let's have it," the fellow directed, flinging
his hand at the edge of the porch. "Shoot!"

"There's nothing to it except that I want a boat, and
want it bad," answered Arthur, sitting down beside him.

The other sucked at his pipe.

"How much is there in it for me, and where do you want
to go?"

"Land me anywhere in Brooklyn or New York, and I'll
split the bundle with you. Can you do it?"

"Oh, I can do it, all right, all right! I've got a twenty-
two-foot motor-boat in a cove back here. But the bundle
— how high does she run?"

"Search me! I don't know."

"What? Ain't looked at it yet? Ain't weeded the
leather?"

"Haven't had time. Whatever it is, I'll go fifty-fifty.
Isn't that O. K.? Take a chance?"

"Sure I will!" the other exclaimed with elation.
"You're 'right,' I see. But you must want a boat some to
put over an offer like that!"

"You're right I do. And I want it quick. Get busy!"

"Sure I'll get busy. But we'll split first. Let's have a
once-over at the package."

"That's fair. Give us your flash-light here."

"Nothin' doin'! Come inside. I got to get some gas, anyhow, for the old boat. And some clothes, too. It's goin' to be some chilly sailin', bo. No; come in an' we'll have a look at what you got. Say!"

"What?"

"Didn't I hear some firin' off there somewhere, half an hour ago, or maybe fifteen minutes?"

"Firing?" Arthur parried.

"M-m-m-huh! I just now happened to think of it. This surf here makes some noise. I didn't know for sure. Was there some gatts goin', kid? Good play with the old pepper-pots, or how?"

"Search me!" denied Arthur. "*I* didn't hear anything."

"Didn't, eh?" asked the other suspiciously. "Well, maybe not. I kind of thought perhaps you was in on it. None o' my funeral, of course; but —"

"Forget it and let's get busy with that boat!" exclaimed the fugitive, standing up and waiting for the other to light the way. "Nothing that's past amounts to a damn now. I want your boat, and I'll cough up right for it. So go to it!"

The ruffianly fellow grumbled a moment to himself incoherently, then turned and flung open a rickety door. The flash of his electric beam flicked white light on rough walls and disorder. Arthur, none too well pleased by this turn of affairs, yet in his desperation forced to chance it, followed.

Inside the door he paused, peering about him with the wise caution that had come to birth in him through his prison experience. At his right, a mulling fire of driftwood-knots showed a fireplace of rough brick. The dull glow of it lighted a squalid room, singularly disordered. Arthur had barely time to note more than this general impression, when his host struck a match and lighted a tin lamp on the table.

The unshaded light revealed a wretched interior — a rough-boarded room with a few nets hung on nails along the walls; a stove on three legs and a brick; a tumbled iron cot; dirty cooking-things; miscellaneous odds and ends of iron and ship-chandlery in one corner, gleaned from the beach; a barrel nearly full of corks near the door.

Beside the fireplace lay a heap of driftwood, drying. The only discordant note in the whole symphony of squalor was a telephone on the table, standing among unwashed dishes.

That telephone struck Arthur with a peculiar and disquieting force.

What could its use be? Why had it been installed in that lonely hovel out there on the edge of nowhere? What possible use could a broken-down beach-comber and casual fisherman have for a telephone?

Turning these questions in his mind, Arthur looked at the man himself, curious to know what manner of creature now held fate in his hands.

The strange fellow was bent over the fire, poking at it with a long iron bar that had once done duty aboard ship. Arthur could not see his face as yet. He had caught a glimpse of it when the man had lighted the lamp, but had not yet been able to form any clear picture of his host. Now, however, as the man turned with some grumbled words of complaint about the chill dampness of the November air on the marsh, the fugitive saw him plainly and frowned.

His was, in fact, a face to give most men pause. In Arthur's plight it seemed doubly disquieting. Nothing good, everything evil was written there in lines of disease, hardship, vice and crime. King Alcohol had set his brand on that low countenance; and wicked thoughts and purposes, bad deeds and criminal schemings had well seconded his work in making the man an object of repulsion and of fear.

The chin was square and bristled with a pepper-and-salt stubble; the nose was broken and twisted awry, as though by a terrific blow; a scar lividly wealed the right temple from the eyebrow up into the tangle of unkempt hair now disclosed as the man flung his sou'wester upon the floor and kicked it away into a corner.

All this was of ill augury; but his eyes were still worse — his eye rather, for he had but one. The left had been gouged out in some of his obviously numerous battles, and now the lid drooped empty. The remaining optic blinked red, inflamed with drink and smoke; an evil eye if ever man possessed one; the eye of a human beast of prey.

Arthur surveyed this person, clad in a reefer, a torn black sweater and a neckerchief, supplemented by corduroy trousers and sea-boots. So violently unpleasant was his impression that he could not entirely suppress its effect in his look. The beach-comber observed this and grinned maliciously, showing broken and yellowed teeth.

"I ain't such a much in the beauty line, am I?" he ejaculated. "No, strike me dead! I ain't no Venus de Medicine, and that's a fact. But what d'you expect? We can't all run a high grade of work like you. Some of us has to pull the rough stuff. So what you kickin' about?"

"I'm not kicking," replied Arthur. "Cut it, cut it, and get busy! Get your things on, cop the gas, and I'll split even with you, whatever I've got. Go to it, now!"

For a moment the man seemed about to obey. He nodded, turned and shuffled toward the fireplace, the iron bar still in his hand. Then he stopped and once again faced Arthur.

"Suppose you make that two-thirds?" he suggested. "The price of livin' is dognation high down here, 'specially gas; and what little I can pick up on the beach don't amount to a damn. It ain't worth a celluloid cat in Hell. Corks used to bring —"

"Oh, forget it!" interrupted Arthur, his temper rising. "Fifty-fifty, I said, and that goes!"

"Nothin' doin'!"

"What?"

"It's *my* boat, ain't it?"

"See here, are you trying to skin me alive?"

"You can pay it — an' you're goin' to, see? Now, dig!"

No mistaking the look in that one glowering eye. Arthur felt his temper getting the upper hand. The man obviously had determined to wring him dry or hold him up altogether. The drag of the pistol in his pocket gladdened him. A little more now, and —

"Well, how about it?" demanded the thug. "Are you goin' to cough, or ain't you? Maybe you'd like to hoof it up the bay with all the bulls scoutin' after you?"

"Is that right?" asked Arthur. "Two-thirds, and you do the job?"

The other nodded.

"When I say I'll do a thing, I do it!" he growled.

He peered curiously at Arthur a moment, then again came nearer.

"Say, bo!" he demanded roughly.

"What is it now?"

"Where d'you get that hair-cut?"

"None of your damned business!"

"Up the river — eh, kid?"

"What of it? You've been there yourself, I bet a million?"

"Maybe I have, maybe I have! Some place, ain't it? Strike me blind, but it's some place! A con would come across with everything he's got, wouldn't he, to beat a dump like that?"

With a quick gesture of his left hand he knocked Arthur's

hat off. Arthur flung up his arm, but too late. The hat —
Slayton's black felt — spiraled away and fell upon the dirty
table.

"Some hair-cut! That's right!" gibed the ruffian. "I
got your number, bo. That an' your white-paper face
would give you a free pass back to Sing Sing any day.

"Just out, hey? And a fresh job on your hands? An'
them after you? Say, look a' here! No two-thirds goes
now — see? You hand over the whole wad, kiddo, or —
Get me?"

He leered horribly at the telephone.

"Come across! Come across!" he menaced, squaring
his jaw. "It's worth it."

Infuriated as Arthur was, trembling with passion and
hate, he still recognized the infinite advantage this brute
possessed. Without his help everything was lost. Against
his opposition nothing could be done. Arthur knew that he
must yield, even to the ultimate penny.

"Take it all, you hog!" he cried bitterly. "After it's all
gone you can't get any more, anyhow. Here — take it!
And get busy! Now that you've cleaned me out, get busy!"

He drew out the wallet, opened it, and pulled out bills —
greenbacks, yellowbacks — without even trying to count
them. He flung them on the table, all but a single "X."

"Here, you, quit holdin' out on me!" snarled the ruffian.

"You can spare me this, to stake me when I strike the
city. I haven't got a cent of my own, I tell you. You've
got to let me have this ten!"

"Like Hell I will! You got an overcoat there you can
put up for a little coin. You got friends. You can make
a touch. I need the coin — see? And — Here! Gimme
that now! Quit your holdin' out!"

With his left hand — the right still held the poker — the
thug snatched both wallet and bank-note. His brows wrinkled in a villainous, low expression as with his single red

eye he studied the pocketbook.   Then a change came over his face.   His mouth dropped open.   The yellow teeth showed.   He stared at Arthur in amaze.

"Say, strike me blind!" he ejaculated.   "If it ain't Slayton's poke!"

"What — what d'you mean?" gasped Arthur.   "You — know him?"

"Know him!   Do — I — *know* him?" bellowed the other in a passion.   "He asks me if I *know* him!   Me, hired to watch an' keep him from — from —"

"What?"

The thug made a quick step, seized Arthur's overcoat and flung it back.

"His overcoat!   His suit!   You got his suit on!"

He turned, snatched up the hat from the table, and peered inside it.   There he saw three little gold-paper letters:

```
W. H. S.
```

"His lid!"

Arthur faced him, livid.

"What's the matter with you, anyhow?" he demanded hotly.   "Crazy, or what?"

"You've cleaned out Slayton?" roared the beach-comber, his face a study of wicked rage.   "You've maybe croaked him, hey?   You've croaked my meal-ticket, have you?"

"Can that and get busy with the boat!" cried Arthur, shaking with rage.   "You've got the wad; now go to it! Get to work!"

"Work!   Ha!   I'll get to work, all right, you son of a dog!   But it won't be the kind o' work you mean.   No boat for yours, kid!   Nix on the boat!   The only boat you'll

get will be the Black Maria.   I'll boat you, all right, all right
— strike me dead if I don't!"

Wheeling, he reached for the telephone.   Arthur staggered back, horror-stricken.

"You — won't do that!   Not *that!*"

"Won't, hey?"

He brandished the heavy poker in a gesture of deadly
menace.

"I won't?   You just wait an' see!"

Arthur's eye measured the distance to the door.   The ruffian stood between him and it with the iron bar in hand.
A sudden madness possessed the fugitive.   Something like
a red haze seemed to swim before his eyes.   Now, just at
the very moment of escape, this hideous, vicious, degraded
creature for some unknown reason was about to deliver him
to the police.

Arthur's hand slid into his pocket.   It closed over the
butt of the automatic.   On the instant the ugly black
weapon whipped up into the air.

With a beast-like cry the thug sprang and struck.   The
iron bar smashed on Arthur's forearm just as he pulled trigger.   The report crashed through the room; splinters flew
from the floor.

The fugitive's arm dropped, paralyzed.   He tried to duck,
to guard with the left elbow; but the swinging bar caught
him.   Fair on the head its crushing impact descended.   No
hair shielded the boy's skull.   His brain took the full shock
of the savage blow.

Reeling, he crashed against the table and fell.   Black
obscurity mercifully enwrapped him in its pall.

CHAPTER XXX

A VAGUE consciousness of pain, mingled with a steady, drumming roar, ushered the fugitive back into the living world again. Where the pain might be or what the roar might mean he could not tell. He knew only that he was lying motionless somewhere; that a dim gray light crossed by black lines now appeared and now vanished; and that mingled with the drumming sound came momentary gusts and shakings as of a great wind.

So much he seemed to sense a while, then again relapsed into vacancy. But before long he found himself awake once more; and now with greater clarity he could take cognizance of his surroundings, his bodily condition and his prospects.

The pain, he found, was localized in head and right forearm. The one he could move; the other, strive as he might, remained fixed. Not quite understanding, he blinked at the gray light, perceived it was a small-paned window, and now recognized the place where he lay — the villainous beachcomber's shack on the dunes.

Memory of everything returned, and with it energies that had lain in abeyance he could not tell how long. Some hours obviously; for when the iron bar had struck him down it had been black night, and now the leaden hue of a rain-swept November morning showed him the ugly desolation of the hovel.

Arthur's first impulse on regaining even partial comprehension was to cry out, to struggle, to fight his way clear of the obstacles that only too clearly were detaining him. But his shrewd keenness, product of the cell, whispered:

"No!"

He therefore continued to lie still, there on the iron cot where he now found himself. And, lying thus, he took stock of his own status and that of his surroundings.

His head was surely wounded, though how badly he could not know, since both his arms were securely lashed to his sides and his whole body was immobile. He could neither stir nor lift a hand to his aching cranium. The right arm, as he tried to tense the muscles, gave him exquisite anguish. It seemed swollen, too. Rightly he judged that the blow with the poker had broken one of the bones. With a grimace of pain he raised his head and cautiously peered round. Even though he could not move, he might at least take observations on his prospects.

The room was as he had seen it the night before, save that by the dull morning light it looked even uglier and more depressingly filthy. On the hearth the fire had died down to powdered white ash, with here and there a vagrant spark of red that winked and blinked at him as in derision. A fire was burning smokily in the stove, on which stood a coffee-pot and some other utensils, all dirty and rusty. Momentarily the smoke gusted out, driven down the rust-red pipe by the buffets of the sea-wind.

Along that pipe dripped and drizzled rain-water, seeping in through a crack in the piece of tin where the pipe went through the wall. This water ran down the pipe till the heat of the fire sizzled it into steam. The roof and the whole crazy structure groaned, creaked and rattled under the drive of the storm that had come up from the sea in the wake of the thickening clouds of the night before. At some particularly vicious drive it seemed almost as though the shack would be bowled clean off the dune and flung over into the salt marsh behind it.

Arthur, exhausted by his straining observations, lay back on the cot where he was now a prisoner and tried to think. Just what had been the cause of the beach-comber's attack he could not fathom. Just what was now going forward he knew not. But he understood in a general way that evil fortune had led him into the power of some dependent or attaché of Slayton, and that now nothing was written on the books for him save delivery into the hands of the police, and then Sing Sing, and then — death.

Arthur laughed bitterly. He did not struggle. Weakness and suffering had rendered him powerless, he knew, to break the bonds that the vicious beach-comber had knotted about him during his unconsciousness. Cruelly tight those cords were, cutting his flesh in numb lines and ridges. He could hardly stir in them. Evidently the fellow had not entertained the slightest idea of letting his prisoner escape, even though the lashings should cut and paralyze him. Not even the protection of the overcoat now shielded Arthur from the net cording. The thug had peeled this off the helpless fugitive, and now it hung behind the stove on a peg with Slayton's hat atop.

"Hey! Hello! Hello!" Arthur suddenly hailed. "Where are you?"

The effort made him wince with pain in head and arm. Yet he repeated the call. Where the ruffian might be he knew not; but if within hearing he might consent to loosen the bonds a little. Surely, now that Arthur was unarmed and wounded, he could not refuse to ease the cords a bit.

No answer to the cry. Nothing save that steady pounding of the rain, the slatting of the wind against the hovel, and the rising, falling, never-ceasing thunder of the surf along the sands.

Arthur lay quiet a while, trying in vain to ease his suffering. Added to the physical torment, greater agonies assailed him — swift, vivid pictures of events now sure: recapture, the cell, trial on another murder charge, conviction, the death-house, the chair, the end of everything under the glare of merciless incandescents, with black-coated doctors and scientists watching his death-agonies produced by a calm electrician at a switchboard.

The hideous injustice of it all maddened him. Neither the first crime nor the second had he committed; yet for the first he had received life imprisonment, and had already served two years in Hell. For the second he was bound to die, murdered in cold blood by a blind, deaf, inexorable power of injustice called the State.

If Arthur had cursed Slayton before, ten times more bitter now his curses were. The Judas had first betrayed and crucified him, and then in dying had with horrible cynicism buried him beneath the crushing weight of fresh accusations. The exquisite irony of the situation wrought powerfully on the boy's fevered mind. He laughed again, then cursed, then struggled — heedless now of all his pain — then howled in rage and vain appeal.

At last, exhausted, he lay still; and all at once again, as at first in the Tombs and later in Sing Sing, thoughts of his mother and of Enid Chamberlain drifted across his mind to soothe and comfort him. He saw the dead mother's smile, the lost sweetheart's loving, trustful, appealing eyes. Through the rain-drive and the wind and surf he seemed to hear echoes of those words that two years ago had stayed and solaced his sad heart:

Yea, though I walk in the valley of the shadow of death, I will fear no evil, for Thou art with me. Thy rod and Thy staff, they comfort me . . .

. . . .

Arthur awoke from an uneasy, fevered sleep, opened his eyes and beheld the beach-comber standing there before him in a suit of disreputable oilskins, dripping and drizzling like a huge, evil water-rat. Whence the man had come he knew not; but there he stood, grinning and leering with that single inflamed eye of his. Arthur's face contracted with repulsion and hate.

"Sleepin' like a baby, so nice an' comfortable, hey?" gibed the ruffian, flinging his hat upon the table. "An' me out in Hell's own storm! It don't seem fair, does it, when you tried to croak me with the old puffin'-rod, for me to have to go hikin' out in it on your account? An' you layin' so nice an'—"

"Can that!" blurted Arthur. "When are they coming?"

"Who comin'?"

"The bulls. You've been out pigging on me, of course. Well, when?"

"Wrong, kid!" retorted the thug. "Back up! Not that I love you, for I don't. But I ain't pigged yet. No need to go out for that. I could get 'em on the wire any time. Will, too, when I want 'em. But I don't just now."

"What's the idea? What did you go for?"

"Well, as you're my guest I don't mind tellin' you."

The beach-comber threw off his oilskin jacket and kicked it under the table. He twirled a chair around by the cot, sat down, fished up pipe and tobacco, and fell to smoking.

"No, I don't mind. Here! Look a' this, will you? Some wad comin' down the pike my way — what?"

From somewhere in his tatters he withdrew a Staten Island paper, wet and drabbled. This he opened up on his knee, then held it before Arthur's eyes. The wounded man read:

BANKER SHOT DOWN

CASHIER SLAYTON OF THE POWHATAN NATIONAL MURDERED IN HIS HOME

ESCAPED CONVICT SUSPECTED

$25,000 REWARD OFFERED FOR HIS APPREHENSION

Speechless, Arthur stared at his captor, who nodded amicably in the best of good-humors.

" Quite a haul I'm goin' to make — eh, bo? " he queried, gusting vile smoke toward the leaky roof. " Some haul! I kind of thought there'd be a good offer out this mornin', as quick as I doped the lay a bit. So I didn't call 'em, after all. No; I waited. Lay low an' wait is a good motto. That's what I done, kid. And strike me dead but I was right, at that! "

He hit the paper a blow with the back of his hand and whirled it over on the table beside his dripping hat.

" Dead right! " said he with gusto. " It's all comin' as I figgered. Old man Chamberlain, the bank president, 'phoned that big offer to headquarters; said if the bank's directors didn't make good on it he would pers'n'lly. Well, who's goin' to get it, the bulls or me? Not them, you bet! They jobbed me once an' lagged me for a finif for a job I never even touched. No love lost, believe me.

" Also, I want the stuff, and I'm goin' to have it. No bulls here! Nix on that! 'Long towards noon, when it's about time for the old buck to breeze into the bank, me for him on the wire. Confidential report — see? Reward guaranteed before I tell him where to come. That is, of course, *if* I produce the man, which I will.

" Get me, kid? Some wise guy — hey? I may not look like such a much, but when it comes to pullin' down the bundle, I'm there with the bells on, believe *me!* "

Arthur watched him with intense repugnance and hatred. He longed for release from this degrading bondage. Even the police would be welcome, it seemed to him, to rescue him from this foul creature, buzzard of unclean pickings at any dirty job.

" Loosen up on these ropes, can't you? " he suddenly demanded, while the ruffian sat and smoked with anticipatory joy. " You've got me, all right enough. Busted my arm,

I guess. Beaned me with the poker. Frisked my gun. Put me down and out. Now, there's no use cutting me in two with these ropes. Let me up!"

"Nothin' doin', kid!"

"What do you mean?"

"I mean you're twenty-five thousand bucks, dead or alive — see? I got you where I know where you are, an' you're goin' to stay."

"But I tell you my right arm's broken! It's swelling. I can't get away. You can loosen me up a little."

"Nix on the loosenin'! It ain't all on account o' the twenty-five thousand, neither. I got other reasons."

"What reasons?"

"Well, for one thing," answered the thug, tamping his pipe with a foul thumb, "when you put his nibs, there, up the escape, you done me out of a good job. And, besides, you went fer to gat me. Now it's my turn. You're there, an' there you stay. Get me, Steve?"

"I get you. What do you mean — I did you out of a good job? Were you working for Slayton? And, by the way, I didn't croak him, after all. I —"

"*Poof!*" spat the beach-comber. "Tell that to Sweeney!"

"All right, but that's on the level. No matter, though. I don't give a damn what *you* think, anyhow. What about this thing of a good job? Was he employing you?"

The beach-comber smoked a moment in silence with his single eye blinking at his captive, while rain and surf and wind wrought their wild symphony without the shack.

"I don't know as I mind tellin' you." he finally answered with deliberation. "The wad I got off you is in your favor. I guess I owe you a little info., if it don't hurt me none.

"You see, it was this way: I was hired by a gink up in the city to kind of look out for Slayton, like. He was a queer guy, Slayton was. Sort of down in the mouth at times. Had spells when he kind-a wanted to blow by the suicide line. A few times he used to walk out on the iron pier down below here an' size up his chances; an he done other stunts, too. The marshes interested him a lot. I guess I saved his life one or two times, all right, all right!"

"Saved his life? What for?"

"For so much per, of course. You don't think I gave a damn about him any way else, do you?"

"You mean your job was to keep an eye on him and head him off from —"

"You're on. Some questioner, ain't you? But I don't care. He's through now, and you're about through. Might as well tell you if you want to know. Yes; I had to watch him sometimes an' report on that there wire — see?"

"Who to?'

"Oh, a man that had some kind of stake or other in keepin' him alive! That was my job — see? My meal-ticket. An' strike me dead if you didn't blow along an' put the skids under it!"

"I get you," said Arthur, beginning to see daylight through the mystery. "But look here! Who could have any interest in keeping him alive? What for?"

"Hell! How do *I* know?"

"It wasn't somebody he owed money to, was it? Somebody that was getting a rake-off out of him?"

The beach-comber shrugged his shoulders non-committally.

"What was his name?" persisted Arthur.

"Search *me!*"

"Was it — Jarboe?"

No answer. But the quick, involuntary start the beach-comber made and the furtive glance in his rat-eye convinced Arthur he had struck home.

"It *was* Jarboe, wasn't it?" he demanded. "An old money-shark up back of Trinity?"

"Dead wrong!" affirmed the ruffian. "It was a guy named — named — Brown. A real-estate guy."

Despite his physical pain and mental anguish, Arthur could not help laughing.

"As a liar, some punk liar!" he gibed. "If you didn't frame a smoother one than that on the stand, no wonder the bulls jobbed you that time. Well, forget it. He's gone, anyhow; and I'm here, and these cords are cutting the eternal tripe out of me!

"Loosen up, can't you? I ask you again. And give me a drink of something — anything. I've got a fever, and I'm all stove up. Have a heart, can't you?"

"Drink? Sure thing! You're goin' to be worth twenty-five thousand to me, bo. I can afford to be generous. What 'll it be? Little drop of gin? Mouthful of brandy? Rye?"

"None of those, thanks. Coffee would go better."

"Coffee's right! Have all you want."

"Loosen me up, first."

"Nix!"

"Just one hand! Just enough so I can move a little. This is paralyzing me, I tell you! It's worse than the jacket up the river! Just one hand out. I'm all in, I tell you, with that wallop you gave me and the broken arm!"

The beach-comber scratched his head reflectively. Suddenly he nodded.

"One hand out, hey?" he asked. "All right; one goes. But no funny biz now, remember. First crack you make I give you the gat. Strike me blind if I don't!"

Arthur lay back, exhausted with the long conversation and the vehemence of his appeal. The thug after a moment's hesitation drew Arthur's pistol from the pocket of his oilskins and laid it eloquently on the table. Then he bent over the cot, undid a few knots and loosed the cords

so that Arthur could withdraw his left arm.   The right was
too paralyzed and agonizing to move.

He then lashed the cords back again as tightly as before.
" I'll take a chance," he grumbled.   " Steve did.   Stretch
now, if you want to.   And don't forget I'm on the job;
see ? "

Arthur flexed and extended his free arm with inexpressible relief.   Over his head he stretched it hard.

" That's fine ! " he exclaimed in gratitude.   " Now if you
could let me have a cup or two of coffee while we're waiting
for the bank to open —"

Nodding and grumbling to himself the brutish fellow
turned toward the stove and began preparing the drink.

" Time enough !   Time enough," said he.   " Couple of
hours yet.   Make yourself comfortable, bo.   You got a
lively road ahead o' you ; but for now, make yourself comfortable.

" Some doin's up at Slayton's, kid.   I stopped there a
while, gettin' that paper.   They're havin' a hell of a time.
I guess the ' front office ' has had the biggest dragnet throwed
out they've got.

" They're after a trail they think they got o' you in the
city.   Two or three have ' made ' you in Manhattan already — an' you here, stowed away safe an' sound in my
cottage by the sea !   Lucky for you I was here, kid.   If I
hadn't been —"

" Oh, for Heaven's sake cut that out and let's look at the
paper ! " interrupted Arthur, maddened by the creature's
formless monologue.   " And then, coffee !   You owe me
that much anyway, and more ! "

Leering, the beach-comber brought Arthur the paper, then
returned to his coffee-making.   Arthur held the paper in his
left hand and eagerly read the sensational account of the
crime.   Forgotten were his aching head and shattered arm

for the moment, as his eyes devoured the columns of false-
hoods, wild assumptions, wrong deductions from impossible
premises and all the vicious tissue of lies once more flung
out to tangle and to kill him.

He dropped the paper with a groan. The first case, two
years ago, had been terrible enough; but not as terrible as
this. The horror of it surged over him — his near approach to escape, the fearful misfortune of his meeting the
beach-comber, the calamity of his capture by this mercenary
beast, the swift on-drawing of the inevitable end. Cov-
ering his eyes with his hand, he gave himself to bitterness
of the spirit and to anguish of the soul.

The beach-comber roused him with a shake of the arm.

"Here's your boot-leg!" he exclaimed.

Arthur blinked up at him.

"Oh, thanks!" he answered, taking the cup — a heavy
cup of the ware known as stone china, almost unbreakable
and of massive mold.

He raised his head and sipped the steaming liquid — a kind
of chicory hogwash — with deliberation. Vile though the
stuff was, it warmed and comforted him. The beach-comber
stood there near the cot, hands on hips, peering at him with
that one sinister optic. When Arthur had drained the last
drop —

"More?" asked he.

"Thanks, yes. Just one."

"All right. Give us the cup."

He filled it again and brought it back, then sat down on
a broken chair near the table, picked up the paper Arthur
had dropped, and bending his one eye close to it, began
reading the article aloud, halting, mispronouncing, mutilat-
ing it, and stopping now and then to chuckle with amusement and intense satisfaction.

"Twenty-five thousand beans, hey? Some rhino!" he
jubilated in great good-humor. "I ain't never had much

luck; but now by God! I make good. Strike me dead if I don't — strike me dead!"

"Strike me dead!"

The phrase transfixed Arthur's vivid attention all in a breath of time.

"Strike me dead!"

The captive held in his hand the heavy mug, now half emptied of the vile liquid. Calculatingly he weighed it, not yet quite sensing its possibilities, but with some vague perception of them in his mind.

"Strike me dead!"

Why not? There sat the ruffian hardly eight feet away, bent over the paper which he had spread upon the table by the pistol — the pistol to be used in case Arthur made one single move for freedom, one solitary act of resistance.

Close to the paper his one eye had been brought. The blind socket was toward Arthur. For the moment the captive was positively secure from observation. That moment might end; it might forever pass and be lost and done for. That golden opportunity, once fled, could never come again.

"Strike me dead!"

It rang and echoed in his feverish brain, seeming to pound in his temples with the pounding of his pulses like hammers on anvils:

"Strike me dead, strike me dead, strike me dead!"

Silently Arthur lowered the heavy cup beside the bed, and soundlessly poured out the rest of the coffee on the floor. He raised the cup again and swung it to and fro, taking careful aim.

The beach-comber, having finished one page of the paper, sat up, turned the sheet and then sank down again, without having glanced round. Arthur, his heart in his mouth, again poised the cup.

There lay the gun. The threat was clear. Arthur knew

death awaited him in case of failure. Either he must break that bestial skull with one blow, or the thug would inevitably pistol him as he lay there, bound and helpless, on the cot.

Swiftly he weighed all the chances, and chose action. Nothing but death awaited him at any rate — inglorious, shameful, horrible death. If he died fighting that were better than to die strapped in the chair, writhing in impotent and dumb abandon of unutterable torment.

Twice, thrice he swung the missile. His eye never for one second left the aimed-for spot — the right temple, where the cranial bones were thinnest — his only hope for liberty, for life.

Lashed as he was, unable to bring his shoulder-muscles into full play, and obliged to use his left arm, the feat became well-nigh impossible; but on it life depended.

Four times he swung the cup, and five.

Suddenly the beach-comber raised his ugly head a little, as though he had finished reading. Slowly he began to turn with meditative deliberation.

A fraction of a second more, and Arthur's last opportunity would be past and gone. The doors of Fate would clang shut on him forever and forever.

" Some rhino!" exulted the thug again, chuckling with supreme satisfaction over his haul. " Some real rhino! Strike me dead if it ain't! "

Flinging into his strained muscles every ounce of strength and nervous energy his battling soul could muster, Arthur wrenched himself a little up from his bonds, aimed with desperate precision, and pointblank hurled the heavy cup.

CHAPTER XXXI

FLIGHT

SPED with the terrific force and accurate aim of desperation, the missile crashed home full on the scarred brow of the beach-comber.

Hardly a grunt he uttered, but fell backwards, knocked clean out — if indeed not killed — while the heavy cup skidded across the table, dropped to the floor and lay there, blood-spattered.

Arthur, staring with wide eyes, trembling and shaking and with teeth that clattered in a chill of nervous anguish, began tearing with his free left hand at the knots of the cords that bound him. The man might be dead — he hoped so fervently — or he might be only stunned. His head looked a horrid sight as he lay there on the dirty floor. Arthur had at any rate won first blood in this battle.

Could he maintain the advantage? Could he yet escape?

Everything now depended on haste, should the ruffian be only stunned. In case he should revive before Arthur could get free, the end would come in short order. The pistol, lying there black and ominous on the table, vouched for that.

Savagely the captive toiled. His nails broke and the flesh, beneath, commenced to bleed, but he felt nothing. With a violent effort he managed to get one of the knots within reach of his teeth. Fingers and teeth together wrenched the cords, worrying them as a dog worries a rat. And all at once a knot gave. The supreme gratitude Arthur felt at that second had never been surpassed in his life.

One knot eased another. Desperately he worked. Soon

a second one was loosed — a third — a fourth. Now Arthur could fling back a whole coil of the stout netting-cord. He drew it round under the cot and attacked more knots. His shoulders were free now — and suddenly his bonds seemed to fall away from him. Some master-knot has eased them all. He was free!

Numbed, lame, dizzy, with a horrible sick feeling in the pit of his stomach and a blinding pain in his bruised head, he managed to draw himself out from the web of lashings that the scoundrel had hauled about him, and supporting himself with his left hand made shift to sit up on the edge of the cot.

To save his life it seemed to him he could not immediately have stood up and walked. His legs were paralyzed. The toes would hardly respond to his will as he tried to move them. It seemed as if the whole lower half of his body were dead.

Often at Sing Sing he had heard tales of paralysis from the strait-jacket. Now he was experiencing the effects of great stricture long applied. Powerless to stand or take a step at this most terribly vital moment, he looked upon the inert body of the beach-comber and from the bottom of his embittered soul heaped vitriol of malediction on the thug.

The pain in his right arm drew his attention. He pulled back the sleeve, examined the bruised and purple flesh, observed the swelling and gingerly felt the bone. This caused him excruciating pain.

"Broken, all right," said he. "That's another debt you've got to pay, you spawn of Hell!"

For the present he could do nothing about his injury. Whatever pain it might cause would just have to be borne with set teeth. Other and more urgent matters were at hand. It was imperative that he should recover the use of his legs before the ruffian might revive — if indeed he still lived.

Arthur rubbed and massaged his own body, thighs and legs as vigorously as he could with his one effective hand. Soon a prickling sensation commenced, and he knew that the circulation was starting in again. Recovery was rapid. In three or four minutes he could move his legs a little. In ten he had managed to get up on his feet and, by holding to the table, to drag himself far enough to get possession of the gun. Now let the beach-comber revive!

It was obvious already that sooner or later the thick-skulled brute would come to. Arthur had not after all succeeded in making way with him. That massive skull and dull brain had resisted the blow, and though the ruffianly face and neck were seeped with blood, nothing had resulted save a flesh-wound.

Another man in Arthur's place might have put the automatic to that villainous head and finished the job. Almost any other would have felt himself justified in that deed. But Arthur, despite everything, still shrank from taking human life. Twice falsely accused of it, hounded, harried, tortured, ruined and damned for it, even now when murder might save his life and free him, he hesitated.

Twice he brought the gun to bear and twice turned it aside. It seemed to him somehow that Enid stood there between him and that prostrate hulk of vice and degradation which was still a living soul. Not for his life could he pull trigger. In a fight he could have shot the thug down; but helpless and inert before him the man was absolutely safe.

Angry at his own weakness, he shoved the pistol into his pocket, with an oath. Kneeling beside the unconscious brute, he examined the injury. He saw it was superficial. The effects would soon pass. That meant Arthur must take immediate measures to restrain the beast when he should awaken from his stupor.

Leaving the beach-comber where he had fallen — indeed, to have tried to move him now would have far exceeded

Arthur's shattered forces — he gathered together a quantity of the net-cord, took a case-knife from the table, and set himself to work making the man his captive.

Arthur's right hand and arm dangled helpless. The blow, beside having broken the radius, seemed to have paralyzed the whole arm — a condition by no means improved by the subsequent cruel lashing on the cot. Arthur could barely move it at all. With his left hand he raised it and thrust it into his shirt, thus making a temporary sling. Later he would attend to the injury, but for the present he must work and work fast to trice up the fallen thug.

With some difficulty Arthur drew both the man's hands behind his back, and then began binding them. Round and round he passed the cord, hauling it tight with all his strength, which now in some measure had begun to return. Unminding his wounded head and throbbing arm, he labored.

The process was slow. He had to crouch there, using his right elbow to hold the man's hands down, while with the left he pulled the cord tight. But he persisted, and after a while got his erstwhile captor firmly trussed.

This done, he bound the thug's feet together, knotting them hard. He next poured water on the lashings to set the knots and swell the cords. Then he stood up, surveyed his work and knew it was good.

Considerably recovered, Arthur set immediately at work to put himself in shape for flight. He bathed his wounded head, examined the gash as best he could in a jagged bit of mirror tacked to the wall of the shack, and decided that his injury, though ugly, was inconsequential. Choosing the best of the beach-comber's few surplus garments, he painfully disguised himself therein, assuming the final appearance of a rough-and-tumble waterman. The oilskins and sou'wester could not have been improved upon as a make-up. A pair of big sea-boots completed it.

He broke in pieces a wooden box that had held canned

goods, cut some splints and with great difficulty applied these to his forearm, which he wrapped with net-cords. He fashioned a sling out of a bit of tattered sail-cloth and through this slipped his arm.

He next emptied Slayton's clothes, which he had discarded, of their contents. He found a few valueless papers and memoranda, which he burned; some loose coins, a silver match-box and some minor miscellanea. The idea came to him that perhaps the wig might help disguise him; but having tried it he found he could not make it fit, and therefore had to abandon that plan.

He stuffed the wig into an inner pocket of the ruffian's clothing he had put on, saved the matches and coins, and did up all the dead cashier's clothing, with the match-box, in a compact bundle weighted with a heavy piece of junk-iron and securely lashed with net-cord.

He now was ready for the urgent business of flight.

The hour, marked by the beach-comber's alarm-clock, was just a little past eight. Outside, wind and weather still were rising, and the rain came hurling against the shack in long, driven curtains that half-obscured the sea. Rather formidable waves had begun to build in the Lower Bay. Standing at the leaky window a moment, peering out, Arthur watched the ravenous curl and slaver of their tongues, anxiously yet without real fear. Better to end life there and now, he was thinking — infinitely better — than a few weeks later in the chair of infamy and torment at Sing Sing.

He turned back into the room, poured some more hot coffee and drank two cups. Bread and cold meat stood on the foul shelf that served the beach-comber as a pantry; but Arthur, fevered and in pain, could force himself to eat nothing. He viewed the man's drinking-water with suspicion, and though athirst confined himself to liquid that had been boiled.

If he were to get away at all, he knew he must bestir himself. His original plan still held. He was still determined to try for the Long Island shore, to enter Manhattan through Brooklyn. Not all the trains and cars could be watched. The police could not take cognizance of everything. Once on Long Island he felt positive he could reach the city undetected; the more so as the fellow had told him the police were working on a clue that reported him already in the city.

First of all Arthur needed money. He proceeded to "frisk" the ruffian with great thoroughness, and very speedily recovered the wallet. This time he counted the contents. They assayed to the color of one hundred and eighty-six dollars. The thug's own pocketbook yielded eleven.

Arthur smiled, well pleased. On this, one could travel far. Even though justice were denied him he might still escape from persecution, win life, a chance to stand erect once more and be a man somehow, somewhere, sometime!

The launch, now — where might it be?

"Out back there in a cove," the fellow had said.

He had also remarked that it needed gas.

But where was the supply? And could Arthur, crippled as he was, start the engine and navigate that plunging turmoil of wild waters in a twenty-two-footer? Grave questions all. Grave in the extreme.

But the fugitive did not hesitate. His mind made up, he went calmly to work in carrying out his plan. For the immediate present in that obscure hiding-place he felt safe. The future — well, the future must look out for itself.

First of all Arthur cut the wires of the telephone. The shack was now wholly isolated. He took the instrument, carried it to the door and gave it a heave out into the rain-swept desolation of pools and dead grasses behind the building.

A barrel on horses under an old tarpaulin suggested gasoline. The suggestion proved correct. Now all Arthur needed was to find the boat itself.

This task proved not difficult. A few minutes of meandering through vague paths among the marshy areas brought him to a black mud-banked tidal slough along which a dozen or fifteen rickety wharves had been rudely built. At one of these rode the launch, innocent of paint or brass, but stoutly engined. Arthur climbed down into it, bailed it out, examined the motor with care, found he understood it, and after five minutes' experimenting under the lashing November downpour started it satisfactorily.

Having proved that the engine would serve him, he stopped it and returned to the shack. The injured ruffian on the floor was now beginning to show signs of life. He was groaning rather loudly, and from time to time his body twitched in spasmodic contractions. Arthur paid no heed to him, but sat down at the table and with Slayton's pencil wrote on the fly-leaf of a greasy old novel:

Keep quiet and don't strain yourself trying to get free. You can't. You won't starve in twenty-four hours. I'll see that you are released. Thanks for the use of the boat. That about balances the wallop you gave me. Good-by.

This message, scrawled painfully with his left hand, Arthur laid on the floor close beside the fellow, so that he must in all probability see it when he should revive. Arthur then took a final look around to be sure he had left no incriminating traces of his presence there, carried the bundle of clothes down to the boat and tossed it in; returned and got a water-pail, and in two trips filled the gas-tank of the motor-boat.

This done, he cast off, started the engine again, and with no further ado navigated under the pouring rain-drive and wild-blustering November wind down the slough toward the tumbling wildness of the Bay.

Five minutes later the motor-boat, guided only by his left hand, was fighting through a savage surf, smothered in spray, shipping a bucket of cold brine at every wallow. That was a wild, ugly sea to buck; but Arthur held her nose to it, and through she went.   Then, slanting away northeastward, she swooped from crest to trough and back again, a wallowing, diminishing speck in the mad dance of the storm.

Presently the scudding mist and rain dimmed even this, then swallowed it completely.

Trackless, the fugitive still held a course toward — what?

CHAPTER XXXII

IN HIDING

SHORTLY before noon a disabled motor-boat, its engine skipping badly and navigated by a solitary waterman in tattered oilskins, limped painfully into a slip on the North River and came alongside a flight of landing-stairs.

Cramped and numb, the waterman clambered out, made fast and looked about him with keen eyes under the dripping brim of his sou'wester. Buffeted by wind and rain, he stood there, peering with sharp intelligence. Two or three members of a tug's crew, loafing at the stokehole door of their craft in the slip, noted that his right arm hung in a sling.

" Some nerve, damned if he ain't! " growled one, " to take 'er out that way, worst blow we had in two year! "

" Nerve is right," answered another. " Only. *I* call it bughouse! "

They passed a few remarks, idly interested as the boatman climbed the stairs and vanished down the pier.

" He ain't left his boat in no very choice spot," the first speaker commented. " This ain't no public landin' nohow. He's li'ble to get in a mix if old man Hawley sees that there la'nch where she is now."

The other answered nothing. A third man behind them asked for a chew, and the subject shifted to things whereof landlubbers wot nothing.

The worst blow in two years had indeed landed Arthur at a place he had not chosen, yet which after all might serve his purpose better than any other. Half way across the Bay, engine trouble had weakened his power. Wind and wave had taken him with savage violence. He had been forced to run before them, straight up through the Narrows in the Upper Bay; and only when within a mile of the Battery had he been able to stop bailing. Exhausted, he had steered his lame boat through a dangerous puzzle of harbor-craft into the North River; and so knowing not whither he went, suffering agonies from his shattered arm, half-frozen, drenched to the skin through his torn oilers — all in all a sick and broken man — he had come once more to land on the fringe of the vast, hostile yet sheltering hive of men, New York.

Under the very eyes of police and "bulls" watching cars and ferries, the disheveled waterman passed. In safety he traversed the broad, cobbled space of West Street, between the pier-houses and the row of buildings opposite. The swinging lattice of a low groggery swallowed him. Five minutes later, in the back room of that dive, he was devouring a horrible beef stew mixed with "punk," and — very much against his taste but merely to divert suspicion — drinking a tall beer wholly innocent of hops or malt.

After the wild and storm-racked experience of the past three hours and more, this haven seemed beatific. Filthy, smoky, crowded with the roughest offscourings of the waterfront — an "ink-pot" where a murder could be bought for two dollars, for one, nay, even for a drink of rye — it still offered peace and rest and opportunity to pull together for the next step of this terrible pilgrimage through the wilderness of a society organized to lay hands on him and slay him.

Here, for a time at least, he was safe. Here he could eat and drink and sleep — for up-stairs a vile doss-house offered beds at fifteen cents. Here he felt the eye of observation would hardly reach him. His protean changes of disguise, largely forced on him by the extraordinary circumstances through which he had passed, seemed to him almost

a complete safeguard for the present. Having started in
convict garb, he had then become a hobo. He had shifted
to a gentleman, and lastly to a waterman in oilers. No less
than Sherlock Holmes, he reflected over his meal, would have
been required to spot him coming — of all ways and in all
places — via a motor-boat to that landing on the North
River.

Had he planned all and been backed by unlimited re-
sources, he could have done no better; and yet all, or mostly
all, had been the result of nothing but chance.

Fate had played his hand for him, not he himself. Bar-
ring the broken arm and the lost vengeance on Slayton, for
which loss he had already grown profoundly grateful, mischance had passed him by. It was with a deep and vast
thankfulness that he sat there among those vile, shouting,
ribald, cursing outcasts in that hideous " kip," devoured his
nauseous food with his left hand and thanked high heaven
that freedom still was his.

Too deeply schooled in the bitter wisdom of the underworld was Arthur now to make any false steps. He carefully refrained from laying his sou'wester aside, even though
it seemed to band his head with a ring of heat and pain.
The big, drooping-brimmed hat admirably protected from
observation that clipped, wounded, aching poll of his.

Too wise was he to flash even a V in that den of thieves
and cutthroats. Had one of many there suspected his identity, piped that cranium or known even a fraction of the
wad he carried, either he would have been snitched on in
ten minutes for the reward, or " big Peter " would have been
slipped to him in a knockout dose, or outright butchery
would forever have ended his bitter quest for liberty.

No; the fugitive took no risks. He kept his tongue in his
cheek, his sou'wester on his head and his wad in his pocket.
He made no talk with any. He paid his score with a few
loose coins from among those he had found in Slayton's coat

— coat, overcoat and all now lay at the bottom of the Bay, sunk deep by that piece of junk-iron he had lashed into the bundle — and thereafter spent some hours in reading newspapers crammed with sensational misinformation about Slayton's "murder" and about Mansfield, the hideous criminal. During this perusal he consumed just enough beer and tobacco to entitle him to shelter from the storm.

Sitting there in hiding in the darkest corner, he pondered many things — the curious ways of justice; the fate that had taken him, clean, straight and whole, unsoiled by criminality, and had made a hunted man of him, a man accused of two murders by the whole world, a man seared by the penitentiary, a man broken in body and embittered in soul, a man yet to be dragged down and harried to his death.

He pondered on Enid too, now millions of miles away from him and forever lost; and felt tears start in his eyes and a lump choke him as he recalled her ways and words, her look, her gestures and endearments of the other, better days.

Had she still faith in him? he wondered. No, no! Impossible! Up to the end of his time in Sing Sing she had believed in him; this much he knew. She had continued writing and had never ceased protesting her faith and trying to instil hope into him that some time the vast wrong should all be made right. She had treasured the one letter a month which constituted his total writing allowance in the Pen. Through all she had "stood by." But now —

Now, Arthur sensed right well, the end of everything had come. His escape, the shooting of Slayton, all the circumstances now had surely condemned him, even in her pure and trusting eyes. And as he realized the loss and felt the last strand breaking which had bound him to resolves for upright conduct, he knew he was standing on the narrow brink of Hell.

One impulse, one deciding factor now might plunge him

irretrievably into the Pit. Society had condemned him, blameless. It had thrust him down into the underworld and held him there. It now sought his life with blind and deaf stupidity as savage as it was unreasoning.

Well, there was the challenge. If society insisted on his playing that game, why not play it after all and play it hard?

No upward way beckoned, but only downward ways. Very well, so be it. The world had flung him out and spat upon him as an enemy. It had refused to hear him, to believe him, to accept him as anything but a foe.

Why not snatch up the gauntlet and — since the rôle had been forced upon him — play it pitilessly and well?

Arthur suddenly aroused himself from these black musings with a start. He had just recalled the fact that the motor boat, still moored in that rain-swept slip, constituted a grave peril for him, a clue that might yet lead him to the chair.

How could he have forgotten it so long? Such folly seemed incredible, yet the fact remained; he had not disposed of the boat, and it must be made way with at once.

But how? He dared not leave the joint. Suffer as he might with his cut head and his broken arm still swelling in its soaked bandages, he was determined to remain hidden there till night at least; perhaps for some days. Yet the boat must be got rid of. This new problem quite dispelled his melancholy musings on the injustice of society. He forgot to ponder future vengeance in his sudden anxiety to fend off present pursuit.

He glanced about him wearily, seeking some face that promised compliance with his will. The hour was now past five. Outside, a rainy night had settled down, dun, chill and drear. The brutal glare of incandescents lit the bar garishly; but in the back room where Arthur sat only two or three were burning. By their light he observed the present personnel.

Sordid and low those unfortunates were — 'longshore-men, sailors and roustabouts of the worst types; a Portu-guese or two; a Bermuda negro; a furtive-eyed crimp; a few miscellaneous bits of human riffraff cast up like débris along the lip of the sea.

One of the 'longshoremen appealed to Arthur's eye, now by reason of his prison-life well versed in gauging criminal character, as the fellow for his purpose. Arthur judiciously approached him, entered into *pourparlers* and in fifteen min-utes had the man coming. The prospect of a twenty-two-foot boat, given away absolutely for nothing, would have lured a more virtuous soul than he.

Arthur furnished full data as to the place and appearance of the launch, frankly stated it was stolen and exacted a promise from the 'longshoreman that he would never snitch and that before nightfall the boat would be safely hidden in some obscure, marshy lagoon up the Passaic River. There paint and a change of some details would effectually disguise it. Arthur and the man had another drink together, and the man departed, glad in his good fortune, leaving Arthur's mind far easier than before.

Next the fugitive's mind reverted to the beach-comber, in all probability still lying bound and helpless in the shack on the dunes. In justice Arthur might have left him there to starve and rot. But his promise had been given, and it must be kept. Not yet had all feelings of humanity been stifled in his heart. All the monstrous houndings of society had not yet been able to destroy his simple kindness and brave honesty.

He now proceeded, therefore, to free the captive by the simple means of notifying the police. He got writing mate-rials and a stamp from the waiter — who though gorilla-like yet appreciated the argument of a ten-cent tip — and, printing with his left hand, bent over the beer-wet table, produced this masterpiece:

Police hedquaters, Dear sir, this to notify you a man was held up an robbed in a shack on the beach 1 ½ miles east of station at oakwood hites, staten iland, this morning. about the middle shack in the settelment north of iron pier. the strong arm man made his getaway, the other one is tide hand an foot there an may die if you dont get him. this is no jolly but strait dope. Yours truly,
WISE GUY.

This done, he sealed and addressed it:

POLICE HEDQUATERS,

Mulbery St, city.

and, having observed a mail-box on the corner across the street, took a chance and posted it himself.

His duty now all done and more than done, he bethought him of a little rest. The morrow must find him ready for still other and greater exertions. Despite his broken arm, constantly growing more painful, he must push on, seeking fresh disguises. Once the police should rescue the beach-comber, his oilskins and sou'wester would be known and sought for. By morning, at latest, he must be afar in some other hole or cranny of the hive, in other clothes and under different circumstances.

As Arthur paid his fifteen cents for the luxury of a night's doss he realized his proposterous folly in having written that letter; and yet he did not regret having written it. Had he left the beach-comber there to die, he himself might have been safe for some days Perhaps nobody would have discovered the man in a good while. Possibly not until old Jarboe should have investigated would anybody have ventured out across those marshes, flailed by the November storm. Meantime Arthur could have rested and recuperated at his ease. The price he now would have to pay for having saved that vicious, worthless life might be his own.

Had he only shot the man and dumped him into a quicksand, as impulse had dictated, how vastly safer now he must have been! Yet in his heart he rejoiced that he had not done so. He cherished the image and the vision of Enid Chamberlain, lost to him now yet still living in his soul — the vision that had stayed his hand, the vision that still seemed to guide him through the dark and formless ways of persecution and of flight.

Not yet had he done murder. With her to uplift and strengthen him he could not do it now. So long as Enid's blessed memory should abide with him, hunted though he was and hounded through the rat-pits and sewers of the underworld, he could not kill.

His heart rose surging up to her in love and gratitude supreme.

"*De profundis!*" he murmured fervently; and for the first time in long weeks of anguish he felt the burning solace of tear-drops starting in his eyes.

CHAPTER XXXIII

"PULL the rope there, Bill!"

Bill, clerk of the doss-house up-stairs over the saloon, being thus adjured by a human wreck slouched far down in a broken-seated chair beside the pot-bellied stove, twitched the cord that drew back the lock of the wire-grated door. Doss-house doors must always be kept locked from the outside. Otherwise the fifteen-cent-less would inevitably prowl in and sleep gratis.

Bill surveyed Arthur, who returned the observation. The clerk seemed constitutionally in need of a shave and con-genitally hard of heart. No appeals unbacked by cash could conceivably procure free sleep from him. He moved a shirt-sleeved arm, notably unclean, and jerked his thumb toward the inner regions.

Arthur was free to enter the pearly gates of slumber. The ticket in his hand — the ticket that the wreck in the chair had noted, even as he had observed Arthur's obvious lack of familiarity with the customs of dosses — entitled him to go through. He accordingly passed from the outer region of bare benches and tables with ragged old news-papers on them, the region adorned with recruiting posters and many indubitable proofs of the tobacco habit, to the inner region of tiered-up rows of cots, whitewashed walls, and numerous signs prohibiting everything in general.

Appallingly foul the air was, worse even than the fetid air of Sing Sing. The filthy bunks in superimposed tiers repelled the newcomer. Hardly more disgusting than these

had been his bunk in his cell on "the flats." Four or five
down-and-outers had already crawled into their lairs.
These were probably men who the night before had "carried the banner," and who now by hook or crook, having
got hold of the coveted "pad-money"— more precious far
than coin for eats — had with the drawing-on of night gone
to their slumbers at the first possible moment after the
opening of the doss. Heaven knew — perhaps — when
some of them might sleep under a roof again!

Only with the greatest repugnance could Arthur force
himself to choose a bunk in this iniquitous den; but his
throbbing head and swollen arm, joined to a vast weariness
of flesh and spirit, forced him to lie down among these outcasts. He chose a flop in the very farthest corner where
the light was dim. Shucking only his boots and outer clothing, which he warily rolled all up together and used as a
pillow, thus safeguarding himself against disadvantageous
exchanges of apparel, he sought repose. Over his clipped
head the sou'wester still extended its protection.

For a few minutes physical pain and mental anguish kept
the fugitive awake, but gradually exhaustion claimed its
due; his ideas and sensations grew vague and uncertain,
and he slept.

He awoke suddenly, not understanding where he was,
sat up on the bunk, and blinked around him. The place
was full of unfortunates, most of them snoring or groaning dolefully. So thick and heavy had the air become in
that tight-closed pit of social misery that the one or two incandescents burning there seemed dimmed thereby. The
clock on the farther wall marked nine-twelve. Arthur had
slept four hours like one dead.

With returning plenitude of consciousness he found that
an intense pain in his arm had wakened him. Despite the
splints and wrappings, it had continued to swell. The bone
had been broken some twenty hours before. Exposure,

hardship, rain, lack of proper care had all wrought havoc with it. Arthur realized as he sat there on the edge of the bunk, feeling of the arm and peering at it by the vague light, that serious developments were forward.

" I'm liable to lose this," he muttered, " if I don't do something for it, and do it quick! "

Inwardly he cursed the luck which, playing him as a cat plays a mouse, had let him escape only with this injury, which might yet drag him down to capture and to death. Were any investigation of his hurt made, it must inevitably lead to exposure. He dared not ask for help, yet help he must have. The *impasse* loomed up appallingly before him.

All at once out from the back of his subconsciousness the image of Dr. Harland Nelson rose and stood before him — Nelson, the cold, calm, scientific man whose testimony had finally convicted him; Nelson, the impersonal; Nelson, who had admitted on the stand that his science had no explanation of those half-dozen gray hairs found in the clutching dead fingers of old man Mackenzie.

Nelson!

The idea of Nelson possessed him suddenly and with strange power. Once more he weighed the half-formulated plan he had already entertained — the plan of taking the gray wig to the doctor, of telling his story, of driving home its truth upon that chill and calculating brain, of enlisting the scientist in his cause.

A forlorn hope? Maybe. Nelson, largely responsible for having sent Arthur away for life — would he, could he now afford to reverse his opinions and champion a man he had helped damn? Could scientific honesty and ethical uprightness so far overbalance the natural human pride of opinion?

Arthur's mind and body were in no condition for analysis. All that he realized as he sat there, suffering torment on that dirty cot in the doss-house, was that the idea of Nelson, of the wig, of justification, had suddenly obsessed him once more; and that, moreover, he stood in direst need of medical attention.

Enough!

Arthur's decision, swiftly made, settled into firm mold with equal swiftness. Standing up, he drew his clothing on again and fixed the sou'wester down close over his telltale stubble of prison-cut hair.

Nobody noticed him in that sad place; none questioned and none cared. He sat down again, hauled on the beachcomber's huge sea-boots, and clumped to the door. At the right, Bill sat yawning over a pink sporting paper and inhaling a cigarette. A little row of butts stood on his greasy desk, upright like tenpins. He gazed at Arthur with a watery eye, scratched his bristling chin, and then resumed his study of the shapeliness and valor abundantly portrayed in the pink pages.

"Give us a slant at your telephone-book there, Jack!" demanded Arthur, simulating the speech of the gutter.

The clerk in silence shoved it over to him. He turned the pages eagerly, emotions at his heart as violent as though the gleam of a new hope over the inky wastes of despair had been a ray that dazzled him with its strange light.

Neff — Neiss — Nelmes — Nelson. Albert E. Edward F. Nelson, Harland, physician, 127A Madison Avenue.

Arthur stared at the address, burning it into his memory

"Thanks!" And he shoved the book back again. The bristly clerk merely yawned.

"I'm goin' out a while. Got a return-check there?" asked the fugitive, keen on maintaining an illusion of belonging to the underworld.

"Nothin' doin'," answered he of the watery eye, sticking another butt at the end of the row. "No checks. If we had 'em, maybe three or four boes would relay sleeps in one night. You either stay in or stay out — see?"

Arthur raised a plaint, but to no avail. He finally had to leave without the desired check. Two minutes later, with the beach-comber's clothes upon him and Slayton's one hundred and eighty-six dollars in his pocket, he was on the street.

The storm had cleared off cold and freezing, with a promise of moonlight again through the scudding clouds. Ice coated the sidewalks and skimmed the little pools between paving-stones or in gutters. Pedestrians hurried past, their breath blowing in vapor-swirls.

Arthur, not yet wholly dry and suffering acute pain, shivered as the nipping air searched through the ragged garments of the beach-comber. He turned into Christopher Street and walked rapidly toward the Ninth Avenue "L," keeping a sharp eye peeled for trouble.

Unmolested he reached the "L," got off at Twenty-Eighth Street, and caught a cross-town car to Madison Avenue. Some few persons regarded him with curiosity, for the figure of a waterman in oilskins and with a broken arm hanging in a sling of sailcloth was no every-day sight. Yet nobody spoke to him, nor was he disturbed in any way.

He passed near two policemen, but neither one stopped him. Few detectives would have been able to "make" him in that outfit. Police, plain-clothes men and detectives all alike were on the lookout for Arthur dressed in Slayton's clothes, the loss of which had been noted. That suit now was lying safely at the bottom of the Bay. The oilskins, sou'wester and huge seaboots were life-savers for the fugitive.

Some few minutes later Arthur approached the physician's door. In front of it a magnificent limousine was standing with a blasé chauffeur yawning on the seat. Arthur mounted the marble steps and rang the electric bell of a door which bore a shining plate of brass, engraved with the name:

HARLAND NELSON, M. D.

Physician and Surgeon

A maid in cap and apron presently opened the door, surveyed this rough-and-tumble figure with disapproval, and shook her head. Her voice was colder than the night wind, which was chattering Arthur's teeth, as she announced:

"The doctor's hours are from seven to nine. You can't see him to-night."

"A doctor's hours are whenever he's needed," shivered the fugitive. "I must see him!"

The maid stared at the sound of this kind of voice and expression in the mouth of a 'longshoreman, but stood firm.

"You can't!"

"I can, and will!"

He pushed past her into the hall.

"Go and tell him it's urgent!"

"He's got company to-night, and —"

"He'd leave anything if he knew who was here. Go get him!"

Fairly outplayed and dominated, the maid shut the outer door, peered a moment with indecision at this extraordinary visitor, then waved a hand at the curtained doorway on her right.

"Step into the office, please," bade she.

Arthur nodded in silence and clumped in over the polished hardwood floor, his big sea-boots making a formidable clatter of hobnails that augured no good for the parquetry. The maid stared at him in indignation, then turned and flounced up-stairs. This peculiar, tall, big-shouldered waterman, who kept his sou'wester on in the house, whose oilskins showed many a rip, and whose rough boots scarred the waxed floor, yet whose broad brows commanded and whose blue eyes and low-pitched voice somehow stirred her heart, surely was the most disconcerting patient ever she had ushered into that office in all the three years of her service.

Thus, piqued, angered, yet underneath it all well pleased to serve him, she ran lightly up the broad stairway. The doctor had told her positively he would see no more patients that night, and had settled down to a game of chess with his friend, while his wife and the visitor's daughter had a bit of Brahms and Dvorák in the music-room. Yet the 'longshore-man had commanded, and she had perforce obeyed. Biting her lip, she did his bidding.

Arthur, listening at the office-door with contracted brow and a poignant nervousness gaining on him moment by moment, heard the murmur of voices up-stairs. He caught the tones of Nelson's dry, cold speech, well-remembered from the trial when the doctor had so dispassionately, so impersonally blighted his prospects and sealed his fate. And at that sound again his uninjured hand clenched hard, his face grew harsh, and in his blue eyes a glint of steel seemed to flash and quiver.

The maid's pitty-pat of footsteps, descending, made him draw back into the clear-lighted, immaculate and splendidly equipped office — the office of one of New York's most eminent and successful practitioners. A bit embarrassed, the girl entered, announced:

" He'll see you in a few minutes," and — having cast an appraising glance at the patient — disappeared.

Left to his own devices, Arthur took stock of the place, listened to some vagrant chords of music that floated down from the upper regions, picked up a copy of the *Lancet* and tried to read, but by ill-luck opened at an article on " The Rôle of the Specialist in Criminal Jurisprudence," and hastily threw it down again. He nervously felt in his pocket for the hundredth time to assure himself he still had that all-precious wig; then stood up and paced the floor, trying to keep a grip on badly frayed nerves that now were struggling to get away from him.

He no longer seemed to feel much pain in his scalp-wound or in his broken arm. The intensity of his emotions, now that he stood at last on the very threshold of defeat or victory, obliterated physical anguish.

This thing he was about to do was freighted with most tremendous consequences. It meant life or death to him — no less. He, an escaped convict now accused of still another murder, was about to present himself to a medical assistant closely connected with all the powers of the law — the very man who had been instrumental in convicting him.

Just on the story he was to tell now hung everything. If that story failed to carry, death stared him in the face.

Could it, backed by nothing save that wig as corroborative evidence — a wig that might have been bought in any one of a hundred shops — batter down the mountains of proof against him? Could it clear his name and restore to him, so far as ever now could be restored, his good name and his chance to live?

Impossible, it seemed. Something whispered to the fugitive:

" Away, away, before it is too late! Out of this house, and save yourself! You may yet escape by flight. Remaining, you are lost! "

Arthur stopped in his pacing, faced the door and took one step toward it. His face had gone paler than ever. As in a chill he shivered. Life or death — which was it to be?

On this cast of the coin of fate he might win all or lose all.

Flight meant that he never could be justified. It meant an admission of blood-guiltiness. Remaining, telling his story and trusting to the facts presupposed their truth. It might win for him. Yet the chance was desperate. Racked by terrible emotions, Arthur stood undecided, with a heart that beat so thick and fast its drumming choked the breath in his throat.

Then suddenly he decided:

Flight!

He could not face the issue. His story was too frail, the only bit of evidence in his favor too tenuous to warrant gambling his life upon it. In a court-room again, any tenth-rate attorney could riddle it and fling it to derision. And on this had he pinned his faith?

A sudden revulsion of feeling swept over him. A branded fugitive he had been, was and still must be. Safety for him could mean nothing but the safety of the hidden and the fleeing. To stand, to turn, to fight meant annihilation.

Fully decided now, he tiptoed toward the office-door as quietly as his big boots would let him. Now he was almost there. A moment more and he would be in the hall, through it, out of the door and away.

But he did not enter the hall.

Instead, with a look of wonder, astonishment and incredulity on his wan face, he grasped the jamb of the door with his left hand and stood there listening at the opening in the portière.

People were coming down the stairs. He heard them distinctly. There must be three or four. Their footfalls sounded plainly on the hardwood steps. And their voices, too, were clearly audible.

One voice in particular it was that had thus transfixed

him ; that had paralyzed his muscles and inhibited his flight. A voice he would have known anywhere in this world, at any time, in any anguish.

It was the voice of a woman.

It was the voice of Enid Chamberlain.

CHAPTER XXXIV

STARING with wide blue eyes that peered through the little space between the curtains, listening so intently that he forgot to breathe, this wreck of a man — maimed, scarred, clipped and in vile rags — stood there peering out to see the beautiful and gracious woman who had once promised herself to him.

To see her — aye! And hear her, too, for just a moment, a brief, heart-wringing moment, before the final scene of the tragedy should be acted and the mocking hand of fate should signal:

"All lights out!"

Arthur knew at once that Enid and her father had been the guests whereof the maid had spoken. Their evening at an end, their call probably terminated by the announcement of an urgent case in the office, now they were on their homeward way.

Arthur grasped the significance of that splendid limousine at the door. It was much like the one wherein he in better days had ridden with the girl. A swift thought of himself riding there now with her in his present wounded, hunted, desperate plight, filled his cup of bitterness to the brim and spilled it over. Oceans, worlds and universes lay between them now — between that woman and himself, between all that had been and all that was or could be.

Chamberlain was speaking, his voice strangely tremulous and aged, already "turning again toward childish treble." In that voice the fugitive clearly understood how the tragic hand of fate had broken the old man. And now, glimpsing his bent figure stiffly coming down the stairs, that kindly face still framed in the magnificent white mass of hair, Arthur felt a pang at realizing how Chamberlain must have suffered — all for the dead and execrated Slayton's evil deed.

"A bit too strong for me to-night, you were, doctor," the old man was saying regretfully. "Just a little bit too strong. That was a smashing attack at the end with both rooks, the bishop and the queen. Double check. Impossible situation. Either your play is improving or mine's going back. A year ago — no, sir! You couldn't have got me into a corner like that!"

The doctor laughed dryly.

"Your variant of the *giuoco piano* was hardly successful," he answered. "It cramped your play. You didn't develop your pieces early enough in the game. Personally I prefer the Ruy Lopez. A great gambit, that! Better luck next time, Chamberlain. You'll have your revenge next week."

The banker nodded, smiling with his thin lips only — his sad eyes never smiled now — and as he reached the bottom of the stairway with the doctor, paused for his coat and silk hat. He put these on with Nelson's help, then stood looking up the stairs at his approaching daughter; while behind the curtain Arthur shook and trembled with a wild, yearning passion of eagerness.

"Come, Enid," the old father said gently and affectionately, as he always spoke to the girl, loved better far than his own life. "We *must* be going. It's later than I thought, and the doctor has a patient waiting. You and Mrs. N. can finish up that discussion to-morrow or the next day. Come along."

"All right, father," she answered from the landing. "I just want to tell her I don't believe it even now. She and you — yes, and the doctor, too; he's worse than either of

you — are bound and determined I shall.   But I don't even
yet, and never —"

"Come, come, Enid!" her father interposed.   "You
haven't·begun that again, have you?   Didn't you promise
you'd drop it for a while?   Say good night now, and come
along."

Arthur, risking discovery by pushing the curtain a little
outward, was now just able to see the beloved figure on the
landing — a sight that set his pulses leaping and that dimmed
his sight with emotions unspeakable.   Instinctively he raised
his hand, swept off the battered old sou'wester and dropped
it to the floor, leaving his gashed and close-cropped head
quite bare.   In her presence he could not stand and watch
her, covered.

Mrs. Nelson, motherly and warm of heart to an extent
that almost balanced the cold, impersonal character of her
husband, took both Enid's hands in hers and drew the girl
close and kissed her.

"Good night, dear," she said.   "Thursday?"

"Thursday," assented Enid, pulling on a long, pearl-gray
glove.   "That is, unless I call you and tell you I can't go."

"Come, come, Enid!" again the old man begged, raising
a beckoning finger.

The girl turned and came on down the stairs, a charming
figure in her silver-fox coat and little fox toque trimmed
with a single rosebud.   Arthur's hungry, famishing glance
swept her from that bud to the tips of her patent-leather,
gray-topped boots.   He trembled so violently that he had to
lean back against the door-jamb to support himself ; and two
big, heavy tears rolled down his wan cheeks, down over his
unshaven, bristling chin — rolled down and dropped upon
the floor at his feet.

Poignantly in that one moment he understood the wreck
that Slayton and society had made of him ; that the hard, un-
intelligent precision of the law had made of him ; that

"justice" had made of him. And, added to the prescience that justice had not yet wrought its fill upon him, but that it still reserved more anguish even unto death, came now the full comprehension of what the law had ravished from his arms.

There she stood, that girl, at the bottom of the stairway with her father. And the convict looked upon her through his tears; beautiful and pure he beheld her.

Her smile, he saw, had saddened. New lines he had never seen in her face had written their story of her grief and faith and struggle. Her eyes, as she looked up at the doctor, giving him her hand, had changed. Arthur had known her as a girl. She was a woman now. The tragedy and pain of these two years had made her one.

"Good night, doctor," said she.

"Good night. And mind, now, no more brooding!"

He spoke jestingly, but a deeper tone of seriousness lay beneath his words.

"I never allow a patient of mine to brood, you know. I haven't pulled you through nervous prostration and Heaven knows what else, to have you drop back into the Pit, with worrying over what can't be helped."

"I'm not worrying, doctor," she answered simply and quietly, her eyes on his. "Not a bit. I'm just going on and on as I have from the first — trusting."

The doctor dropped her gloved hand, raised both his arms a little at his sides and let them fall again in his familiar gesture of despair when anything passed his bounds of power or patience.

"Miss Chamberlain!" he protested.

"Doctor!" she resisted with adamantine firmness.

"Come, Enid!" her father once more interposed with as near an approach to irritation as his loyal and gentle old soul could ever simulate.

He took her by the arm, and together they passed down

the hall. Enid walked on the side nearest the office-door.
She passed not one foot from the opening in the portières;
hardly a foot from the eager, burning gaze of the hunted
man. The little breeze of her passing wafted a faintest
breath of perfume to his nostrils — *lys du Japon* it was, delicate, elusive, supremely feminine. He quivered, recoiled
into a chair, sank down and buried his face in his left hand,
breathing hard.

He heard a few parting words, the opening of the outer
door, its closing, then the hum of the motor as it drew away
from the curb. Enid was gone.

The doctor's step sounded in the hallway. It entered the
office, stopped, then came on again.

" Hmmm!" the doctor ejaculated. " What's the trouble? "

Arthur raised his head and stared at the physician. Nothing much about him had changed in those two fateful years.
He had grown a little more bald, perhaps; but the same
toothbrush mustache still covered his lip, the same keen eyes
still looked out through the same shell-rimmed glasses. The
same impersonal air of calm and abstract science still distinguished him.

" Well? " asked the doctor. " What can I do for you, my
man? These are not my regular hours, you know, but the
maid told me it was urgent. Fracture, eh? And scalp-
wound? Fighting, or what? "

Arthur faced the doctor, his heart beating thickly. Obviously Nelson did not recognize him. The doors of retreat
had not yet closed behind him, then. He could have his
injuries treated, pay the charge and go, unmolested. Go?
Yes; but with the same horrible pursuit behind him, the same
hideous charges still hanging over his head. Go — still a
fugitive.

For a moment the struggle whether to stand his ground
or flee once more racked his soul. But almost instantly Ar-

thur's decision strengthened again and vanquished his weakness. He would not go until his story had been told. Now, face to face with the supreme moment, he would stick to the task and live or die by the result.

Arthur, pale as death and shivering all over, took three steps and confronted the physician, who stood there regarding him through those round glasses with as much personal interest as he might have had in an insect under a lens.

" What's the matter? " demanded Nelson. " Can't you talk? How did you get hurt? "

" I got hurt," answered Arthur slowly and with twitching lips, " I got hurt trying to win justice."

Nelson laughed dryly.

" One of the most prolific methods of acquiring injuries," he commented. " Well, who did it? And what with? Maybe that will have some bearing on my diagnosis."

" None whatever," Arthur replied, while the doctor peered at him in some surprise, astonished to hear such words and tones in the mouth of this ruffianly looking water-rat. " None at all. But I don't mind telling you I was struck on the head with an iron bar, and that the same bar probably broke one of the bones in my arm here. Will you repair the damage? "

Nelson pursed his lips.

" You ought to have gone to some hospital or other," said he. " Why take blacksmith's work to a watchmaker? Your case is commonplace and easy. I specialize in the finesse of the art — heart-surgery, ophthalmic work, delicate and complex operations. The stitching of your clipped scalp and the setting of your radius does not appeal to me, my good fellow, and —"

" You're a physician, aren't you? " demanded Arthur.

" So some claim. Others, the contrary."

" Well, if you are, then you're bound to take a case that comes to you, aren't you? "

"Morally, yes. But you must know that my prices are prohibitive for the ordinary run of men."

"What will you charge to do this work for me and look me over and give me an opinion of my case?"

"Since you ask, a hundred and fifty dollars," answered the doctor, congratulating himself that this figure would collapse the fellow, who would then take himself off to the nearest hospital — to some free clinic, possibly.

"A hundred and fifty, eh?" asked the fugitive, reaching for Slayton's wallet. "Good! Here it is!"

He put the wallet on the doctor's table, drew out the roll of bills, and clumsily, with his left hand, counted off the sum. This he shoved over to the doctor in silence, then replaced the rest of the money in the wallet and once more slid it into his pocket.

Equally silent, Nelson counted the sum, shot a suspicious glance at his strange patient — a glance directed especially at his clipped scalp and pallid hue — formulated a question, decided not to ask it, and finally, opening a drawer in the table, dropped the money into it. His expression was one of displeasure. Up-stairs he had a couple of chapters on "The Minor Tactics of Chess" to read, and this interruption was most inopportune.

"Take your coat off," he directed. "Here, I'll help you. Now, then, sit down here. We'll get down to business."

While he laid out instruments, antiseptics and materials, from time to time he cast a wondering look at this peculiar person whose every action was so unexpected. Somewhere, far back in the vague, dark caverns of his subconsciousness, that face seemed to waken ghostly memories. Some time, he thought, it must have passed upon the cinema-screen of his experience, among the swarms of others that his busy life brought him in contact with. Some time, somewhere — but when, where? Shaking his head, he abandoned the elusive quest.

"Here," said he sharply, taking up a pair of crooked scissors. "Now then, your arm!"

Deftly he cut away the sling and the clumsy surgery of Arthur's inexperience, soon exposing the muscular arm all bruised, ridged and swollen.

"Well, well!" said he. "How long since it was hurt?"

"About twenty-one hours."

"Why didn't you have it seen to before?"

"The circumstances weren't such that I could."

"Weren't, eh?" sharply, as he washed his hands. "Something irregular?"

"Very."

"Oh, indeed!"

"Very much so. And beside," added Arthur, fixing his eyes on the doctor's face, "I wasn't where I could see you."

"You mean you were set on having *my* care?"

"I was determined to see you even before I got hurt."

"The deuce you say! What are you driving at, anyhow? Why did you want to consult *me?*"

"Doctor," answered the fugitive slowly, "I once on a time had an important demonstration of your precise, scientific, highly efficient methods. I have never forgotten that lesson. Now on account of it I've come back to you."

"You mean to say I've treated you before?" asked Nelson, preparing an antiseptic wash.

"Emphatically, yes!"

"Hmmm!" growled the doctor, beginning his work on the broken bone with a deft skill beautiful to witness.

He made no further comment, however; and Arthur, racked with pain, kept silence with stoic endurance. Twenty-five minutes later, his head and arm patched with supreme skill, Arthur sat gaunt and exhausted beside the table. Nelson poured him a stiff glass of whisky.

"Here!" said he, setting it before him. "I prescribe about four ounces of *spiritus frumenti*. I don't want you keeling over on my hands, and for a fact you look mighty white."

Arthur pushed away the glass.

" No, I thank you," he declined. " I don't care for any. I'll be all right in a minute or two.   The pallor I've got now can't be taken away with any four ounces of *spiritus frumenti.*"

" I thought as much," the doctor answered, giving him a caustic glance. " You don't mind telling me, do you, what clipped your hair and bleached your face? "

" You mean the principal factor? "

" The principal factor."

" Well," replied Arthur, fixing a steady gaze on him, " the principal factor in my imprisonment, when we come down to that, was very largely — *you!* "

CHAPTER XXXV

WHEN SCIENCE LIES

A MOMENT'S silence followed, while each man's eyes searched the other's face. Then the doctor, frowning, rubbed his close-shaven chin.

"What do you mean?" he asked in his usual cold tones. "I a factor in your imprisonment? How so?"

"You don't understand?"

"No."

Arthur raised his left hand to his clipped and wounded head.

"Doctor," said he, "it was you who brought this infamy and this wound on me."

"I?"

"You see this prison pallor?"

"Well?"

"You put it on my face."

"How so?"

"You, doctor, did all this to me, and so much more that I couldn't tell you all of it in a week. Unless you know what Sing Sing really is you can't understand the depths you plunged me into."

"I plunged you into depths?" demanded Nelson, his face for the first time betraying a little uneasiness.

The presence of a deranged man always is disconcerting, especially when that man has a fancied grievance and may be armed. Nelson now took this extraordinary patient for nothing else than an insane man with an obsession. Swiftly he calculated his chance of reaching the gun in his table drawer. His eyes sought the drawer.

334

Arthur seemed to interpret the look and the thought behind it.

"Doctor," said he, "I stand here before you with a terrible grievance, and I am armed. I could shoot you down in your tracks. But you have nothing to fear, nothing whatever.

"I didn't come for vengeance, but for justice. I got these injuries in the course of a quest for justice. Justice is what I want, and mean to have. To kill you would accomplish nothing, would prove nothing, and would only make me guilty of a real crime after having been falsely accused of two that I never committed.

"Besides, there's an influence at work on me now, as there was then, which makes killing anybody an impossibility. So you haven't anything to fear. I'm here not to kill you, but to talk with you, ask you some questions, get some facts and demand a little justice. Is that clear?"

"Perfectly," answered Nelson, drawing a chair up beside the table and sitting down. "Quite so. No intimidation here, you know. But all the explanation you desire. Is that understood?"

"Absolutely."

"All right! Put your gun on the table there!"

"I will," acceded Arthur.

He drew it from his pocket and laid it on the table under the circle of lamplight.

"Do you recognize it, doctor?" asked he.

Nelson shook his head.

"No more than I do you," he responded. "I see so many revolvers and knives and such things in a year, you know. So many faces. So much tragedy and blood and trouble of all kinds."

"You don't know that gun?"

"Absolutely not."

"You've seen it before, however. In a court-room."

"Possibly," the doctor replied, nodding. "But when and where?"

"You've seen me, too, at the same time and place."

"Name them!"

"Doctor," the fugitive answered, "if I do and tell you who I am, I'm taking my life in my hands. Even now at this moment I could go free from here and get away unquestioned. You know nothing of me. I'm here as a patient. I've been in jail, that's obvious and admitted. But for all you know I may have served my time out and be a released man. You can't detain me.

"After I tell you what I'm going to tell you, however, you may act differently. If I can't impress you with the truth of my story and waken your sense of justice the results will be fatal to me. Remember one thing: A guilty man at large will *not* expose himself to danger for the sake of getting justice."

Nelson pondered a moment, then nodded comprehension.

"Very good; very good indeed," he answered. "A distinct point in your favor. You mean that you are under accusation and that you risk much in coming to me for the justice you fancy I can give?"

"Exactly that, doctor. I not only risk much, but I risk everything I have to give. I risk my life!"

The doctor stared at Arthur hard through his round shell glasses.

"If I were quite convinced of your sanity —" he began.

Arthur laughed bitterly.

"Don't worry about that, doctor!" he exclaimed. "I'm sick and sore and hunted, I'm wronged and outcast and a fugitive, but I'm not insane. You'll see before I get through that my mind is clear and that I'm normal, all right. All you've got to do is listen to me and I'll convince you of that."

" All right; assume you're sane. What now? Who are you? "

" Take a good look, doctor. Don't you recognize me? "

Nelson studied his face a long minute, then shook his head in negation.

" No, I don't ! " he answered.

" Do you mean to tell me, doctor, that you can go on the witness-stand and deliberately give testimony that condemns a human being to the living Hell of prison, or to death, and then not even remember his face? "

Nelson paused before replying. Then he nodded.

" Yes," said he. " That's the fact of the matter. In a year, you see, I make so many examinations and autopsies, do so much work for the coroners, and testify in so many criminal and civil cases that I simply can't retain all the details. I am called for blood-tests, handwriting-examinations, bacteriological work, and a great many other branches. If I ever testified against you, sir, I must confess I've entirely forgotten you. Your prison experience has no doubt radically altered your appearance; don't forget that."

" I know it, doctor," answered Arthur. " And yet it seems hard to believe you can utterly lose track of a man whom you help send away for life."

" For life, eh? How — how do you happen to be here, then? "

" We'll discuss that later. The main thing now is that you don't remember me."

" Not in the slightest. When I testify, the accused is not a man to me. He ceases to be a human being and becomes a case. I work without prejudice, favor, animus of any kind, strictly on the facts. Science knows neither good nor evil, but only truth."

" Yes, doctor," Arthur rejoined. " I heard you remark as much in court the day you proved me — an innocent man — a murderer ! "

"I proved you a murderer, and you weren't? Impossible! Science never lies!"

Arthur laughed bitterly, leaning forward and setting his left elbow on the table.

"She doesn't, eh?" asked he. "You're wrong, doctor. Sometimes she lies horribly, wantonly, fatally. When she does lie, she goes the limit and then some! She went the limit on me that time, all right!"

Nelson shook his head in negation.

"Impossible!"

"See here, doctor!" exclaimed the fugitive, shivering with emotion. "You say yourself you rely on facts wholly and entirely. Now suppose I can give you facts to show you were wrong? How many would you need to be convinced?"

"Only one," replied the physician. "One absolute fact, *contra*, will upset the finest hypothesis under heaven."

"Very well, then! I win and you lose!" declared Arthur, suddenly flushing a little as the blood leaped through his arteries.

"How so?"

"I've got that one fact!"

"What is it?"

"This!"

Speaking, he drew from his pocket Slayton's gray wig and flung it upon the table.

"There's your fact, doctor! I win!"

Absolutely at a loss to understand, the doctor regarded this peculiar exhibit with blinking eyes, owl-like through those round shell bows. For a moment he sat motionless. Then he took up the wig, studied it intently, turned it round and over, and finally dropped it once more on the table. He peered at Arthur with puzzled eyes, where, nevertheless, a certain nascent comprehension seemed to glimmer.

"What does all this mean?" he suddenly demanded.

"You're talking riddles when I want and must have facts! Come, now; no more of this beating round the bush! My time's valuable. You've already taken an hour of it. If you've got anything to say, man, for the love of Heaven say it! Who are you, and what does all this mean?"

Arthur's blue eyes held the doctor's black ones as he answered:

"It means that the riddle of the Donald Mackenzie murder, in the Powhatan National Bank, two years and more ago, is solved at last. It means that I, Arthur Mansfield, accused of that murder, convicted — largely by your scientific evidence — and sentenced to life imprisonment, have escaped, have found the proof of my innocence, and have brought it to you! It means —"

"*You*, Arthur Mansfield?" cried the doctor, starting up with more emotion than he had felt in years. "*You?*"

"That's my name. I'm the man!"

Nelson walked round the table, took Arthur's chin in his hand, and turned his face more to the light. For a long minute he studied it. Then he released his hold.

"Yes; I remember you now," said he. "The wide brows, the contour of the chin, straight nose and blue eyes — I recall you. But with your head clipped, half a week's stubble on your face, the pallor — you used to be ruddy — and the awful clothes you've got there, can you blame me for not having 'made' you, as the professional saying is?"

"Not in the least," answered the fugitive. "I think my disguise *is* rather good. It has got me here anyhow, right into the hands of authority, intelligent authority, through the dragnet of stupidity flung over the city. Glad you like it."

"I do. It's excellent. So you're Mansfield, eh?"

"Yes."

"You know, of course, you're also accused of killing Slayton?"

"Naturally!"

"You know I ought to call police headquarters and —"

"Not till you've heard the truth! I tell you I'm just as innocent of this second murder as I was of the first one."

"Impossible! The facts are conclusive."

"So they seemed in the Mackenzie case. Yet they lied. I wouldn't have come to you and put my head deliberately into the noose unless I'd had something pretty strong to clear me, would I?"

"It doesn't seem so, as I said before," admitted the doctor, going back to his chair. "If I were a man given to popular locutions of the day, I'd say this entire situation gets my goat!"

"Wait till you hear the whole of it!" exclaimed Arthur, striking the table with his fist. "Wait till you really know what that means — and that — and these!"

He pointed at the automatic lying there before them both, and at the wig, and then at the beach-comber's clothes he wore.

"Wait till you hear and understand. My life now depends on making you believe the truth!"

"If you can convince me what you say *is* true, have no fear," the doctor answered. "Now, your story!"

CHAPTER XXXVI

WITH an intensity of earnestness that bore weight even with the coldly scientific doctor, Arthur fixed his eyes on the physician's face.

" Convince you? " he cried. " How can I help it when I tell the living truth? "

" Go on! Speak! "

" I will. But first — tell me — one thing —"

" Well, what is it? "

" When she — Enid — left with her father just now, I was standing right inside that curtain there."

He pointed at the hall-doorway.

" She passed right near me, only a foot or two away."

" Yes. What about it? "

" I realized then, doctor, that I've got her to live for, if not myself. Realized it as never before. If I don't make good now she'll have this burden to carry all her life. Make good? I've *got* to — for Enid! Now, tell me — tell me —"

" Tell you what? "

" What does she — think? What does she believe? I heard her say a few words there in the hall. Were they about me? Had you been discussing me and this last murder? What does Enid think about that? Does she still — trust me? "

Nelson nodded reluctantly.

" I'm sorry to tell you she does," he answered with regret.

" Thank God! If *she* can still believe in me —"

" It's most unfortunate that she can and does. You see, she's been a patient of mine for some months now. Nervous disorders caused by the tragedy. Just as I was getting her straightened out, why — *this* came along.

"And now I'm very much afraid there'll be work to be done all over again. Mansfield, if you're responsible for the wreckage of that white little, brave little woman's life, by God, sir! you *deserve* the chair!"

The doctor spoke with unusual emphasis and brought his fist down with a bang upon the table. Under that calm, unruffled exterior fires perhaps still burned; who could tell?

Arthur laid his left hand on the doctor's as it rested on the table.

"Listen!" said he, his voice shaking. "I'm here to save her more than I am to save myself. Does that mean anything to you? Is there enough of the human being left in you, doctor, to grasp that? Do you understand me?"

Nelson smiled dryly. His eyes quivered for just the fraction of a second, and a curious look altered his dry face.

"I am perhaps more human than many suspect," he answered; "but that's not to the point. Your motives are of no importance now. All I'm interested in is your story. Let's have it."

Arthur gazed at him for a moment of tense silence. Then, paling still more, he began to speak.

While the doctor listened intently, weighing each fact and the manner of its presentation, the fugitive recounted the long, strange and eventful sequence of misfortunes which had plunged him, totally innocent, into this nethermost pit of woe and exile and death.

From the very beginning he told the tale — surely one of the strangest ever woven in this sad, mad world of ours — forgetting nothing, slighting nothing, excusing nothing, exaggerating nothing. He spoke clearly and well, with entire command of his narrative, developing it in perfect sequence, pouring out in half an hour the accumulated result of months of study and reflection.

Carefully he explained his own first misdeed, his visit to Slayton's house, and all the events leading up to the fatal accusation. From time to time the doctor interrupted with a brief word or question to expand or illuminate some point of special interest. Deathly pale, shaking a little, holding fast with his uninjured hand to the edge of the table to steady himself, Arthur answered everything with clarity and force.

His eyes, unnaturally blue with excitement, shone in that white face with startling vividness. They seemed burning with the fever of his vehemence. His voice cut the silence like a knife. Thus, winged with forces as of fire and steel, he drove his message home to Nelson.

He told of his reflections while in Sing Sing, his piecings-out of all the evidence, and his conclusion, at the end — an irresistible conclusion — that the cashier himself had done the murder. He admitted his determination to escape and to avenge his wrong by killing the man who had thus wrecked him. He narrated his journey to Slayton's home at Oakwood Heights in every detail, and followed it with a complete account of all the events at the house of the dead man and at the shack on the dunes. Thereafter he brought his story down to the immediate present.

"You have it all, now, doctor," he concluded, panting a little with exhaustion and the eagerness of his tale. "Now the complete series of facts is in your hands. I couldn't possibly have invented any such story. Every investigation you or the police may undertake will bear it out. And, on top of all, I want you to recall one point of the trial, two years ago — a point that at the time completely baffled you — a point you had to ignore, even though you admitted it might hold the key to the entire mystery, as indeed it does!"

"What point?" asked Nelson, elbows on the table, hands joined and chin upon them, while his spectacled eyes bored penetrantly at Arthur. "What point do you refer to?"

Arthur paused a weighty moment before replying.

"You remember those six or eight gray hairs found in the dead fingers of the old watchman?" he demanded.

"Perfectly."

"And you recall that of all the evidence they alone baffled you?"

"Yes."

"I can explain them now!"

"Explain them? You mean —"

"I mean they came from *there!*"

And Arthur brought his fist down with a thud on the wig that lay before them.

"From there?"

"Those hairs were pulled out of that wig, doctor. No doubt about it in this world. Slayton must have been disguised when he did the job. In some way or other Mackenzie got hold of that wig. In getting it away from him Slayton left a few hairs in the old man's clutch."

"It couldn't be — and yet —"

"It could and was, I tell you!" the fugitive insisted.

"And yet it might."

"No other possible hypothesis will explain those six hairs, doctor, in that dead grasp!"

Nelson pondered a moment, eying Arthur with sharp intelligence. Mentally he was weighing the other's truth or guile. Could a man possibly have fabricated so ingenious and consistent a story and have capped the climax of it by that theory of the wig? For a moment Nelson was almost convinced.

But just on the verge of it his old belief and certainty came rushing back — the wholly conclusive mass of damning evidence that had swamped Arthur in the beginning now once more asserted its power over the physician. He shook his head and frowned.

"You found that wig on Slayton's desk, you say?"

" I did ! "

" That's too thin, Mansfield.   You might have got it anywhere, and —"

" Make a microscopic comparison of some of these hairs
and the ones that figured in the trial.   That will be absolute
proof, won't it ? "

" Not necessarily.   You may have had the wig yourself
the night of the murder.   You seem to know a lot about it,
Mansfield.   How can I tell but what you took it when you
were at Slayton's house and —"

" And kept it hidden all this time and went and reclaimed
it after my escape?   Nonsense ! "

" Stranger things have happened, as matters of record.
You're asking me to throw away a most tremendous mass of
evidence, to stultify all my conclusions, to call the law a liar
and a fool and to acquit you as blameless on the strength of
what?   Just your own story and that wig !   No, no, Mansfield ; there must be more than that.   It's not enough ; it
won't do ! "

Arthur clutched the table desperately.   Beneath him the
ground was falling fast away.   His calculations had mis-
carried ; his supreme effort had ended in doubt and impending failure.   A bitterness as of death gripped his soul.
Ashen-faced and trembling, he leaned across the table.

" Doctor," he exclaimed hoarsely, " As God lives, I swear
to you that I'm telling the absolute, unvarnished truth.   You
can't give me up to the police now with even the doubt in
your mind that I've awakened.   You can't do it — you
mustn't !   I've established enough of a case so that I can
and do demand protection —"

" Justice is all I'm interested in," coldly interrupted the
physician.

" Protection for a day or two until I can prove more.
That's all I want ; just a couple of days in this house to pull
together, collect some more proofs, go over the story with

you again and let you cross-examine me. I guarantee on
my honor that if you can pick hole or flaw in my story or my
reasoning, or prove it false in any detail, I'll let you give me
up without a struggle. We're not at the bottom of this case
yet.

"Give me two days. That's all I ask. Do I get them or
not?"

The doctor considered.

"I don't want to shelter a fugitive from justice nor yet
compound a felony," he slowly answered; "and yet I can't
make up my mind to refuse you, Mansfield. Personally, I
still believe you guilty of two cold-blooded murders. Still,
certain factors puzzle me. Why you didn't kill that beach-
comber who stood in your way I can't understand. A man
who has done as I believe you have wouldn't have hesitated
in that case. So much is in your favor.

"Again"—and he checked the second item on his
forefinger—"your coming here at all is a favorable symptom
— indication, I mean. Third, this wig has possibilities.
On the strength of these points — yes; I'll give you shelter
for two days. Do your best till Friday. After that we'll
see."

Arthur bowed his head, kept a minute's silence, and then
raised his eyes to the doctor's again.

"You'll make an examination of those hairs?" asked he.

"Yes."

"Then I can ask nothing more."

"Nor will I offer anything except to take care of your
hurts, as I would those of any other patient, and let you lie
hidden above-stairs. No word or sign of mine shall betray you. In return I demand a promise."

"What promise?"

"That you won't try to escape. Even though the verdict
goes against you, you'll stick? You'll take your medicine?"

"To run away would be a confession of guilt — and I'm innocent!"

"You'll stick?"

"I will!"

Nelson put out his right hand. Arthur's left grasped it in a firm clasp.

"All right, then. Agreed! And now —"

A sudden stridor of the telephone interrupted him.

"Hello! Hello!"

.   .   .   .

"Yes, this is the doctor speaking now."

.   .   .   .

"Important developments, eh? In what line?"

.   .   .   .

"Yes, I can handle that, I guess. Chirography is something of a hobby with me, you know. I say, Inspector! Have you any guaranteed sample of his writing?"

.   .   .   .

"Oh, that letter to his wife, eh? That's right. I forgot that. Very well; I'll be down at once."

.   .   .   .

"Good-by!"

The doctor hung up briskly, and swung toward Arthur with a smile.

"Always something to do, you see," he commented. "I've got to go down to Headquarters. Don't be alarmed. I won't betray you. I think you're a consummate murderer, Mansfield, but my word's been given and I'll keep it. You'll have the benefit of the doubt for a couple of days. If you can clear yourself nobody'll be more pleased than I!"

"You forget Enid, doctor. You forget me!"

The doctor vouchsafed no answer, but showed his guest

to a room at the back of the house on the third floor, and
bade Arthur turn in.

Five minutes later Nelson was in his car, whirling down-
town to Mulberry Street in answer to the urgent summons
of Inspector Burton of the Detective Bureau.

CHAPTER XXXVII

A S he briskly entered Burton's inner office the inspector looked up from the paper over which he had been bending with a powerful reading-glass, under the strong down-beating glow of an electric light.

" Hello, doc! " he greeted. " You're the man I want to see. How's your goat? Tied up good and tight? "

Nelson shook his head in negation.

" It was an hour ago," he answered, laying aside his hat and coat; " but to tell you the truth, Burton, I've just been through an experience that has mighty near cut its rope and let it out of the pen. But no matter about that. What's the trouble? Something urgent, I take it, from the way you 'phoned me."

" Urgent is right! Do you want it in sections, easy like, or all in a bunch? "

" You might as well communicate it all at once, Burton. I don't believe much in the delaying of important matters. What have you got there, anyhow? "

He pointed at the paper on the desk, peered through his round glasses, and blinked, as was his habit.

" Ask me! " said the inspector, scratching the back of his neck, which was thick and red. " If I knew, I wouldn't be sending for you, doc. I've either got the most amazing piece of forgery, plus the most ingenious piece of fiction, ever put across, or else you and I, and the courts, and the law, and the whole works are an A B C set of fools that ought to be walloped with a shingle and put to bed without our suppers. Now, then, which is it? "

" What do you mean? "

For all answer Burton jerked open a drawer of his desk and took out a letter. This he handed to Nelson.

" Draw up that chair," he directed, " and sit down and look at *that!* Take a good look and tell me what it is! "

He handed the letter to Nelson, who obeyed. After a moment's inspection the doctor answered:

" That is the letter Slayton wrote his wife on the night of the Mackenzie murder. The letter you mentioned to me just now over the wire. Why do you ask? "

" It's his writing, positively? "

" Positively. That was proved at the trial."

" And you could identify it in another specimen? "

" Yes. That's part of my job, identifying writing."

" Well, then! "   ·

The inspector passed over a page of the writing he had been examining under the lens.

" Now tell me, doc, what's *that?* "

With hardly more than a glance at it Nelson answered:

" Slayton's writing, of course."

" Sure of it? "

" I'm never sure of anything till I've applied the methods of exact science; but so far as humanly speaking goes, without the exhaustive tests of the chirographic expert, I'd back that writing for Slayton's against the world."

" By God! so would I! " exclaimed the inspector, bringing his fist down hard on the desk. " That's what's got me all up in the air. That's what is going to put the double-crossed kibosh on the department and on all of us, make us look like six plugged nickels, and give us the ha-ha! from here to Hackney! If this was only a forgery, now! "

" A forgery? What do you mean? You wish it were? "

" Do I? Some! It would let us all out, then. But now — suffering cats, doc! We're all of us in bad, from A to Z! "

"What the devil are you driving at, man?" ejaculated Nelson, reading a few words of the paper he held in hand. "What's up, anyhow?"

"That paper there," the inspector answered in extreme dejection, "was found late this P. M. by Jaffrey and Howard in the basement of Slayton's house at Oakwood Heights. They were digging out clues of the man that did up the cashier and got McNulty through the leg in that pistol-battle on the marsh.

"Well, doc, down there in a kind of wood-bin under a lot of kindling, what do they get hold of but this thing? Nobody knows how it got there, but the outrageous part is that it *was* there with bells on, all right, all right."

"Outrageous? How so?" queried Nelson, reading a few lines with contracted brows.

"How *so?* Well, if it proves us a bunch of E. Z. Marks and come-ons, isn't that outrageous? If it shows us up as a lot of muttonheads, and clears the man suspected on this last case — the man already safely 'buried' for life on the first case, track 13 and a washout — isn't that outrageous? If it —"

"Hold on, there, hold on!" cried the doctor, his impersonal face reddening slightly, a sure sign of the greatest degree of anger he ever permitted himself to enjoy. "What are you driving at anyhow? What do you mean?"

"Read that and see!" cried Burton, shoving two more sheets into the doctor's hands. "I just gave you that unimportant part there for you to 'make' the writing. Now you've got the whole infernal thing. Read that and tell me you wouldn't give your hand to have had it burned before those two lunatics found it and read it all through and brought it here to me, grinning like chessy-cats, confound 'em!"

"You mean it's something that possibly may reverse the

case and work some measure of tardy justice in an irreparable wrong?"

"Yes, damn it! you've said it! And where do we get off *then*, I'd like to know?"

The doctor surveyed him a long moment through his glasses with a scorn so withering that even Burton's thick hide smarted. Then with a marvelously eloquent "Hmmm!" he found the beginning of Slayton's extraordinary confession and started reading.

Hastily his keen eyes passed down the paragraphs, absorbing the dead cashier's farewell to his wife, the statement of the causes of his trouble, the explanation of the "plant" to convict Arthur, and the confession of the murder itself

They paused a while over the matter of the gray wig. The doctor's face grew coldly analytical as he read and re-read this paragraph, weighing its truth, unmoved by any blame or ridicule that might fall upon himself for the terrible miscarriage of justice he had engineered. Burton meanwhile fumed and muttered oaths, lighted a cigar, forgot to smoke it, and, finally standing up, began pacing the floor in a growing rage.

"Sit down, you idiot!" snapped the doctor. "You keep me from understanding just how big a fool I've been myself!"

Burton subsided, and the physician continued his reading, ending with the personal details about the disposition of the dead man's property and his urgent request to have the confession put at once into the hands of the district attorney.

When he had quite finished he sat there pondering a silent minute, then glanced sharply at Burton.

"It's genuine!" he snapped. "We're all damned fools! The boy was innocent all the time — as innocent of Mackenzie's murder that he was ruined for and served two years of Hell for as he is of Slayton's death that he's being hounded for this minute! We're all a pack of blazing luna-

tics and have been all the time. Slayton made monkeys of
us all, from you and me right up to the district attorney
himself. And now —"

"And now! Now that Jaffrey and Howard have read
this, how are we going to stand from under?" Burton demanded, raging.

"We aren't!"

"If they hadn't read it we could damn soon make 'way
with it and not be laughing-stocks for all —"

"You cur!"

Nelson wheeled on the inspector suddenly with something
very like real, human rage. Right in Burton's astonished
face the doctor shook the confession till the paper crackled.

"You cur!" he cried again, his eyes blazing. "Here a
good, clean, honest boy has been through Hell and damna-
tion and at this very moment is sick, wounded, desolate and
wrecked — has lost name, place, prospects, and even his
chance at happiness with a girl that *is* a girl — all because
science played us a scurvy trick and because Slayton, the
black crook, made suckers of us all!

"Here all this happens, and now we know the truth; and
instead of crying: 'My God! How can we make it right
with him?' you whine and cringe and shiver for your rotten reputation, and want to make 'way with the evidence
and think how you can stand from under!

"Bah! You sicken me! And to think the detection of
crime and the administration of justice ever touches *your*
hands! Holy heavens, what a farce! Look here, Burton!
In the course of my work I have to inspect microscopic specimens, some of them only one one-thousandth of an inch in
diameter or less — often much less. Beside your heart and
soul those specimens are whales, mammoths, megalosauri!
Now you know what I think. Good *night!*"

Without another word, but with a look of infinite scorn,
the doctor seized his hat and strode toward the door. Open-

mouthed, Burton stared after him, a kind of sickly, ashen hue spreading over his usually red wattles.

Then, all at once energized by the sight of those papers in the doctor's hands now leaving his possession, the inspector sprang up with a cry.

"Here, doc! Where you going with that confession?" he shouted angrily.

"Going? Home!"

"You aren't going to take that? You can't! It's —"

"It's mine for the present!" retorted Nelson, turning at the door and shaking the papers at him. "Perhaps you'd like to have me repeat what you've just said, eh? No? All right then! Keep still!"

The door banged, and he was gone. Burton stared round in dumfounded amaze, then sank back into his desk-chair, let both arms fall limp, and murmured:

"Well, by God!"

Nelson meantime was hastening to the telephone.

"Hello! 24679 Riverside!"

Impatiently he waited, the papers still clutched in his hand, which, despite all his scientific aplomb, now shook a little.

"The cur!" he muttered. "The swine!"

Somebody answered the 'phone.

"Hello, hello! Is this Mr. Chamberlain?"

. . . .

"Yes. See here, Chamberlain, has Enid gone to bed yet? No? All right. Something of the most extreme importance has just happened. No, no; I can't tell you over the 'phone. Won't under any conditions. No; it can't wait till morning. Positively can't!"

. . . .

"Now see here, Chamberlain! I've got to see you and Enid at my office immediately. It's only 10.45. You can

come down in the car in no time. I insist. Hurt her?
Heaven bless you, man, no! No, no, *no!* I prescribe
it, I tell you! I'm her physician, am I not? This is part
of my treatment! The most important part I've ever given
her!"

.   .   .   .

"It doesn't matter whether you understand or don't understand. I tell you I've got to see Enid to-night, right
away, and you've got to come with her! No, no; this is
imperative!"

.   .   .   .

"All right, then. I'll be there. Good-by! Mind now,
you both come as quick as the Lord will let you, or, by Jove,
I throw up the entire case! Good-by!"

Nelson hung up with a bang, stuffed the papers into his
pocket, and — blowing his nose rather hard, the while his
solemn eyes winked with unusual rapidity — hastened out
to his car, jumped into it, and, with a single command:
"Home! Quick!" slammed the door as though that act
afforded him an infinite relief.

CHAPTER XXXVIII

SPED swiftly homeward by his powerful machine, Nelson flung off hat and coat in the front hall, and, with unusual celerity — for he was of deliberate tendencies — mounted the stairs to the room he had given the fugitive.

The house was still. Mrs. Nelson had already gone to bed. The servants had departed to their own place. Through the mansion calm and quiet reigned, as befitted the well-bred house of well-bred people. Nothing could have been farther from the spirit and the tradition of that house than any strong emotion, any disturbance, anything, in fact, but just well-ordered rationality and a harmonious peace.

Nelson rapped twice on Arthur's door.

"Come!" sounded a voice.

He entered. The fugitive was sitting on the edge of the bed, still dressed, with his left arm clasping his injured right and his head bent in dejection.

"Hello! Not in bed yet, sir?" demanded Nelson, trying hard to give his voice the same impersonal tone it had possessed in his previous conversation with the boy. "I don't allow my patients to disobey me! What does this mean?"

"It means that nothing matters," answered Arthur. "I was just sitting here thinking, that's all. Thinking how infernally peculiar it is that a man can tell the truth, the exact truth, the whole truth, and nothing but the truth, and the whole world will rise up and call him 'Liar!'

Yes, the whole world — even its best thinkers and keenest analyzers, like you, doctor. Isn't it worth pondering?"

Nelson blinked and rubbed his chin. He was boiling inwardly with desire to haul out that confession and thrust it into Arthur's hands with a:

"Look! Look here! You're free!"

But he restrained himself. He had his plan, had Nelson. Somewhere under that cold, formal and precise exterior still lurked hidden fires. Beneath the mask of science still lived a man.

"Worth thinking about, isn't it, doctor?" the fugitive repeated, fixing a keen blue gaze on his host. "It's the one great problem that has been gnawing at my vitals for two years, and now is sharper than ever because the events of the past few days have doubled its scope. Seems to me a man might go insane stewing over a thing like that, an injustice like that, and —"

"Please try to forget it, Mansfield," the doctor begged, lifting an inhibiting hand. "What I'm here for just now is to ask you a question or two — a purely hypothetical question, you know. Suppose by any means or other you should be cleared of the two charges now resting on your name and be rehabilitated in public estimation, what attitude would you assume toward the world? What profession would you follow — banking again, or some other? And — hmmm, hmmm! — in regard to Enid — Miss Chamberlain —"

"I don't see what you want to turn the iron in my wounds for," Mansfield answered slowly. "You don't believe my story yourself, and surely if *you* don't nobody else will. You're just holding up a kind of dazzling bait before me to see me snatch at it and then jerk it away again. That's not fair and it's not kind. If I'm condemned, let me alone. Don't make me think!"

"But I *am* going to make you think!" retorted the doctor with some heat. "I didn't say your case was hopeless. I simply said that I couldn't quite accept your version as yet. Suppose I should to-morrow and should succeed in clearing you, what then?"

"Oh, then," said Arthur, his voice breaking, his chest beginning to heave, "then —"

"Would you be vindictive and revengeful and try to get square with those that have wronged you, or would you turn your back on the past and face the future with a brave heart?"

Arthur pondered a minute, then shook his head.

"I don't know," he answered slowly. "Heroes in novels always forgive and forget, but I'm not a hero and this isn't a novel. I'm only a human being and this is fact, here and now, in New York State. While I was up the river there, nothing mattered but cutting Slayton's heart out. But when I escaped and really saw him dead I found I didn't hate him after all. I could almost forgive him.

"I suppose if I were free I'd let things slide. The thing I'd really like to attack would be the procedure itself that made such a hellish thing possible in my case and lots of other cases, and that still makes it possible."

"You mean you'd quit banking and go in for law?"

"Yes. And by God, doctor, if I ever could get where I could hit a wallop at this way of doing business I'd hit it — hard!"

He brought his fist down on his knee with a resounding thump. Nelson covertly smiled, his eyes bright with an unusual joy.

"And Enid?" he asked. "You still —"

"Don't, doctor! Don't, don't, don't!" pleaded Arthur, dropping his face into his hand. "Please don't talk about *her* — please let me alone now. No more, no more — please!"

Below-stairs the trilling of a bell caught the doctor's ear.

With one long, appraising look at his bowed shoulders and
bent head, the doctor laid a hand on Arthur's arm.

" See here! " said he. " In five minutes, not before, you
come down to my office. I want to see you there. Remember! Five minutes. And wait there till I come.
Will you? "

Arthur nodded.

" What for? " he asked in a choked voice.

" No matter. I have your promise. I want to go over
the case again with you. Don't forget now! "

He left the room and, with a step almost as light as a
boy's, his face radiating sentiments for many years quite
foreign to its scientific aspect, ran down the stairs to answer the bell.

" My dear doctor, what in the name of all that's erratic
does this mean? " demanded Chamberlain as he and Enid
came into the dim-lit hallway. " To summon us in such
haste, at such an extraordinary hour of the night and on
the pretext that it's part of Enid's regimen —"

The doctor laid a hand on the old banker's arm.

" My dear Chamberlain," said he, " you will tremendously
oblige me by not asking any questions just now. Do me a
huge favor, will you? "

" Anything you ask, my dear doctor; anything you ask."

" All right! Go into the smoking-room there and shut
the door and help yourself to the best weeds I've got, *and*
stay there till I come. Will you? "

" How extraordinary! " exclaimed the banker while Enid
stared in amaze. She was clad, as before, in the soft gray
foxskin with the little rosebud toque. Her eyes, very dark
blue — or were they black? — widened with astonishment.
Not only was the doctor's request a thing to wonder at,
but the doctor's whole personality seemed to have under-
gone some indefinable change, some rejuvenescence not to
be accounted for, some subtle and benign expansion.

"Why, doctor!" cried the girl slowly. "Whatever in the world — ?"

"No questions, please!" dictated Nelson, taking the banker by the arm and leading him toward the smoke-room. "My time is very limited. I only ask you to trust me for once — and to obey."

When Chamberlain, still protesting, had been duly and safely sequestrated, the doctor returned to Enid.

"My dear," said he, laying a hand on her glove, "will you come into the library?"

Understanding nothing, she nodded assent. He followed her and closed the door. The other door between the library and the office stood ajar. To this he went and closed it also. Then he returned to her, standing on the Shiraz rug beside the table with its book-racks, its leather mat, its opalescent lamp which beautifully and graciously shaded the oval of her cheek with delicate, warm tones.

"Enid," said he, "you have been my patient for a long time now, and I feel that I know you almost as your father knows you. I am no longer a young man. You can confide in me. As your physician I am also your confessor. I am going to ask you a question or two, and you must answer them truthfully. On those answers everything depends."

She said no word, but looked at him in silent appraisal as though striving with her deep gaze to fathom and to read his hidden meaning. For a moment their eyes sought each other. Then, blinking nervously, the doctor recommenced:

"Let me hypothecate a case, Enid. But first let me ask you again whether you still cling to your idea that Arthur was innocent of that first murder and that he is likewise innocent of this second one?"

She nodded gravely.

"It isn't an idea," she answerd. "It's absolute faith. Positive conviction based on a better knowledge of him than any you or anybody else can have. Yes; I still believe him innocent. Why do you ask? "

Nelson, thus put to the question direct, stammered a moment, rather unprofessionally moved, and finally answered :

" Why? Because I want to make an hypothesis, as I said a moment ago. Listen carefully and answer with absolute sincerity. Will you? "

" I will! "

Enid had gone a little pale, it seemed; but her eyes held steady and her voice betrayed no tremor as she said again :

" I will! What's your hypothesis? "

" This! " answered Nelson, showing signs of nervousness as he heard a step upon the stair — a step that entered the office and stopped there. " Suppose, my dear Enid, that any such improbable series of incidents should arise, or any fact become known which might entirely exculpate Arthur Mansfield; and suppose you were to see him not as an idealized man, but a cruelly wronged, wounded, broken and shattered wreck of his one-time self — a wreck, yet still a wreck possessing all the possibilities of the former man, and far, far more, because now he had become a man in thought and character and a boy no longer, and — and —"

The doctor, his rhetoric entirely tangled, with no possibility of ever going straight again unless the Gordian knot were cut by a fresh beginning, paused, drew out his handkerchief, and swabbed his brow.

" Bless my soul! " said he. " It's terribly warm in here, to-night! "

He glanced at the thermometer hanging on the chandelier. It registered 61. He made another try :

" Suppose this man were to appear as a fugitive, innocent yet hunted — a fugitive in preposterous clothing, all rags and dirt — more or less — and with his arm broken, and with a wounded head — a head all clipped and shaven in the infamous prison way — but innocent, you understand, and perfectly true to you — not a thought of anything but fidelity, you understand —hmmm! hmmm —"

The doctor was becoming extraordinarily hoarse. Unable to continue, he thrust a hand into his breast-pocket and fetched out a folded paper, closely written.

"Where is he, doctor?" cried the girl in a low, eager voice, seizing the doctor's hand in both her own.

She had begun to tremble all over with an unconquerable nervous chill.

"Where is my boy? Where? *Where?*"

Nelson thrust the paper into her hand and opened the door into the office.

"Enid," he choked, "take this, and God bless you! He doesn't know what it is any more than you do. Read it — together —"

At sound of Enid's voice, Arthur turned his head. He stood up, chin high, shoulders square, a sudden blaze of wonder and of glory in his eyes.

"Enid!" he cried, his voice thrilling like a bugle-call.

"My boy, my boy! What have they done to you? Oh, Arthur! What have they done?"

In her furs and warmth and beauty she ran to him, ragged and torn and wan.

"Don't forget to read that paper!" shouted the doctor huskily, then shut the door. "The young fools! The damned young fools!" he swore, tears streaming down his face — the face so long a stranger to tears. "If I were given to popular locutions, I'd say this — gets my — eternal —"

The smoking-room door swung open and Chamberlain mildly appeared, his benign old face haloed by that splendid mane of white.

"Eh? What's all this?" he demanded. "By Jove, doctor, what's happened? Where's Enid? You're crying? Here, here! What's the matter with my girl?"

He started toward the office, terrified, but Nelson seized his arm and dragged him back.

"Keep out o' that, you old fool!" he croaked, letting the tears run unheeded and unashamed. "You were young once yourself, and I — even I am human — in spots! No, you don't, sir! Not a step nearer that office-door!

"Who are we to intrude at such a time? We're only human, you and I. And those two, Enid and Arthur — she all faith and he as innocent, by God! as the babe unborn — they're with the immortals at the Gates of Paradise!"

THE END